The Power of Being

To Sandi,

Embracing our own power of Being is often the only requisite to make our dreams become reality

Always,
Monica Cufin
8/12/13

Published by
CloseKnit Books
232 W. Washington St.
Madison, GA 30650

The Power of Being
ISBN: 1475075235
ISBN-13: 9781475075236
Library of Congress Control Number: 2012905304
CreateSpace, North Charleston, SC

First Edition

Book Design & Photography
By
Barbara A. Powers

Printed in USA

Also by Mónica M. Culqui
To My Capricious Love

The Power of Being

by

Mónica M. Culqui

Published by
CloseKnit Books
Madison, GA

Mónica M. Culqui © 2012

*To
Adria*

Acknowledgements

People who know me would always refrain me from writing yet another book when I just need to type a note, an invite or in this case my thank you to all those who have been great instruments in helping me to write the material on these pages. I guess I could easily type their name and say thanks, a simple task. However, I feel the need to extend my most humble gratitude to all individually because every one of them is a part of this creative endeavor.

Barbara Powers: A true, honest and the most altruistic person with the genuine gift of friendship and great heart. Barbara has been the most instrumental and sweet angel who has pushed me to finish "this dog gone paper, manuscript, novel whatever you want to call it, but finish it for heaven's sake!" had been her words. Her enthusiasm at reading the stream of conscious and correcting my lack of idiomatic expressions has made us both appreciate the cultural differences between us. At the lowest point of my life after my divorce she has been there to lift up my spirits, restore my faith, and appreciate the beauty of life. She is my sister, my friend, my number one advocate of all the creativity within me. Without her I would not be writing my too long acknowledgement page. She would tell me now 'don't forget the essential editor *par excellence*,' which would be her.

Tara Hottenstein: A very smart and wonderful soul who indulged me by listening to the idea of my story at its very beginning and suggesting that I should name it as Amy Tang's *The Bone Setter's Daughter* honoring my father's craft of being a diamond setter and call it "The Diamond Setter's Daughter." We had many chuckles on her suggestion, talked about Tang's book in our 'two' people Book club of sorts, and she added with great conviction that I was imaginative enough to come up with my own title. Tara asked me to continue with the writing to tell her how the story ends. Thank you for your friendship, advice and faith that I can be a storyteller.

Melina Lambert: My beautiful niece who had finished her B.A in English and I thought what a better person to tell me if my story had merit and wrote to her. She was kind to say, "Yeah, I will be more than happy to read it and give you a critique. I'll try to be objective." I asked nothing more than her objectivity and her answer was like a teacher to a pupil, "It needs character development and more dialogue," Melina wrote back in awe of the story and she too asked me to continue to see how it ends.

Beth Scott: who became excited at the prospect of reading and correcting my paper. She liked what she read but became stuck on part two and with a strong evaluation that perhaps it should have dissuaded me to continue, she gave me 'fire' to go on and edit part two to make it flow with the story.

Saye Atkinson: A very kind and erudite man who was the first to read, review and call it a 'manuscript.' The times I had wanted to give this baby up, I have gone back to the three page email he sent with his critique which included his comparison of me to Louise Erdrich, *Love Medicine* and unbelievably but true to the Hispanic author Gabriel García Márquez, *Love in the Time of Cholera* in the way I described certain parts of my story. Thank you for such an immense kindness.

Karen Wibell: who as a member of the Madison Writers Guild, after hearing my then prologue, suggested I enter it to have it evaluated at the prestigious Harriet Austin Writers Conference and to also attend the conference where I would meet upcoming writers that could share the story of how to write and publish a book. It was a positive push in the right path. I went to have an evaluation and I still keep the notes from the evaluator who told me that indeed my 'paper' now a manuscript had the potential to become a novel. A literary work, I screamed and cried and I felt the 'surreal' feeling like being pregnant again with a baby growing inside of me.

Steve Jordan: A lovely, kind man who loved me conditionally for a short time, allowing me to grow while storing strength to withstand his surprising end to us. 'Like the caterpillar, he allowed me to think that my world was coming to its end, only to realize I was being transform into a butterfly.' An anonymous quote.

Marcelo and Elva Culqui: who are my protectors, my guardian angels and in their filial love I feel secure to go on dancing in the clouds like my protagonist.

César Culqui: my father who patiently sees his middle child transform herself into that elusive butterfly he likes so much. Thank you for your love and patience to see me still forge the dreams I have within.

The Power of Being

Rocío Díaz Luis Calderón*   *Luis' cousin
                          Mamita María José m. Miguel Ángel
         |_____|
                    | Tío Miguelito fathered by
                    | Antonio Altero
         Paloma Díaz (m. Antonio Galarza)
         |_____|
                            |
Froilán Isabel **Micaela** (m. Edward Sims) Rebeca Andrés
                            |____|
                                Annabella

Part One

In the fecund Andes Mountains of South America, a story begins full of poignant and perilous details resembling the many precipices of its terrain, yet allowing a young girl to navigate with such care and tenacity that her journey became her power of being...

Thoughts on Paper

Finding the most illuminated room of the house, Micaela stood in awe looking at the splendid sea scape before her. She stood breathing in the salty air that rushed through the large windows. The motion of the wind circulated around her, brushing against her skin lightly, rekindling a remembrance of things which were now only dusty abstract relics in the alcove of her mind. She thought of how she had always craved and loved light. The earth-weathered deep-ledge and whitewashed solid windows, which allowed the light to enter in such a way as it did, were as much the reason for buying this little Grecian cottage as any. Perched on a promontory overlooking the Aegean Sea, the house had belonged to a very wise old woman once regarded as the matriarch of the small seaside town. Feeling afraid that she might wake up from this wondrous dream, she got close to the window ledge and caressed the thick painted walls and exhaled, what seemed a lifetime of sorrows and joys. She whispered to herself, "I'm finally home..."

Micaela had finished writing her book and the response was as good as she had hoped. She often told people of how she would write this book, the story of a woman awakened by the 'light,' becoming aware of the many boundaries and struggles she would have to overcome to arrive at the realization of a lifetime. The strong husky voice of Liam Griggs, her partner, lover, friend and every other noun for couples, except husband, brought her back to the world that was now a part of her dream made into reality. She referred to him as her salvation and her joy personified. She would recount how this handsome, tall, blond, blue-eyed man with the panache of a young Roger Moore came into her life by a serendipitous accident that made her love him and cherish him all the more.

"What are you thinking now?" Liam asked her.

"Oh, just thinking how much I love to stare at the horizon... and...wonder what is beyond it," she said it in a contemplative voice.

She reached for his hands, caressing them ever so softly and kissing them. She looked at him saying, "Thank you, for helping me dance with the clouds, fly to the sky and share moments like this with you," inviting him to rejoice in seeing the panorama before them.

He caressed her back and started to play with her hair, and softly told her how much he had loved her all these years, how much he had loved to see her dance at times with the innocence of a child and often with the sensuality of a fertility goddess. His look became intense and sweetly focusing on her lips, he asked very softly, "I still want to know, what makes you sometimes so sad and lonesome? And why do you sometimes push away?" he continued.

Micaela had always wondered about these questions herself, and as she perused her thoughts, she focused on that force that instilled the false sense of pride, her zest for life, her insecurities and the sadness still pervading her soul. Paloma Díaz de Galarza, her mother, had been that strong domineering force, the one who loved her in the most capricious and conditional way, not knowing that by doing so, she had bestowed upon her female middle child the gift of an overpowering might that had made her grateful for all things. For it was Paloma's way of loving her that made her strong and gave her the sense of awe that kept her going through all the seemingly hard times she had encounter.

Micaela thought of Virginia Woolf's remark from "A Room of One's Own... A woman writing thinks back through her mother's writings." She thought that the journey of her life could easily begin with her own mother, not so much the writings, but rather her mother's strong sense of oral tradition.

It had been her mother's life which Micaela thought was like a *pequeña novela* worth retelling. She had always wanted to recount her mother's life. She had heard it told time after time back in the old country, her mother's beloved Ecuador. It was told with such a grandiose tone that one had the feeling of seeing a part of a scene in a big theatrical production that left everyone who came wanting more. She remembered how sometimes it was told with sadness making the listener interpret the stories as life lessons much needed to be learned. Sometimes it was told in a reminiscent colorful way as if looking at scattered pictures ready to be put in an album. What she remembered most fondly were the circumstances in which the story was told or rather the times when it was told.

Micaela must have been around eight years old when the first memory of her amidst family and friends had come rushing through her thoughts. When compared to her beautiful sisters, she was ordinary looking as a small-framed, skinny little girl, with a page-boy haircut. She remembered how insignificant her mother made her feel permitting her to do as she pleased. Micaela felt Paloma did not really pay attention to her whereabouts. She remembered always being so active and curious of her surroundings, much to the annoyance of her elders.

On many weekends, they would trek to her mother's adoptive brother's house who Micaela knew as *Tío Miguelito*. He lived in the nearby town, about thirty minutes away by bus, an hour by foot. As they got closer to the house, they passed by an old and simply decorated white church mounted on a massive stone pedestal.

Micaela loved to run up the stairs alongside the church, running her way to the front of the church, down the front set of stairs and then repeating this exercise until her family seemed to disappear off into the plaza farther down the road. They turned right onto the narrow cobble-stoned street, lined with houses, separated only by the pretty pastel paint of each individual dwelling. They were adorned with thick brown painted window sills creating geometric patterns that were not uniform, alluding to the musical notes that sounded in harmony as the road converged at the other end. Micaela loved to stand at the corner and see this phenomenon take place, wondering to herself what made the street seem narrower at the other end.

"Mami, Paloma...why does the street get narrower at the other end?" she would ask her mother.

"What kind of question is that?" her mother would ask back, irritated at the question.

"Well...come here and see for yourself, Mami!" Micaela would add.

"Hurry up! Why do you have to look at and question everything on the road Micaela?" her older sister would intervene seeing Paloma's annoyance at Micaela's precociousness.

Much later in life she would learn about linear perspective, and then it would all make sense. She would chuckle at this childhood memory knowing that she had always questioned and analyzed the minutest detail of some of her days and the conversations she had, especially with the people who matter the most. She knew then that her mother's love would not be given to her so freely, and that she would have to work and strive with a compelling drive to earn her approval and love.

When they arrived at her uncle's house, they never entered through the front door. Instead, they would enter through the patio door that was to the right of the front entrance. It opened onto a long and narrow paved pathway leading to the courtyard in the back of the house. They were greeted by the loud barking of the old collie

named Lassie (of course!) Micaela, upon entering would run, grab a ball and throw it toward the courtyard. "Go get it girl!" she would yell.

After getting rid of Lassie, her mother, Paloma, would nudge her, telling Micaela in a stern voice, "Are you going to say hello?"

"Good afternoon, *Tío Miguelito*...how are you today?" she would comply in the most gracious way.

Her uncle would smile at Micaela with an inconsequential look that made Micaela wonder, *why do we have to say hello when he does not even care about the little ones!*

On the other hand, her aunt, Marianna, the middle-aged woman with curly hair, porcelain skin, and an extra pound or two, would extend her arms and show how glad she always was to see the family.

"Hi, my sweet and skinny girl!" her aunt would exclaim pulling Micaela's small head up against her well-endowed bosom, placing a kiss on the top of her forehead.

"You smell like bread!" Micaela would excitedly exclaim and under the same breath she would continue, "Are you baking my favorite bread?"

"Of course, I knew you were coming, so I had to make your favorite *pan de agua*!" her aunt would respond, indulging the child with her love and affection.

Micaela would extend all the salutations and pleasantries to the relatives, and finally, when all this was done, Micaela would stop and smell all the flowers that ran along the side of the pathway. She loved the hydrangeas, the round clusters of white flowers reminiscent of huge cheese balls. But the strong smell of chlorophyll from its leaves after she pinched them made her make faces. Her aunt, Marianna, would wink at her by saying, "If you make ugly faces like that, your face is going to stay that way!"

Micaela also loved picking honeysuckle flowers and their fragrance for she knew the sweet liquid at the bottom of the stamen would be ready for the taking. She would buzz like a bee as she thought, *this is a good dinner!*

She smiled and ran carefree with Lassie, who interrupted her snack at the honeysuckle bush by bringing the ball back, "Good girl!" she exclaimed, petting the animal.

Micaela would go inside the house by the kitchen door and the smell of brewing coffee would enshroud the whole house. She knew fresh baked bread was coming and her favorite cheese was already being cut. With a melodramatic gesture and sounding very formal she would ask her aunt, "Is my coffee ready yet, my dear?" as she plunged herself on the sofa drawing her small hand to her forehead in a dramatic swoon.

"Such travel has left me famished!" she continued.

"I must sit a spell or two or three and rest my weary tired bones under the eucalyptus tree!" she added. Rolling her eyes, with the languid motion of her hand adding to her playful distress, she would continue, knowing that her melodramatic tactics annoyed everyone in sight, especially her two unimaginative sisters.

"Stop being ridiculous and sit up straight!" her mother would admonish.

She loved these visits to her uncle's house. She knew they would spend the night talking and reminiscing as more fresh cheese along with hot fig preserves would be the salty-sweet manna served to appease the foretelling gods. In a vast living room, with chairs placed all around and a guitar almost placed on cue nearby, she knew it was time for the retelling. *Tío Miguelito* would play the guitar, and his wife, Marianna, would sing while Micaela's mother reminisced all the way to her beginnings in between songs. This is how her family began creating moments, that with each telling, became clear pictures that would shape not only the woman Micaela would become, but also some of the most pronounced likes and dislikes in her life. Micaela held dear the retelling of the stories, for it made family and friends understand her mother, the idiosyncrasies she possessed for which she never apologized, and for the stoic aloof legacy given to her children at the time of her passing.

Some years earlier, Micaela had started to gather these memories, putting them down on paper. She had wanted to do this because the rich oral tradition she had as a child growing up in South America was becoming lost among her family. She and her daughter were far away from the family circle and were no longer active participants in the usual gatherings where talking about the old times continued, but with added new perspectives, since the only person that could correct the way it should be told was no longer there. Her mother, Paloma, had passed away a couple of years before Micaela decided to write it all down. She felt that by putting her mother's life on paper, she and future generations would know about the stern Paloma Díaz, the unforgiving matriarch of the Galarza Díaz family...the very woman who held the family together. Micaela's mother had markedly shaped her life, a life that included a failed marriage and an unrequited love tryst, only to be awakened by the 'light' and celebrated by the warmth of her sweetest friend, lover and companion, Liam.

Rocío Díaz and Paloma's Painful Beginnings

In between songs, bread, cheese and figs, the story of Micaela's mother, Paloma, revealed itself with great bravado from the lips of its major protagonist. Micaela's biological grandmother had been a young girl from a prominent family that had owned a large part of land in Quito, Ecuador. Her name was Rocío Díaz and she had only been fifteen at the time of her kidnapping by the majordomo of the adjacent hacienda. From the time of the *conquistadores*, their goal was to obtain not only the gold of the indigenous people but also the vast land of the most unexplored, fecund and beautiful Andes Mountains. Rocío's ancestors followed in the tradition of the many people who came prominently from Spain to make their mark in the new world. The importance of Micaela's mother being of Spanish descent was pertinent, since it separated their social upper class status from the indigenous people, and the *mestizos* of the land where her ancestors had come to live.

Micaela always felt a sense of demarcation between the two cultures. To be from Spain was better than to be from Ecuador, because most Ecuadorians were *mestizos* and not full-blooded Spaniards. The sense of false pride that one culture is better than the other nagged at Micaela's heart from a very young age. "Why is it so important to be a Spaniard and not an Ecuadorian Indian who after all, had the riches that the Spaniards desired?" Micaela would find herself asking this question, never getting an answer as she grew up.

Micaela teased her mother by saying scornfully, "Yeah, everyone who comes to South America is from Spain...God forbid to be a *mestizo*...or even worse an Indian!"

Calling her mother a *mestizo* or Indian became a weapon for Micaela as she grew up. She learned to push buttons that allowed her to see people's weaknesses or idiosyncrasies and to drive her mother crazy with ire.

"I do not know if everyone came from Spain, but my great grandparents on my mother's side were full-blooded Spaniards!" Micaela's mother, Paloma, would exclaim proudly.

"My mother's grandfather had arrived in the new world in the middle of the nineteenth century. He had acquired a large part of land where the airport stands now," she continued.

Attentively and wanting to catch a remark that would give Micaela a reason to argue with her mother, she would protest, "I don't believe that such a vast piece of land was once ours!"

Micaela, with a doubting tone, would pose the question, "What happened to all that? Why did your family lose all that land?" She would keep asking, trying to get to the bottom of what had happened to her family, to have lost so much.

"My grandfather was too proud and too ambitious," Paloma would say, full of contempt for her ancestors. She almost had a smirk of disdain when she thought how her mother's family had lost all their land and the hard work it took to procure it.

"Rocío's father, my grandfather, instilled in his family this ambition. It was almost innate for him to desire and obtain more land and to keep what he had inherited. It did not matter at what cost this land was obtained and the hefty price my mother would pay in order for her father, my grandfather, to keep his land." Paloma's voice would then become somber and contemplative.

Micaela at a young age could see and understand the array of emotion that became obvious in her mother's facial expression making her think, *why were they so ambitious and proud?* It would become Micaela's preoccupation to fully understand why her biological great-grandfather had done these things, because every time his name was mentioned, the anger, anguish and heartache was easily visible in her mother's eyes.

Thus, in the many conversations among the family, the prologue for Paloma's life story started with Rocío's ancestors and their blind greed for obtaining land and more land, which ended up costing Micaela's great-grandfather his most precious possession, his only child, Rocío.

Micaela's uncle, Miguelito, would start singing an old song from the Spanish Golden Era's famous trio *Los Panchos*. The song was always *"Sin Ti,"* which inspired the adults to retell their memories of times gone by with an added zest for life, although the song is about big regrets and loneliness. Micaela would grow up cherishing and relishing these moments in which the lyrics of an old song would add to the passion that the adults in her family had for *la vida*.

Paloma would start the retelling with, "It was almost my mother's fifteenth birthday and she had been looking forward with the girlish dreamy way of adolescence to her coming of age party, *la quinceañera*."

"The event would have been my grandparents' way to introduce Rocío, my mother, to society and to start looking for the most eligible bachelor," she would explain.

"Needless to say, that would be the one that owned the most land, so that this land could be passed on to the next generation. He also would have to be from Spanish descent, especially from the fair-skinned Spaniards of Northern Spain!" Paloma would be emphatic about this detail as she spoke.

Someone in the crowd or one of Micaela's older siblings would interject to make sure their mother did not forget such an important note, which always gave Micaela the opportunity to speak her mind. In a patronizing, and with a disrespectful grimace Micaela would add, "Don't forget they have to be white, blond and blue-eyed!"

"She said the fair-skinned Spaniards from Northern Spain!" someone else would reiterate Paloma's pride on being from Spanish blood.

Micaela, at such a young age, intuitively felt how cunningly her mother tried to inculcate the prejudicial culling of the better-type of skin in her children. She was so proud of her Spanish origins that to choose other than that would be to insult her roots.

Rocío's family had emigrated from the Catalonia region of Spain, a region with its own language, folkways and cuisine. Micaela's mother would take pride in her culinary mastery and talent by stating, "It is in my blood to be a good cook!"

"Mom, please continue with your story. You always deviate and start another fable, and it takes forever to listen to you!" Micaela would protest as she nibbled from a bit of figs and cheese.

Paloma would reprimand her daughter's insolence by saying, "Well, if you do not want to hear it then go play with your cousins and their dolls!"

Micaela admired her mother's swift change of demeanor into a disciplinarian as she became annoyed at her child's lack of manners, correcting the behavior and gracefully, nonchalantly going back to the rest of her story. Micaela relished seeing her mother so swift and beautiful as she handled every aspect of a circumstance, like a director perfecting a scene.

"It was at this time with an avaricious desperation to get bargaining power that the rivalry between my grandfather, Esteban

Díaz, and the neighboring landowner, Mr. Sandoval, had become most volatile. In order to procure the property between them, Mr. Sandoval, the owner of the *hacienda* instructed his foreman to kidnap my mother," Paloma would continue.

The foreman, Luis Calderón, a married man in his early thirties with children of his own, took the young girl up into the hills and kept her there until the landowner would send for him to bring her back. Rocío's demise through an unfortunate sequence of events started at this moment in time. The foreman, Luis, eyed the young girl of the fairest skin, rosy cheeks and long auburn hair. Her hair shimmered with the quality of the richest Dupioni silk, enhancing her features and bringing the viewer into exquisite delirium. People often thought that it was unusual in the land of mestizos to have this countenance, which resembled many of Raphael's *Madonnas*.

Luis had been watching and monitoring Rocío's riding schedule. Every morning at the break of dawn, unbeknownst to her family, Rocío would ride her favorite horse, *Relampago*, up to the hills nearby and then race the poor beast back to the ranch to be on time for breakfast and not to be discovered by her parents. On this morning, when Rocío reached the top of the hill she got off the horse. This was something she had never done before but she spotted a bush with pretty lilac buds and wanted to pick some of the pretty flowers. Suddenly, she realized that the bush had fresh dirt surrounding it, telling her it had just been planted and before she knew it, the figure of Luis stood before her. Startled by his presence and feeling an ominous sensation of been ambushed, she tried to reach for the reins only to see him grab them first and hand them to her. With an unsettling feeling, she accepted them only to be grasped by his strong hand, making her mount the horse before him. He motioned the horse to turn around as they rode in the opposite direction of the ranch.

"Don't bother screaming for help. At this hour no one is up to hear you," Luis told her.

"I am not scared of you. I am scared of what my father will do to you when he finds out what you have done," she rebutted.

"Don't worry, we are just trying to have some leverage for land negotiation with your father and you are the prettiest leverage yet," he chuckled.

"Where are you taking me?" She wanted to know.

"It does not matter. You do not know this part of the mountains so you would never be able to find your way home without me," he continued.

Feeling defeated and scared but trying not to disclose her feelings she gave in and did not move nor talk the rest of the way. Farther up the hill she saw a dilapidated cabin. They stopped, dismounted and he extended his arms to help her down. She obeyed afraid of being hit or abused.

Her hair shimmered in the sun. Her blouse had opened leaving her round, voluptuous, adolescent breasts exposed, making her already virginal loveliness exude a sensuality that caught him off guard. Luis noticed the young girl's beauty for the first time and felt angst for her circumstances as he tied her to the bed post in the lonely barren cabin. As the days passed, bringing her food, he would look at her and in her defeated yet hopeful circumstance he could detect her wanting him to take her back home. She looked even more beautiful and innocent. Overwhelmed by her sultry demeanor yet youthful innocence, he managed to set aside his feelings of lust. However, tired of fighting these feelings time after time, and seeing the beautiful young girl pleading with her eyes but never saying a word, he fell prey to his lust and took advantage of the child who cried after being forced against her will. Rocío's beautiful rosy cheeks became pale and somber and her desperate look of fear replaced the lovely serene semblance she once possessed. Anger and hatred became apparent as she would hear him come in bringing her the food she never touched. He would continue with his monstrous act and in one of these attacks, Micaela's mother, Paloma, was conceived.

"I heard *Mamita* say, 'That brute took advantage of the poor girl not only that one time but many times after that because the negotiations between landowners took a long time,'" Micaela's mother would then add, "He was a very weak, selfish and stupid man." At this point in the story, all the women would become agitated, and they would agree or disagree that it had been Rocío's father's responsibility for taking so long in these negotiations without even thinking about his daughter's fate. They all sat around the dining room table looking at each other as if with their individual glances the story would change. *Tío Miguelito* would take a break from his guitar playing in the nearby living room and would come to sit down among the women and hear the story as though it was for the first time. Micaela would look around at the grownups and ask herself, "Haven't they heard this story a thousand times? Didn't they live the story as well?"

Paloma often let Micaela listen to what the grownups talked about. She remembered how she learned to read people's expressions and as though having telepathic abilities, she would specifically turn to *Tío Miguelito* who had a look of disbelief, having the same question as hers. She would then imagine carrying on a conversation with the uncle who was so aloof and made everyone feel inconsequential that to connect with him this way made Micaela feel ten feet tall. They both looked at the women becoming agitated for the thousandth time even though they had heard the same story over and over. *Tío Miguelito* would have a smirk on his face that told Micaela he was about to leave the scene, which he did. She always laughed because if *Tío Miguelito* or any of the other adults knew what she was thinking about this story and the women that seemed so silly, her mother would never let her participate in the story telling.

"The child was kidnapped and abused, for heaven's sake!" an aunt or cousin of Micaela's mother would exclaim in disbelief.

"The ambition and greed of my grandfather had blinded him, and he did not relinquish his land, can you believe it?" Paloma would say. The rhetorical question was always added at this point of the story. And with the innocence of a child, Micaela would look around to see the expressions on the faces of the women hearing the story for the thousandth time.

It never failed that one of them would say, "God only knows how horrible things really were up there."

The rest of them would roll their eyes, and some would even make the sign of the cross, as they lamented the poignancy of the moment stating, "Poor girl!"

Later when Micaela was a little older and became aware what conceived meant, she would condescendingly ask them when they got to that point of the story, "What went on up there?"

Paloma would ignore Micaela's questions, as though emphatically stressing the fact that a child should not be asking these questions. However, Micaela's persistence sometimes ended in a bad note from her mother.

"Didn't you hear me?" she would ask as if the whole conversation was directed to her.

And with the same arrogance of her great-grandfather, Micaela would retort, "He kidnapped her, hid her in the mountains, fell in love with the girl and mom was conceived. So what went on up there?"

At this point her mother's ire was well awakened by Micaela's inquisitive and rude attitude and she would admonish and oust her, sending her to play with the rest of the children. Micaela always managed to apologize and make some excuse only to sheepishly sneak back in and be part of the inner circle of rich oral tradition. Her mother, Paloma, sometimes would make excuses for Micaela by saying, "This one was born with a gift of advocacy and verbosity. It is hard to keep her quiet."

"This one was born old! I tell you, she will grow up to be a writer or philosopher, you silly skinny girl," her aunt, Marianna would add. "I know you'll be something extraordinary!"

reaching for Micaela's head and placing her messy tresses into place.

"As much as you like to talk and try to get away with murder!" she would add smiling, caressing Micaela's small face.

Ignoring the disrespectful child, Micaela's grandmother, or rather the woman she grew up thinking was her grandmother, María José, would resume retelling the most cruel and poignant part of the story; sounding astounded and resentful, "The child, the product of rape, did not look like Rocío at all. Instead, the tiny baby was born with the softest olive-hued skin, jet black hair and big brown almond-shaped eyes that would become one of her tools to get the things she wanted in life," she would add with a sadness that made Micaela question what was so wrong with being olive-skinned?

Rocío, Micaela's biological grandmother, had contempt for the child from the moment she pushed it out of her womb until the day she passed away. Micaela remembered how the women in the family lamented this event.

María José would add, "The silly girl, Rocío, did not know anything about anything. That is why she gave the baby away."

Aunt Marianna would ask, "So she did not give the baby up because it was the product of the worst perfidy, right?"

In the same breath, Marianna would continue, "But rather because she was olive-skinned. That is absurd!" she would exclaim with a grimace of pronounced dislike, throwing her hands up in the air as if to say, "I do not want to hear anymore!"

"She was as cute as a button and those brown eyes...who could say no to those beautiful brown eyes?" Marianna would add with a gesture of pride and confusion as she again extended her arms up in the air.

"I know," María José would agree with indignation in her voice.

"Rocío gave the baby up because she was not fair skinned enough," and then María José's would become sad and contemplative.

"Then why did she marry that Indian boy, who was as dark and unwanted by society as her own child?" Marianna, the aunt, persisted with questions she would end up answering herself and to which everyone already knew the answers. Listening to the rhetorical questions among the protagonists of the soap opera often made Micaela sneer, for which she was always reprimanded. Micaela would never understand why these women knowing full well how painful the story was, would continue emphasizing the most poignant details while forgetting all along that Paloma was the baby of the story and was sitting right there being treated as the third person. Even more so, why would her mother allow such irreverent behavior from the women in her clan?

"Was it to rebel against the family and bring more shame to her parents?" Marianna would add, trying to elicit the answer that had already been heard a thousand times, maybe in the hope that there had been a mistake or perchance a different answer would be given this time.

Micaela knew the answer already, for she had heard these comments all of her childhood years in South America. At the young age of ten, she would ask herself, "What difference does the color of one's skin make? How could marrying an Indian boy be shameful?"

Micaela would continue silently, elaborating these questions that she knew better than to ask any adults around her for fear of what further atrocities they would come up with, these people are crazy giving babies up because they are not fair skinned enough! She would lament in the same manner as the adult women, but only to her as she played with balls of yarn the women often had around the house. As she grew up, hearing the same conversations, Micaela came to realize that these were some of the lines drawn that separated not only people and societies but, sadly enough, families and who they considered loved ones.

Even as a child, Micaela could not accept that the color of one's skin had so much to do with how you were seen in the world at large. She resented her biological grandmother for thinking that being "olive-skinned" made a person inferior to one of a lighter shade. She grew up thinking what a waste of time and energy to be thinking about this and not about how the person was from the inside out. Micaela loved her adoptive grandmother, María José, for loving and caring for the tiny olive-skinned baby. For her continued love and support of Paloma and also for loving her children. From the time Micaela was able to reason, she thought her grandmother, María José was strength and unconditional love incarnate. She grew up feeling grateful for having loved her the way her mother never could.

Nonetheless, for Micaela, her mother Paloma was the loveliest creature; she would die for her if she was ever asked. Micaela wanted to be like Paloma because she was beauty, elegance, dignity, and fun in the flesh. In addition, Paloma was like a majestic butterfly that fluttered about sitting upon the most grandiose and colorful dahlias like she grew in her garden, which inspired Micaela's own gardens in her adult years. Her mother, Paloma, was a beautiful human being with so much love and compassion for all those around her that Micaela could not fathom the idea that someone like this could be given up at her entrance to this world. Most important, Micaela wondered, why someone like her would show so much contempt to her middle child as if taking revenge of the wrong done to her.

"That was it!" Micaela would say later on in her adult life.

"That was it!...That is why she loved me the way she did...to show me the way!" Micaela quietly would say to herself as she wiped tears away while trimming the dead dahlias in her own garden to let new ones grow.

María José Calderón: Paloma's Adoptive Mother, her Salvation

Thus, the way for Micaela in her younger years was clearly marked by the scornful watch of her mother, yet she was nurtured with the loving tenderness of her adoptive grandmother, María José Calderón, the woman who not only was the guardian angel in Paloma's life at the most opportune moment to save her from the abandonment of her 'parents' but also to protect Micaela from the mother who chose to ostracize her. For this also olive-skinned, dark-haired, small-framed petite woman with a strong, marked stoicism loved Paloma's children as her own in the most strict, yet unconditional way.

She was the cousin of Luis Calderón, Paloma's father. Micaela remembered her as a woman in her late sixties with graying hair and a face with very few wrinkles to be of such an age. Her small mouth seldom smiled, her eyes were small and filled with melancholic nostalgia that only added beauty to the few wrinkles that made her whole semblance. She wore only long gray skirts, black cardigans, never any with color, and beautiful woolen shawls that draped around her head and shoulders making her look like the aged *Madonna* in the *Deposition* renditions of the churches they often visited. On special occasions, she would wear her precious white antique linen blouses with Madeira-embroidered edges at the collar that would soften her face and stern disposition. Micaela detected that she wanted to hide away this feminine side of her persona by wearing the somber and old fashioned every-day attire. One day, Micaela would come to find out why this was the case.

Nonetheless, it was Mamita María José who indulged Micaela in her acting and dancing skits she put on for her younger sister and cousins who often came to visit. She loved to see Micaela dance and would often play a record just to see her twirl and move freely across the living room, clapping as the music came to an end. Micaela would bow, running into her arms to feel completely loved and approved by this woman who would whisper in her ear "*Brava, bravisima.*"

Micaela loved listening to her beloved *mamita* María José recount her cousin Luis Calderón's ordeal. Micaela knew whatever *mamita* said was from the 'horse's mouth,' so to speak and she believed everything she heard. She would tell how her cousin Luis felt remorse about his atrocious act toward Paloma's mother, Rocío up in that mountain cabin. After finding out that her family had inexplicably blamed her for her own demise to the point of ousting her from the family, he decided to help the girl. The fact that Rocío had become pregnant made the situation more difficult and complex. Luis panicked and did not know what to do with the young pregnant girl. Adding to his surprise, Rocío had fled into higher mountains without anyone knowing about it, only to return after the birth of her child. Rocío's contempt of her own baby girl at the time of her birth worsened the circumstances causing Luis great angst and regret. Seeking advice, he sheepishly told *mamita* María José, "Rocío gave me the child to dispose of or do whatever I wanted."

"What do you want me to do?" she asked, shrugging her shoulders as if she did not care.

"I don't know, can you take her to your place of work. Isn't that an orphanage?" he added sadly.

"This is your problem not mine, I already have my own problem to deal with." She scornfully continued referring to 'the problem' as her own son, Miguel who became *Tío Miguelito* for the later generations.

Tío Miguelito was María José's only son. He had been born illegitimate but later had been legitimized as his father lay dying. *Tío Miguelito's* father had been in the Ecuadorian/Peruvian war of 1941. He had been fatally shot but before his death, summoned María José to marry him, thus, making the child legitimate to carry on his last name.

"Where is Rocío?" María José asked Luis.

"She is still hoping and praying her parents would send for her," he responded.

"But I don't think it is going to happen," he added looking away from the child who squirmed in his arms.

"They told me her father is really ashamed of the whole situation and does not want anything to do with her."

"How does that make you feel? You idiot. Huh!" María José retorted.

"I hope you feel proud, ruining their two lives, not to mention your entire family if they ever find out about this *bochorno*."

"That is why I have come to beg for your help," Luis said pleading to María José.

"I do not know if they would take her in at the orphanage!"

"Moreover, you do not want your own blood to be raised in a place like that!" she went on.

"The nuns are good to the children there, aren't they?" Luis continued.

"Yeah! With children who really are orphans, and as far as I am concerned she has both parents and her mother comes from a wealthy family," she exclaimed, reaching for the tiny babe, which caused her to change her manner to a gentler and tender way.

"Maybe I can keep her for a little while, or at least, until you find a reasonable remedy to this situation." María José Calderón suddenly looked at her cousin with contempt. Looking back at the sweet baby in her arms, María José felt sadness at the lonely prospect of this child, she added, "I will keep her only for a little while, no longer than a month you hear me?"

However, María José felt not only contempt for her cousin's actions, but also pity for this baby whose own mother at the time of her birth had disowned and damned the poor infant. So the days turned into weeks, weeks into months and months into a lifetime of selfless love for the tiny babe who was born under such sad circumstances. She decided to keep and raise the child as her own in the company of her son Miguel Ángel.

María José Calderón became *mamita* María José, the adoptive grandmother of Paloma's children, who protected and defended them. She was a proud woman whose own circumstances in life were not too happy. She was a no nonsense type of woman whose demeanor seemed to say, "Stay away from me, I don't need anyone in my life." Yet she gave of herself with noble grace and kindness and she was Micaela's favorite *mamita*.

Micaela's memories of her beloved *mamita* María José went back to the same apartment complex where they all lived at one time. They lived in a building which seemed like a fortress. The bedrooms and living room were on the upper floor, the kitchen and dining room were below. However, there were no inside stairs connecting the two floors. Instead, to get to the bedrooms and living room, one would use a long concrete outdoor stairway, which also led to the street and patio. *Mamita* María José lived in the lower part of the fortress in a room near their kitchen.

Micaela called it a room because that is all it was; a small, dark room with no windows. You entered through double doors made of old pieces of gray massive wood that arched at the top, with a gothic looking dead bolt requiring a huge key to open it. At her young age of eleven, Micaela thought the doors were beautiful in their shape and character. The gray wood had highlights of darker hues of gray and brown deep set in its nooks and crannies in which she could see many shapes and forms inviting her to come see the texture of the wood. Micaela believed this is where her love of doors began. These old doors, as ominous as they sometimes seemed, also represented the entrance to some of the sweetest childhood memories she would have throughout her life. She learned to pray and question things in that room. She learned to listen to the silence and to be afraid of the dark in that room. When you came into the room and shut the door, it became permeated with darkness and only a trickle of light would seep through the bottom of the door, and once your eyes adjusted to the lack of light, you would see shadows in the darkness of it all.

Everything seemed so huge and mysterious in the dark room. A bed stood to the right of the door facing the wall at the other end of the room. The right side of the room was separated by a temporary wall that was decoupage with pictures from old black and white fashion catalogs creating a whimsical area that did not agree with the inhabitant of this room. Farther to the right side of the bed, indented in the wall, there was a cubbyhole that served as a shrine. There was a crucifix in the middle and pictures of the Sacred Heart, along with that of the Virgin Mary, flanked by these two highly adorned statues of St. Anthony and The Virgin Mary and Child, votives and keepsakes of every religious holiday one could think of growing up Catholic. The side of the room behind the temporary decoupage wall was off limits to Micaela and anyone for that matter. Micaela always wondered why she could not go back there.

On the left side of the room, a table made of the same old sturdy wood as the doors held a baked enamel washbasin with dents and nicks that added beauty to the old receptacle. A tightly woven basket held beautiful oranges. Their aroma mixed with burning wood from the wrought-iron wood stove engulfed the walls of the room which *mamita* María José called her home. A mirror and some books sat on a very large table. Next to this massive table, there was an immense and bold looking chest, which seemed too old to even know when it was made. The chest was impressive and intimidating for a child roaming through the room, especially when you were not allowed to look inside.

Micaela remembered talking to this huge chest and saying to it "Why can't you be friendly and let me see what is inside, huh?"

"You know you cannot look inside of me" Micaela would pretend to sound like an old man and would proceed to have a conversation with herself.

"You must think I am crazy by talking to you," she would say back to the chest.

"No! I don't think you are crazy. You are just a mischievous and very curious little girl," she would respond in the deep male voice.

"How do you know these things?"

"You do not know me, you know?" she would add.

"I do know you, you are here all the time and at times you pretend to be asleep, in the hopes you will get to see inside me when your *mamita* goes away," she would add in her deep male voice.

"You are a liar," she would exclaim turning around, moving toward the high set bed.

Once, not too long after her 'conversation' with the trunk, Micaela pretended to be asleep only to accidentally see where her *mamita* hid the key to the ominous chest and its mysterious contents. Micaela even as a child laughed at how silly she had been not to realize the obvious place for the key to be hidden. It was in the statue of Saint Anthony, the Catholic patron saint of lost items, the poor and travelers. His roots being from Portugal played a big role in the secrets her *mamita* held so dear in this chest. She revered the statue in the most unusual way even for the devout Catholic she was. Saint Anthony wore a beautiful and extremely well adorned cape with silk embroidered flowers. In the back interior of the cape there was a pocket that held the key to what became the most revealing yet secretive tidings Micaela and María José would ever share.

Fate would have it that one Sunday Micaela woke up to find *mamita* had left for mass leaving her behind. She had done this in the past and many times Micaela would become frightened by the darkness only to be comforted by a big cup of warm *café con leche* and a large animal cookie left behind for her when she awakened. This time she took a bite and turned to the chest and talking to it said, "So...today you are going to show me what you have inside even though *mamita* never wanted to show any one, not even me!"

"Well, you have the key, so open me up," Micaela said in her deep male voice.

"Will you be afraid of what you might find?" she continued in the deep voice.

Even at the young age of eleven, she had a strange feeling that whatever she was about to find, it would make the bond between her and *mamita* even stronger with never having to say a word about it to each other. *Mamita* María José was perceived as an enigma, but after finding the key to the chest and seeing what was inside; Micaela realized that she was not only private and reserved but also a very sad and lonely woman who seldom let her guard down.

Micaela put down the cookie and approaching the shrine with reverence and making the sign of the cross, she took out the key hidden inside St. Anthony's cape.

"This is why they call you the patron saint of lost things, because you also help find things out, huh, huh?" she told the statue.

With a big cleansing breath she got close to the chest and placing the key in its keyhole she struggled turning the key to the right in order to unlock it. She knew time was of the essence because soon enough *mamita* would be returning from mass. The clicking sound of success made Micaela smile and whisper to herself, "I did it!"

Not realizing how heavy the lid would be, she struggled to lift it while making grunting noises that sounded in harmony with those the old chest made and desperately tried also to refrain from making more noise than necessary. She finally managed to have it open and holding the top straight up, Micaela saw her *Mamita*'s beautiful and neatly folded Madeira blouses, along with her woolen shawls made of the softest merino wool. Trying very hard not to disturb a bit of their folds and creases, Micaela picked them up to see what their beauty really hid because she always had sensed that when María José wore these garments something deeper than her flesh was hidden under them. Below these garments was a small box made of Mother of Pearl. Its presence made Micaela quiver and she had never felt like this before. She did not want to open the box but at the same time she could not stop herself from doing so. Pushing aside the garments, she pulled the box out and gently placed it on the nearby table to open it. There, to her amazement, was a picture of a very handsome young man in a linen suit and Panama hat stretching his arms to the viewer in a very inviting stance. She nodded her head and with a deep frown, a puzzled look filled her young face.

Micaela sensed her grandmother to be the viewer but how could she be the viewer? She had never spoken of this man before. Who was he? She thought to herself. She turned the picture over and on the back it had a name Antonio Altero, Madeira Portugal.

The next picture, adding to the surprising awe and bewildered emotions making her heart race, she saw a much younger *mamita* María José in a beautiful small flowered print chiffon dress hugging the man named Antonio Altero from behind, wearing his hat and smiling in the most flirtatious way a young woman could smile. Love was in her eyes and in his as well. Who was this man? Micaela became excitedly curious because he did not resemble any of the males of her clan. He did look like *tío Miguelito* in one of his pictures when he was young. She thought this was most strange since he did not match the description of the man who had summoned *mamita* María José to legitimize their son.

She continued to examine the rest of the items in the box and she came across an envelope with a letter in it that seemed to have been crushed and then smoothed out again with regrets of having crushed it in the first place. The energy she felt from the letter was something Micaela would carry with her for the rest of her life. What were all those feelings that came from these mementos? Why did *mamita* sometimes put the pictures and letter close to her breast and say a prayer in the most fervent way? An array of thoughts rushed through her young mind and she proceeded to open the letter which read,

> "My Dearest Ma. José,
>
> I am very sorry to have to write this letter and tell you that family circumstances prohibit me from coming to Ecuador and making things right for us. You need to understand that with the passing of my father, I must tend to my family estate and marry my long intended to comply with my father's wishes. I want you to know that forever my heart will only belong to María José and I only hope that you also remain true to our love. It is selfish and absurd to ask this of you but I would die if you should ever entertain another man in your life. Please tell our child how unfortunate life can be at times but that I will always love you both. Only loving you always, Antonio"

Micaela could not believe her eyes. What she was reading was astonishingly different from what she knew of the stoic and strong *mamita* María José. Another envelope still remained at the bottom of the box. Micaela reached for it and opening with urgency to see what else she did not know about her beloved *mamita*. This letter felt different from the first. The energy was serious and dignified, something unreal to be felt by a young girl. Before she read it she went directly to see who signed it and it was Miguel Ángel Benavides, *tío Miguelito's* supposed father who wrote to María José before dying.

> "Dear María José,
>
> I hope all is well for you and your son. Antonio tells me that despite the circumstances, you have decided to honor me by giving your child my name following Antonio's

wishes. I know it must be very hard for you to accept what has happened, but do know that I expected more from Antonio than what he has delivered. I know this does not help but I can assure you that he truly loves you and wants to rectify his wrong doings. I do not know why his thinking is the way it is now, but that does not help you at all. Anyway, Antonio has asked me to do him a great favor and because I love him as a brother and I was a witness to the love you shared for each other I have decided to grant him this wish. He has entrusted me with the financial affairs of your son, my godson. I want him to have a normal life without the chiding of not having a father, and thus I have agreed to ask for your hand in marriage to protect your only child. The gangrene has spread throughout my body and my stay in this world is not very long. I know this would come as a great shock but you must understand this is the only way Antonio can make things right for you and your child. I will take this to my grave and I only hope you have the grace to forgive us both and do the right thing for you and Miguel Ángel Benavides He will have a small inheritance from my side plus the military benefits so he can have schooling and medical assistance until his eighteenth year. María José please accept my proposal if only to benefit your son, who you know I would have loved as my own if I had been given more years to live. I hope to be hearing from you at your earliest convenience but please hurry since it is becoming harder and harder to sustain life the way I am. If you decide to come, please bring Miguel Ángel to our ceremony, I want to say farewell to my 'son.'

Respectfully yours,
Miguel Ángel Benavides"

Micaela dropped the letter to the ground and realized she could not look any more at the contents of this trunk because there were too many painful secrets and memories for the woman she loved so dearly. She picked up the letter and accidentally tore it, afraid of being found out she folded it hastily and put it away. She looked at the old clock on the wall and realized *mamita* would be coming soon, she started to place things back. Soon enough, she heard steps and the jingling of keys; hurriedly she finished putting everything away and in her haste placed the key behind Saint Anthony statue and not in the pocket of his cape.

Mamita came in carrying some bread and oranges, and strangely enough she let the door open wide, allowing for the morning light to enter. No longer in darkness Micaela could see all the contents of the room. The stillness of the moment kept her in awe, afraid of what was going to happen if *mamita* found out about her being in the chest. In the light, she could see how everything was in order, pristine and standing still in her presence. Micaela was no longer afraid. It was a beautiful metaphor to see the light coming in allowing her to see far more than the place itself but the secrets of its inhabitant. Micaela pretended she was asleep.

"I know you are awake, you drank all the coffee and spilled some on the table," she told Micaela cleaning the crumbs left on the table and looking intensely at the chest with a frown delineating two lines on top of her forehead, she knew something was amiss. She went toward St. Anthony's statue and did not find the key in its pocket realizing her intuition had been correct. She turned to Micaela and gave her a kiss.

"Wake up sleepy head," nudging her and tickling her. "Did you go in my trunk?"

Hesitating not knowing what the consequences would be if she admitted her guilt, she decided to be honest with the woman she loved and admired so much. "Yes, I'm so sorry."

"It is not nice to be nosey with things that do not belong to you…only rude and uneducated people do that…you must be respectful of things," kissing her cheek she whispered in her ear.

"Promise me that you will be respectful of other people's personal things," she told her brushing Micaela's bangs out of her face. The 'promise' her beloved *mamita* was asking, Micaela knew was the promise to never disclose the contents of the chest.

"I promise," she extended her small child's arms wrapping them around *Mamita's* neck; she whispered back "I love you."

"I know baby, I know."

Without any words, Micaela now knew about real unconditional love. Instinctively, she felt María José's reason for being so sad, lonely and painfully reserved. Furthermore, Micaela could not believe that her *mamita* chose not to sternly reprimand her. Instead she chose to entrust her with an ominous secret, one that only can be taken to the grave. To have this kind of trust bestowed upon one at such a young age was unbelievable. This moment became etched in the deep corners of Micaela's soul and every time life would be unkind she would go back to this Sunday morning where love, secrets and the passion that ran in her veins became tangible gifts creating the power of invincibility and might in her being. Micaela at eleven years old felt proud and honored to be in the circle of women she called family. *Mamita* María José would always let her know she was the special child who held the secrets of her heart.

Micaela came to understand *Mamita's* secret...she had fallen in love with a young man from Portugal, whose name was Antonio Altero. He was from a prominent family in Madeira and had taken María José to introduce her to his family. However, the family deemed her not good enough for the first born and had threatened to disown him if he continued the relationship with the Ecuadorian girl. They had been intimate and Antonio had started a hope chest filling it with the most beautiful linens, embroidered blouses and the merino wool shawls she had come to use only on special occasions. Antonio was the long lost love for whom, she fervently prayed to St. Anthony, pleading to bring him back to her, but to no avail. She never loved anyone else and kept to herself until the day she died.

As the years went by, Micaela learned to cherish her *mamita* even more for the selfless way she loved not only her own mother,

Paloma, but all the children in the family, especially her. Micaela knew that as she grew older she would emulate her, love everyone the way she did and she would also wear pretty soft Madeira-embroidered lacy collar blouses with the woolen shawls, so that she would appear as enigmatic and romantic as her *mamita* María José. Many times she would wonder about these first memories and becoming aware of the difference between the two women who loved her as a child. One trusted and loved her without any questions asked, and the other despondently questioned everything Micaela did and wanted to accomplish in her life.

These many memories from her youth often came to mind in later years. Sometimes they were voices telling her to let her imagination run wild and add to the story of her family as they unfolded in her imaginative soul. They nagged at her heart as though telling her that these were the makings of a writer, the makings of a story teller and she must follow through and write down everything she could so they would not become just splashes of memories but a story to be shared with everyone. She would think of the family's secrets and how she could use them to add to the climax of a story but then she would have to refrain as not to expose the trust and love given to her by those who truly loved her. Micaela would think back to the old dark room and look for answers while questioning her writing aspirations that she knew her parents would not approve of and she always thought back to the mysterious grandmother she had.

Mamita's unconditional love not only gave Micaela the beginnings of her power of being but also helped Paloma's story come alive with each telling. For it was María José who stood behind Paloma in the many family gatherings to serve as her understudy to continue with the story when the memories were too painful for the protagonist to recount.

"Go ahead, darling, keep telling the atrocities done to you... but it is okay, you are a wonderful woman with princesses as daughters. There should be no regrets." María José would tell Paloma as she embraced her and looked into those big brown eyes. Micaela felt the unspoken love between them ran through her veins, rushing through her heart and making her want to exhale at the overwhelming emotion it produced in her. Paloma's crying and blowing her nose would bring Micaela back to the story line where she would hear about the torment in her mother's life.

"My grandfather's obsession to obtain more land clouded his judgment. He wanted to keep the land rather than bear the shame of what had happened to his daughter, my mother." Paloma would say in an agitated manner. Micaela admired, from a young age, the stoic attitude her mother took when stating how her own mother had disdained her. However, she felt sad for all the turmoil it brought to the surface and she could feel the sorrow of her own mother; so that many times in her young age, Micaela wanted to take away the pain from her mother and make it her own.

She admired and revered her mother so that all she wanted for her was to have never felt the pain she had felt as a child. Paloma would continue, "His imprudent behavior would cost him his daughter and his family."

After finding out that her father was more interested in the land than his daughter, Rocío had vowed she would never return home and that the shame her father felt at the disgrace of his only child would be a hundred times worse. She renounced her family, moved to the city, and married an Indian young man with far less social and financial status than her parents would have wanted for her. The "Indian" as he was referred to by the whole family had parented Rocío's two other girls, one who had been perfectly healthy and the other who had been still born. Micaela remembered how the choice, Rocío had made to marry the Indian man still resonated with contempt by the family and no one really liked to talk about this.

Micaela's mother, Paloma, never heard from her half sister or her biological grandparents except to know her grandfather's bad judgment had cost the Díaz Ruiz family all the land they had once possessed. The most interesting aspect of the 'land myth,' as Micaela started calling this part of her mother's story, was that a large area of this land was where the airport of the capital city now stands, and is exactly at the north section of the airport where Rocío's house once stood.

Sounding deeply regretful María José would say, "If it wouldn't have been for mere stupidity, my child would be rich now," referring to Micaela's mother, Paloma.

With great pride and contempt for the circumstances María José would summarize Paloma's beginning: "Rocío had sworn never to come back to her parents' house and the child she was carrying was the *maldición* in her life. She never wanted the child and after her birth, she gave her to Luis to keep since it was the act of his rape that produced this olive skin, brown-eyed girl, who reminded her of all the pain she had to endure not only at the time of the kidnapping but of her parents' abandonment."

With softer candor, holding Paloma's hand she would add, "Yet, here she is looking more beautiful than as a child, with a husband who adores her and children who remind her that life is nothing but a bitter sweet struggle where only the strong survive to tell about it."

These two women would embrace in a stoic manner that would bring pride in the faces of those gathered around seeing them hold each other after all those years of adversity and sadness. It made Micaela love them all the more not knowing that in her life the recollection of this precise moment would come to mind, saving her from her desperate and agonizingly empty moments her own life would bring at times.

Paloma Díaz: Micaela's Overpowering Force

Paloma Díaz, the unwanted child conceived out of the worst perfidy, had been born with the exotic features of a Mediterranean Queen. She was petite and well proportioned. She had beautiful soft olive skin, jet black hair, a button nose and large almond-shaped brown eyes that could speak louder than her small red lips. The vivacity and precociousness of the child gave way to the social butterfly of womanhood. It was Paloma's conduct of propriety foiled by her superb social graces that forged her daughter Micaela's character. It became an example for her as she grew older, and like vignettes of a great production, Micaela would often go back and peruse them to show her the way to handle some of the difficult circumstances of her own life.

Micaela remembered her mother meeting people on the streets, asking about their well being, always smiling in the most proper way. So it was no surprise that many times the parties and celebrations of secular or religious nature would happen at Micaela's home. Especially, when they finally moved from the "fortress-like" building they rented to a small house of their own with a backyard containing a small garden where Paloma would delve into her love of gardening. Soon after moving to their new house,

Micaela's mother, Paloma, announced that the family would be getting together with family and friends to celebrate All Saints' Day Feast, the day after Halloween in America, November first.

The celebration would include a sweet porridge made of blueberries and pineapples called *Colada Morada*. It would be eaten with freshly baked bread shaped like dolls for the children and braided wreaths for the adults. The preparation of this meal was something of a feast in itself. Micaela loved how the women gathered around in the small kitchen and each had a task of their own. While joking and teasing, they tried to outdo each other in making the bread and porridge. Paloma would come from the market with big blueberries and fresh pineapple.

"Boy! It is becoming harder and harder to get the blueberries and pineapples for this dish," Paloma would exclaim as she proceeded to put the enormous blueberries in a colander to wash them.

"Froilán! Could you come and give me a hand with the pineapples, please," she would yell for her son to do the perilous job of peeling the hard and prickly pineapple skin and cutting it into small pieces that would become the blueberry porridge's garnish.

The house soon had the smell of blueberries and thyme cooking in water with lots of sugar and cloves. The aroma of the bread baking in the oven would intertwine with the sweet smell of blueberries and like spirits of the sublime world; these aromas would dance around the house. They would enter, meshing with the curtains that swayed along with the breeze flowing through the windows, taking a whiff of the smells and seizing the movement of the people gathered in the kitchen. It continued a mesmerizing flow of intense energy that made Micaela's spirit soar at the innocent age of eleven. She would run back and forth from the kitchen to the dining room making sure that no one touched her bread doll which glistened in the afternoon sunlight making the sugar crystals appear like diamonds spread out on a blanket made of amber. Micaela knew moments like these would never leave her memory and she would use them as tools to create her own family environment.

The year this ritual became engraved in Micaela's memory was the year that while making the bread in the shape of dolls, *Mamita* María José told the story of the time when Micaela's mother, Paloma, had refused to partake of this holiday because she was angry with her real mother, Rocío. When she heard the story, Paloma, a grown woman, wife, and mother of four children, instantly became the eight-year-old who had refused to eat the *Colada Morada* in protest of her mother's rejection. *Mamita* María José went on to say it had been the afternoon of All Saints' Day when she had taken Paloma to see her mother, Rocío, to ask for her blessing on this holy day. Paloma had stood in the doorway apprehensive to ask for the blessing. Rocío never welcomed or invited her inside the house. Instead, in a scornful way, she told Paloma to go away, "Take the *colada morada*, bread and go home!"

As Paloma continued to take the goods, María José admonished Rocío asking her, "Why won't you give her your blessing? She is your child after all!"

While *Mamita* María José still insisted Paloma ask for her mother's blessing, she had also convinced Rocío to approach the child to bless her. María José left mother and child to deal with each other trying to escape the poignant friction of the scene. However, Paloma could feel her mother's unwillingness to do so, to which she reacted by not wanting to take the bread doll nor the porridge. Paloma became indignant and proud and ran out to the street to catch up with *Mamita* María José. When she reached her, she had neither the porridge nor the bread, upon seeing this *Mamita* María José asked Paloma,

"Where is the *colada morada* and bread your mother gave you?"

"I don't want anything from that woman... She does not like me!" Paloma responded angrily.

"You go back to her house right now, and apologize for leaving your gift behind. It is not polite to reject a gift, especially one that represents this holy day." *Mamita* María José scolded her.

"Where is your humbleness child? she added.

"You do not need to be proud like this, Paloma!" Gently grabbing Paloma's little arm and pushing her toward her biological mother's house.

She proceeded to tell her, "Nothing good ever comes from being so proud." And as if all the reproach was not enough, *Mamita* María José added sternly, "She is your mother and you must always love her despite her feelings for you!"

Apprehensive and full of pride, Paloma, went back and told her mother, "Thank you, for the gift. However, you do not have to do this ever again! I will never come back for any gift or your blessing."

Rocío grabbed the small child by her face and intensely looking at her daughter said, "If it would have been up to me, you would not be coming to me and asking for a damn thing. I hate the way you ruined my life and for that I will despise you as I despise my own family, the ones that could have prevented all this from happening!"

In astonishment and fright, Paloma's reaction came unexpectedly in the most surprising way. Pushing Rocío's hands away from her face, she yelled back, "Don't you ever touch me again! You are nothing but a poor excuse of a mother! Damn you and all your rich family!"

She turned away proudly and without looking back, she walked out of the portico and onto the street. She found the cold air coming from the Andes peaks refreshing, washing her tears away from her red angry cheeks. Grimacing and sticking her tongue out, she hurried down the cobbled stone street trying to catch up to the person she called *Mamita*. Reaching for her hand while passing her the bread, she glanced at the porridge and softly looking away, she said to herself, "I will never go to that house and see her again!"

A year after this incident, at the young age of twenty-three, Rocío, Micaela's biological grandmother passed away from child birth complications.

When *Mamita* María José had finished her story, Paloma would think back to this moment reiterating her thoughts and feelings. She would never forget how proud she felt at her own refusal of her mother's contempt for her. With a false sense of pride that made her think she could hide the poignant details of her young life, she would add, "At the time of the porridge and bread episode, I felt the finality of our relationship enveloping my soul with the same cold air that came from the Andes peaks washing my tears away. I knew then there would never be another moment in my life where I would allow anyone to make me feel so discounted, so belittled, and who ever tried to do that would only know of my indifference."

Micaela watched her mother become angry and resentful just as if it was happening at that moment. Little did Micaela know at the time, that in some inexplicable way, Paloma would treat Micaela the same way her own mother had treated her. She would become very critical of Micaela's behavior and would watch over her to the point of making her feel inadequate and at times she would show Micaela so much indifference that she knew firsthand how her mother must have felt all those years ago being rejected by Rocío. Ironically, it would be the cold and unreachable ways of her mother's conditional love and how she seemed to deliberately misunderstand Micaela's precocious and vivacious nature, much like her own, that would become the force that saved Micaela from all the pains and sorrow that would come her way.

Mamita María José would look to the people around and say, "After that day I never took my *guagua* to see her again. Not even, right before she died when Rocío asked to see her one last time."

Micaela also could not understand the pride these women felt and the anger they harbored toward Rocío. Micaela would often ask herself, "Why are they so hateful?"

Without realizing that she too was harboring the same contempt for her biological grandmother as the women of her clan, she murmured under her breath, "It wasn't my mother's fault what happened to her, you idiot!" Each time she made sure no one heard her, except once, when she did not notice *Mamita* María José looking at her intensely. *Mamita* continued to reprimand her by saying, "You should not call names to the dead."

However, Micaela would keep questioning...*Why didn't she love her baby? Why was she so mean to a little girl?* And this was her first lesson in obstinate pride. *No one will ever make me feel so unloved and hated!* She thought to herself, becoming distracted by the people who started to enter the dining room where the food was being served. Laughter and noise would march in taking away the sullen feelings of hurt that the retelling of that part of the story would bring to mind. They would eat the bread and porridge that had a bittersweet taste, just like the story her *Mamita* María José had just told.

Thus, it seemed every family celebration of religious holidays, birthdays or festivities were the places and times where the story of her mother's life would enter Micaela's ears infusing her soul with an intuitive sense of might preparing her to guard her being just like the women in her clan. The words became engraved in her mind like the engraved, stone monuments in a cemetery and it created these wonderful vignettes and ideas that as a child, Micaela could not understand, nor could she make sense of the despair they brought to her. As she grew up and heard more stories, she came to understand her mother's loneliness and her quest to be loved as a child, as a woman, and as a mother. Micaela came to understand her mother's relentless pride and indifference to those who tried to cross her even in the smallest ways. This was Paloma's way of protecting herself from her mother's rejection, from so much pain that came at the beginning of her being. Her mother's way of protecting herself would be the one thing Micaela would fight against all her life in order to become her own person and not the bitter, resentful obstinate proud woman she knew her mother to be and sadly, her two other sisters as well.

As such, from these stories, Micaela understood the way her mother loved all of her children, as well the expectations she placed on each child. And from the time they moved to America, Micaela took personally and very much to heart, her mother's high expectations of her and how dutifully she would try to meet them. She learned to listen quietly while her mother addressed her in the most stern and, at times, unloving way. However, as Micaela grew up her mother's critical eye became a point of friction and contention between the two of them. At times, it made her want to be like Paloma...hurtful...speaking in the same way as Paloma had told her own mother: "Do not worry, I will never ask for your blessing again." Little did Micaela know that at the time of her mother's passing, the ritual of blessing her children would become a poignant moment in her own life.

Micaela remembered Paloma's stories becoming like religious parables, full of wisdom teaching a lesson or two, like the time when Micaela had borrowed a shirt from a classmate that suited her pants better than the one she owned. Her mother became agitated and distraught at Micaela wearing someone else's blouse and proceeded to show her the skin condition, *Vitiligo*, that Micaela knew had nothing to do with borrowing other people's clothes.

"Look, this is what will happen to you if you wear someone else's clothes. You do not know where they have been nor if they are healthy and clean," her mother exclaimed throwing her arms up and showing great distress by running her fingers through her hair to which Micaela would often roll her eyes and grimace in contempt. Vitiligo is the loss of pigmentation in patchy areas throughout one's body and is caused by stress. Well, Paloma used this condition to instruct all her children not to borrow other people's clothes, shoes or anything else for that matter. Her *Vitiligo* story would begin with *Mamita* María José's place of employment. She had been a laundress at the Vincent de Paul orphanage and convent. *Mamita* María José would take Paloma with her to work, and because she was such a beautiful and vivacious child with big brown eyes, the nuns would let her stay and watched over her more than they did the other orphans. Micaela would often imagine the big white walls of this convent with the nuns in their brown and white habits running around like Julie Andrews up in the mountains singing, "The hills are alive with the sound of music." But her mother would remove all that romanticism and replace it with the gothic, scary melodrama of her story.

The convent was far away from the main road perched up on a hillside near a long cliff that had an eerie feeling of a precipice. A narrow dirt road led down to the river where most of the laundry was done. The drudgery of climbing down the hill, washing in the river and then climbing the hills back to hang the wash on laundry lines near the patio of the convent must have been dreadful for those doing the work.

"What torture! How long did *Mamita* María José do this job, mom?' Micaela would ask.

"Oh, she did that for a long time, she retired from that job." Paloma would answer.

"No wonder, she is so strong," Micaela would say very proud of the determination of her adoptive grandmother to work so hard for the pension she received each month that would provide independence in her old age.

The convent was not white walled and pristine as Micaela had it in her mind, but rather it was old and grimy with beige walls that needed painting. The nuns were strict and often mean to the orphans, but her mother was loved. Paloma remembered the kitchen area where the employees would gather and receive a pint of milk with freshly baked bread.

"The nuns loved me so, that they gave *Mamita* two portions; one for me and one for her," Paloma would say full of pride and longing for the warmth of the gesture.

As the years went by, and Paloma became an adolescent, she met two orphaned girls, one was a mulatto girl named Sylvia and the other a girl named Rosalba. The three girls had become friends. However, the friendship with Silvia became disastrous because of her envy of the fact that Paloma was not really an orphan, but rather the daughter of a worker in the convent, a girl who came and did as she pleased just because the nuns liked her. Rosalba on the other hand, was a sweeter and more understanding girl than Sylvia and became a good friend to Paloma.

Rosalba and Paloma remained friends many years after Rosalba left the Convent at the age of eighteen. Paloma had attended Rosalba's wedding and they visited each other as the years went by. Rosalba lived half-way to the city bordering the southern part of town where Paloma, María José and the four children lived. Many times Paloma, Micaela and her younger sister, Rebeca, would walk downtown and if there was a down pour, Paloma and the girls always stayed at Rosalba's house until the rain subsided. She lived near the convent where they both grew up. Rosalba would serve them coffee and bread, and they would laugh and share stories of the envious Sylvia.

"Do you remember Sylvia?" Rosalba asked Micaela's mother on one of those visiting days.

"Of course! How could I forget her? I still have the white patches she gave me," Paloma would say with reproach in her voice.

"Well, I saw her the other day. She doesn't look good for her age," Rosalba added.

"Where did you see her," Paloma asked curiously, as Micaela with great anticipation also wanted to know where this woman was now.

"At the Woman's Center. She asked about you." Rosalba told Paloma.

"You are kidding!" Paloma retorted.

"No. She said someone told her you directed that center and maybe you could help her with a health issue she is now facing." Rosalba lamented.

"I told her that you probably didn't want to see her. After all, she is the girl who gave you vitiligo. She had this condition and never told anyone, until the day you saw the white blotchy areas on her skin when she changed her clothes," she said indignantly.

Rosalba would preach to Paloma's girls: "Your mother contracted vitiligo from Sylvia, so never wear other people's clothes, and listen to your mother when she tells you not to, because this really happened to her."

Micaela would roll her eyes and think it was nonsense, but that is how her mother taught her children never to wear borrowed clothes. The story would always come to mind, especially when Micaela came across the picture of Rosalba and Paloma as teenagers in bathing suits, posing for the picture at the river bank. It was Micaela's favorite picture of her mother as a young person with her friend. Looking at the two girls in the black and white picture with their big smiles and zest for life, Micaela could see the vibrancy of their youth echoed by the ripples and splashes of water in the background as the river flowed with the same energy of the two young females in the picture, laughing, seemingly carefree of what the future would bring. For they seemed really hoping for better futures despite the circumstances of their birth. Paloma with parents who did not want her and Rosalba, the unwanted orphan.

These bits and pieces of her life were told many times and from that Micaela would make the story of her mother. She knew they were true, because the happy stories would be happy and the sad ones would always bring Micaela's mother down. It became apparent that indeed these things happened because every time they were told, the feelings of resentment, envy and anger filled Paloma's eyes and she would become distant and aloof. Micaela at a young age became aware of how her mother guarded herself by retelling the stories that helped her create and maintain the big walls that kept her intact, in a place where the hurt of contempt, and the pain of being given away would never touch her heart.

Paloma's unyielding pride helped her create walls and separations at times when they were not even necessary. Micaela at the tender age of eleven would ponder a story that she heard and try to make some sense of it, but she did not know why. She remembered the 'parable' where her mother instructed that beauty is in the eyes of the beholder and that physical beauty does not last but integrity and dignity stay with you in times eternal. This part of her life would always be brought up when a cousin of hers, Grecia, who was an enigma in and of itself, would come to visit. She was a woman in her late fifties with a few extra pounds but her age lines and added weight could not deny the beauty she must have been in her younger years. She was always perfumed and impeccably dressed when she came to visit. She had an opulent presence that was like an oxymoron because of her brutally honest manner and saucy vocabulary. None of the well behaved cousins and women relatives would dare to be like Grecia. For Grecia's opulence came for her 'hard earned money, laying on my back,' as she would say sending the proper Paloma into a hissy fit asking Grecia to hold her tongue. The ritual of coffee and fresh baked bread around four o'clock in the afternoon would take on a more festive and urgent feeling as the good china would be brought out because Grecia was visiting. "Micaela go to the bakery and get us some piping hot bread. Do not linger talking to everyone in sight, do you hear?" Paloma would instruct her child who gladly took any and every chance to leave the house to explore the neighborhood.

It was a precious and delicious trip for Micaela, who still at the age of eleven would wander off to do errands for her mother, and while doing them, would imagine all kinds of stories and talk to the characters in them. On these occasions, she became the great impresario of a big production, and in the instance of buying the bread for the afternoon coffee, her imagination took her off to a jungle. She knew the few houses down the block had fig trees by their fences and she always went underneath the branches pretending it was the jungle.

It has been days since I have eaten anything, I am famished and thirsty! She would think as she went underneath the first fig tree, pretending to push the leaves aside and once she got to the corner where she could see the entrance to the bakery two blocks down, she would exclaim, "It is a mirage, do not be fooled by the aroma of the fresh bread!"

As she looked both ways for the oncoming traffic, "watch out for the cannibals nearby Micaela. You made it to the 'mirage' and the smell is so overwhelming, it must not be a mirage. It's a miracle, a bakery in the middle of the jungle!" she would exclaim in a melodramatic motion always making sure no one was looking.

It never failed, as she approached the bakery, the smell of bread would make her hungry. She would enter this seemingly long, dark tunnel that allowed the red, piping hot ovens at the end to give light to the commotion of the men in white, pulling the baking pans with the beautiful mounds of golden brown bread. She would wait until the bakers put other loaves of bread in the oven. She watched the dough rise in a matter of minutes. The loaves would come out of the oven, the sweet aroma of fresh baked bread rising from them.

Micaela would talk to the bakers, "How long does it take to make the dough?"

"All day long, sometimes," they would answer as they winked at the precociousness of the young skinny girl.

"Do you want to try making bread?" some of the bakers would ask Micaela.

"Yeah, so I can bake it and eat it as it comes out of the oven all day long," she would mimic the bakers' comment, winking back at them.

The bakers knew Micaela's family and they were nice to her, sometimes even entertaining her vivid imagination. They would ask, "So, did you fight any cannibals today as you came into the jungle?"

She would then make up some elaborate story to tell them and out of kindness, the owner would give the precocious child a couple of extra loaves, which she would devour on the way home. It was payment for the story she had told, bringing laughter and amusement to the bakery owner, a sweet lady who also knew her mother and was a good friend of her family.

"You are going to be writer one day, you know it?" the shop owner would tell Micaela.

"You have such a vivid imagination, for such a young girl!" she would add, making Micaela wonder about the statement.

Micaela would trek back home, bringing in the bread, with its fresh smell still lingering, almost waiting for the moment she entered the small kitchen. The smell of freshly made coffee would marry the smell of the freshly baked bread. A warm feeling would come over the people who gathered at the table, talking about the day. After welcoming cousin Grecia, the stories would begin.

"Remember the orphan mulatto girl, named Sylvia?" Paloma would ask.

Paloma's cousin would respond, "The one that gave you vitiligo."

"Yeah, that one," was Paloma's answer.

Micaela would take a bite of yet another piece of bread, rolling her eyes at this remark, because she knew it was the signal to get comfortable, to listen to the coming parable.

"After Sylvia left the convent she went to work. I could not go to school because mom did not have the money." Paloma lamented the latter part of the statement.

"So, we both got a job at this manufacturing company where they made stockings," she continued.

"I started to do some clerical work because I was good with numbers." Paloma proudly would state.

"Sylvia, on the other hand worked in the production part of the plant," Paloma added with a condescending voice.

Micaela took note of her expression and even as a small child, she thought, *Why is she being condescending about a production* line? It is an honest job, so why is it such a big bad deal to be in that part of the plant?

Paloma's eyes would light up at the retelling of the story. She was a vain little woman and this job would give her the means to buy hosiery. She foolishly thought that made up for the sadness of not being able to afford go to school. She was resigned to her situation and thought the job would provide for other things as well. She would get ahead and become somebody special someday. She was sixteen years old at this place and time. Sylvia had seen how Paloma advanced in the company so she started the rumor that Paloma was where she was because no one could say 'no' to her pleading brown eyes.

"God only knows, what she did to get her job," Sylvia started saying around work.

The boss was a middle aged man who took the rumor to heart and thought maybe there was something to find there. Paloma was tending to her work and out of the corner of her eye, she had seen him approach her desk and asked her to stay after work.

"I need you to finish some reports after work tonight. Of course you will be compensated for this time," he told Paloma.

Later that evening after everyone had gone home, Paloma was alone in his office and as she started to put her papers away, he entered the room. As he came closer to her, he whispered in a deliberate seductive way, "Of all the girls here, you are the one I want to give my time to."

"How about your wife?" Paloma responded.

As he grabbed her by the arms, Paloma pulled away from him and shouted, "Even if you were not married, what makes you think I would want you!"

The man was indignant at Paloma's denigration and attempted to accost her again as she started running out of the office. She turned and kicked him hard. He came at her and grabbed her by the leg. She screamed and fought her way free of his grasp.

"I kicked him where it hurts the most," she would say with a triumphant look in her eyes.

But as she tried to escape, his watch had snagged one of her nylons and ripped it. When she realized what had happened, she was angry at the man for trying to force himself on her, but she would say with a cynical smile, "He dared to rip my nylons! Can you believe that?" Everyone would start laughing.

Micaela could never understand why such a grave story would be made light of. *What about her almost being raped?* She would think to herself. However, this was Paloma's way of recounting this horrific night. Years later, Micaela understood why her mother made this story as light as possible. She would say, "When we focus on the positive things, we take care of ourselves and who we are inside, and then no one can touch us negatively."

Is this a riddle or what? Micaela would think. Then she added what became her mantra as she was growing up: "All these grown-ups are crazy!"

"We keep our dignity and integrity by never allowing ourselves to be in perilous situations, so we can take care of the things that really matter, allowing us time to pay attention to the small details," Paloma continued saying.

"I should have known better than to put myself in that vulnerable position," she added.

"But I knew from that moment how to be on the lookout for the many men, who after hearing my carefree laughter, would think they could take advantage of me as they wished." She made the didactic point for her female children to know.

Indeed, Micaela knew that there were many men who came to accost her mother because of her genuine love of life. And it was her carefree laughter which made her big brown eyes sparkle like the brightest stars in the darkest of nights, that vibrant vivacity that Micaela wished to possess. To be able to speak with one's eyes as her mother often did was Micaela's dream.

Paloma's beauty indeed almost became a problem until she met the man of her dreams, Micaela's father, Antonio Galarza, the one man who could say no to those big brown eyes and to the vibrancy of her being. Paloma and her mother, María José, had moved to a new neighborhood when Paloma was about seventeen. They had been there only a week, and one morning, when Antonio was leaving his apartment they passed each other by the entrance.

Micaela remembered how Paloma would describe him. Traces of young love were in her mother's voice, but there was also resentment, which as Micaela got older she would come to understand.

"He was a tall and handsome young man, slender and dressed in the clothes of the time, which make him look suave and elegant," Paloma would say, longing to be in the past once again.

"Your father was like a young Omar Sharif," she said, after she saw the movie, *Doctor Zhivago*.

"Marcello Mastroniani has nothing your father doesn't have. *El Italiano* does not even do justice to your father, he was that handsome!" she would exclaim with her eyes lighting up, just the way a young girl's eyes light up at the moment of her first kiss.

Micaela loved to hear this part of her mother's life because she hoped one day she too would be loved by a man the way her father loved her mother. Paloma had encountered him one day in passing and looked at him with the demure eyes of a damsel in distress. Upon seeing her eyes, Micaela's father would later tell her, "I just could not help but fall in love with those eyes."

One day, one of the neighbors who raised turkeys in her backyard had been robbed and in the commotion of determining who took the turkeys, these two people, Paloma and Antonio, had gone to the scene of the crime and struck up a conversation. They both were young and upon meeting for the first time, their love became the cliché "Love at first sight." They knew Micaela's mother was too young to be seeing anyone, however, they devised ways to meet. Having Rosalba as their accomplice, they would sneak to the theater and to the river bank. They would see each other after work and Antonio would walk her home. The temptation proved to be too strong and the two became lovers giving into their passion and desires, Micaela's mother bore her first child at the young age of nineteen. Needless to say, this part of the story of her life would be told with the most reverence. It was the most important story that Micaela would hear because it taught her that you must always wait and not give into the pressures of "love," and Micaela would wonder what pressures? She later would know the importance of this lesson.

Paloma would say, "After the turkey incident, I had to get married. Thank God your father was good looking because it made things easier." She would add with a smirk on her face.

Easier for what if they loved each other? Why does it have to be so hard? Micaela would wonder. And with her melodramatic antics she would leave exclaiming, "I don't think I will ever fall in love. It just all seems so hard!" Her mother would look at her nodding her head in disbelief at how dramatic this child was. She would then tell her, "I will remind you of these words one day, young lady!"

The wedding day of Paloma and Antonio in the church nearby came sooner than they expected. "It was an overcast Saturday morning that promised rain," Paloma would describe her wedding day.

"*Mamita* María José was upset at the whole thing, and when your father's mom came to ask for my hand in marriage, she was rude and unwilling to cooperate," Paloma added.

"I was too upset not only because of the embarrassment of the pregnancy, but also because I was hormonal," Paloma would say with the same anger of the past.

"However, I was mostly upset because of how I had imagined my wedding to be; full of people coming to the church where I would make my own dress with the finest lace and silk, adorned with tiny pearl buttons and flowers that signify the purity of the white gown, the church filled with flowers and both families waiting in anticipation for the union to begin. But no, it did not turn out this way," she continued.

"The chances of a white wedding gown were nil, flowers, much less, and I could forget about a party of any sort. The ignominy of my actions was not allowed in those days, and as such, the event could not be celebrated in any sort of way, according to my mother," Paloma added didactically.

Instead, Paloma had bought herself a very pristine, *a la Joan Crawford-style* blue suit and a hat to match. On her wedding day, she walked through the narrow streets of the old colonial part of town in which she lived toward the Church of San Sebastian with *Mamita* María José. They walked the cobblestone street in complete silence trying to say many things but unable to speak a word. They looked at each other with compassion and then looked away so neither one of them could see the tears in each other's eyes. Slowly the white exterior walls of the convent gave way to the large wrought iron doors and entrance to the church.

"I saw myself open the door with *Mamita* María José behind me, and what I knew should have been a moment of joy, became a moment of sorrow, for I disappointed the woman who had taken care of me and wanted better for me," she would say in her saddest voice.

In anticipation, Antonio was already inside the church waiting for Paloma to arrive. His mother had objected to this day since *Mamita* María José was not willing to cooperate and make the necessary arrangements like Antonio's mother had suggested. As if in a bad sequenced dream, Paloma would remember this day and the way she told the story, one could see the sadness of the occasion that was a quick flash back, "We entered the church, the priest unaware that I was with child, went through the Catholic ritual, gave us the blessings and we went home. No pictures, no celebration or fanfare." They had gone home and without much ado, their young love and marriage began, lasting some forty years.

"That's it?" Micaela would ask in astonishment.

"Why, didn't dad buy you a wedding dress, a cake, flowers or something?" she would add but was ignored.

Quickly dispelling any lingering sadness at the retelling of their wedding day, Paloma would add, "Your father made up for the lack of fanfare on that day by calling me *mi negrita linda* everyday since we got married. He will always call me pretty, and how my eyes made him weak at the knees every time he saw me, so I guess I should be happy with that, no?"

Micaela's father, Antonio, after forty years of marriage would still say, "Your mother was pretty and still is. Look at her, *mi negrita Linda*!" Paloma was very pretty indeed. At the age of thirty-eight with four children, she was nominated to enter a beauty pageant. Micaela could never forget the time her mother won the contest where only married mothers could participate and the winner became the Queen of Mothers. It was a sight to see her mother on her throne in a boat-collared '60's dress made of off-white brocade with matching pumps, gloves up to her elbows. Paloma sat there surrounded by her entourage which included Froilán, her escort and first son. Protected, admired and loved, she looked beautiful indeed. With her black bouffant hair, she was crowned with a shimmering tiara only to be eclipsed by the translucent sparkles of Paloma's big brown eyes that spoke volumes of happiness and joy.

At the sight of all this pageantry, Micaela knew almost instinctively that for her mother, it was a victory over all those years of pain and rejection. She suffered as a child and hid her pain, but it did not matter as she sat on this throne, she was victorious, the Queen of Mothers and no one would reject her now; no one would dare to have any contempt for her. Victory indeed was sweet for the poor unwanted olive skinned child who had grown up to be the most dutiful mother her women's club possessed and they had bestowed upon her the title she so rightly deserved, Queen of Mothers.

This all came about from her involvement as a volunteer at one of the Catholic Charity Associations, where she blossom teaching illiterate children. She had enlisted at the center for a class on speech writing and had become one of the most eloquent speech writers for the association. She wrote poems and short stories that she never let anyone read for fear of being rejected. Rejection was something Micaela's mother understood, but was never able to accept. Yet it was something Micaela would not only feel first hand from her 'dutiful mother,' but felt she was expected to accept. Micaela was happy for her mother's achievements and qualities but often wondered why such a compassionate person with the world at large could be so critical and despondent at times with her own precocious middle child. It was as though Micaela was reliving the cycle of her mother's life as the ostracized child, much like Rocío, her own mother, had chosen to feel about Paloma at the time of her birth. The only contrast between Micaela and Paloma was that Micaela would never stop trying to get closer to her mother's heart, in order, to feel the love and affection Paloma gave freely to others but not to her.

Micaela remembered how creative her mother was because she also knew how to sew like a professional seamstress. Paloma would bring beautiful bolts of colorful fine fabrics home and put them on the large dining room table. She would then get her scissors, a French curve and tailor's chalk. Then measuring here and there on the material, she would pick up the scissors and would go at the material like a mad woman, cutting and tracing and pinning and transferring all these pieces to the sewing machine, and then like magic, a beautiful dress would be made. Paloma would wear it or Micaela's older sister, Isabel, would be the model as they both looked beautiful in the dresses she made.

Micaela would try to copy her mother, using the remnants to make the same beautiful outfits for her dolls that looked like Barbie, but were not. She wanted to be so much like her mother but to no avail, she was disappointed to see that her mother would not share her enthusiasm, expertise, and help Micaela's emulation of her sewing abilities. Micaela would feel inadequate, discarded and would end up feeling frustrated at the way her outfits turned out to be mediocre in comparison to her mother's. She also tried to keep a journal in which little speeches where written just like her mother's but instead of praising Micaela for trying she was always admonish by Paloma who told her, "That is nonsense, you need to study your academic subjects so you can achieve excellence."

Micaela knew then she would never stop wanting to be like her mother, a writer who delivered eloquent speeches instructing women to be strong and mighty like her grandmother and her own mother. She too would be the social butterfly and would have the many friends and acquaintances so she can entertain just like her mother did. At the tender age of twelve, she took the opportunity and started writing in a composition book the things that touched her soul the most in the course of each day; like the incident with the pharmacist that was about to happen in one of her school breaks that allowed her to roam the neighborhood on her brother's bike when her mother was away.

A pharmacist friend of the family, Dr. Fernando Rodriguez, relocated his store and while cleaning up, discarded some old note pads. Micaela saw this and asked him if she could have them. He was curious as to why Micaela wanted the pads and asked, "What are you going to do with them?"

"Well for starters, I am going to write some of my adventures on them." She smiled.

"Oh, so you are going to be a writer?" he asked looking at the languid skinny child caress the note pads as if they were some kind of sacred relics never seen before.

"Are you really going to use these pads?" he inquired.

"Of course! This is good paper and it should not be thrown away. The story of my life is what these pages are going to contain!" Micaela exclaimed in her dramatically way.

Looking at the child's enthusiasm, Dr. Rodriguez went inside the store and brought a box full of note pads, a binder and some pencils and pens, "Here you are Miss Story Teller, you can write to your heart's content with the story of your life. When you publish it, let me know. I want to know if you wrote about me or not."

Micaela's mouth dropped open surprised at Dr. Rodriguez' generosity and most importantly, at his acknowledging something so dear to her. That day standing in front of the pharmacy counter she knew she would write about everyone and everything, whether her mother liked it or not. "Dr. Rodriguez you will be in the pages of my life story in the kindest way, and I will write a poem that will rhyme with all the medicines you sell in your store. How would you like that?" Micaela exclaimed. She ran home with such excitement. She could hardly contain herself.

When she got home, she realized no one was there for her to share the great news that she had been given pens and paper to start her literary career. She put down the box of 'sacred relics' and ever so gently, pulling out one of the insignificant preprinted pharmaceutical pads, Micaela touched it as if it was paper made of fine linen that could only be used to write the lost golden religious scrolls. She placed the stiff note pad up against her cheek as if her thoughts could be transferred onto its pages. She exhaled a deep breath closing her eyes and caressing the pad that made her smile with genuine happiness. She immediately started to write down what had happened when she heard the front door slam shut. She got up from her bed full of note pads and pencils and tip toed toward the window so she could see who had just arrived. It was her mother. Her gut feeling told her to hide Dr. Rodriguez' gift under the bed. Paloma came into the room and seeing Micaela come out from under the bed, questioned her, "What are you doing? What are you hiding? Are you in trouble again?"

"Good afternoon Mami. How was your meeting this morning?" she asked trying to evade the interrogation.

"I asked you a question. What are you doing under the bed?" Paloma said, raising her voice.

"I was looking for the paper shoes I made for Rebeca. She could not find them and I thought they might be under my bed. She will be mad if I lose them. Have you seen them anywhere or did the dog chew them up - huh Mami?" Micaela quickly made up the story of the shoes and after her mother was appeased with her lie, she was left alone in her room. She wrote it all down on the new pad with a title "How Quickly One Can Be Fooled."

Without realizing it, she started to make some doodling on the paper to go along with her shoe story. Micaela's mother appeared in the doorway and saw all the paper and pencils.

"What is all that? child!" she asked indignantly, realizing she had been lied to by her daughter.

"It is just some paper Dr. Rodriguez was throwing away. He gave it to me, he said I could start writing the story of my life," Micaela said sheepishly knowing her mother's wrath was about to be unleashed but instead what happened became more hurtful.

"The story of your life, the nonsense you make up in your head, who would be interested in that story? You are nothing but a constant reminder of how dreams made of sand are just as easily destroyed, you silly girl. Put those papers away and go outside and play with your little sister!"

Micaela sadly listened to what her mother said, trying to stop the tears from rolling down her cheeks. She collected the papers and putting them inside the binder, she saw a tear splash onto a pristine white sheet. It created a perfect round, grey circle that expanded by its absorption into the paper. In awe, she thought of what her mother had just said and even though the dreams of sand made no sense to her, she knew that her mother's approval of her wanting to become a writer would be unreachable as was her love and acceptance. As much as Micaela tried to earn her mother's approval of becoming a writer, Paloma would always dissuade her. Micaela's aspirations of becoming an eloquent public speaker, as well was shattered by the inspiration itself, her mother. But with the same obstinate determination of her ancestors she wrote when no one was looking.

She would take any moment her mother was not present to write on her beloved note pads. She loved to go to her *Mamita María José's* apartment and fake being asleep so she did not have to go to church, but instead, stay by herself to drink the milk and eat the cookie as she wrote little episodes of school and neighborhood events of the week before. She made notes of some of her mother's designs or just copied poetry from the many books she borrowed from the nearby library. It became a ritual to go under the ironing board when the laundress, Carmela, came to iron their linens, and being a good reporter, she would ask her many questions about her life. She would then write a story using the answers Carmela gave her and read it to her the next time she came. Much to Micaela's delight, Carmela listened to the story she was telling with a genuine appreciation and understanding that Micaela had taken the time to do something like that for her. Micaela often went in the back of her mother's garden to secretly write when her mother was away. She loved to hear some of the adults who took care of her talk about her in the third person upon seeing her efforts in continuing with her writing despite her mother's disapproval. They would say to each other, "Do not disturb the writer. She is in her element right now. Can't you see the steam coming from her little head as she is cooking up another story?"

Micaela did not mind the adults making light of her choice at such a tender age because she knew in her heart of hearts, even then, this is what she wanted to be...a writer...a story teller so she can share her love of books and their written word.

However, the ominous cloud of Paloma's unrelenting ways of raising her children was ever present. And in between all the stories told of her life, Micaela learned how proud her mother was. She was proud to a fault and the poignancy of her stories had made her a bit detached even from her own children. To be a writer or approach any creative endeavor was not good enough for her.

"I learned the craft of sewing to help your father...not to be just anybody's artisan," she would say haughtily. Yet Paloma's desire to see her children achieve more than what she had by marrying so young, blinded her at times. She became intransigent when picking the field of study for her children. They all had to be professionals in some illustrative career...a doctor, a lawyer, an engineer. How dare a child choose a creative field? This cold and detached way her mother inculcated in her children to become 'somebody' made her become aloof and distant. Micaela could not even remember when her mother kissed her or gave her a hug. She never heard any words of praise even when Micaela would appear in the skits at school. She remembered being a Spanish flamenco dancer with castanets and a tall mantilla on her small head hoping to have anyone give her praise on how authentic she looked, but, not even her mother mentioned such a detail. She was a wise man and an astronaut in her school productions, yet she would never hear her mother say anything nice, or for that matter, indifferent about the roles she played.

Even more unfortunate was the preferential treatment Paloma had for her older daughter Isabel. Who because of her beauty always played an angel or the Virgin Mary, and had been chosen to participate in a pageant. Micaela always thought, *I cannot wait until I grow up so I can be in a pageant or two.* The afternoon her mother and sister were choosing fabric for the garments to be worn in the pageant, Micaela overheard a conversation her mother was having with the next door neighbor and best friend, Cecilia. While looking at the beautiful pieces of cloth, Cecilia went to say, "Isabel, will look even more beautiful than she already is dressed in these beautiful fabrics."

"She really is a pretty girl. You really have some pretty daughters," she added.

Micaela's mother, just like a peacock, spread her wings to show the pride she felt for her daughter Isabel.

"Indeed, Isabel is a beautiful girl. Ever since she was born, she has had that immaculate beauty. She is my Snow White," Paloma replied.

"All three of your girls are pretty," Cecilia added.

The reply that came out of Paloma's mouth, Micaela would never forget. Micaela carried the pain throughout her life, wondering why her mother would say such a thing. "I know my girls are pretty. Isabel has always been gorgeous with soft white skin and rosy cheeks. She looks like Rocío, her grandmother," she said reflecting on the beauty that had been her own mother.

"Why couldn't I have looked like her?" Paloma would ask aloud.

"Maybe if I looked like her, my mother, Rocío would not have given me up," she said with a twinge of jealousy and a sadness that would pass as quickly as she continued admiring her third and younger daughter, Rebeca.

"My little Rebeca, on the other hand, is an exotic beauty with those almond-shaped eyes, jet black hair and soft olive skin like mine. She is delightful too," she added.

Paloma concluded the appraisal of her daughters by saying, "I really do not know what happened to my Micaela, my skinny Micaela. She is just my ugly duckling."

They laughed and continued to look at the beautiful fabrics, unaware that Micaela had heard this appraisal of the Galarza Díaz girls. Micaela was only twelve then, but remembered how the words pounded in her ears and the feeling of inadequacy that flowed through her veins. At the time, being as young as she was, she was very hurt and did not understand why she was described as the 'ugly duckling.' Years later, she would realize that the pain the comparison caused was just a waste of time, because if one remembers the story, the ugly duckling becomes the beautiful swan. It would take years before Micaela accepted that she had become the beautiful swan and that the love of oneself is far more important than even a mother's love.

The following year, her father came and spent the summer with his family. Eight years earlier, Antonio Galarza had moved to America in search of the "American dream." It took him all these eight years away from his family to make the necessary money and bureaucratic appeals for the family to immigrate legally to America and reunite. According to Micaela's mother, it had been the longest eight years of her life. She could not help but feel resentment toward

Antonio to be left behind especially with a baby on the way. He would not be there to see their fourth child born, something that is held as sacrosanct. Paloma had always said letting her husband go to make things better for the family was their biggest sacrifice. But as the years passed and her life continued alone, she wondered why it took him so long to come back to reunite the family. In a Latin country where many men do not respect women, being a woman all alone with her fourth child on its way, was just asking for trouble from men similar to the one who had accosted her before she was married. She suffered by herself without a husband to support her and share the responsibilities of the marriage. Paloma did consider herself fortunate having *Mamita* María José always standing by her. Despite her abandonment, people envied her stoic ways, not knowing that it often came from the woman she called mom, María José.

In the eight years she was separated from her husband, Paloma devoted herself to raising her children and in all those years, she was never reproached by her peers or neighbors. Instead, they admired how such a young, beautiful woman could handle the responsibility of raising all those children by herself. But most admirable was her ability to understand and allow her husband to be away for so long to God only knows what vagaries. After the eighth year, she had enough and told her husband, "You have three choices…bring the family to where you are, come back home or give me a divorce. Then you can go your way and I will go mine."

Antonio, indignant at her demand, believed Paloma had another man in her life. He accused her of being unfaithful, and so to end her coquetry and 'double life' he decided to take the family to America. As she got older, Micaela heard the story many times never knowing for sure if her mother was bluffing or whether she was really giving her husband an ultimatum. The following year, they moved to America, however, the bubbly, effervescent woman that Micaela knew in South America would become an even more detached and stern mother in the new foreign place. Remembering and sadly repeating the last conversation Paloma had with her *Mamita* María José would be the most poignant story yet. She tried so hard to tell it as if by doing so the connection of her adoptive mother and her would still be there, but she could never tell it to its entirety for the sobbing would ensue and the lamenting would not end. Paloma would say how María José foretold the future and how painful it was going to be without her. Knowing too well how close Micaela had been with *Mamita* María José, Paloma never knew nor cared to find out how hurtful it was for Micaela to hear this. Looking back she realized she left without saying a farewell to the woman of whom her secrets she zealously held and how much she missed her unconditional love. The stories Paloma would tell in America would become more like scattered pictures that Micaela would take upon herself to place into some kind of order to make sense of her own life.

Part Two

New land, new experiences and the emotional nakedness leading to self discovery on the perilous route of adolescence ending in a painful destination of womanhood.

Lessons Learned

In the hot, dry air of a summer afternoon in 1971, July first to be exact, Micaela and her family arrived at Los Angeles Airport. Looking outside the small window of the aircraft, Micaela could not believe her eyes at the immensity of the place. The runways had many planes coming in and others taking off; their sound was astounding and frightening. She became mesmerized seeing the traffic and commotion of workers who looked rather small because of their distance from her. She had a strange feeling of excitement combined with the worry and sadness that was flowing through her. She wished her *Mamita* María José would be here to hold her hand and tell her, *just say a little prayer to the Guardian Angel and you will be okay*, Micaela thought to herself. She would keep this advice from her grandmother, and as time went on, it served her well. When she needed to listen to her heart, she would say the prayer and everything managed to be okay.

All the documents for her siblings and mother were in perfect order, however, hers were somewhat amiss and the whole family had to wait for Micaela's immigration papers to be rechecked before they let them leave the airport. The others sat in a waiting room nearby and Micaela could hear her sibling's lambasting her for delaying them to meet with their father.

"We should have known that the only papers to be messed up would be hers. We should have left her behind anyway!" Isabel, her older sister, exclaimed.

Micaela tried very hard to stop her eyes from welling up with tears but the immensity of the place, the uncaring insensitivity of the officials and the mean remark of her sister made her feel as the inadequate 'ugly duckling' that perhaps her mother should have left behind. She closed her eyes to stop crying and quickly wiped away a tear that had escaped. After what seemed to be an eternity, they were all granted their resident visas and on their way they went, only to be disappointed by their father's lack of consideration at their traveling for the first time. He was nowhere to be found and the excitement of seeing him after all those years of separation became filled with uneasiness, angst and fear, for they all knew Paloma would not take kindly to his inconsideration. She became agitated trying to keep up with her children making sure they were not wandering off like Micaela had become so accustomed to doing. She kept them very close to her, almost as if trying to shield her own fears behind them. They were headed to the baggage claim area being directed by this 'Amazon' Anglo Saxon woman who kept talking louder as if that was going to make them understand English.

"Your father will pay for this! Who does he think he is...and why is this *gringa* talking so loud?" Paloma kept repeating this to her children, trying to disguise her own fear and trepidation of being in this strange land with the odd language which she had failed in high school. The woman pointed to the long square tube that was spewing luggage onto a carousel that moved like a merry go around. Micaela looked at her mother as though saying, "May I ride it mother?" and in return the look in Paloma's face was that of Medusa turning Micaela's action into stone. Micaela knew somehow that she could not do things as she had done them back home; she would have to assess her surroundings before she would go off into the 'jungle where the best bread ever made awaited her.'

They were all mesmerized by the carousel, except Paloma whose ire became very pronounced in her small sweet olive face.

This major oversight by, Antonio, Paloma's husband would be brought up time after time and the somewhat peaceful loneliness of being raised by one parent became a chaotic, yelling match between her parents as they started their reunion, their new beginning in a new land.

Standing on the curb, watching many cars coming and going, Paloma looked angry and disillusioned at not having been greeted and attended to by her husband. She looked everywhere to get a glimpse of the man who had made her come to this strange new place. All of a sudden, they were all startled by the speeding blue Nova screeching to a halt in from of them. Micaela's father jumped out of the car rather hastily, and looking somewhat disheveled tried very hard to act excited at the sight of his family standing right in front of him. He reached for Paloma. As her parents embraced with their children encircling them, Micaela could feel the anguish and disappointment in her mother's tense body as she tried to keep the decorum expected of people of her class.

Micaela realized that she was in a new place, with new people who did not resemble any of the people she knew. They were mostly blond, blue eyed, some with pale skin, and others with different bronze tonalities making them look unnatural. They looked nothing like the people where she came from. She liked what she saw but became totally self aware of her image. Her physical self awareness and the unspoken tension between her parents being together started to brew in Micaela's young heart an ominous feeling of uneasy bewilderment. It was not the idealistic reunion the children had envisioned for their parents to have. Instead it was a reunion with so many mixed emotions. The tense air of expectancy added to that ominous feeling of discord bringing Micaela's first concern to mind on how was this going to affect the ever fragile relationship she and her mother already had.

As they drove along, she looked up at this immense architectural sight that looked like something from the future...an arched open dome extending out on four legs, with a structure attached at its middle. "That is a restaurant that moves around so that people who are dining here have access to a 360-degree sight of the airport to enjoy."

Micaela was in amazement having heard her father inform them of this 'outer space' building, as he hurriedly drove away from the airport. She thought, *Wow! Things happen too quickly here; first my father shows up late and without any pomp and circumstance he does not apologize for being late, he really does not remember mom's wrath. Poor thing he will pay for his nonchalant attitude and that building is scary!*

She was only twelve years old, yet the new environment and unfamiliar sights made her feel grown up, like an adult who had been on this planet longer than twelve years. She seemed to know 'things,' and she knew about her preoccupation with them, but what did it all mean? She had no clue. Micaela made it her lifelong goal to make sure she discovered what these 'things' really meant. The intense enthusiasm of being in a new place would never leave her soul, as the passion for living an extraordinary and zealous existence would always nag at her being. She would dream of doing all that she could, knowing in her heart no one would ever be able to stop her. She had these thoughts from an early age, and she would become all consumed in these feelings; her spirit soared and flew high, higher than the 'space-age' structure that had caused her to be in awe.

Her father's car was a spanking new 1968 Chevrolet Nova. She knew they had never owned a car before but now that they were in this strange and exciting huge place, they had one. Her older siblings thought it was very impressive and thrilling not having to take the bus everywhere they went, but for Micaela, the most important matter was that both parents were together and she could care less about the car. Although, sadly enough for the young girl with playwright dreams, the bus rides she had taken downtown had allowed her imagination to go wild. Now that would have to be traded for an easy ride listening to the often trivial chatter of her family.

She kept thinking of how long she had waited for this moment--the reunion of her father and mother...and the whole family. Micaela's thoughts flashed back to how she longed to make Father's Day presents at school and to give them to him in person instead of just making them only to be forgotten on some hallway's chair at school. Consciously, or not, she left them behind, telling her mother she lost them when leaving the Father's Day event, the production honoring the fathers. "Why bring it home where mom would only criticize my bad craftsmanship on every inconsequential trinket I make for a person who would rather stay away than be with his family," Micaela had always said this under her breath. But now she felt awkward because her father being so late to meet them at their arrival and seeing her parents' tense embrace. *What is going to happen here in this new place...why am I so afraid? I wish Mamita María José was here,* she thought as tears again welled up in her eyes.

On their way to their new home in America, Micaela was filled with anticipation and for a short moment forgot the sadness of not having her beloved *Mamita* María José nearby. However, the angry moods of her parents, the delay in getting out from the bureaucracy of immigration and the immensity of the place became a gamut of feelings encroaching her young being. Micaela realized she no longer had that strong loving person to help her out in times of despair by simply hugging her and applauding her twirling around. No more would there be a dark sanctuary that Micaela found her apartment to be...no more oranges, the animal cookies with milk and coffee waiting for her to wake up. For the first time in her young life, she felt what a panic attack must feel like because she had no one to run to. She desperately tried to stop her tears but the chiding of her two unsympathetic sisters made her longing even more sad and lonesome. She tried to pray to the Guardian Ángel but she momentarily forgot the words and before she knew it they had arrived at the pristine neighborhood which they now would call home. She felt the excitement of being in a new place that came with a hefty price to pay. How did she know this as a young girl of twelve? She knew it...but she did not know why she knew it.

The immensity of the airport clashed with the small house they drove up to. Micaela's puzzled look emphasized her thought, *How are we all going to live here?*

She entered her new home. It was a four-bedroom house with a large living room, one bathroom and a small kitchen. It was empty and the bright mustard colored carpet helped accentuate the light that came in from the windows. "This is nice. I love the windows!" she exclaimed and started running to see the rest of the house.

Her older brother, Froilán, turned on his transistor radio and the first song she heard was Rod Stewart's "Maggie May." Micaela liked the tune and although she could not understand the meaning of the lyrics, she was surprisingly proud she knew some of the words. It was a new experience for her much like Stewart's song, which ironically enough, is about an unhappy experience in the life of the young man being adulterated by the older woman, but still it is about a new experience. As life would have it, it was perhaps a prelude to the many unhappy romantic experiences Micaela would have in this new land. She could not understand what he was singing about, but as her life would unfold its mysteries, the heartache of the song would become a part of her being because at that moment, something inexplicable in the song kept nagging at her young heart. Without much thought, she let the external stimuli of being in a new place and her family together again dismiss the ominous feeling she subconsciously suppressed in trade for the excitement of the moment. Micaela felt a sense of freedom, but freedom from what at the age of twelve? However, she knew she felt free, in this vast land where she knew no one and no one knew of her. At her young age, she knew this was an exciting revelation she would continue to seek as she traveled in later years.

She went down the hall, which at the time seemed rather long. To the left of this hallway, she entered the bedroom she would share with her two sisters. She looked at the windows and their rectangular horizontal shape that ran along almost the entire width of the wall. They were positioned very high.

This struck her as funny, and different from any windows she had ever seen. She had to get on her tippy toes to take a look out at the backyard, which was next to a huge garage way in the back. She looked at the grass and saw that it needed water. She hoped then that she did not have to water this grass as she had to in the backyard of her house in South America. *Dad is here now; he will make Froilán do it!* She thought with a smirk on her face.

She looked at the tall fences separating her new house from the neighbors and found herself missing the shrubs of honeysuckle that ran on top of the fences at her old house.

"There are neither roses nor dahlias in this backyard. I know Mom will soon start planting everything, and we will have a jungle in no time!" she said out loud.

The crooning of Rod came back into her ears and she heard him say something about "going back to school," and this prompted her to run back into the living room being aware that she understood a whole phrase.

"When do we go to school?" she asked her father.

"All in due time, *mi flaca*," her father answered in an aloof and patronizing way.

Luggage and things that were brought from the old country were starting to be put in place.

The commotion created by her brother, sisters, and now mom and dad being together, made her feel whole. She saw the family united and with that innate and innocent wisdom, she gave thanks to God and said the "Lord's Prayer," watching her father and mother exchange a caress.

With the sage of her old soul who knew everything, she remembered that back in South America the perception of the American way of life was that money grew on trees and that one could do whatever one wanted. With this in mind, on the evening of her arrival, her siblings decided to go out and roam the new neighborhood. Micaela, in one of her melodramatic moments, picked up a bedspread that her mother had brought from the old country, which was too sensational for home decor. It was cotton twill with a large print of exotic flowers, bordered with a ruffle of highly polished green chintz, the color of the green flowers in the print. It was a gaudy bed spread and quite large for her small frame. She grabbed it and wrapped it round her shoulders as if it were a cape.

"You look silly, take that off...do not go out in the neighborhood like that." Her mother proceeded to tell her.

Micaela turned, with the impudence of a twelve-year old drama queen, and exclaimed, "In America, anything goes!"

They reached the door and out the four of them went into the excitement of the unknown, trying to dispel the unspoken fear of their mother's wrath at their return. As they heard their father side with them by telling Paloma, "Let them be and do not worry. The block is rather small for them to wander off too long." Micaela felt then that her father as referee would be an edge only to find out later in life that he would not only be physically absent with many hours of work but emotionally as well, for Paloma took the reign of their new life. She ruled with a despotic attitude, the result of her resentment of being plucked away from the old and placed in the new strange land.

Testing the waters they still went, excited at the prospect of seeing many new things. It was a nice warm summer night and they went around the block to the main avenue. Coming to the wide brightly lit street, Micaela imagined herself on a big stage where her cape was being admired by everyone. As they walked around, she found herself being stared at by the passersby, but moreover she became well aware of the children's snickering at her unusual appearance that made herself look out of place. Never again would she say, "Anything goes! No way, no how!"

How ironic, that her first lesson of propriety as an adolescent, she learned in America, at the time when free love and carefree days abound and people thought that in America anything was acceptable. She would later explain to people, especially those who were not aware of her being in America for more than half her life, would dare to ask "So how does it feel to be here?" as if she just got off the boat. At times, when Micaela felt it was appropriate to speak her mind, she would point out that to fall prey to the stereotypes of a culture or individuals is always a mistake. She would tell her little story of her first day in the land that became her home, just to prove her point.

Months later, after their arrival in the new country, her mother announced she was pregnant. It was a moment of mixed emotions for the whole family.

"I do not know what I am going to do now, by myself with this child," Paloma told the older siblings, realizing that *mamita* María José would not be there to help her out.

Her mother had wanted to work and be somebody in America, but she knew with a baby on the way it would keep her at home and she would have to continue being the mother, and housekeeper. "Your father is upset with the whole idea of having this child," Paloma kept saying to her older children. She was indignant at his almost blaming her for the 'oops.' They hardly spoke and the tension between the parents made for a life of being quiet and despondent much like the parents themselves. Micaela longed to walk through her 'jungle' to sort all these new feelings and attitudes but to no avail she felt entrapped almost paralleling her parents' mood and demeanor.

Isabel, Micaela's older sister, the pretty one, the one who won pageants and always got the school roles of Virgin Mary and beautiful Angels, had become unbearably depressed and more rebellious than she had been in South America. She refused to go to high school in the United States. Coming from an all-girl, Catholic school, she could not adapt to the co-ed system of a public school. She demanded to be sent back to South America. Micaela's mother knew better, what she missed the most was the boyfriend she left behind. Much to the surprise of the family, Isabel's boyfriend had announced that he was coming to America to marry her and take her back home.

"These upcoming months are going to be the most hellish nine months of my life," Isabel retorted at the news of Paloma's pregnancy.

"Why do you say that Issy?" Micaela questioned her sister with an intent look wanting to see how she was going to react.

"Well, because we will have to take care of Mami and the new baby, and you know how Mami gets when she is sick and all," Isabel answered with the most annoyed demeanor.

"Well, what do you care...you will soon go back to the old country," Micaela told her older sister, insinuating that the responsibility would be hers since she was the second oldest daughter of the clan. She knew it would be hers, and the memory of the embrace between her mother, Paloma, and her beloved *Mamita María José* long ago came to mind. It filled her with the same stoic feeling as when she first saw it as a child, and with a somewhat supernatural force, she felt a strength overcome her. She knew at that moment she had acquired the invincibility to face the task at hand and make her previous generation of women proud. She knew then that this memory would visit her often throughout the seemingly hard times. Her resolve was taking shape and she knew that the story of her life would have many poignant yet beautiful moments and events worth retelling and making her power of being a force transcending places and time, making those family ties even stronger. Little did she know that as strong as she was becoming, so was the struggle between Paloma and her.

"Well then, it will be okay because you like to be in charge, care for people and most of all be the adventurer among all of us," Isabel continued with a sarcastic sounding tone.

"Yeah, I suppose it does not matter so much to you what will become of your family and what we do after you leave us all," she added with an obvious resentment.

Isabel had been catered to all her life. Micaela remembered how the chores were delegated so Isabel could have it easy. It was too much for Isabel to go buy bread at the bakery in town. It was too much for her to go downtown and buy buttons and notions for her mother's sewing projects. *Yet, she now wants to go back to South America with that awful excuse of a man and marry him of all things, go figure!* Micaela thought to herself.

Soon after Micaela's youngest brother was born, the preparation for Isabel's wedding started. Paloma had made some friends, and the kids had made some friends, so, within three months after the birth of the youngest child all these new people and compatriots that knew the family came and attended the wedding of Isabel. Micaela's mother was opposed to the wedding because Isabel was only eighteen years old and needed to finish school. Paloma was reminded that now Isabel was eighteen years old, she was an adult and she could do as she pleased. Many hurtful words were shouted and exchanged between mother and daughter.

According to Micaela's mother, she did not care how old you were, if you were living in her house, you were to do as she said. It was the tradition, the norm, and anyone who went against it might as well be dead, because the indifference Paloma would treat you with was worse than death. Micaela remembered how much she hated to make her mother upset because she would become even more detached and indifferent than she already was.

"If someone hates you, that is still a feeling they have for you, whereas, if someone is indifferent to you, that will kill you. Indifference kills, remembered that!" Paloma told her children time after time.

Micaela grew up hearing that statement, and it became a lesson that made her proud to a fault. She discovered later on in life that she too could become indifferent to people who somehow annoyed her, and the title of 'Ice Queen' was bestowed upon her. Micaela hoped that by acting that way, her mother would be proud, and approve of the child she called her 'ugly duckling.'

Isabel, on the other hand, had always been obstinate and chose to rebel against her mother's wishes until the day she went back to the old country. A decision she regretted for the rest of her life and one that she never admitted to herself or anyone else, that marrying the man she married and staying away from the family circle came with a hefty price.

After Isabel got married and left, Micaela assumed the role of the oldest daughter, and became her mother's assistant, translator and nanny for the two smaller children. She would look after them and see that the youngest was okay. Her mother's fainting spells became more frequent and severe. She would almost be incapacitated, and it was Micaela's responsibility to look after the whole family. She would miss school to take the baby to the doctor for his checkups. She remembered her little brother, so tiny and beautiful, with pretty round cheeks, looking up at her, smiling and embracing her as if he knew it was Micaela who would protect him. As time passed, Micaela became his second mother, the one to whom he would come later on in life to ask for advice and make her his confidante. She learned to be a housekeeper and mother at the young age of fourteen. Although Micaela seemed not to mind much, taking things in stride, always learning and accepting the responsibility that came her way, she did resent having to miss school to help with the chores around the house or tend to her mother's malady. She resented the fact that her childhood was becoming extinct and that any free time to do the things most teenagers do would not be in her daily routine. Her time to read books and wander off to her imaginative places would be replaced by the making of schedules to fit everyone else's routine. She learned that she could not voice her resentment and that her beloved prescription pads would not be filled as much as she would have liked. Her artistic and creative voice would be squelched much like her spirit and sadly she went on about her teenage days trying to live up to her mother's critical expectation of her while thinking to herself, *Why, why can't I be with the girls and be in a school club? Why do I have to come home to be a prisoner in my own house, where I cannot say what it is on my mind, or share of my day? Why can't I be left alone with my books, even if they are just my school books? Why do I have to sit with the family watching those stupid novelas?*

"Your mother is sick today, Micaela, you need to stay home and care for your little brother," her father would say as he woke her up very early to help her younger sister get ready for school.

"Micaela, make sure you do not put too much oatmeal in the water!" her mother would instruct from her bedroom.

"Don't forget to put in a pinch of salt," her mother would add.

"I know how to make oatmeal, mother," she would answer back rolling her eyes in desperation.

"Are you talking back?" her mother would retort.

"No, Mami," she would say as she looked out the window to see the trash man lifting the trash cans off the sidewalk and emptying them into the back of the truck. He jumped back on the truck when he had finished and continued to the next house.

Why couldn't I be the trash and be dumped far away from here so I do not have to put up with this mess? She would think to herself at times, "because you are not trash, and where you should be dumped is at school with your brother and sister," she would add, out loud.

"Micaela, where is your sister's clothes? She is going to be late for school. Oh how I wish I did not wake up sick and have to see your ineptitude at such simple tasks," Paloma reproached Micaela's help.

"Is your father's breakfast ready?" She would add under the same breath.

Feeling tired already from the morning's commotion, Micaela would stay home and help clean and put things in order, prepare dinner for her father and siblings, and maintain the household routine under the critical direction of her mother.

She often wished that there was a bakery around so she could walk there and get some bread, pretending she was in another world and have her 'reward' like the many afternoons in South America. Little by little, however, she felt encroached by the ominous feeling she had had when she first arrived in Los Angeles; little by little pieces of her spirit were taken away from her, little by little she started to believe she was the 'ugly duckling' after all...otherwise why would she be treated that way. Why so much hostility, so much disdain when all Micaela wanted was to assimilate in this phenomenal place and become phenomenal herself to earn the approval of her parents, especially and hopefully the love of her mother.

But now Micaela had to resign herself to go shopping in the large supermarket that was just around the corner being entirely different from the bakery she knew. The bread there was packaged in white bags adorned with different colored dots and it did not taste the same. She would pick this strange bag up and put it in the buggy with the rest of the groceries. The neighborhood her father had chosen for her family was mainly affluent white people, and her inability to speak the language made it difficult for Micaela to make friends with the children of the neighborhood, who after staring at her gangly skinny self, often would wave and say, "Hi." All these things made her feel inadequate and being swallowed up by the immensity of the place where if she would get lost, she knew no one would care or bother to come after her.

One time, Micaela heard a young girl pass by their house and wave at her brother saying, "Hi" she ran to her father and asked, "Why do they say hi?"

"That is another way of saying hello, good morning or afternoon," her father told her.

"Well, why don't they say, Hello, how are you?" Micaela would ask, astounded by the way salutations deviated from the salutations in her English book in her South American school. She wanted to go to school so she could learn English and the little nuances of this interesting language, and the necessary tools to be able to assimilate into the society to which she now belonged.

She had been in the country two years and she was now in the eighth grade, she was still learning how things worked. She was still learning English and the customs of her new school. One day, at the very beginning of the year, she heard a commotion coming from her English Second Language class and they told her that there was going to be a fight. She had befriended three 'Cuban' girls who informed her in Spanish that Micaela was going to be part of this fight.

When she was told this, Micaela retorted, "But girls do not fight! That is only for uneducated boys to do! If I get in a fight, I will be in trouble not only because you don't fight but I am a girl!" As soon as Micaela had said it, a girl grabbed her from the back and made her fall down.

"I am going to hurt you, snobby bitch!" the girl told Micaela.

They tumbled down and the girl punched her, yelling, "You think you are so smart, you stupid bitch!"

Micaela did not remember how she reacted to this attack because all she could remember was waking up in the nurse's station and waiting for her parents to come take her home. She was admonished by the principal, but Micaela was not going to get blamed for something she did not do. In an angry voice, she told the principal, "You cannot blame me for all of this. I do not even remember what just happened...that girl is in my home economics class, but I have never talked to her before," she continued.

"I had no idea this was going to happen. You have to believe me," she pleaded, as the secretary announced her parents had arrived.

"Hello Mr. Galarza, Ms. Galarza, please come in. She is in the infirmary," the principal told Micaela's parents.

"Luckily for Micaela, her English teacher saw everything and she tells me that it was not your daughter who precipitated the incident but rather a classmate of hers," the principal said.

Her mother sighed and felt relief. God forbid her daughter would have started a fight, and she exclaimed, "I am so glad that it was not Micaela who started it; she knows better than that!"

"Is she alright?" Her father asked sounding more concerned about his daughter's well being than the sense of decorum and propriety the mother held so dear.

"It has been known among the teachers that Alina Pacheco is a troubled child who likes to pick fights with the new students, especially the ones with the airs like Micaela's," the principal started to explain. "By airs, I mean that your daughter is rather reserved and has not tried to assimilate into the clubs and friendships that she could have here at school." The principal kept explaining, but abruptly Micaela's mother interjected by indignantly saying, "My daughter does not come to school to socialize or to be a club goers."

"I understand that, but they tell me that she does not talk to anyone and she keeps very much to herself. That is not going to help her in the long run," the principal added.

"You should not be concerned with how many friends my daughter has. You should be concerned with the trouble makers. Try making this school a place where children are so busy working that they don't have time to get into this type of nonsense!" Paloma exclaimed, becoming very agitated that the principal's view of Micaela's introspection was seen as a lack of her social skills that led to being attacked by another student.

"We need to see my daughter. Where is she?" Paloma finally asked to see Micaela.

"Let me take you to the nurse's station," the secretary pointed the way.

"Good afternoon, Mother, Father," Micaela said so formally that the nurse was amazed at the reverence the child had for her parents.

"The principal tells me you walk about having 'airs,'" Paloma retorted to Micaela.

"What airs? I do not talk to anyone?" Micaela defended herself. "I think the principal wants me to befriend someone, anyone, but all these kids are so dumb and ignorant of things that they should know already. They do not even have an idea where the United States stands in reference to world politics or even that it is a part of the North American continent...there is really no one to talk to in this school, so I do not bother. Please forgive me for being so uptight and arrogant perhaps, but I'd rather keep to myself," she went on to say, explaining why she did not want to have any friends.

"These girls who wanted to fight were mad at me because I did the fractions much faster than they did in our cooking class," she kept on explaining.

"It is okay, *mi flaca*," her father said to calm her down. "You can come with us, unless you want to stay," her father added.

"She needs to see a doctor to make sure she is okay," the nurse told her parents.

"She fainted and a doctor should tell you why," the nurse added.

"Okay then, let's go," her father picked her up in his arms and carried Micaela out of school.

Micaela, being that close to him and feeling the protection of his arms around her as he carried her out of the school grounds, felt for the first time as if he was her knight in shining armor, the one who would be there to defend her and protect her; and for a fleeting second she felt truly loved by this man who often times was emotionally and physically absent for his children. A memory she would hold very close and dear in her heart.

When they got home, ominous feelings suddenly came over Micaela and entered her being making her chest feel as heavy as a ton of bricks. She tried to hurry to her bedroom so she could hide from Paloma's wrath that she had felt brewing on the way home from school. As she started down the hallway, she felt her mother's presence behind her. They both entered her room and Paloma shut the door. What happen next Micaela tried very much to erase from her memory but she became branded by her mother's brutality as Paloma proceeded to slap and hit her, making Micaela fall to the floor.

Paloma took a belt and struck Micaela's small frame while repeating at the top of her lungs, "You do not embarrass our family like you have done today! Do you hear me, you sorry piece of insolent trash, because that is what you are when you behave the way you have behaved today! You have always been a thorn in my side! I should have never tried to find you the day you got lost... you do nothing but hurt me. Why! Why! Why! Must you always hurt me the way you do?"

Never again did Micaela approach her mother looking for the tenderness she craved. From that moment on, she knew that like a beautiful piece of china that had fallen breaking into many tiny pieces, trying to glue it back together would just be a futile act. Sadly enough, their gradual estrangement began at that moment in time.

The experience of the fight became a strange, bitter-sweet lesson for Micaela and Alina Pacheco both. Alina indeed, had a bad reputation of being a bully and picked on students at her whim. Thus for Micaela to have stood her ground against this 'ruffian in go-go outfits' as she referred to the bully made everyone even Alina eventually like and respect Micaela. As the story of the attack was told, after falling on the cement walkway, Micaela had gotten up, and put her backpack aside, and she waited for Alina's reaction, which was to throw herself on Micaela. Micaela had grabbed her by her hair and kicked her foot, making her fall down. Then Micaela grabbed her and started pounding her head to the floor with such anger that everyone helped Alina Pacheco by pulling Micaela off in fear of Micaela really hurting the girl. Micaela could not remember these moments to save her life. She knew then that she could never be put in situations where her demeanor would change so drastically that she would become Jekyll and Hyde-like. She promised herself never to allow anyone to get her that upset.

After that incident no one would bother or say anything to Micaela. She was not proud of her actions. Instead the incident in which she had lost her decorum and dignity, made her feel embarrassed and ashamed for reacting in such a physical and violent way. She really did not have friends except for the three 'Cuban' girls who had their own little clique. They allowed Micaela to enter it at their whim. Micaela really did not care, she was too busy reading English books, so that by some chance, osmosis might take place and she would be able to speak English much more easily. She hated having to depend on the 'Cuban' girls to help her with her English, especially when it came to being friends with the boys.

She had always been suspicious of people, and even at the tender age of fourteen, she did not trust these girls for fear that they would make up things or rather 'lose' things in translation. There was a boy for each of these girls respectively; Martha would be matched with John, Aleida would be with Peter and Lisbet would be with Pablo. John, Peter, and Pablo were the cutie-pies of the school and every girl wanted them. Tony, a friend of theirs, was the so-so guy that the girls picked for Micaela. Micaela, on the other hand, had already picked her cutie pie and had chosen Pablo to be "hers." The girls who supposedly were her friends; knowing that she liked Pablo had decided not to allow her to date Pablo.

Well, well, well. You do not pick for Micaela, she thought.

"Only Micaela picks for Micaela, and I choose Pablo," she told herself looking in the mirror and decided to document this challenge on one of the prescription pads which she had managed to bring from her old country. Often times she would pull a little cardboard box out holding her notebooks given to her by Dr. Rodriguez. It would almost be like they were quietly waiting for Micaela to open their pages and document more experiences from her young life, especially now that she lived in this new exciting place. She dated the note in which she picked the boy who would be her first love. The invincibility of Micaela at the age of fourteen was something she would never lose, as well as the innocence of her soul. For these two things were the major ingredients in making her resolve stronger and stronger, which eventually helped the 'ugly duckling' become the beautiful swan.

Fighting and being recruited into the 'Cuban' girl's club was the highlight of her middle school years. Micaela had managed to get good grades despite her inability to communicate one hundred per cent in English, and was proud of how much understanding of the language she had acquired as the summer of '73 began. Come fall, she would start high school and what a thrill that would be. She would be treated as the young adult she had become, studying all she could study, and introducing a third language. She looked forward to learning French, even though the 'Cuban' girls advised her against it.

Micaela and the 'Cuban' girls, as her mother often referred to her friends, were all spread out on the floor of her bedroom, being teenagers, looking at the upcoming schedule of classes and at the teen magazines of the day.

"Why are you going to take French when Spanish would be much easier?" Aleida had asked as they perused through the class schedule of their freshman year.

"Why not French, we already know Spanish, what would be the challenge in that?" Micaela retorted.

"You are stupid!" Aleida added. "You make your life harder than it needs to be," she went on.

"I think we should expand our minds and broaden our horizons!" Micaela exclaimed as she paced back and forth with a book in one hand and the other hand behind her back.

"You look like a teacher already," Aleida laughing and mocking Micaela's stance.

"Well, I would rather look like a teacher than a stupid girl looking for boys who are not even paying any attention to you," Micaela said it with contempt.

"Well, if you are going to be like that, we are leaving!" the 'Cuban' girls said in unison as they proceeded to leave Micaela's room.

"Where are you all going?" Paloma asked the girls. "I am bringing figs and cheese, that is Micaela's favorite snack," she added.

"No, thank you Mrs. Galarza, we are going home," they politely said in unison.

"Is there not anything you can do or say alone?" Micaela whispered under her breath.

Micaela saw how tight knit their friendship was. They did everything together, finished each other's sentences and never decided on something by themselves.

How sad it must be to have to do everything other people are doing, no originality, Micaela thought to herself.

So the summer started on a sour note since the 'Cuban' girls were not going to include Micaela in their little "clique" anymore. She knew then that she would not only need to learn more about friendships, but also about the nuances of the English language that were never taught to her in the old country. Two years in middle school in America proved to be very interesting, although it was nothing compared to what would have been expected of her in South America.

Here everything was very slack and relaxed, the demeanor of the teachers was not as strict as the ones in Ecuador. The major difference between the two countries educational system impacted Micaela's attitude and she saw how her classmates were drastically different from those in her own country. In South America, the elementary years being first to sixth grade are a foundation to prepare you for the secondary grades which are seventh to twelve, but more importantly they are crucial in preparing young adults for life. Secondary years are extremely demanding and important and students are serious about their studies because otherwise there is no mercy for those who are not willing to work hard and be successful in their chosen professional fields.

Micaela yearned to get back to school where she would delve into her studies, to absorb all the literature she could learn and be the responsible high school student she was expected to be. Instead, the responsibility of high school students in America was lacking among her classmates.

In addition, the little adolescent melodrama of the 'Cuban' girls dropping her as their friend became augmented by her mother's decision to go to South America, taking her baby brother with her, leaving Micaela with the burden of taking care of all the household chores, and looking after her two siblings and father for the entire summer. Again, she had to assume the responsibilities of an adult until her mother's return which she never knew when that would be.

At times the desolation she felt at the absence of her baby brother made Micaela not only feel abandoned by her mother but in a very strange way, a sense of betrayal by the person she could no longer trust to be kind to her in any way. She would clean the house in the morning, made sure her younger sister took a bath every day and she would prepare breakfast, lunch and dinner for everyone in the house leaving her no time for herself. Luckily for Micaela, her older brother who had a part time job would sometimes come home in the afternoon and watch their younger sister, Rebeca. Micaela would seize this opportunity to take her bicycle down to the park where she knew the 'Cuban' girls and boys would be. Nonchalantly she would appear, and irritate every girl with her presence. They did not want her there, and their annoyance was readily seen.

Pablo would come and say hello. Shyly and meekly she would respond back, "Hello."

She thought it was funny, the reaction she saw from the boy. It taught her that boys like it when girls act like meek little lambs and she thought it was absurd. She went on to walk away from the girls while able to maintain Pablo trailing behind her. She became aware of how manipulative one can become by mere body language. She would never forget this detail as she grew into the independent woman she knew then that she would become.

"How come you always say, 'hello,'" he asked.

"I do not know, what other word could I say for 'hello'?" she responded.

"Well, you could say 'hi,' like everyone else," he added.

"I'm not like everyone else and I did not know that there was another way to say 'hello,'" she lied. She remember her father's comment on that.

"Yeah, it is a shorter way and no one really says 'hello,'" he said.

"Next time I come to the park with you guys, I will say 'hi,' but only to you. Would you like that?" She winked, while moving her eyes just so, to match her mischievous smile.

The playful way in which she said that made him feel like the man he knew he was going to be. Soon she would find out Pablo's schedule for the summer because he was a jock playing baseball and football and was part of the popular clique. His schedule consisted of being in the park as much as time allowed, to practice and be ready for the season. Micaela was on a quest to conquer this young man despite what the 'Cuban' girls felt about it. But one afternoon in the park she was told with the malice of a teenager ready to hurt another teenager, "John asked me to go to the church dance, and Peter asked Aleida. I know Pablo will ask Lisbet if he hasn't done so yet," Martha told Micaela.

Micaela could not help to be hurt a little bit, but then she realized maybe he had not asked Lisbet yet, and she proceeded to exclaim, "Well, maybe he will ask me!"

Martha continued with added scorn, "I don't think so. I heard Pablo tell Tony, 'Why don't you take Micaela to the dance?'"

"What gave Pablo the right to ask Tony that?" Micaela said it indignantly.

"I do not know...why don't you tell Tony?" Martha continued.

Micaela felt as though something fishy was brewing and decided to drop a thought for her to ponder, so she told Martha, "I probably cannot go anyway. My parents won't let me,"

Micaela made it sound like there would be no way her parents would allow her to go. Taking away Martha's conniving hurtfulness and preparing for her own attack. Micaela picked up her bike and headed back home and called a friend of Pablo, Saulo.

"Hey, Saulito how are you?" she asked with a smirk on her face knowing damn well what she was about to come up with.

"Hey, Micaela. What's new?" he said surprised by the call, because he had asked Micaela why didn't she call the guys like the other girls do. "Because I am not allowed to call boys. My mom checks my calls and I do not dare disappoint her," Micaela had told Saulo once.

"Nothing...are you going to the school dance?" Micaela asked him.

"No, I don't think so, I don't have anyone to take," he said.

"Has Pablo asked you yet?" he added, "He told me he was going to ask you."

Micaela realized then that the 'Cuban' girls had always lied to her and were not really her friends. Saulito as he was often called, told Micaela that Pablo liked her a lot and he really like the fact she came to his practice games and watched him play, and that it wasn't his idea to ask Lisbet, but was told he should. Pablo had also told Saulo that he liked that Micaela rode her bike to see him in all of his scrimmages and that the other girls did not do that. Instead they stayed home, expecting the boys to call them.

Micaela understood then that she would never belong to a clique of girls who waited by the phone, she knew then that there were more important things to do. Waiting is for people who do not want to live life to its fullest. "No, no, not me," she said to herself and looking up to the heavens she added, "Those who want, seek, and Pablo will be mine, and he will call me without expecting me to call him."

With that in mind, and more books to read, the summer passed and high school was about to begin. However, an unexpected and frightening incident occurred before school started. Tony had heard about the 'Cuban' girls picking him for Micaela, so he had attempted to pursue Micaela in "going together." Micaela found Tony attractive with his tall, slender frame, light brown hair and beautiful green eyes. He had come to the house one afternoon and had asked Micaela if she wanted to go to the park.

"Okay, but I have to be home by four. My dad comes home at six and dinner needs to be served then," she told him as they went to the garage to get her bike to ride down to the park.

They started toward the park and realized that it was already kind of late. Tony, besides being cute, was also funny and amusing, something Micaela liked in a person. Losing herself in her adventurous way of being and trusting Tony she followed to his pointing of the nearby church courtyard where a swing set and a jungle gym welcomed them under the warm afternoon sunlight. The church was closed but the entrance to the beautiful garden in the middle of the tall buildings was open. The fountain's running water and the splashes against the afternoon light created little rainbows as the water hit the ground.

Tony and Micaela sat down near the fountain and watched the water fall. Tony began to tell her how pretty she was. She never believed that she was pretty because her own mother did not think so, much less a boy she did not care about. Tony looked at her in a strange way that made her uncomfortable. He got up and wanted to explore their whereabouts. Micaela did not feel right, yet she continued to follow him in his exploration of the playground. "Come on Micaela let's go see what's in that building," he said pointing to a structure that look rather scary. With a puzzled look on her face, she went on to be the adventurer she was, following him to investigate the building that was empty and desolate.

Her mother's voice came into her head stopping her in her tracks and she heard herself ask Tony, "Where are we going?"

In a playful way he said, "Come on pretty girl. Let's go find the treasure."

"Don't call me pretty!" she protested.

"Just accept that you are and that I think you are and that should be enough!" getting annoyed with her.

Feeling uneasy by the time she reached the dilapidated doorway and seeing nothing but darkness she turned in desperation realizing her big mistake of following him. To make matters worse, he pushed her into this long dark hallway, where he grabbed her by her waist and while pressing his hand against her breast, he told her,

"You need to put on a little bit of weight. You're really skinny. There is nothing here."

Again her mother's voice came always telling how skinny Micaela was, that she needed to straighten her hair up, and that she needed to dress up more often. Lost in the criticism of her mother, Tony came closer to her and clutched her face, forcing a kiss on her that she was not expecting as well as trying to take off of her blouse. It seemed surreal and confusing why her mother's criticism of her appearance would come at such a deplorable and devastating moment. *Am I so loathsome that everyone would take such little regard for the 'ugly duckling' as to use me and hurt me in every way?* The thoughts came rushing into her head that was spinning and trying to make sense of what was happening. She wanted to cry and scream but something very powerful stopped her and all she could think was to absorb the anger she felt entering her being. She stopped abruptly in front of Tony, then heard herself scream out, "Stop it and get the hell away from me you piece of shit! I will hit you so hard your head will spin making your balls turn blue."

She pushed him away with such force that surprised them both. She ran out and heard Tony running behind her yelling at her in a hurtful way, "Pablo doesn't like you and he never will you stupid girl!"

Again the same strength overcame her, she stopped and giving Tony a hard look, Micaela asked him, "So, you are the best I can do...? Worse yet, I should settle for second best?" she yelled back at him giving him a gesture of disdain that would have made Paloma very proud.

"Don't be stupid Micaela, we can go to dances and things, and we can go steady, don't you want that?" Tony asked her, now regretting his trying to persuade her to go with him.

"No! Are you crazy? After what you just tried to do to me, HELL NO! YOU DISGUST ME!" Remembering some melodramatic moment from one of those Spanish novelas her mother used to watch, she told Tony with a straight face, "Plus know this! If I cannot have Pablo, I do not want anybody else!" Her acting out one of those cheesy scenes worked, because at the very beginning of the ninth grade, everyone knew how much in love Micaela was with Pablo, and as such, the summer came to its end.

In the past two years since coming to America and being reunited with her family, Micaela learned quickly that her world stage was much more immense than she would ever have thought possible, only to know of but never to be a part of it. Paloma her mother would take care of that. She became aware that she was different, not so much because she was from a different country but because Micaela, at a very young age, had a different mentality. An intellect of a much older person and view of life all of her own, at such a young age she was her own person, with her own ideas and she was not ready to give up on the things she already believed and held dear. Micaela knew that in her new world she would be misunderstood just as in the old world but most importantly, in the world between her mother and her. Each day that passed their views of life grew wider apart. Sadly she would look at the beautiful, vivacious woman she once knew to be her mother become transformed into this aloof and distant person, unhappy to be in this new country.

Micaela learned to be a mother without bearing a child, to defend herself despite the repercussion of her actions, to be her own friend and belong to her own clique. Life, as she started to comprehend was going to be hard with many ups and downs. Her spirit would be shattered and the 'ugly duckling' would only be able to hide in the books of the library nearby.

Moreover, it was Paloma's unhappiness that made her relentlessly repudiate her middle child, Micaela, not knowing that by doing so a passion, a force, a power started to brew in her young being. Micaela's lessons learned were to guard and care for herself and keep very close to heart the things she loved most, to do the right thing for her mother and family, burying herself so deeply into oblivion that she sometimes forgot precisely those things that she loved most; like the writing of her little short stories, the poetry that came to her as she walked to school, her trips to the library where she would touch the spine of every book going through the stacks, listening to the silence of the place where she cried in desperation yet very quietly suppressing every primal scream that was ready to roar cleansing her of the resentment she started to harbor at the unfairness of her life after coming to America. She learned to find herself in the memory of an embrace between the two women she loved so dearly allowing for the strength to become her driving force in a world where her most precious desire, that of writing, would have to wait.

First Love's Angst

Summer ended; fall and school began. Nothing was different, only the location. She was in high school with the same people from middle school. The 'Tony' incident at summer's end put her on guard and she only thought of her books; her goals and aspirations perhaps of being a writer one day made her days bearable and Micaela looked forward to going to school to quench her thirst for knowledge. She truly hoped high school would be at least a little more challenging than middle school. She anticipated going through the many rites of passage that most teenagers experience and these feelings would contribute to her writing arsenal even if it only meant to be for the prescription pads she still held on to. She tried every night to write down the daily occurrences whether painful or mundane.

"The words, the sentences, the paragraphs must be written down to give shape to the story at week's end," she would tell herself smiling, trying to compose something at the end of each week.

She wanted to know how her first real kiss would feel and although there would not be any serenades from young lovers at her window bay as it would have been growing up in South America, she still thought about how an American boy would court her, how he would tell her sweet nothings in her ear especially since the rectangular windows of her house did not lend themselves to a romantic mood.

Seeing herself caught in the middle of these cultural differences, the nagging ominous feeling when she first heard "Maggie May" came over her, and instinctively Micaela knew her mother would put an abrupt end to all her teenage growing pains in America. Trying to resign herself to the thought that her first love angst would be very painful, she was totally unaware that it would also be the beginning of a life of disappointments due to the choices of men she would make from an early start. She came to understand that in the matters of the heart she had antiquated ideas and ideals; being in love for her meant to be loyal to the death and loving only one person. Sadly for Micaela this was not the case in this era of peace and love...a more carefree outlook was in vogue. Even more unfortunate to her romantic heart, here in America, her girlfriends were choosing who would entertain her first young love. Little did the so-called girlfriends know, that she came from a long line of pain and suffering where the only thing left for one to keep face and stay intact was to manipulate situations to the highest and best self interest.

The 'monster' of cold manipulation brought on by the brutal attack of her mother, the disdain of leaving her behind to take care of the family, the attempt of Tony to rape and cunningly take away her innocence had started to enter her young soul, and made Micaela astutely manipulate every romantic relationship she would have. In the fall with the starting at a new school, Pablo would be the first romantic endeavor she would make sure came her way. Around the middle of December, after she had turned fifteen, Pablo asked her if she would come to the football scrimmage.

"I have to ask my parents, call me later and I will let you know," Micaela told him.

She did not have to wait long. Around eight o'clock his call came through.

"My parents told me no, I can't go. They are rather strict," she said feeling annoyed.

She was upset because she knew that he was a catch and the too many 'no's' would dissuade him from asking her to go steady.

"It is okay," Pablo whispered to her over the phone.

"Why are you whispering?"

"John and Peter are here and they are going to the Winter Wonderland School Dance," he told Micaela.

"Are they going to make fun of you if you do not go?" she asked him.

"Well, maybe," he said trying not to show that he was worried about that. His friends were making fun of him for choosing a sheltered and overprotected girl who could not be allowed to share the antics of most teenagers growing up in the Seventies.

"She is never going to let you go to first base, ha ha ha ha," they told Pablo in unison, laughing and wrapping their arms around themselves as if to be in an embrace.

Micaela could hear the laughter and the teasing over the phone, as well as the last remark by one of the boys. "What does that mean?" she asked him, repeating the comment.

"Nothing, really," he lied.

"You are lying, so tell me what does that mean," she would ask sheepishly.

"Well, I will tell you tomorrow after school," he said, sounding eager for the meeting to take place.

It surprised Micaela to hear the eagerness in his voice. It endeared him to her, with a feeling of uneasiness in her stomach she thought, *Oh my Lord! This is what they mean by having butter-*

flies in your stomach. Becoming aware that although she had gone after the conquest, she was falling for this young man and this made her start a journal to document her romantic feelings for him. Thus, one cold afternoon after school, under the bleachers of the football field, they walked trying to hit each other's hands and laughing at who was quicker at withdrawing. In one of those moments, he was quicker and grabbed her hand.

"I do not want to hit your hand. I want you to be my girlfriend," he muttered looking at her intensely.

Trembling because of the cold weather and the anticipation, he continued, as the warm air coming out of his mouth turned into little clouds dissipating in the air. "Would you go steady with me?" he asked.

Micaela's world was complete. She realized that she did not have to be a cheerleader to have one of the jocks. Smarts and knowing how to play your cards right made them come your way. She felt victorious over the 'Cuban' girls who had told her, "He would never ask you out, 'cause you are not Cuban."

Pablo was from Cuba and was the older of two brothers with a set of proud parents who doted on both boys. Pablo's mother liked Micaela almost instantly, the father, however, kept his reservations about the skinny girl who became their son's first *noviecita*.

Micaela and Pablo went steady for the next two years, and sometimes when she reminisced about her first real romance, she would say, "We were boyfriend and girlfriend for two years, nine months, seven days, four hours, two minutes and three seconds." And only she knew this was precise.

It was taken as a joke but she knew better. What had started as a challenge turned into a young romance with phone calls after her chores were done but only for half an hour. She was not allowed to go to the school dances and the poor boy had to stay home and call her. She often asked herself why prolong the romance but she could not answer.

"You know, you could go. Just because I am not allowed to be there, it should not stop you from enjoying the dance," Micaela would often tell him.

"No, it's okay, we can talk over the phone," he would tell her and sweetly he added, "I would rather stay home and talk to you."

Nine months later when the baseball season started, she was allowed to see him play but her younger sister and brother had to go with her to chaperone. At one of those baseball games, Micaela met Pablo's mother. It was a big event. His mother saw this slender girl with long wavy hair who made her teenage boy stay home Friday nights to call her. She admired her for that power.

"Mom, this is Micaela, my girlfriend... Micaela, this is my mother, Elida del Consuelo, Santa María de la Trinidad Guzman Perez," Pablo introduced them very proper and politely.

"Nice to meet you Mrs. Guzman," she responded.

"Likewise," his mother said, and continued under the same breath, "So you are the sweet girl he cannot stop talking about, huh?"

Micaela began blushing from the mother's statement which Micaela took as a compliment, "I guess...Thank you, ma'am."

"I admire the girl who makes my boy stay home each night waiting to make that call at the same time, every night," his mother told her smiling.

"You are a very pretty girl. I listened to him describe you but you are much prettier in person," she added, giving Micaela a hug.

I wish mom could see this woman praising and hugging me, like the way she should, she thought, feeling ecstatic at the warmth of this woman.

Pablo's mother liked Micaela very much from the start, and she would cook lunch for both of them and send it with Pablo to school. They would eat on the benches, outside the cafeteria, and

Micaela thought that it was cool having this food prepared just for them. She had always loved different ethnic food, so for his mother to send lunch like this was just an added treat.

The following summer Pablo and Micaela had been going together for a year and a half. Her mother had decided to go back to South America with her little brother for the summer, again! It meant that Micaela would have the house to herself and Pablo could come over whenever he wanted. Indeed, he would come around noon and have lunch with them. She pretended to play house with him and it was fun. She pretended to be in her own apartment once she moved out of her parents' house and no one would tell her how much salt her oatmeal should have. The chores she had to do were made less tedious with him around. For the first time in her life since coming to America, she was glad to see her mom go off the way she did, but also felt a great sense of guilt at feeling this way. She would clean the house by making the beds first. One day, as she was making the bed in her parents' room, he came from behind her and pushed her onto the bed and started tickling her.

"Stop, you should not be in this room...this is my parents' room, are you crazy?" she scolded him.

"If Rebeca sees you in here, she will tell my father, and he would kill us both," she told him pulling him off the bed trying to push him out of the bedroom.

"Don't you want to play mommy and daddy?" he said as he grabbed her and gave her a juicy kiss. To this day, Micaela thinks back to those days, when in the craziness of her teen years she might have indulged in the sweetest young love. But, she did not, afraid to disappoint her mother.

"Stop it and get out, we both need to leave this room and forget about playing mommy and daddy!" she told him sternly.

"We are only sixteen and if we play mommy and daddy we are bound to become mommy and daddy and then what will we do, you silly boy!"

She knew already what it was to get up and feed a child at dawn or in the middle of the night. She already knew how helpless one feels seeing an infant with a high fever and having to wait until it breaks or even worse having to take him to the hospital. It was not a fun game raising a baby, helping her mother with the last sibling was an eye opener that made Micaela always guard herself sexually.

However, she also wondered what happened to the raging hormones, she always heard about, weren't they working? What was that force that made her stop even though deep inside she wanted to be with him. Instead, she always thought what if? She wished she wouldn't have thought that way, but every time she wanted to give in, her mother's voice would take over and she would hear her say,

"Where is your dignity and pride?... Did I not raise you better than that?"

Micaela always remembered thinking back to a time in South America when she overheard a conversation between her mother and her mother's best friend, Cecilia. Paloma thought her oldest daughter, Isabel had gotten pregnant. The disgrace this would bring to her family made Paloma cry and cry with such melodrama, only to find out she was not pregnant. But the sight of her mother's distress had made Micaela tell both of them, "I will never make you cry like that. I promise. Not over boys anyway!"

Her mother had dismissed her innocent exclamation. But Micaela had persisted and told her mother that when she marries she would be wearing a white gown. "Otherwise, I will also, wear a blue suit like you did for giving in to the pressures of love." At which Paloma ignored Micaela's promise by asking her to go outside and play. With Pablo's insistence on having sex at such a young age, she knew indeed about not succumbing to his sexual desires that could have easily led her to disappoint the only person whose approval she still so fervidly yearned for, that of her mother's. She remembered how she had sworn to herself and perhaps it was that promise that prevented her from doing things that she knew she would live to regret later on.

The relationship with Pablo became more strained because of her refusal to be sexually active.

"Come on, Pablo you know I will never do that," she would tell him.

"Just hold it and stroke it, pleeease," he would plead, as he would grab her small hand, directing her into his pants.

"My dad looks out here, checking on me, and I don't want him to see me doing this to you...It will only be detrimental to your life," she would say looking in every direction.

"I really should not be doing this," Micaela told him as she got really close and grabbed his extended penis, but quickly releasing it afraid of being seen by her father.

"You are my girlfriend," he would say with frustration in his tone.

"I know that! But I can't," she would respond feeling ashamed and embarrassed for both of them.

"Please leave and come back when you have cooled off, okay?" she would tell him sending him off the porch.

Needless to say, he was only sixteen and his hormones were raging and soon thereafter he decided to break up with her. The reason she remembered the exact date it happened was because she had counted the days to see how long this boy would put up with her virginal attitude. The night he broke up with her, Paloma had gone to school to learn English, something she struggled with all of her life. Micaela's father had stayed home to look after the kids while she was in class, and he had been working on some jewelry settings for a customer of his.

The telephone rang as always at 8:00 p.m. but she felt an ominous feeling as she picked up the phone, "Hello,"

"Is Micaela home?" Pablo asked.

"Hey, it's me! Can't you tell it's me?" Micaela asked, puzzled by the formality in his tone.

"I did not recognize your voice,"

"What are you doing tomorrow after school?" he asked.

"The same things I always do after school." She was still feeling that ominous feeling and puzzled at his aloof behavior.

"I will probably have to help mom with some chores and then do my homework. Why?" Micaela asked him. She felt instinctively that something was wrong.

"Well, I just need to talk to you about something," he said.

Again, she felt the hollow feeling in her stomach, "What is going on?"

"I will tell you tomorrow," he said after a small hesitation.

"No, tell me now," she insisted.

"Well, I just better tell you in person."

"No, tell me now."

"I really cannot do it over the phone... I think it is rude," he added sounding anxious.

"Whatever it is you need to tell me, it can be said now," she said distancing herself emotionally from him. She could not understand this new feeling but she was a bit angry at what she knew he wanted to say.

"Well," he started. "I want to put our relationship on hold," he continued.

"Just like that! Like if it was a phone call, excuse the pun," she could not help but let go of a nervous laugh.

"You mean, we are breaking up and you are going to see other girls?" she asked, afraid of the answer, because she knew it would be yes.

"Well, yes I will see other girls, but I am not going to be their boyfriend or anything like that!" he tried to explain.

"Well, if you date other girls, I will be free to date other boys, right?" she asked.

"Well, no! I do not want you to date any other boys."

"That does not seem fair, not that I will have the time for that anymore since I have to prepare for my SAT's and fill out my college applications."

Micaela's started to fume, at his stupidity and thought to tell him, *Who do you think you are telling me what to do and you are leaving me for some girl who you want to...what is the English word, fuck, yeah that is the word, yet I cannot see other boys. Poor imbecile!*

Bringing her thoughts to a screeching halt, she listened to what was the most absurd statement he could tell her, "If you go to college then I really want to break up with you because I do not want you to go to school."

Micaela was dumbfounded and responded with indignity, "Well then, this settles things. You go find a girl who can screw you and your stupid head, since you seem to want it that way. I, on the other hand, am going to college, NYU in New York City to be precise."

"New York City?" he was incredulous at hearing her say screw and then where she was going to school. "Your parents would never let you go to NYU," he added, secure of his statement.

"Nevertheless, I am applying to NYU and majoring in Literature," she confidently added.

"Why are you going to NYU?" he curiously asked her.

"To be a screen writer and write plays that people will love," she added.

"Well, good luck...then...Can I call you from time to time?" he asked, dismissing her interest in becoming a playwright.

"No, you cannot call me from time to time, what to check up on me?" She said it indignantly, feeling the heat on her cheeks.

"Just do as you please...and...be happy," she told him and hung up.

After hanging up the phone, she felt anger and pain, but most of all she felt relieved. Still, she thought, "After two years, nine months, seven days, four hours, two minutes and three seconds, it does hurt to see him go."

She was in shock because not only did he not love her the way her mother had said a man should love a woman, by respecting them and not asking for sex, but also for not wanting her to develop as a person intellectually. Instead, he just thought about sex and had no intentions of pursuing higher education, something Micaela would always crave as she craved light. She was sad that he believed in that machismo affliction of some Latin men, but really of most insecure men, and she swore to herself that she would never again get involved with another Latin macho man or for that matter, an insecure one. Life would see it differently, unfortunately for Micaela. Plus, her independent *joie de vivre* would become the old adage, 'Never say never.'

She left the den where the phone was and just wanted to cry. It had been a bitter sweet journey of conquest, love and enlightenment. She had forced a situation only to show her prowess to the 'Cuban' girls but found Pablo and his family to be nice and loving to her. How could she have miscalculated her own manipulation and extend their union as far as it did, causing the pain of being dumped before she could do the dumping. The turmoil and the feeling of relief at the same time, made her realize as she looked in the mirror and thought to herself *Why do you feel like crying...*

if you are relieved that it is over? She knew the answer, it was her pride and vanity that were hurt.

Sorrowfully, she also became aware of how much she was going to miss Elida, Pablo's mom. For she gave Micaela the love she could not get from her own mother, it was like finding a surrogate *Mamita* María José when things got bad at home, she would call Elida to appease her fears. It was her she already missed and not her son. She could not understand all the array of emotions the break up produced in her young heart. The fact that all along he did not want her to go to college made her acrimoniously sad since she realized that after two years, nine months, seven days, four hours, two minutes and three seconds, she really did not know this boy. Moreover, he did not know her because she could not fathom the thought of anyone not wanting to go to school and advance educationally. Wasn't he there when she so proudly showed him her beloved prescription pads full of little stories, "Wow!" he had exclaimed, "You wrote all these. Is this box full of them?!"

She wanted to cry but her younger siblings and dad were there, she did not want to make a spectacle of herself. Her mother would not approve of her carrying on. She went into the shower and cried many tears. Her father had heard the conversation on the phone and knew why she went into the bathroom. He, being emotionally absent, would not console her by holding her or feeling sorry for her, instead, he called Micaela back into the den.

Micaela's father had come to America to follow a trade that had helped him overcome poverty and hard times. He had learned to be a goldsmith and in the old tradition of the lost wax method, he sculpted wax to be the mold for the piece of jewelry he designed. He set stones as part of the whole creation and had become a master jeweler and had done quite well for himself and his family. Her father was a very reserved man and all the issues, problems and affairs of the children were dealt with by his wife. If the children needed anything, they first went to their mother, but he gave the last word to their mother, and then it trickled down to the children. Micaela did not remember having the openness with her parents she would have liked. Instead a "wall" called respect separated the two generations. Perhaps, it was also the eight years of separation they had as a family growing up in South America that severed the connection between father and daughter. Nonetheless, here he was this night, out of all nights, giving Micaela a beautiful and surprising experience.

"Micaela, could you come here please?" he called her, looking and inspecting her swollen eye lids and red nose.

"Here, wipe your nose," he gave her his handkerchief.

"Why did Pablo make you cry?" he asked.

She knew her mother was not there, and even if she was, her mother was not very perceptive to her children's pain. She herself had never had that as a child so she did not know how to show genuine concern and empathy. Instead, she would have been upset and told her, "Stop crying and making a fool of yourself." Life would have it that the best lesson of self love was going to be taught by her father. He had been setting some diamonds. He had two small bags and he walked toward the dining room table and asked Micaela to sit down next to him.

"I want you to see these stones and tell me the difference between them," he told Micaela, as he put three luminous diamonds down. He pulled out the other bag and placed another set of four diamonds next to the three already on the table.

Micaela inspected the first bunch and she could see that these three pieces had a crystalline shine with a beautiful soothing soft sparkle in them. She could see very clearly the little tiny spectrum coming from certain angles in the stones. She told him what she saw and then he pushed them aside and brought the other four pieces closer to her.

"Tell me what you see in these," he instructed her.

Micaela inspected the new stones placed in front of her very carefully. At first glance they looked the same.

"I like the first ones better."

"Why?" her father asked.

"These other four diamonds are shiny, even a little more than the previous ones, but they lacked the subtle luminosity I see in the other ones. These were brighter but with no clarity."

"I like the first ones better, they look more elegant," she added. "A subtle luminosity and distinct endless clarity come to your eyes, and a very delicate array of light, without jumping at you like the other ones," she added.

Her father gently touched her cheek, wiping a tear away, told her, "Good that you can see the difference, because you chose the real thing. Those are diamonds; the others are cubic zirconium. They are not real diamonds."

"Unfortunately, Pablo has chosen to leave the real thing. You are the diamond that he is leaving behind. Do not ever let anyone tell you differently. You will grow to shine with the clear elegance of a diamond and will be priceless for the man who knows better. Don't ever forget it, *mi flaca.*"

Micaela cried even more, realizing how much her reserved and ever observing father loved her. How sweet and gentle he was with her at such a vulnerable time; her knight in shining armor was there for her again; 'Carrying' her young bruised heart to a better place with such a comparison. She never forgot this lesson…she was a diamond in her father's eyes and she would not only grow up to shine but she would become eternal she told herself. *With my books and poems, people will know of my pain, my mother's pain and all the pain, sorrow and happiness in women… Women who are strong yet delicate and beautiful as diamonds.* Micaela, throughout her life, would think of these words she had mumbled to herself as she went to bed that night with the pains of a first time broken heart.

Time passed and life continued for Micaela. She opted to delve into her books. Following Mr. Langdon's, her guidance counselor, advice on which college she should attend, Micaela began filling out her college applications. The first one she applied almost in secrecy, was NYU. She felt so proud and looked forward to having an answer of 'Congratulations, you have been accepted into our Literature program' then almost begrudgingly she applied to the schools her parents had expected her to apply to, especially UCLA where her mother knew she would be attending, come next Fall. She was busy studying, working and trying to make herself busy, doing more than time allowed trying hard not to think about her hurt vanity, and not over-thinking how she would tell her parents of her going to New York. All of these thoughts dispelled the feeling of having been dumped by a stupid boy. After all, she was the diamond that was just beginning to get polished to shine to her full potential.

The bittersweet happiness of that moment when her father had compared her to a diamond was eclipsed by the hurtful thing her mother did one early morning. It was about a month after Pablo had broken up with Micaela, and her mother came to her bedroom around two o'clock in the morning and woke her up.

"Mica, wake up!" she nudged, and rocked her back and forth by the shoulders.

"I want you to see that you are wasting away for someone who does not deserve it in the least!" her mother angrily added.

It was hard for Micaela to understand why would her mother want to show her what she was about to show her. Paloma could not see that Micaela early in life found ways to harness any angst, sadness or pent up anger that life brought her way becoming aware of these instances with a clarity unknown to her. The gift of clairvoyance was manifesting itself in her young being. Thus after the breakup she submerged herself in household chores, school work and her beloved books. She loved to read, and she read every chance she got. It was her senior year in high school and she was waiting to hear from the colleges she had applied to so she could decide where she would be going. She got a part time job in an office nearby and was attending a technical night school learning dental assisting. She wanted to see what being a dentist was like, the profession her mother had chosen for her. She was a very busy young woman. She did not really have much time to sit down and eat. She had lost a lot of weight and became even skinnier than before. In a five foot and four inch small frame, she only weighed ninety-nine pounds by the end of the school year. She was skinny but not frail.

Micaela came home around five in the afternoon, grabbed an apple or pear and ran out of the house to go to her dental assisting classes. "This is a good move, *mi hija*. It will let you understand the profession and convince you that this is the path you need to pursue," Paloma, would say.

Micaela already knew what she wanted to be and it wasn't a dentist. She wanted to pursue the literary arts. She wanted to become a writer, a playwright and she wanted to be like her mother, delivering speeches and helping with community theater as Paloma had done back in their country. She saw herself in New York City, coming back to Hollywood where she would become another Cecil B. De Mile or better.

Always, her mother would put a damper on her dreams by saying, "Why do you want to be a writer?"

"You have to be good at it," she would add, with an underlying tone that she did not believe Micaela capable of being a good writer. How would you know if I am a good writer or not?... I do not exist for you and everything I bring home you discard or think of it as insignificant, Micaela muttered under her breath.

Trying not to pay attention to her mother, Micaela submerged herself into her studies, work, and dental assistant training. Time to eat, which she loved very much, became almost nonexistent. She did lose weight and perhaps was approaching anorexic standards, but by no means was this intentional. Her mother thought she was becoming anorexic because of the pain and suffering over the break up. Paloma's solution would be to wake her up from her sound sleep at two o'clock in the morning to show her Pablo making out with the girl across the street. She was a Korean girl who had moved into the neighborhood just a year before Pablo and Micaela broke up. What she did not know was the girl named Kim, had a part time job at Sears, where Pablo also had a part time job. They had started seeing each other not knowing Kim's house was across the street from Micaela.

It did not matter to Micaela when it happened because she knew deep in her heart that no one belongs to anyone, and love and friendship are precious gifts people bestow upon you, so if when they are taken away you just need to be thankful to have had them at all. Her mother saw it in a different way and every time she thought about the incident, Micaela became upset with her mother and thought to herself *How could she do that? Doesn't she know that this hurts?*

She didn't care that Pablo was making out with the girl across the street, but rather the way her mother would want to point this out to her. She became confused at the way her mother showed her how she loved her.

"I do this because I love you and it hurts me to see you waste away," her mother told her.

It was the first time Micaela heard her mother say those words "I love you, and do not want you to suffer."

If this is the way you are going to say it and I have to hurt this much each time you decide to let me know, then please don't say it! She thought to herself.

A week later and in all the emotional turmoil of seeing the ex-boyfriend kissing the new girl friend as her mother pointed out, Micaela was abruptly told by her mother, "I told you all your hard work will pay off. You are going to UCLA." Paloma pulled the opened enveloped from her apron pocket and gave it to her. Noticing that the envelope was addressed to Micaela, she could not believe her mother's intrusion of her privacy, and the disappointment of being accepted to a career that was not her choice made her bitter and angry. For the first time she was forced to lash out at her mother in English knowing that she would not be able to understand fully what she was saying, "I don't want to be a dentist, Mom. Why don't you get it in your thick head, that is what you want, not me, I am not going there instead I will be going to NYU, you get it NYU?!"

"What is NYU?" Paloma asked.

"You keep saying NYU, NYU, what is NYU?...Rebeca come here now!"

Rebeca looking puzzled at the interaction of her sister and mother answered, "Yes, Mami Paloma?"

"What is NYU?...tell me, is it a place?...Why is Micaela always talking about NYU?"

"It is a school in New York City, Mami. Why?" Rebeca afraid of what it was about to happen answered timidly.

"Why do you mean is a school in New York City? And who is going there?" Paloma looking intently at Micaela approached her daughter with a defiant stance making her regret the wrath she had brought on. She knew that this was a moment where she needed to stand strong, but the force of her mother was relentlessly stronger than hers, and she regretted telling her the way she had.

"When did you apply to this school, and who told you, you could apply to this school. Why wasn't I informed of this?...If you think that because you are eighteen years old and are going to college you are going to defy me like this, I would cut you in two before you even realize it. Do not get on my wrong side because you know that my indifference will kill you, do you hear me? You will go to UCLA and become a dentist. You will make your father and me proud of the hard work we have done for you to become better... better than that stupid dream of becoming a writer. Bring me the box of pads I know you have hidden from me, even in Ecuador. Give it to me now and you will see what unfounded dreams become!"

Charging into Micaela's room looking like a mad woman trying to find something lost, Paloma came across the cardboard box under her bed with all her stories on the prescription pads and took it outside, dumping them on top of a small grill. She lit a match throwing it on top of Micaela's precious pads. Paloma yelled at Micaela, "Unfounded dreams become smoke, smoke! Get it through your thick head you will never be a writer...never because you are not good enough!"

Micaela was stunned. She wanted to hit her mother and inflict the same visceral pain she was feeling to stop her from burning her words the way she was doing, but all she could muster was to hear herself saying, "Why, why do you hate me so much. What have I done to deserve so much rejection? It is almost as if you are taking out on me something someone has done to you. I know I am your ugly duckling but it turns into a swan. I will show you one day that I will be the writer you are not allowing me to become, and then I will be so far away that you will not even have my indifference. If this is what you want for you and I, then I bid farewell to the mother who should have never had me in the first place, and all you are to me is a woman to whom I would prove that the words are mine and they are all here," pointing to her temples and heart, "and no one, not even you can take them away." Before Micaela could finish, she felt the hard blow from the back of her mother's hand across her face.

It brought Micaela to the sad realization that she and Paloma, her mother, were done. She stood all alone in the middle of the small back yard with the flames dying down much like her spirit but for only that moment, the moment when she saw her mother turn and walk away.

The next day she went to school without even seeing her mother, for she got up early to make breakfast for her father while Paloma stayed in bed with her usual malady. Micaela did not feel anything for the first time. She did not care whether Paloma was okay or not in her bedroom. All she knew is that she needed to get to school and get lost in the learning. She was shocked when she arrived at her homeroom class and was called out by her teacher who proceeded to send her to the nurse station. She looked at the bruise on her cheek and the nurse started to ask questions. Micaela realized how distraught she had been not to realize or even feel the pain that she was now being made aware of.

"How did this happen?" the nurse asked.

Micaela's reaction was to tell a grandiose story of how she and her brother started to wrestle leading to a tickling match and in the commotion he had stretched his arm letting go of her grasp with such a force that without wanting to, he slapped Micaela to the ground. She played the mean little sister act telling the nurse that she had gotten her big brother in trouble for this. The nurse believed her and gave her a look of disapproval at her gloating which made Micaela happy knowing that she created a believable story. Boasting under her breath, she said, "I am right. My words are mine, they are only mine."

She was sent back to her second period class which was heaven for her since it was her literature class with Ms. Atkinson. In this awful morning, it meant much more than just her second period class, because Ms. Atkinson started the class with a big announcement.

"Sit, sit everyone, I have an important announcement to make. I am so proud that one of my students has been accepted to a very prestigious school with a large academic scholarship. It was the short story she wrote for this class that enabled her to be the recipient of such an honor. I am passing around the short story and she will be glad to sign it for you ladies and gentlemen... Micaela Galarza's: 'My Coming to America: What does it mean to me'." Everyone applauded and started to look at her.

Micaela was in disbelief that her last minute decision to take a literature class and to write a short story for a class project had given her the opportunity to go after the most cherished desire she had been contemplating for a long time, to be a writer. But she was also trying to fathom all the feelings of overwhelming proportions at the happenings of the last two days. Life seemed to have her on a teeter totter that only made her feel powerless and abated. Micaela knew that her dream of attending NYU had been already destroyed and she had the proof on her face, so unfair it all seemed and the most poignant moment was yet to happen. Again, that ominous feeling over her was lurking and she knew of things but did not know what they were or what they meant. She distinctly remembered her mother's objection after she had mentioned her wish to take a writing class. Micaela had all the requirements to graduate in the top ten percent of her class and without thinking about asking permission, she had taken this writing class anyway to fulfill time and not credits. She also remembered how this decision got her first true fan, her literature teacher.

"Micaela, I really liked your short story," Ms. Atkinson told her after class one day. "Do you keep a journal?"

"Thank you...yes, I do keep a journal ma'am. Why?" she timidly asked.

"Well, because most writers have a tendency to keep journals. They write poetry on paper napkins. Painters doodle, writers keep journals," Ms. Atkinson told her in an inquisitive tone.

"All my life I wanted to read all the books in the world and write like the best writers in history. To create images with words, I find it fascinating. How we humans can communicate with the written word, I find it spellbinding," Micaela excitedly told her teacher.

"I see!" Ms. Atkinson exclaimed seeing Micaela's love for writing.

"You seem to go too far away places every time you talk about the book reports and the stories we analyze in class." She went on. "I find it refreshing yet quite astonishing that none of your other teachers did not see this gift you have."

"I have mailed a recommendation to the dean of Humanities at New York University on your behalf. I hope you don't mind," she told Micaela.

"I feel pretty confident you will get in." she added.

"You think?" Micaela asked with wondrous eyes.

"I see you are already in another world, thinking of another story. Am I right?" Ms. Atkinson felt the excitement coming from Micaela.

"Can you see all that in my expression?" Micaela asked her.

"Yes, I think you will be a wonderful story teller," the teacher added.

It made Micaela touch heaven to have such a strong critic already. Someone who knew about English grammar, syntax and all those necessary tools to be an effective writer, calling her a story teller. It make her smile as she thought to herself, *If Ms. Atkinson only knew that many of my short stories I write on the weekends have been written on insignificant prescription pads, free scratch pads from companies used for their advertisement and freely given to me. They were the best thing America had to offer me.*

"That is what I want to be...a story teller," she added with such excitement and determination, incredulously thinking that for the first time she had voiced out to someone other than her family, that she had chosen writing to be her career path.

Ms. Atkinson could not help herself but to extend her arms giving this young lady a hug which also offered her some kind of repose and validation at a such young age. In the next few months, the two would get together for tea. They exchanged book critiques and the latest movies made from novels and how they differed. They would gossip about casting of actors for the novels they had read as if they were producers in Hollywood. They laughed at their choices and how comical they found their authoritative expertise to be. Micaela loved her Ms. Atkinson and the feeling was reciprocated with a such fervor that what Doris Atkinson had in store for Micaela would set her in an emotional down spiral that unbeknown to her, was only her power of being that sustained her through this trying time because even in her mind the memory of the women of her clan seemed to be siding with her mother. She went home to the chilly air of her mother's indifference, her siblings and father's angst at the ire Micaela had brought on to make things so uncomfortable. She stayed in her room and did not mention what had transpired in class earlier that morning.

"Please let it be morning again," she whispered as she went to bed.

She thought about the time when she got together with Ms. Atkinson and she was concocting a way to have Micaela attend the school of her choice for literature and she seemed so happy to help Micaela out.

"Micaela!" her father yelled out with urgency.

"What happened?...Is mom okay?" Micaela asked trying to focus from just being awakened.

The image on the TV news was painfully shocking as the picture of her beloved teacher, mentor and friend appeared to be the victim of a long courageous battle with cancer. A chilling ache throughout her body overcame her, and she wanted to scream but a force stopped her; it seemed like she was having a nightmare from which she could not wake up, a tornado of emotions swirling through her. She left the room as fast as she could to reach the bathroom and holding tight to the cold porcelain of the toilet basin she tasted the bitter bile coming through her esophagus as it made its way to her throat where at the young age of eighteen she viscerally felt the suffering of the human condition, something she would never forget.

Not one tear she shed, yet she felt her chest implode to the deepest part of her being. Ms. Atkinson had never let Micaela know of her situation and she first felt betrayed and then a sense of peace came to her soul not knowing why. Doris Atkinson's gift in life to Micaela had been her affirmation but her gift in death or rather her last wishes for Micaela left her feeling very loved when a package a week later came for her in the mail. A collection of antique poetry books was bestowed upon her. She cried holding the books and the letter that came with them. It made her think back to the moment when she first shared with her about her dream of storytelling and how sweetly the old woman had always supported her. The letter read,

"My sweet and talented Micaela,

I stopped reading these books after you honored me with the poetry I read on your prescription pads. The devotional ones sustained me in my last hour and I knew then you needed to have my favorite poetry books to accompany the many that will be printed having your name on the cover and the gentle sweetness of your heart on every page.

In addition, I must tell you that I found this antique leather bound and exquisitely embossed journal beckon to me once, and my wishes to have it became real and more special because it was a gift from my mother who wanted me to be a writer. It meant so much to me I did not want to take away from its beauty with the simplicity of my thoughts. Throughout my adult years, I have looked at the pristine empty linen pages and listened to the soft rustling of its rice paper liners knowing someday the pages will have wonderful words written on them to tell the world about the writer whose thoughts would rival the exquisite nature of it. I want you to be the new owner and your remarkable words to be the work of art contained within. Only then I will be content knowing that the graciousness of your soul merits being on every page. I regret that I must part now and not be able to attend the many signing occasions you are bound to have.

Your humble and devoted fan,
Doris Atkinson.

PS: Its writer, you, will be awesome, because you are already an extraordinary young lady!"

She cried quietly and stoically like the Victorian refrained woman her teacher had been. She felt lonely with yet another loss and she thought back to all the lonely times she felt since coming to America and how much it had paid off to stay away from 'friends' and all the fun stuff as she went through the process of assimilating into the new world her parents had brought her to. The many lonely nights studying for tests and reading to learn English had gotten her excellent grades enabling Micaela to get scholarships to the two choices presented to her.

She had taken the writing class against her mother's wishes. Again, her mother told her, "You already know how to read and write. Why must you insist on becoming a writer when you can be a dentist? You love to read and you work hard at your studies, which is the discipline required for you to become a dentist and be more successful than your father and me," her mother continued.

Micaela felt desperately lonely with no support from her family to share the excitement of being accepted to NYU and her future as a writer. The only person who would have shared this joy was now gone. Such a crossroads, having to choose between her love of writing and her respect for her parents. It weighed heavily on her, and the more she thought about it, she hoped her parents, especially her mother, would be understanding of this vulnerable time she was recovering from. She deserved to choose her own profession in which she could excel just by the love of being in that profession. Being a writer would lead her to become eternal with every word. Micaela always wanted to be eternal like the stories she heard as a child. And what better way to become eternal, by composing symphonies with the arrangements of sentences, or creating works of art by merely describing a place or feelings in the most eloquent prose she would think to herself as her tears would stream down her face knowing this would never be.

A Destiny Truncated by Choices Made

The darkness and disquiet of young Micaela's life weighed heavily on her heart. As she prepared for another rite of passage, the senior year traditions such as Ditch Day and the prom, she knew she would not be allowed to take part in any of them. She no longer cared about anything most eighteen year old girls look forward to and she only yearned for some solace now that she had resigned not to go to New York City to follow her dreams. In this morose and almost catatonic attitude, she met a handsome boy.

Blake, tall and slender, was a cashier at the grocery store where Micaela went shopping every Saturday with her mother. Blake had beautiful, baby blue eyes that could only be compared to the soft blue skies at the break of dawn. She was enamored by their color the first time she laid her own brown eyes on them. She thought they shined like the softest light coming from a pair of pale Brazilian aquamarine stones that would make anyone melt at the mere sight of them. He had a provocative smile, and blond, wavy hair that shimmered in the splendor of the fluorescent grocery store lights. Like a religious ritual, after coming back from the farmers' market and leaving all the fresh fruit and meat they bought in the refrigerator, they would then go out to the grocery store. Sometimes, Blake would be there and as an eighteen-year old girl in turmoil, Micaela would find herself staring at him as he waited on the people ahead of them.

They would exchange glances and smile at each other. Their smiles and glances continued for the next few months. Without thinking about her recent heartaches, and totally forgetting about the college choices needed to be made for that one moment, she became aware of a cunning idea or so she thought...He is cute enough to take me to that notorious prom. Her turmoil dissipated by the urgency of having someone like the grocery boy take her to the prom. It made her shift focus on how to go about getting him. Time was of the essence and she knew she had to work fast.

In desperation, as well as the excuse and inspiration of following the current women's movement, she thought, *This is nineteen, seventy-seven. Why do I have to wait for the boys to ask me out? All he can do is say, 'No!'* She repeated this to herself and with the naiveté of youth (for we cannot say it was innocence) she performed a deliberate act. Just before closing time, she went to the market to buy milk for her mother. She took with her a little piece of pink paper on which she had printed her name and telephone number. Micaela made sure no one else was nearby and then entered Blake's checkout line. She looked at him, smiled, and while paying for her purchase, passed the little paper into his hand saying, "Only if you want to." And with the coquetry of a young girl in desperate need to have a cute date for the prom, she smiled, walked to the door and glancing over her shoulder just once, she exited.

She hoped he would call her. She had already imagined her grand entrance to the prom, and being eighteen, Micaela was very sure her parents would not object to this one special school dance. She would take Blake. They would look so beautiful in prom attire. All the girls and Pablo would be jealous. Blake was much more handsome than Pablo and he was American after all. Most of the Latin kids stuck around Latin kids, so for them, this would be a shock that she dared to 'cross that line' and date a white boy, especially one as handsome as Blake. Micaela's cultural rebellion proved to be much more interesting than what she hoped for. She dared to push the 'race envelope' to see how it would feel to be stared at, *I wonder if it feels like being an animal in a zoo...something for people to look at?* Micaela thought this racist attitude was absurd. She realized of her 'mistake' after telling this bit of detail to her mother one day.

"I think it is wrong to date out of your social status and much worse out of your race," her mother told her, with strong conviction, as if to tell her "You better not do it."

"So you would object if I dated other than Ecuadorian or Latin men?" she asked, knowing that the stern and conditionally loving mother would definitely have something to say about the matter.

"You are not old enough to date men, or any *mocoso* who comes your way!" she told her. "And when the time comes, you better never date, a boy who is black or Indian or illiterate!" Paloma told Micaela glancing at her with penetrating eyes, with the intention of marking the information in her brain forever.

"Why?" Micaela asked, nonchalantly.

"Why?" her mother repeated the question.

"Yes, why?" Micaela asked again.

"Because, do you want people to talk badly about you?" her mother continued.

"What could they say?" Micaela asked.

"Are you being smart with me?" her mother asked, frowning at her.

"No, I just want to know what would be so wrong with dating an Indian boy or a black boy or a white boy for that matter," she stated.

"Because people would look at you like you were animals in a zoo," her mother said, looking intently at Micaela.

Micaela smirked, as she thought of the statement and realized she had heard that from her mother before. Knowing her mother would object to her next statement, she went on to say it as she walked away, "That is one way to get attention. So what if I am like an animal in the zoo. I just have to adjust to being seen by everyone that way."

Occasionally, her mother was receptive to Micaela's adolescent growing pains, but scolding and sounding indignant, she said, "Micaela, you know better than that!" Paloma felt the need to instill in her daughter the painful act of being prejudice and continued saying, "If you should marry anyone who is inferior in any way or does not even compare to your own upbringing, I would take that as a threat and as defiance against the family and a sign you do not want our love." Micaela's mother said it very coldly and matter of fact, "Now, is that what you want?" she asked Micaela.

"I dunno" she responded and thinking to herself, *What love? There is no love, only criticism and put downs. How can you call that love?...Making you eat until your plate is clean regardless of the gluttony of such an act. Making you miss school and making a child do things that only adults should be responsible for...Stealing one's childhood, How can that be love?!* Startled by her mother's sudden proximity to her, she tried to escape, but to no avail.

"That does not sound right to me, and I don't speak English very well," Paloma added, expecting Micaela to speak properly.

"I do not know!" Micaela repeated as she walked away from her mother's presence. She remembered that as a child in the old country, a scene like this one had been played out before in the panorama of her young life.

That time it had been her beloved *Mamita* María José who tried to teach her about the separating lines between people. It was a rainy afternoon, her mother's laundress, named Lucrecia had come to do laundry and iron linens for the family. Lucrecia had a daughter, Rosita, the same age as Micaela who had come with her that afternoon. She spread the bed sheet over the ironing board creating sort of a tent underneath the board. Micaela had told Lucrecia's child to come and play with her and her dolls underneath this huge tent made by the linens. Kids will be kids and they played in their made-up house. In the middle of playing Micaela heard *Mamita* María José's voice calling her.

"Micaela, could you come here for a minute please," she called out.

"Shh," Micaela told her playmate.

"She is going to get mad at you," Rosita responded.

"Shh, that is why we need to stay quiet so she will not find us." Micaela smirked, staying quiet and still.

"Micaela, where are you, sweet child of God," María José kept at it.

"Lucrecia, have you seen Micaela?" María José asked.

Without the need of words, Lucrecia, pointed down below the ironing board telling on the poor children.

"Micaela, come out of there at once," her grandmother had sternly demanded.

"I am coming, *Mamita* María José," Micaela responded, feeling a bit nervous, for the tone of her grandmother's voice was not ever like that when talking to her.

Nervously, coming out from under the bed sheet, she looked up at her grandmother who was looking at her in a very cross way.

"Come here," she told her.

"When I call you or anybody calls you, you answer, 'Yes ma'am I am coming,'" she scolded.

"Do you understand?" she added, making sure Micaela understood about being well-mannered.

"Yes, ma'am," she responded.

Her adoptive grandmother made some tea and sat down with the child in a very somber manner. Micaela knew something grave was about to happen because only when the lesson was hard or a delicate issue had to be dealt with, tea time made its presence. Coffee was the routine of everyday, but tea time was for serious talk or hysteria among the women of her clan. Tea was considered a soothing and tranquilizing drink to deal with matters that at times were of life or death.

"Now, I know you are lonely sometimes and you want to play with whomever is around you, but you must choose correctly," her grandmother told her.

"What do you mean?" she asked, instinctively afraid of what her beloved grandma was going to say.

"Well, the laundress' little girl is not from your same background. She is the daughter of the hired help. You do not play with the children of the hired help," she told her in an ominous voice.

"But what difference does it make that she is the child of the hired help, *Mamita* María José?" Micaela asked her grandmother.

"There is a lot of difference and for now you do as your mother and I tell you!" her grandmother scolded.

Micaela could not believe someone who loved her so would tell her not to play with another child her own age. She was sad that she was told she was better than that little girl and from then on she had to be careful about the company she kept, especially when the older women of her household were around. How hypocritical that was and how non Christian it was for her family to see the distinction of class. It was the first time in her childhood she was made to see the lines between people, which then and ever since then she thought were absurd. She realized that she belonged to this group of people that for better or worse, were her family.

The turmoil she felt then as a child was multiplied by the conversation her mother and Micaela had just had. Micaela slammed the door of her bedroom and threw herself on the bed. Grabbing a pillow to cover her head she let out a loud scream.

"What is the matter with you?" her younger sister shouted.

"Nothing — nothing is ever wrong with me, you or anybody in this family!" she exclaimed angrily.

"You are so weird!" her sister added, "Why can't you be happy with things as they are?"

"Be happy with the *status quo*. Is that what you are telling me?" she asked her sister.

"What does that mean?" her sister asked.

"You see! If you do not ask, learn words, phrases and things, you will never know anything and then you will be complacent, living in a world that never changes. That is the status quo from the Latin; 'the existing condition,'" she went on to give her younger sister a lesson on how to read the dictionary, Micaela's favorite book.

"Oh! See how you are! You are so weird!" her sister stated.

"Whatever!" Micaela exclaimed knowing that it was absurd to debate a point of importance with a child four years younger who thought even then, that cheerleading was an important task to accomplish.

"You are just as complacent as the other people in this house!" she told her sister, leaving their bedroom to answer her mother, who was calling her name.

"You have a phone call!" she indicated to her with an acrimonious look.

"Thank you," picking up the receiver.

"Don't stay on it too long. See me afterwards. I need to talk to you," her mother added with a disapproving tone.

To her surprise, it was Blake and a heavenly bliss she felt for the first time came over her. Micaela also knew the reason of her mother's disapproving tone. Blake started calling Micaela almost every day to chat about almost anything. He was two years older than she. He was attending the community college near his house which was in another neighborhood. He had asked her if she would go there after graduation. Sounding snobbish she told him, "No, I got accepted into U.C.L.A and my parents really want me to go there. But where I really want to go is N.Y. U."

"New York City!" Incredulous, he continued to ask, "Why so far?"

"Well, I will be far away from my overprotective parents, and I will be learning something that I want to learn...like writing."

"So you want to be a writer, huh?" He said with a twinge of *je ne sais quoi*.

Between phones calls and groceries being checked out, they got closer and closer, and one day he asked her out to see a movie. She was already eighteen years old, but somehow she knew her parents would object to her going to the movies with a 'white' boy they did not know anything about as well as never meeting his family. Her mother already had heard his voice and told Micaela that she did not know this boy and thought he sounded too old for her. Micaela thanked her lucky stars for the day she had agreed to go to see the movie, for a family friend coincidentally had just arrived from South America, and of course her mother would not have a chance to protest and make a scene. She would be too busy showing her friend the crazy ways Americans do things and entertaining them as she would have done in the old country. Her mother's sense of decorum and keeping up appearances gave Micaela the opportunity to go see the movie with this cute American boy without any chaperones. She snuck out of the house and to the movies they went to see Sylvester Stallone's "Rocky."

Micaela was in heaven. She had never been out with a boy to the movies, alone! It was such a big move on her part that she was filled with excitement and a surreal sense of being. Blake looked beautiful in a navy blue turtle neck that made his blonde locks look like little rays of sunshine coming to take a peek at his blue eyes. He looked like a blonde John Travolta and was just dreamy with a cleft in his chin that became accentuated as he smiled in a devilish way, making Micaela weak at the knees and making her question "Why, why, why, is this boy going out with me?" She could not believe that she waited for more than an hour to enter the movie theater and while in line all the girls were staring at her date, HER DATE!

Once they got inside, he asked her, "Do you want anything to drink?"

Oh my gosh, he is going to be a gentleman and buy me a drink, WOW! She thought, and in the same breath she heard herself say, "I'd like a coke if that, if that is okay?"

"I am going to get some Milk Duds. Do you want some too?" He asked her as he bent down to her cheek and gave her a kiss.

"Be back," he whispered and disappeared into the darkness of the movie theater.

She looked around and all the couples sitting next to her smiled at her, as if they were saying, "You go girl. He is really cute!"

He came back with two drinks and candy in his pocket, and told her, "Hey, get the candy from my pocket, would you?"

She approached his pocket as if it was a relic she did not want to disturb. She felt so nervous for being in his personal space, so soon and so quick. She blushed as she reached in his pant pockets for the Milk Duds. With trembling, shaky hands, she pulled the small carton and as soon as she tried to open it, she was not aware of her own strength and they went flying all over the floor.

She was so embarrassed but gently he told her, "It doesn't matter, don't worry about it."

"Come here, sit with me and let's watch the movie, we will pick up the Duds after the movie is over, you messy girl, okay?" He told her teasing her and nudging her knees.

Oh my gosh! He is so sweet! She thought. All she remembers from Rocky is Stallone running up the stairs on the Philadelphia Museum, then his screaming "Adrian!"

She would laugh years later when she remembered all that she did that night was stare at this beautiful blond young man who once or twice would look at her with a smile on his face that accentuated his dimples. A twinge of desire would peek into her soul, wanting more of his smile, more of the look in his eyes when he saw her. Micaela could not describe that look but it made her feel so full of life, vibrant and wanted. She felt as if she was the honeysuckle flower about to be peeled apart to partake of its sweet insides and a sense of success was so sweetly palpable.

Blake, on the other hand, could not believe that she had never been to a movie with a boy and would playfully tell her, "You are lying. You are eighteen. For sure you have been to the movies with a boyfriend or two."

"Oh sure! I did...couple of times...same boyfriend," she said sarcastically, "I went to see the "Exorcist," with my boyfriend, father and two other siblings." She would smile and continue laughing, "My father sat next to me and every time we would hold hands, my father would clear his throat, rotate his head around like Linda Blair, at which point the hand would let go and we would all resume watching the movie. You needed to be there," she told him, winking at him and with a carefree smile becoming infectious, something that endeared her to Blake, unaware of just how much.

Micaela's laugh became contagious as she laughed with *gusto* imagining the sad romantic picture of being in America in the seventies and having the chaperones all around her like a scene from the "Godfather." They both laughed, and as she moved forward to grimace in imitation of her father looking after the young couple in the dark, he felt her long hair and told her, "I like your hair. It is so full and incredibly thick yet soft."

"I do not understand, with a face as cute as yours and hair like this, how could you only have had one boyfriend. I bet there are a bunch of boys who try to grab hold of you," he added. He stroked her hair with an intensity that made Micaela think back about when the women of her clan talked about the "pressures of love." *If this is how the 'pressure of love' feels, I want more 'pressure,'* she thought with a guilty yet wicked smile that Blake mistook as 'do it some more' and grabbed her hair again which made Micaela feel warm. *What is this tingling sensation I just felt?* She thought trying to compose herself from the awkward embarrassment she started to feel.

"The first time I saw you at the store was when you were getting the milk, and as you reached down, your hair just cascaded around your face and all I could see was the small mouth you have," he told her, approaching her lips.

For the first time she became aware of her hair and lips. *Were they that attractive as to make a boy wonder about me?"* she thought to herself.

"Naugh! He is just saying this!" she told herself in disbelief and blushing, creating a glow on her face which Blake became aware and made him feel more special than he had ever felt with any other girl.

"Stop making fun of me," she told him.

"Why do you think I am making fun of something as pretty as your hair and lips?" He added feeling a bit awkward at her inability to accept a compliment.

He drove her home and before they got near the house, he asked her, "Should I kiss you good night here or can I do it in front of your house? Something tells me that I would not be able to do it in front of your house," he said in the same breath.

"Well, there are many ways to kiss me that would be acceptable to do it in front of my parents even," she chuckled.

"Show me!" he added.

"Well, there is the European kiss which is both cheeks. There is the Latin American kiss where you only kiss one cheek," and before she could explain the other kisses, he gently grabbed her with his hands around her head, massaging her ear lobes with his thumbs he told her, "This is my French kiss...for my sweet Micaela."

She stood there feeling flaccid as if a vacuum had removed every organ and only her skin remained standing, about to fall and become a pile on the ground, but in the same milli of a second her heart raced and the thoughts in her head were about to explode. She could never write about this moment in time, she quickly thought to herself...*How could I write about my first amatory feeling ever?*...when the moist sweet taste of his lips touched hers as she opened her mouth. She felt his wanting come rushing into her mouth with his tongue which only asked to be held to make him feel all the passion she never imagined she had, but he knew it would be all his.

Micaela would think back to this instance much later in life, and at times would find herself longing for this specific event to help her dispel her feelings of insecurity that made her feel unattractive or when she thought her mother was right in thinking that she was an 'ugly duckling.' Sade's "Sweetest Taboo" would come to mind and the melody would suffice for the lack of tangible feeling. "You give me, you give me the sweetest taboo You give me, you're giving me the sweetest taboo. Too good for me..." Blake had given her the sweetest taboo in his French kiss which made her love him through most of her college years. He had made her aware for the first time in her life that her erogenous zone was in her lips. How sweet it was to be kissed with the wanting and beseeching way Blake had kissed her then. Her feelings of self discovery of the woman she would become, she would hold dear waiting for those feelings to be there again one day.

The next day, she went to Sears wearing bell bottom hip hugger pants that were tight on her small body. She had a striped sweater that accentuated her skinny untouched body which was still reverberating from the heat of the moment brought on by the kiss of the previous night. She went to the hardware section of the store where Pablo would be, she walked by the counter, where Kim, his Korean girlfriend, was looking at her with questioning eyes, as if to ask why was Micaela there. She asked herself this question, but the answer was that in Blake's kiss a feeling of empowerment had started to unleash the force, the force that was her power of being. Micaela had felt betrayed by Pablo leaving her and now she wanted him to see her transformation and regret his choice.

Yeah! Let's look worried, little girl. See who has the upper hand now, you who have him...or him, wondering what if Micaela would have been more open to a sexual encounter! ... All those wasted summer afternoons...wondering why she did not give of herself to me, when all along she could have! Micaela thought to herself and came to the realization that indeed her power of being did not need a validation or affirmation. Yet she realized that the experiences of being a young woman were becoming like the skin of an onion been peeled away layer by layer, exposing not only the strong scent of its make up but the subtle flavors that helps a meal become enticing and full of gusto much like her young spirit taking shape from girl to womanhood and she left the store before making a spectacle of herself. She smiled at Kim, left Sears, and never saw Pablo again.

The next Saturday before going to the farmers' market, she asked her mother if she could cut her hair. Skater Dorothy Hamill's hair cut was in *vogue,* and she cut it that way to go along with the changes she was feeling; the feeling of empowerment and confidence. The next morning, about nine o'clock, she got a call from Blake asking if she could have breakfast with him. She told her parents she was going to the library which was in the opposite direction of the grocery store, but off she went hoping her mother would not decide to water the front lawn at this time and catch her going in the opposite direction. She went to the store and there he was in blue jeans and a denim shirt that made him look like a tall "James Dean." He stood leaning up against his yellow 1965 Chevy truck. He looked surprised to see her short hair. He opened the door helping her to get in and asked her, "What happened to your long hair?"

"I wanted to look like Dorothy. What do you think?"

"Well, I like the long hair better, but this style is cute on you. It makes you look younger...like a little girl," he told her, reaching to kiss her on the cheek.

They went to "House of Pancakes." They never met for dinner nor would he come to see her after work. She lived very close to the supermarket where he worked so it was not that he had to go out of his way. For a while, they went out only during the day and it was sporadic. In the six months that they had been going together, they went out to another movie only to find it sold out. They went walking on the strand instead. Once he took her to an amusement park and they had a blast. It was the first time she went to a restaurant and had dinner with her date. She often wondered, Is he my boyfriend, or am I just a friend? especially when after the amusement park closed, they stayed in the parking lot watching everyone leave.

They started to kiss and fool around. She loved this playing with him because she was never allowed to horse around in the house.

"Ladies don't play around like that!" her mother would say.

So to be in his truck and Blake playing with her short hair, tickling each other, it was heaven. She loved to tickle him as he tried to get a hold of her wrists and once he did, he would put her hands behind her back pulling her face close to his and kissing her like a wild man. They laughed and caressed and all of a sudden they both stopped and ever so slowly and softly he would let go of her hands and she would caress his face. They would embrace and this one time, he lay on top of her, kissing her throat going down on her chest getting very close to her breasts trying to undo her bra. No fighting, no objection came from her. Instead the fire centered at her groin. She felt it would only be dissipated by him undressing her totally and in return she would give in to the 'pressures of love.' But fate would have it that he was a gentleman and as if he was directed by her mother, he stopped and said, "Your parents would not approve of this...I better take you home."

Sadly enough, after that night, the dates started to happen again only in the morning light. She started to wonder why all the dates happened only at lunch or breakfast time. She got even more curious because come March there was the Sadie Hawkins dance, and that is when a girl would ask a guy. So one day, she asked and he said he could not go. She was hurt but shrugged it off.

A month later the big announcement was made that the prom was coming up and she thought she would make a beautiful gown from her own design and no one would have this dress along with the handsome young man she found Blake to be. "All eyes will be on me, wearing a beautiful gown on the arm of a knock out boy. Pablo is sure to regret leaving me!" She would exclaimed out loud letting her vanity get the best of her.

However, when it came time to ask him, he again said he could not go with her. At that moment she became really upset and decided to find out why the dating was only in the daytime. He always said no to the school dances and Micaela felt something fishy was going on.

They were on the phone and she heard herself saying, "I need to know why you always say no. Is there something wrong with me that you do not want to be seen with me, or what?" she added.

He stayed quiet and after a long pause he muttered, "I need to talk to you but not on the phone."

"Can you come out for an hour or so?" he asked her.

"Where do you want us to meet?" Micaela responded, somewhat annoyed because this was *déjà vu*. The same thing Pablo had told her about a year ago, at which point she had told him,

"Whatever you need to tell me; you can tell me over the phone."

She felt he did not merit her trying to go and meet with him, especially when she needed to fool her parents somehow about leaving the house at night, "All this trouble just to be dumped is not worth it," she muttered to herself.

Blake pleaded with her and for some unknown reason, she knew this time was different. There were too many questions that needed to be asked and answered face to face.

"Come to Manhattan pier," he went on.

She agreed and said, "I will see you in fifteen minutes, okay?"

The Manhattan pier was only about fifteen minutes by car from her house. She loved to go down there in the afternoon and listen to the "Carpenter's" sad songs. She loved to watch the sunset trying to count the many shades of red, orange, gray and blue as the sun said 'good bye' to her and disappear, lonely, into the darkness of night. She wrote some of the saddest poems when she and Pablo broke up looking at that sunset. She took her small journal where her melancholic thoughts of past times were recorded. "Here we go again, little book," she whispered. She got into the car and pictured the darkness of the sea already in place as the late afternoon went on to become night.

"Why can't they just love me the way I am? I do not put out!" she told herself.

She drove through the busy streets and as she got closer to the pier, the area was filled with commotion of passersby. Micaela parked near the pier and searched for Blake's yellow truck. She did not find it there, so she thought he was late. *I hope he shows up soon enough so I do not have to wait here looking at other couple's embrace. That would not be good,* she thought.

As soon she muttered the words, there he was turning near where she parked. He looked handsome with the same turtleneck sweater he had worn to the movies that first time. She felt weak in the knees, and just wanted to put a spell over him and make him want to stay with her. She knew the inevitable break up was coming. She got out of the car and he gave her a kiss and a hug.

They slowly walked along the boardwalk approaching the pier that extended into the ocean. It ended in a circular area where the Marine Museum stood surrounded by benches for the fishermen to fish, and lovers to sit down and watch the sunset. Neither one of them said anything, until they reached the museum area. The soft melody of the ocean waves coming ashore told her to be strong, not to cry when the crescendo of the good bye notes would vibrate in her ear, burning holes in her soon to be lonely heart. "Stop it with your melodrama!...He is going to ask you to marry him, not!" she chuckled quietly as they reached the end of the pier and the vast darkness of the ocean at night covered the couple about to be pulled apart. He looked at her with a quiet intent, a lot of trepidation in his eyes, almost embarrassed about what he was about to say.

"When you gave me your phone number, I had a girlfriend," he started to say looking away from her.

"Why did you call me?" she asked, a bit annoyed at his dishonesty.

"Well, I can't or maybe do not know how to answer that."

"Well, I know it was very forward of me to ask you out like that!" she added without apologizing.

"But, you did not have to agree to call me," Micaela added trying to see the emotions in his face.

"I know, I could have said no, but I liked seeing you with your mom every Saturday. You seemed to be such a caring young girl translating for your mom the labels on the items you both sometimes were so entranced by. You standing in line, flirting with me the way you did was so new and refreshing. I just wanted to find out more about you," he responded reaching for her hand.

Micaela pulled away not wanting to be touched. As she turned around and walked away from him. Blake came from behind her and grabbed her by her arm. He had a pitiful look on his face. Micaela could not say let go of me. Instead she reached for his arms and gave him a hug. Blake hugged her back and continued.

"She found out about you and asked me to choose," he said still holding her in his arms.

She smelled his scent and wanted to freeze this moment in time, but she knew she could not and a tear showed up in her eye. She got even closer to his chest and dried her tears on his sweater, trying to avoid him looking at her crying.

"She was upset and wanted an answer right away," he continued.

"I did not want to choose, so she broke up with me," he went on.

Micaela listened and wanted to hide and cry even more. She felt bad because she felt responsible. If she had not given him her phone number, she would not have come between these two people.

How could I have done this? She reproached herself.

She heard herself saying, "I am sorry, about the whole thing. It is my fault, since I initiated our relationship, if one can even call it that!"

"I don't want you to blame yourself. It is my fault too," he added.

Micaela did not want to be there anymore, because what he told her after that made her realize it was her inability to answer her raging hormones that made him go back to the other girl and break up with her. *Why can't I succumb to the pressures of love? What makes me so rigid and cold? Don't you like these boys?* she reproached herself again.

"After a while, she came back and because I had strong ties to her, I felt I needed to go back with her," he said looking away from Micaela and entering a place all of his own.

"What other ties?" Micaela asked him. He continued to look away.

Oh...the ties...the ties that mean having to put out and have sex with these bastards! She thought with an indignation and anger because she knew she could not go there.

There is yet another 'pressure of love' and this time it hurt much more, Micaela would say to herself, because there was much more at stake. The prom was approaching soon and fast and this was her only chance to shine in front of all the other people who she knew were laughing at her expense. The cheerleaders, of course, that Micaela learned later had been with Pablo while they were dating. The 'Cuban' girls who attended the *quinceañeras* and told her about the good times they had. The prom was supposed to make up for all the lonely nights, Micaela was unable to participate in the teenage rituals of high school because she came from a different cultural background. She came from a frustrated mother who was suspicious of the world because of her own inferiority complex. She realized at this poignant moment how trying high school had been. How miserable she sometimes felt and how close she stood to the abyss of teenage angst for been a studious geek. She was aloof at times to keep her sanity, and all her hard work and attending her chosen school would not be in her future.

Micaela wanted to lash out at this beautiful boy who had played with the emotions of two stupid girls, but thanks to the melody of the waves coming ashore, she was able to appease her mind and to soothe her soul. She refrained from making a spectacle of herself. Every splash told her to compose herself and not to let him see her cry. The sea cried for her with every splash against the rocks. In the stillness of the moment, nature's grace came to her rescue. Micaela could hear the splashing of the water up against the rocks with the same fury she was feeling at the moment, but the rocks remained solid letting the water run back into the sea. She emulated the rocks' strength and stood there watching the motion of the waves, the splashing of water and felt a darkness encroaching her soul with the fervor of the night. The moon afar smiled upon her, as if to tell her to be faithful to herself and not let her dignity be betrayed by her own loneliness. The stoic embrace of the two most important women in her life came again to mind and she knew she had to let go and be strong. To be strong, that is what she was learning now, with every goodbye, with every deception, with every frustration and decision made abruptly, she was learning to be strong.

"Be strong, be sure of your next move, for you must let him go...he was never yours," she muttered in silence trying very hard to convince herself of the right thing to do in order to carry it through without damage to her dignity and fragile sense of being.

The salty chilly ocean breeze made her feel cold, and a feeling of detachment ensued. The scene was a romantic one. The two lovers were stopping in their tracks. They never would play again. She told him, "I am sorry for getting in the way, I really am. But it is true, you could have stopped all of this. One thing though, Blake, if I had been your girlfriend, no matter how strong the ties were, I never would have made you choose."

"I did not want to choose!" he answered stupidly.

"Well, be that as it may, I would have had to let you go, like I am letting you go now." She continued.

"I still want to see you," he insisted.

"It is not fair to either one of us. She came back to you after knowing you cheated on her. So she must really love you, and the ties you are speaking about...you will never have those ties with me. It is better you go and make those ties stronger...Who knows, she might be the mother of your children one day." She said it half smiling, half sad.

Micaela suddenly realized they had walked all the way back into the parking lot and she stood in front of her car door, uneasy trying to get her keys in the lock while trembling in anger and desolation. He grabbed her hand to help her and she pulled away giving him a scornful look as she managed to open the door and get in her car. Stevie Nicks would keep her company as she cried over yet another loss. Fleetwood Mac's "Dreams" was playing on the radio. This time Stevie Nicks was saying, "Lovers only love you when they're playing..." She thought she would change the lyrics to, *They only love you when they get what they want.* She continued listening to the song. She thought it was very fitting to her mood. She would play that song over and over until the tape broke in the cassette she bought a new one a week later.

Reflecting on the reasons why the boys in her life were breaking up with her, she became angry at herself for being such a prude.

Why did I not let him touch my boobs that night after the amusement park? she thought of all these kinds of stupid questions.

"What is the worst that can happen, Micaela?" she continued the conversation with herself out loud.

"Get pregnant...that is the worst thing that can happen!... Fall prey to the stereotype of many uneducated women who stay barefoot and pregnant," she told herself calming down, trying to be the logical and the methodical person she knew she could be.

"So it's my predicament that I am going to be a spinster because in the 'age of Aquarius' I am the only girl who keeps her legs together and a good lid on the virginity bull shit!" She said this to herself as she drove away from the beach. The ocean became farther away in her rear view mirror and the pier got lost in the darkness of the night. She thought of the darkness of happier days, seeing herself in the darkness of the movie theater and the good feelings she had then. This time the darkness made her think about the loss of the blonde locks and blue eyed boy smiling at her. As sad as this experience felt, she also knew deep down that she had made a promise she was not about to break, not for Pablo, not for Blake with his Norwegian looks and beautiful eyes.

I wonder who will be the next boy who comes into my life and leaves frustrated realizing my inability to be sexually active?...unreal! she thought as she reached her house and crossed the front lawn.

It was about ten o'clock in the evening and her mother was waiting for her.

"Where have you been?... It is kind of late for you to be out roaming the streets, don't you think?...Girls shouldn't be out at this time of night by themselves. What are the neighbors going to think?" Micaela's mother asked her in an angry stern way.

Micaela listened to her mother and she thought, *The neighbors don't even speak Spanish, so what difference does it make what they are thinking? I swear I am on the way to becoming the virginal spinster, the first one they will send to the moon, since they are sending everything up there; tang, monkey and now me, the virgin!* The thought of deep space which frightened her, made her laugh nervously as she thought, *I have to put out, I have to put out, I really don't want to be sent to the moon!*

Her mother asked with an infuriated voice, "Are you laughing at me? I will smack you silly if you are! You need to be more respectful of your mother."

I have lost someone I cared about very much and realized he doesn't care about me, and there she is yelling at me. Micaela thought to herself.

"If you only knew how much I respect you, you would not waste your time yelling at me. Instead you could see my pain, hold me and tell me everything will be okay. For once why can't you see me, hear me and love me...your daughter, and not bother with your concerns for other people!" she muttered those words as the tears rolled down her cheeks.

"Are you talking back to me?" her mother retorted.

"No, mami, I am just saying I am sorry and you are right. It will never happen again," she told her mother wiping her tears away.

The prom came and she never attended, she even forgot what she did that night; it was lost in oblivion as the years went by. She would go to the grocery store and if Blake was there, she would try to avoid him at all cost. Buying groceries became a chore that she would continue to hate through the years. The twelfth grade was coming to an end and she was glad. She would no longer see Pablo flirting with the cheerleaders and pretend that he did not see her. She would go on to college and become better than these people with their small mentality where a person who attends the prom is cool versus one who does not.

Besides been the Valedictorian of her graduating class, she had also been in the French Club throughout her high school years, and she went on to win the Bank of America Foreign Language Award at the end of the school year. It made Micaela feel good, standing among all her peers as she was recognized and given a trophy for her ability to speak French fluently. But most importantly, she felt proud that after being in America for only six years she was able to write and give her speech eloquently and to see the 'Cuban' girls sneer, Pablo's longing look and her parents both tearing at her words even though her mom did not understood half of them. But her ugly duckling stood in her own splendor under her golden robe decorated by the sashes and cords which announce her academic accolades. She had the scholarships to UCLA and NYU, but she knew it was UCLA and forget NYU.

Micaela's mother told her, "No daughter of mine is going to leave my house unmarried to roam the world."

Her father, the wanderer incarnate, who made the trip to America to better himself could not help her. Instead he agreed with Micaela's mother and told Micaela, "I can help with the car insurance so that you can attend such a prestigious University as UCLA, but still it is necessary that you commute so that you can help at home."

It was a forty-five minute drive to Westwood on the freeways on a good day. In a traffic jam it usually took her about an hour and a half each way. She could not say no. Instead, Micaela said good bye to her dreams of becoming a writer and resigned herself to look into people's mouths for the rest of her life, and become a dentist; all this in return for her mother's approval.

She started attending UCLA the next fall and what she discovered there was something she was not even aware of, because the transformation from ugly duckling into the beautiful swan was about to begin whether she wanted it to or not.

Her schedule was grueling. She had decided to major in Biology and Minor in French. The first year had been hard to adjust to; it was not only the size of the campus that intimidated her but also all the brainy kids who were her classmates. They represented a competitive challenge that perhaps would have been easier if her heart had been in the subject matter. She did not feel right being there and she started to make doodles in her note books and write little poems about the architecture and landscape of the campus.

Micaela befriended a Middle Eastern young man, Bezhad, who followed her every where she went. They became good friends and would take classes together and shared car rides. Christmas came and she felt a sense of relief as the semester ended. She managed to pass all her classes but it had not been easy due to her lack of interest. The only classes she had enjoyed were French and English composition. She could not stop writing and kept a journal of everything that happened in school and the people with whom she came in contact. She got a part time job at May Co. in the Junior's Department, where she could still see all the new fashions and keep her sense of style alive. She never wanted to be trendy but rather have her own look with pizzazz and a little bit of old world class that gave her a presence wherever she went and became one of her best attributes.

At the end of the year, her mother had a New Year's Eve party and invited some people from Chile. They were from South America so her mother felt good about that. Most of her friends were from the old country or some from other countries in South America. Micaela's mother was very picky about whom she befriended in America trusting no one. Along with the people from Chile there was a young man from Argentina who reminded her of the class mates she was taking a break from. His name was John and he was a 'brainiac.' John brought a gorgeous friend, named Fabrizio. He was foreign looking out of the pages of *Paris Match*, Micaela's favorite magazine of the time. They were introduced and they had only eyes for each other. Her mother approved so it made it even better.

Maybe we will be talking marriage, come the new year, she thought with a devilish smile as her mother prompted them to go sit on the back porch. She liked him a lot because he was raised in Ethiopia and was fluent in French. They talked about everything and anything and made fun of the adult ways with their own cultural idiosyncrasies.

She went back to school and did not see Fabrizio until the summer. They went out to the movies and family gatherings. One day he announced "I have been accepted to UCLA, and I am starting next semester. I will probably see you there," he told her with excitement in his voice.

"What are you majoring in?" Micaela asked.

"Biology...Isn't that your major too?" he asked.

"Yeah. What do you plan to do with that?" Micaela asked him

Fabrizio wanted to become a doctor and that suited her family to a tee. Unfortunately, Micaela's mother fell ill and she had to a postpone going back to school that year. This really made her angry and made her resent her mother for being so prone to having these spells for which no doctor could explain the cause. Without any protest she resigned herself to helping with the chores of the house, looking after her younger brother and sister, while maintaining the household as perfect as her mother always demanded it to be.

The whole year was brutal because she not only had to give up her dreams of going to NYU, the school of her choice, but now she could not even attend college, something she cherished with all her heart. She would help clean the house, tend to her mother, rush to work and come home as soon as her younger siblings got out of school, make dinner for them and rush to the nearby community college to attend her literature classes at night. She did not want to take time away from her studies totally, so she had enrolled in a couple of literature classes to keep up with the routine of reading and writing papers. She wanted to write more eloquently in her new language, something that was still rather difficult for her. Keeping herself actively involved with reading and writing would be to her advantage.

She was surprised one day by seeing Blake at El Camino College and then remembered that he had mentioned this is where he had planned to go. It had been almost two years since their break up. They both were at the bookstore as they encountered each other. After realizing who he was, she darted for the door.

He came running after her and asked, "Micaela, wait! It is so nice to see you here, but I thought you were going to NYU?" he said, surprised but happy to see her there.

Micaela felt weird realizing he remembered a detail like that.

"My mom got sick so I am taking some time off from my courses at UCLA. I came here for some English classes to keep me reading and writing and not forget my ABC's," she explained trying to be funny and hide her embarrassment of seeing him again.

"You are such a good daughter, always thinking of your mom's health first." Blake said

"Can we have a cup a coffee? Or I can buy you some Milk Duds and you can spill them again." He smiled, teasing her with the memory of their night out. "We can go to the cafeteria and have something to drink, if you do not drink coffee."

"Remember, I come from one of the major exporting countries of coffee in the world and you think I would not drink coffee?" She smiled at him while taking a long look at the beautiful blond curls coming down his forehead to find his beautiful aquamarine blue eyes that told her...He was really glad to see her.

"What classes are you taking?" he asked again.

"Poetry and English. How about you?" she asked him back.

"I'm taking some welding classes," he said rather shyly. "I am not the scholastic type, like you."

They walked down the long hall toward the cafeteria and she thought of the time at the amusement park and the fun they had had. She was happy to know he remembered the movie incident with the Milk Duds. A warm fuzzy feeling came over her.

"Do you take cream and sugar?" he asked as he prepared two cups of coffee.

"No, I like my coffee black and strong like my men," she laughed with her devilish laugh.

"You have changed…I thought, they were blonde and blue eyed, the men you like," he told her as he winked back at her.

"No, they tend to hurt you, so I stopped liking that type," she added sarcastically reaching for her cup.

"Ouch!" he replied.

They sat down and chatted for a while.

"So, are you working too?" he asked.

"Yeah, I'm still working at May Co. in the mall," she added.

"How about you. Are you still at the grocery store or have you moved on?" trying to confirm what she thought since his truck had not been there for a long time and no matter what time it was he was not in the grocery store where they had met.

"Yeah, I am working at this body shop, sort of like an apprenticeship," he told her

"You like it?" she asked.

"Yeah. It is what I always wanted to do," he told her sadly to think that she had forgotten about something so intimate and special to him.

"That is nice. Do your parents approve?"

"Well, they don't really care, as long as I am doing something I like, and I like welding," he told her.

She looked at her watch and realized that it was near ten o'clock and her parents would be worried thinking she had run away from home.

"I would have gone to NYU if I had been your parents' daughter," she told him with half a smile thinking about her dreams and wishing her parents were like Blake's.

"Then, I could not have dated you," he said it smiling a smile that accentuated the cleft in his chin, and getting closer enough to touch her nose he added, "Maybe I will see you again, to have another cup of coffee?" He tilted his head and asking sheepishly, getting very close to her.

"What about her?" She asked annoyed at his request and actions.

"She is no longer in the picture," he responded.

"Is that so?" she asked in disbelief.

"Well, maybe, but I am always busy. I do not know if I will have time," she went on to add trying not to show her real emotions in turmoil.

"Make the time, please?" He pleaded.

"I have to go, see you" she waved and turned away.

As she started to head for the parking lot Micaela thought, "What if he wanted to go back with her. No, you cannot succumb to those pretty blue eyes, he will hurt you again. You know that." She told herself out loud.

She got home and like always, her mother was waiting in the living room and as she entered, she asked, "Where have you been? Do you know what time it is?

"I was delayed by an old classmate who is attending the school right now."

"Is it a girl or a boy?" her mother continued.

"A boy! But what difference does it make? He is only a classmate, Mami," she exclaimed annoyed at her mother's critical ways.

"Don't take that tone of voice with me I am still your mother and you need to respect me, always!" she retorted.

"Yes, Ma'am." Micaela responded.

She changed into her pajamas and talked to Rebeca, who was telling her all about her cheerleading camp and that she would be attending another one soon.

"My little sister can be a cheerleader and go away to camp, but the older and responsible me has to be home by nine!" she told her sister as she opened the pages of Steinbeck's "The Red Pony." She thought, "Why can't I be Jody?"

She thought of Blake and his wanting to see her again, and she fell asleep, satisfied to know that if you wait long enough, things and people can come your way again.

The following day she was surprised when Blake called and asked her to go to a dance at the college where they both were now attending. However, she knew then that she could not go down that path again; it was already too late. It was her mother's pride that made her turn away from the boy whom two years back had made her really happy and then sad in a very short period of time. She could never trust him again. If he cheated once he would cheat twice and this time he would be cheating on her!

She called him back and told him, "I am sorry but I do not think it is a good idea for us to go the dance."

"Why not?" he insisted.

"Well, because my mother's friend wants me to go with her son. My family is very fond of him," she told him.

"Oh is that your new boyfriend?" he asked curious to know.

"No, he is not my boyfriend, he is just a friend of the family," she told him matter of fact.

"I really want to see you again, Micaela," he added.

"I think it is a bad idea," she told him again sounding determined and secure that she never wanted to see him again.

Unwillingly she tried very hard to sound determined and uncaring for him. Deep down she knew that it hurt her so much not to be part of the sweet and fun filled relationship they would have had. Full of trepidation she wanted to dispel all the caring she already had felt for this young man who gave her her first outing, her first breakfast in a restaurant and her first French kiss. She dreamed of having more of those moments. He was the first who had taken her to a restaurant to have dinner by candle light. She had all the first encounters of young love with him, *how could he have not been honest and lie to me?* She thought to herself and in every uneasy moment of her life she would go back and start reminiscing of the night they saw "Rocky" together.

In the mean time, Fabrizio had known about the same dance and called to ask her out. She accepted his invitation because her mother was okay with it. Micaela loved to dance and her love for dancing would stay in her forever. She danced in public, alone or wherever she was taken away by the music flowing in her being. It was her love of music and dance that let the unleashed sensuality manifest itself in her every move which was intensified by her genuine innocence of this inner power she was becoming aware.

The night of the dance, Fabrizio appeared looking just as handsome and dreamy as the first day she met him. He did not have blue eyes nor blonde hair, but his Mediterranean flair made him intriguing and refreshing for Micaela who loved to know about other people and their culture. She wore a little cotton dress with a small print of green leaves on a blue background. It had a scooped neck line that gathered in a bow made of the same material. It had a tight bodice accentuating her small and skinny frame with gathers at her small waistline covering the fact that at the age of twenty she had no hips, no butt, nor any curves at all for the gathers to expand around. Instead they fell on their own creases that just made her look elegant yet sensual. Her hair growing out from the Dorothy Hamill look had a natural curl that made her look sassy and cute. As the night progressed her hair became curlier by her sweating from dancing and frolicking with small ringlets gathered around her small oval face which added an exotic touch.

They had gone to the dance accompanied by her older brother Froilán, who went on to find a girl and forgot about his chaperoning responsibilities.

"Thank God for blonde girls so he can leave me alone!" Micaela told Fabrizio.

"Don't worry about your brother. He told me to take you home," he told her pulling her onto the dance floor and hugging her in a swaying move that made her dizzy at first.

"Really!?" she asked excited at the prospect of being a grown up girl living in America without all the boundaries and sheltered attitudes of the old country, and needless to say without all the chaperones that came along to guard her forever virginity.

They danced to "KC and the Sunshine Band" and had a blast. At midnight the dance came to an end and Fabrizio took her home. As he drove the empty streets at this late hour of the night, he came to a red light. When it turned green, he did not move, instead he stayed still at the green light looking at her curls drenched in the sweat. She looked cute with her sweaty face, red as a radish with the wet curls cascading down her face. Her brown eyes looked surprised and questioned him.

"What are you doing?...Why don't you drive now that the light is green?" She asked him in such a flirty way that it made her more sexy than she would ever know. It was her ingénue attitude that was so natural making her more sensual.

"I don't care. I just want to stop here and look at you," he told her.

"But the police might come and get us in trouble for stopping traffic." Her devilish smile came upon her face and extending her arms coquettishly she poked him in his rib cage.

"I do not care. All I care about right now is how I am going to kiss that small mouth of yours that has been teasing me all night and has made me crazy enough to stop at a green light," he said as he reach for her.

"You are a strange young man, you know?... My sweaty and ugly hair is making you crazy? I feel so ugly right now, how can you say you like this sweaty face?" She moved closer to him and pretending not to be ready for his reaction she made faces that made him smile.

He touched her ever so gently and with his thumbs, he felt her lips and holding her head with both hands he brought her even closer to him and proceeded to kiss her like she had never been kissed before because although she tried to forget Blake, Fabrizio's kiss was different than Blake's. His kiss was more about him and not like Blake who had made her feel wanted. With Blake it was all about her for the first time. However, she had learned how to respond to this type of energy and while kissing Fabrizio, a tear drop meshing with her sweat as she thought, *Blake, Blake how sweet it would have been.* For a moment she felt longing for Blake's sweet kiss and not Fabrizio's.

She quickly thought, *This is it!* but as soon as she became aware of her emotions, the promise she made to her mother of wearing a white dress on her wedding day, and then the light changing back to green, stopped her in her tracks. Pushing away from him and pulling her hair back, she told him, "My mom thinks very highly of you. You do not want to disappoint her, do you? She would never let us go out again."

"Do you always have to be this good?" he asked annoyed as he accelerated and headed for her house.

"Can I call you tomorrow?" he asked her, still upset at her abruptness of minutes before.

"Sure! Mom likes you." She smiled and pointed to him that her mother was watching out the window.

Smart man that he was, he gave her a kiss on the cheek and told her, "You do not kiss too badly for a mama's good little girl, you know," she hit him gently on the chest and waved as she entered the house.

"Where is your brother?" Her mother asked.

"I do not know. He met with some friends and left me all alone. Thank God for Fabrizio, who could drive me home," she told her mother in an upset voice.

Her mother agreed. She liked Fabrizio. He was a good boy who was studying an honorable profession, Medicine, so Paloma was okay with her daughter being out with him late at night for the first time, as though the night never happened.

She was giddy the whole week after her second experience of attending a dance with a cute boy and no chaperones. Things may change as she would get older and wiser and would persuade her parents to do as the Romans when in Rome, or something like that. She went to work and nothing could take away her happiness of the night before. However, she was very surprised because as she was folding some blouses, she looked up and saw the beautiful boy wearing the cowboy shirt she had long ago made for him. It was light blue denim that matched his eyes and seeing the cowboy and horse that she had embroidered on the shoulders made her smile. She had taken the time to do this for the young man who had meant so much to her not too long ago.

"Hey, Micaela. Can you take a break?" Blake asked.

"I guess. Let me ask," she said in a contemplative way.

"Mrs. Johnson, may I go to lunch now?" she asked her supervisor.

"Sure, I was about to ask you when you were going to go," she answered back.

"Thank you, I'll be back in 30 minutes" she said picking up her purse and heading for the door that opened to the mall.

They walked around the mall's second floor looking down at the passersby on the first floor. They went down the escalator as he tried to hold her to protect her from falling down the moving stairs. She felt sad feeling so comfortable with the familiarity she had shared with him while they dated. She wanted to tickle him as she had done before but she refrained from thinking back to those fun times. They came to the Orange Julius stand and he asked her if she wanted something to drink.

"No, I am fine. I am wondering...What brings you around to this part of town?" she asked him.

"I wanted to see you and I called your house. They told me that you were at work," he answered.

"You called my house? Now I have to go home and answer all kinds of questions, my mother will ask," she said sounding upset.

"I am sorry, but I really wanted to see you," he said in a soft kind voice.

"Okay. You are here. You see me...now I have to go back to work," she told him abruptly.

She knew then that she could not go down that path again; it was already too late.

"But Micaela! I really want to see you again," he held her by her arm.

"As much as I would like to be with you again, I just can't. The thought of 'her' coming back, yet another time and you fleeing to her to get the things I cannot give you will always be in the back of my mind. You deserve better than that!" What she meant was, "I DESERVE better than that!"

"Why are you so stubborn? Why won't you give us a chance?" He asked her looking contemptuously at her.

"We had a chance, and we lost that chance," she said without even giving a thought to her answer.

"You'll live to regret this. I am sure of it," he said sounding sad and upset.

It had been rewarding to know that he had come back into her life and she was able to be strong enough not to succumb to his pretty face and pleading ways, and allow herself to be hurt. Her mother had built walls around her so as not to get hurt, and now without realizing it, Micaela was starting to do the same. She felt that by being abrupt and relentless she could hide her true feelings... she did want him back but she could not take that chance of getting hurt again!

As the years went by, Micaela would always go back to this moment in time with Blake and his French kiss. This moment etched in her memory of her younger years was her salvation when she became a frustrated woman always choosing to do right in order to appease her loved ones or people she needed to be kind to. She would wonder, *What if I had not been so proud?* She thought she had no regrets, but the questions stayed in the back of her mind always making her second guess her decisions.

The fall came and she was able to go back to UCLA and she knew that she could no longer keep her part time job at the mall near her home, but she still needed a job. She got a job in a place where she would unknowingly meet the man that would put her in the path of desperation, ambivalence and necessary pain in order to give birth to the swan.

Back on campus her middle eastern friend was still attending and had not forgotten her. He told her, "I thought maybe you changed your major to something that better suits you."

"No, I took a break because of sickness in the family," she told him.

"Oh, I am sorry," he said reaching for the books that were looking heavy for her to hold.

"It is okay. My mother is fine now," she added.

She was wearing a rayon jersey dress made by her mother under Micaela's direction of how it should look, it had been the very first time her and Paloma had collaborated and had gotten along fine. It was very plain with a sash gathered at her small waist but the time spent together with Paloma made Micaela cherish the dress much more.

"You look too beautiful to be a dentist." Her friend told her,

"Did your mom make that dress too?" he asked her.

"Yeah. You like it?" she asked him as she twirled around and the easy hand of the rayon jersey played along with her small body.

"I like everything you wear...I still think you should pursue something more creative, I tell you...you are in the wrong field," he told her with a conviction that made her think about the choices she had made thus far.

"Why don't you go and tell my parents that!" she exclaimed.

"Maybe they will hear you and let me go to NYU, huh?" she retorted annoyed at having to think about her future and what will become of her if she continue choosing the things that were not important to her.

"You crazy, your parents will kill us both if they know we are friends...aren't I right, little missy?" he grimaced a John Wayne look and they both smiled and entering their Calculus class they sat down and he looked at her glad to see her back.

Fabrizio who was also attending and taking some of the same classes but a different schedule, kept asking her who her friend was.

"Who is the rag head?" Fabrizio asked her one morning after her History class.

"What did you just say!?" She asked insulted by the racial slur.

"What!...Is he not from the Middle East?" he asked embarrassed at the fact that Micaela would not put up with such a slur.

"Yes, he is but you do not have to refer to him as such!" Micaela told him indignantly.

"Well, you better watch out...If your parents know you are being friends with one of them... they will prohibit you from coming here...and you know it!" he told her.

He is right, my ever judgmental mother will be beside herself if she knew he was my friend. Micaela thought.

"He is really nice...you should meet him...plus he is the same field as yours...Medicine," Micaela told Fabrizio.

"Most middle eastern men are overprotective of their women," Fabrizio went on.

Micaela smiled and told him, "Why are you so worried about Bezhad? He is just a friend."

"He wants you for more than a friend, though. Why won't you realize that!" Fabrizio exclaimed.

"It is so obvious by the way he looks at you, and helps you with your books," he added

"Hey, listen, you are not my father nor my mother to be telling me these things...who I choose to befriend is my business and only mine," she told him indignantly.

"Well as my girlfriend I want to make sure you are aware of how it is," he told getting closer to her.

"Oh, so when did I become your steady girlfriend?" she retorted. "As of now because you are jealous of Bezhad, and want to mark your territory?" She added frowning at him and grimacing a gesture of contempt with her hands on her hips.

He grabbed her and smiling at her he said, "No...you silly!... because I love the way your cheeks turn red when you get mad... and the crease in your forehead makes you look seeexyyy!"

They hugged and twirled around smiling at each other, Micaela thought it was cute the way he had asked her to go steady in a very Latin way, where the actions of the lovers are just enough.

They went to the movies, they went to family dinners, and they became the cute couple whose parents were planning behind the scenes what would be in their future. When they were not surrounded by family and mutual friends they were away on campus of UCLA trying very hard to pass classes and compete with only the best in the field of Pre-Med.

Micaela and Fabrizio would meet at the reading rooms in the basement of the library and they would do homework together. She enjoyed his company and without being aware she had managed to have a boyfriend who was cute. He was of Italo/Greek descent and was fluent in French and made Micaela very happy because they talked in French and often criticized the things they did not like in that exquisite tongue. It was their code language and many times he tried to get her in bed with that romantic accentuation of the rs in his throat. However, the powers that be never let Micaela let her guard down, and needless to say, Fabrizio disappeared into the horizon giving her the excuse that his mother needed his attention.

The thought nagged at her but it was dismissed because she had too many things to do and exams to prepare for were her top priority. But she was disillusioned by the set of events...she remembered coming to class to take a final exam and having to stop in the middle of it because John Lennon had been shot and killed. Even though she had listened to the many songs of the Beatles, she had no idea who John Lennon was.

Bezhad, her friend, was very sad and incredulous at her asking him, "Who is John Lennon?"

The next day, the whole world was devastated by the news. The school's atmosphere was somber even among the brainy kids of the South campus, where all the future doctors, and engineers are put through the rigors of UCLA standards. Many continued to mourn the day of John Lennon's death.

"Do you want me to pick you up and bring you to school tomorrow?" she asked him concerned at his sullenness upon hearing the news.

"Would you mind?" He had agreed and the next day, Micaela stopped at his house took him to school and after school she also took him home and dropped him off.

"Do you want to come in for a second?" Bezhad more than asking was telling her to come in.

"I can show you who John Lennon is...or was," he added sullenly.

"What do you mean?" She asked him.

"Come in and I'll show you," he insisted.

She entered his small one bedroom apartment lacking of furniture and feminine touches. There were pillows here and there made of beautiful colors and texture of materials. The kitchen was not kept up and she was a little bit uneasy. What would her mother think if she knew she was standing in the middle of an empty harem-like apartment with a Middle Eastern boy. She smirked and then she became her own mother thinking to herself, *He seemed like such a nice young man. How could he live like this? Don't be like your mother, making assumptions of people just because they are a little different from you.* She added to her thoughts, as she came to a big beautiful framed mirror where she looked at herself and thought, *What the hell are you doing in this man's apartment?*

She turned around to see what Bezhad was doing. He was perusing through a pile of long play records and he looked sad immersed in finding something in his face told the world this was his treasure. He looked up to see her while pulling the black vinyl record out of its jacket and asking Micaela, "Have you ever heard the song 'Imagine'?"

"Of course, that is a beautiful song!" she exclaimed.

"Well, you know who sings it?" he asked.

"No, who?" she asked back.

The music started playing and he grabbed her hand and brought her close to him and started to sing along with the voice coming from the speaker and he whispered into her ear, *"Imagine there's no Heaven...It's easy if you try...No hell below us...Above us only sky...Imagine all the people...Living for today."* It dawned on her that this was John Lennon and as soon as she realized that she also became aware that this was the only moment as far as she could remember in her lifetime that the same energy she often felt while dancing was coming from this young man who touched her so gently and so calmly with such an intensity that their dancing was pure rapture. The music flowed through him and with every melodic sound he danced with the music in her. Their bodies meshed as one and they swayed along with the lyrics trying in their own small way among the beautiful colored pillows to be one, although they came from different worlds in this moment of time in that empty living room they were just one. They both started to cry, thinking about the loss and Micaela thinking about the times when she had seen prejudice and felt the separation of people because of their differences. Prejudice brings such anger to our world, making people fear each other, creating chaos and disharmony.

"Imagine" was John Lennon's song about how wonderful it would to be able to understand and accept one another, and in this particular moment, it was Micaela's way to help this young man in grieving for his favorite artist, who had come to such a violent end. It hurt her so deeply to see her friend in such a despair that Micaela forgot about her mother's judgments and was glad to be here in this empty living room soothing and appeasing her friend's soul. They danced in the middle of the living room, with every pillow looking at them as they held each other gently with the music playing on, paying homage to the dead song writer and artist. She also knew then that Bezhad had always liked her more than a friend but he knew it could never be. Her mother would never accept a middle easterner to become a part of her family. Paloma had always made it explicitly clear that it had to be someone worthy of her Spanish upbringing. So in her mind only Spanish people from South America or Europe could dare to court any daughter of hers.

"Imagine, how much I could love you," he said looking at her and touching her long hair.

"Imagine, never making the calculus class," she said trying to play it off, as she pulled away from his embrace.

"I must go now," she added afraid that if she would have stayed it would be only to prove to the world that they can be as one regardless of their obvious cultural differences.

How could I do this to mom, she thought looking around for her purse and car keys.

"I know, your mom will kill you...if you are late," he told her with a smile and making a fearful face and trying very hard not to show how sad the situation made him feel. Micaela was beautiful in many ways. She was full of spunk and wit, of goodness and honesty, and full of life but she continued to succumb to her obedient attitude at her mother's whims, her mother who kept a very close and critical eye on this beautiful young woman who perhaps would never realize how beautiful she could become.

"Don't make fun of my family" she told him sounding annoyed but realizing it was true.

"You are almost twenty years old. You live in America...you are going to one of the best schools in the country with an academic scholarship...what more could they ask for from a female child?"

"A husband of Spanish or at least of European descent," she told him grimacing a stoic stance.

"I could be the moor that succumbed to such Spanish beauty and could not help but be overpowered by her tantalizing stoicism," he told her laughing as he touched her hair with a longing look that made Micaela feel aware of how much attraction she also felt for this young middle eastern young man. However, the specter of her mother was there and Micaela could see her finger pointing at her saying, "You better not."

"You are crazy!" she exclaimed smiling at him as she pulled away.

"For you!" he added and went on to say, "I tell you what. When you decide that I am good enough for you, you tell me, and I will be there in a heartbeat, okay?"

"It's not me thinking you are not good enough...it's my mom," she told him. "Plus don't forget, I am Fabrizio's girlfriend remember?"

"I meant to ask you about him. What happened? I have not seen him on campus," he added.

"I thought maybe he quit you and school," winking at her with a big smile.

"I've got to go, really," she said as they exchanged a kiss on both cheeks.

After the next semester, she would never see Bezhad nor hear from him again.

Fabrizio never returned her calls and so she delved into her studies only to realize that the more she studied the more she hated Pre-Med. She hated the math and chemistry she had to take. The upper courses were so intense that she told a friend, Marisa, at work that she could no longer hack it.

"It is not underwater basket weaving, you know?" her friend told Micaela.

"You are studying a pretty hard subject," she added.

"I know, plus I don't like it. I really do not want to be a dentist." She said it with a big sigh coming from the bottom of her gut.

"How long have you felt this way?" the friend asked.

"Ever since I can remember...ever since mom decided it for me...I guess," she said trying to console and convince herself that she needed to go on.

"Well, you need to do what is in your heart, not what is in your parent's heart," Marisa said giving her a hug. "You are too good of a kid, you know!" she added.

"They should be so lucky to have a girl in California, who at twenty is still a virgin trying to make it in one of the hardest schools in the country in a field she could care less about!" she said all in one breath.

"Thank you for listening to me," Micaela told her friend.

"You are the only one I can tell these things to without being judged and trying to make me change my mind," she added.

They talked about where Micaela was at this point of her young life, the feeling of despair ensued. She felt alone and very sad. It seemed that the world was at her feet and that she could do anything she wanted to do and become anything she wanted. After all she was in America, the land of opportunity, she thought. However, things had gone awry and had become complicated. She felt trapped between the world that offered opportunities, and the world of her family which prevented her from taking the road to better herself. She felt divided between the two cultures. They both had their guidelines and expectations of her as a young woman, daughter, friend and girlfriend, never allowing her to be just who she was or at least what she wanted to be. For the American culture, she was made to a tee with her independent and free spirit. She was capable of achieving the most cherished endeavors. On the other hand, her Latin roots demanded that she not be too independent and to follow her traditional footsteps. Micaela always understood these as being suspicious of other people and their idiosyncrasies and that she needed to be true to her parents' beliefs, even the one that prevented her from going away to college, "because no daughter of mine would roam the world unmarried," had been her mother's words.

Going through high school had been hard with its cliques and lack of personality among the players involved. Going through college was becoming even harder since her heart was not in the subject at hand. The 'pressures of love' just left her empty and confused, the love relationships she had experienced had managed to leave her not wanting to offer herself any more the only way she knew how, for sex was out of the question, thus she felt very limited and frustrated. She prepared to be true to herself and drop from her studies, get a job to get enough money to move away from all that she knew and embark on a life of writing and perhaps become a set decorator or costume designer even. Who knew what the future could hold!

Part Three

Trekking up the unconquerable precipice to see peace restored.

Painful Deceptions Revisited

After leaving her job at the mall, Micaela found a job as the Girl Friday for an illumination company, however, after only four months she was told she might be laid off. Micaela did not want to leave this place yet. She not only liked doing the clerical part of the job but she also liked working there because it stimulated her imagination. The company made lighting fixtures for the movie industry and Micaela loved being in the testing room. Standing under a spot light, with the same childhood innocence she had in South America, she would pretend she was the Spanish singer Rocío Durcal and sing her favorite song, *Acompañame*. It always made Micaela think back to the times in the old country, growing up with her cousins. They had singing contests, and though Micaela could not carry a tune, she always managed to win, singing or rather destroying the songs as she walked on their pretend stage mimicking her favorite songstress. Under the heat of the spotlight she felt warm thinking about growing up in such a safe and family-oriented environment.

Her friend Marisa's voice brought her back to reality and she heard her saying, "Hey, listen I got you a clerical job at your rival school in the Architecture Department...are you interested?"

What! USC?...are you crazy?" she said it with a sarcastic chuckle, and under the same breath, Micaela continued, "How much does it pay and for how long?"

"Only for the summer...I figure with your schedule and all you have to do for your parents, you could definitely not have a full time job all year around." Marisa said looking at Micaela with the same warmth as her aunt Marianna had in the old country. Marisa was a middle aged woman who never had any children. She had longed to have a daughter like Micaela and thought the world of the young woman whom she admired for being responsible and dependable. She was able to see the beauty in Micaela's spirit and wanted the best for her young friend. Afraid of the financial cuts the company was experiencing she kept looking for ways to keep Micaela employed and if she needed to get another job somewhere, Marisa was determined to make sure Micaela did not go jobless.

"Thanks! Mari you are a peach" Micaela told her giving her a hug.

Micaela left that afternoon with anticipation and looked forward to her next employment adventure. *If I could just find a job at a newspaper and write a column, it would be a start*, she thought.

Afraid of her mother's wrath, she knew she could not neglect her studies so she decided to work on her electives and leave her core classes for later. She was still driving to Westwood but not with the anticipation she had hoped for. Instead, it became a chore having to drive to and fro with little time to write or read her favorite books. Moreover, the next time Micaela came to work, she had a sullen look coming into her friend's office and lamenting to her. She sat down with a forceful manner crashing her body onto the hardness of the wooden chair.

"The job was already taken," Micaela told her friend Marisa with a big sigh.

"I am sorry, honey...Well there is a new guy coming in today to take Jim's place...Did you know that?...Maybe he'll ask you to stay." Marisa told her.

"Who is it? Do you know him?" Micaela asked without any thought to the questions as she went about filing some papers.

She finished her filing and saw it was time to leave, but she was stopped by her new supervisor. Ten years her senior, he was tall and slim with light brown hair and hazel eyes that had a shy and melancholic demeanor to them, which he tried to hide by looking away at every chance he could. He had been married and had two small children. He seemed nice and personable despite his little bit of bashful manner. Micaela later found out that he had liked her from the beginning but was concerned about the ten-year age difference between them.

"Hi, I am Edward, the new area supervisor," he told her as he came across the hallway.

"Nice to meet you Mr. I did not catch the last name," she added.

"Sorry, Edward Sims," he responded.

"Well, it is nice to meet you Mr. Edward Sims...one 'm' or two?" she continued to ask him.

"Only one 'm,' but thank you for asking," he added.

"Can you please come to my office?" he went on.

They entered his office and a pile of boxes were in the middle of the room. He started moving files and arranging small office furniture around making room for them to check out his new work area. Micaela looked around and saw how disorderly everything was,

"Are you going to need help with these files?" she asked politely.

"Well, they tell me you could help me with this mess. They are willing to let you come in on Saturday mornings to help out with the new office space arrangements...Would you be interested? Don't worry about the lay off... I am impressed with how much you are wanted and respected among the upper management," he told her this as he pulled a couple of picture frames from a box placing the pictures in front of him on his desk.

"Are these your children?" Micaela asked him as she approached the picture frames.

"Yeah! These are my children," he answered with a sullen voice triggered by a detached attitude that Micaela detected right away.

"Where is their mother?" She asked feeling embarrassed at her rude curiosity which was awakened by that intuitive voice that told her something was amiss.

"I am sorry, I did not mean to pry," she added feeling honestly apologetic.

"It's all right," he answered becoming a bit contemplative.

"She left us about three years ago...We have not heard from her since," he went on.

"Oh! I am sorry...you must feel awful about it." Micaela wanted to know because there was not a feeling nor expression of any kind when he talked about the mother of his children.

"Well, I don't feel anything now. At first, I was angry and totally overwhelmed by the prospect of being a single parent with two little tykes...but now, it is okay. We are going to make it, I suppose," he added as he caressed the frame with the little girl.

"She is cute...How old is she?" Micaela continued with her questions.

"She is eight and he is six."

"They are small," she said stating a fact as she started to walk out.

"Where are you from?" He asked her, trying to change the subject.

"Originally from South America, Ecuador to be precise," she said with a pride that had never been there before.

"So you are the exotic type, huh?" he said smiling at her.

"I suppose…whatever that means!" she said it shrugging her shoulders and saying goodbye.

Micaela felt uneasy. Never before had anyone let alone a man much older than she, told her that she was exotic. As soon as she got home and had the chance, she checked in the dictionary to know the exact definition of the word. She started laughing and reread the second and third definition out loud, "Strikingly and charmingly different…I like this one!…but I don't think I can be of or relating to striptease. Mom could not have a daughter gyrating in front of men," she exclaimed laughing throwing herself onto the bed. Grabbing her pillow close to her chest, she stopped and thought, *So my boss thinks I am strikingly and charmingly different.*

"What is the matter with you?…You are so strange Mica!" her younger sister exclaimed leaving the room.

"No little one, I am exotic. Didn't you know that?" she yelled back caressing herself in a mocking sensual way as the door closed behind her sister.

When Saturday came, she went to work to do the new office arrangements. Her supervisor along with other coworkers were there and she said hello to everyone.

"So boys, are you ready to have a feminine touch to your interior design?" she mocked with an authoritarian stance as she passed by the entrance.

"Hello, Micaela!" Her supervisor greeted her as he opened the door for her.

"Good Morning, Mr. Sims," she responded.

"Call me Edward. Mr. Sims is my father," he added with a big smile.

"Well, I would rather call you Mr. Sims if is all right with you," she requested.

"Why so formal?"

"Well, you are my boss and I want to keep that professionalism in place...Is that okay with you?" she asked again.

"Well, if it makes you feel better," he said.

"It does," she responded as she picked up some boxes to take to their respective areas.

Everyone got involved with the task at hand and soon enough, it was lunch time.

"Why don't we all take a break and go to Burger King and have a nice lunch on the company's money?" Mr. Sims said loud enough for everyone to hear and looked for Micaela.

"Where is Micaela?" He asked one of the coworkers.

"She is in your office, placing files in your filing cabinet," the coworker responded.

"She is a hard worker. She has done two offices already and now she is doing yours. Soon she will become a manager of some department here," the coworker added.

Micaela appeared with boxes in her arms and with a questioning look making her supervisor uneasy at her determination to get things done as fast as they could.

"Micaela, you need to take a break," Edward told her.

"As soon as I put these boxes down and get the contents out," she responded.

"Didn't you hear me say we were going to Burger King for lunch on the company's card?" he repeated.

"Yeah, but I do not like Burger Keeng," she added quickly and her Spanish accent became accentuated making her sound cute and quaint to Edward.

"Say that again," he added with a smile.

"What do you mean?...Say what again?" she asked.

"Where do you not like to eat," he added waiting for her to respond with her accent.

Micaela realized what he was trying to do and enunciated King with the right intonation and added a bit annoyed, "I do not mind to be corrected with my English accent, however, please do not make fun of the way I talk or pretend to make me feel quaint with something that I should be doing better, like speaking properly."

"I'm sorry, I didn't intend to make you feel bad...You sound different and cute, that's all," Edward said walking away from her.

"Come on, Micaela. They are leaving us behind," her coworker pushed her toward the exit.

"I am not going. I told Mr. Sims already I wasn't going."

She stayed behind doing all the work that needed to be done, so she would be able to go to the library for a while before getting home at the time her mother expected her. Micaela loved libraries with their solitude and silence. She relished going through the stacks of literature thinking how wonderful it would be to write books for people to become inspired, or to dream about whatever makes them happy or to take them away from a sorry existence just like the many times she felt about her own life. This is why she aspired to be a writer or a poet. What better reason would there be for someone to be able to transport people away in the pages of a book? She would pick out the books she wanted to read, holding them tight to her chest as if to have the information come through her by osmosis. *So many words, aligned in the right sentence structure to give meaning and voice to a thought of someone alive long ago. It just seems so unreal,* she would think to herself as she chose the poetry of Tennyson and started reading "Nothing will Die," she compared it to "All Things will Die" and tried to think what made Tennyson write these two poems that basically have the same words but with different content.

"Micaela? Is that you?" Edward Sims was behind her asking as if it was too incredulous of such a coincidence to find her there.

"Hey, Mr. Sims," she greeted him, amazed and annoyed at the same time to see her supervisor there in the same place.

She first thought, *Was he following me?* Then the two children that came out from behind him explained why he was there.

"Daddy, we missed the children's reading, I told you we were late." The blond pig tailed little girl in the picture frame was telling him tugging on his pants.

"I am glad! I didn't want to be here any how!" the little girl's younger brother next to her exclaimed.

"Micaela, let me introduce you to my children," gently pulling the children in front of him, he introduced them to her.

"Hi, what is your name?" Micaela ignored Edward and walked directly to the little girl. Touching one of her pigtails very gently she went on to asked her more questions about the family.

"I am Marie and this is my brother Edward, Jr.," she responded politely and a bit curious.

Micaela felt very close to this child for reasons unknown to her. There was a thread connecting the two and Micaela wanted to know why could this be. She was eight years old, not shy at all but rather curious about the strange woman her father knew. She was the first born and felt very responsible for her father and younger brother after her mother had left. Micaela, realized that they both shared the sense of taking care of people, and the expectation of making everyone feel safe and Micaela became entranced by the delicate features of the child whose eyes could speak volumes of the inner strength that each of them possessed.

"I like your pigtails!... Did daddy do them?" Micaela asked her.

"No," she laughed as she answered.

"He does not like to mess with my hair," Marie added.

"He does not like to do my hair either!" the little boy, Edward Jr., exclaimed.

Micaela realized how rude she was being with the small male child as she only paid attention to the little girl.

"Oh boy!...So who does your hair?" Micaela asked him as she touched his golden hair.

"Our grandma," Marie answered.

"Yeah! She takes care of us better than daddy," the little boy added.

"Well, grandma is a very lucky woman to have such wonderful kids to play with their hair and take care of them," Micaela told them both, trying very hard not to be patronizing.

"Well, I am sorry they are being chatter boxes this afternoon," Edward Sr. explained.

"Oh!..that is okay... I like when kids can answer questions and tell you things without being shy or uneasy," Micaela said.

"Thank you," he responded, watching this young woman being so tender and loving to his children.

"Well...you should be proud of these two little ones," she added.

"Do you come here every weekend or just today?" Micaela asked.

"Well, I try to bring them every chance I can. This library is close to the house," he told her.

"Yeah, we can walk from here to the house. Would you like to come and see our new play set?" Marie asked reaching for Micaela's hand. It made her feel uneasy, however, in a nice and warm way.

"Thank you, but I need to get home. My mother is sort of strict and would not want me to miss dinner with the family," she told them putting her books in her backpack and grabbing her sweater from the chair.

"Do you really need to be home so soon?...It is only five o'clock," Edward added.

"Yeah, I need to be going home," she repeated.

"Maybe you can come next Saturday to see our play set," Marie insisted.

"Well, maybe... I will ask my mother if it is okay, okay?" she went on.

"You make your mother sound like the ruler of your life and you make yourself sound about the same age as Marie," Edward told her as she passed by him toward the exit.

"Well, most Latin mothers think they are conductors of their children's lives...and anyway as far as my own mother is concerned, I am the same age as Marie!" she told him back with a sarcastic smile and a wink.

"I will see you Monday at work, and thank you for putting my office in order, faster than what I had anticipated," he went on.

"You are welcome...bye little ones," Micaela waved to the children and left Edward with a feeling that a tornado had just gone through him. The refreshing whirlwind of Micaela had touched something within him, especially by the way she had reacted with his children.

She got home and her mother, Paloma, told her that she had called her at work and they had told her that Micaela had left a little before noon.

"Where have you been all this time?" Paloma asked Micaela.

"I told you that I have to do research for a paper and needed to go to the library," she explained.

"Well, you need to tell me this before you leave the house... with all the running around I need to do on the weekends, I could really use your help." She told Micaela in the tone of voice of martyrdom. The few times she could get away with it, she tried to make Micaela feel guilty for not helping out with the chores.

"I am sorry, Mom...but sometimes I don't know what is more important, my school work or the chores, especially when Beca can help with some of them," Micaela told her mother.

"Don't you be impertinent with me, you hear?" Paloma admonished Micaela.

"I am not trying to be impertinent. It's just that I need to say what I feel and it seems when I do; it always upsets you," she added.

"There you go with your mouth! Can you stay quiet?" Paloma added.

"I am sorry," she shrugged her shoulders and went to her bedroom to leave the books she got from the library.

"Micaela!" her mother yelled at her.

"Yes, I am coming," she came out of her bedroom unwillingly to see what her mother wanted now.

"Look! The Lawrence Welk Show is coming up and dinner is not even started...next time make sure to leave the business of the library a little sooner so you can help with dinner," Paloma again went on admonishing Micaela.

"Yes, ma'am," she complied.

The weekend always ended up like this with her helping with the chores to start a new week. Cleaning house, preparing lunch menus for her younger siblings, making sure all the laundry was washed, folded and placed in drawers and closets but foremost everything was left to her to make sure it was done to meet her mother's approval for which she was never given any kind of praise, only to hear the same sentence time and time again, "if I wasn't so sick, I could probably do the same thing you did in half the time." Micaela always repeated that under her breath along with her mother.

Micaela could not wait until Monday, going back to the routine of school and work that took her away from home, away from her mother's critical eye and where she could be whatever she wanted to be. When she was away, Micaela felt a sense of liberation and self worth. People praised her at school and at work, but never at home. On this particular Monday, she became intrigued at the prospect of working for the new supervisor Mr. Sims and checking up on the two little kids she met over the weekend.

"Good afternoon, Mr. Sims," she greeted Edward.

"Hi Micaela. How are you doing?" he responded interested to know what she did the rest of the weekend.

"Very well, thank you and you?" she added.

"Are you always this formal?" he asked her smiling at her.

"What do you mean?" she retorted.

"Well, you are a very formal young lady...It must be all that motherly supervision you have going on," he added.

"Are you making fun of me?" she asked annoyed at his pointing out her mother's overprotective attitude towards her.

"Is she like that with all of her children or just you?" he asked ignoring Micaela's annoyance to his criticism of her mother.

"Well, I guess...She really is overprotective of all of us," she said while thinking that it was not true, but she did not know him enough to start crying on his shoulder. Plus she did not want to sound like a little damsel in distress. She wanted to continue being the exotic one; she smiled to herself.

"Well, it is ok to be overprotected. I wish in a way my kids had a mom like that. You really have to think about how lucky some have it and others do not," he said in a pensive voice.

"I guess you are right, but sometimes it can be rather smothering to have someone breathing down your neck all the time," Micaela said it without thinking and as she finished she realized that she had let too much of herself be known. She needed to stop this right now. However, he talked to her in such an understanding way prompting her to keep telling him about her family life and how much she hated to be criticized by her own mother.

Edward saw Micaela's resentment toward her mother as a way to get into her good graces because he liked this feisty young woman, who was full of life, full of dreams with a compassion that softened her in a most unusual way. The impetus attitude which sometimes came about in the way she talked and expressed herself was always brought down by a melancholic and sullen demeanor that endeared her to Edward. She had been very sweet and docile in the presence of his children. Coming from a Latin background, Edward thought she could be a great mother for them. She could teach them and care for them much better than their own mother.

He knew this just from seeing her work with such a determination and consideration to her other coworkers. She had a way with people and being very personable, she had all the supervisors praising her and giving her more work to do because she was so dependable. Her coworkers always invited her for happy hour every Friday even though she was only twenty at the time. She would order orange juice and many times they wanted to get her some alcohol to spice up her juice but she always said no. Edward thought this was a plus for a person to take care of his children.

"Hey, I saw you this afternoon with a young man who dropped you off at work," Edward said to her as they were leaving work for the nearby pub.

"That was my brother, Froilán. He dropped me off because my car is in the garage," she said.

"So is he coming to get you after work or are you taking the bus?" he added.

"No, I am calling my dad to come and get me," she responded.

"Why don't I take you home?" Edward suggested.

"Oh no! Thanks," she quickly responded with a fear in her voice that intrigued him.

"I promise...I do not bite," he told her.

"Oh no...It's not you that I am afraid of...my parents would not hear of it, my supervisor bringing me home." She added, "They are very old fashioned and they would not like me to be driven by a strange man, of whom the family knows nothing about," she went on making faces as she spoke.

"They can't be that overprotective, are they?' he asked looking at her very intently.

"You have no idea how overprotective they are," she added, opening the door to the pub, where people started to know her, asking each time, "Are you twenty-one yet?"

"Hello, everyone. No... I am not twenty-one yet," she motioned with her arms in a gesture of giving up.

"You are really funny, you know," Edward told her.

"Why do you say that?" She asked back.

"Well, you beat them to the punch every time you come in here and every time they give you a hard time. You are very diplomatic and very sweet the way you get away with turning the tables on them or putting people in their place...How do you do that?" Edward kept asking all kinds of questions that gave her insight to her own being. The more questions he asked, the more uneasy she became, for the questions about her made her aware of feelings and emotions that were deep old relics in the corners of her soul.

"Why do you bring me here and ask me all these kinds of questions?" she asked sounding annoyed at his inquisition of her.

"I don't know... I guess I am trying to get to know you," he answered sheepishly.

"I find you very attractive and intriguing, and I want to know more about the things that go on in that seemingly aloof head of yours," he added.

"Well, I do not want to get to know you... I am not trying to be mean or rude but I want to keep a distance... You are my supervisor and I do not want to be taken advantage of nor looked upon as if I want to move up the ladder of success by sleeping with you," Micaela told him hoping he would leave her alone.

On the contrary, and unknown to Micaela, as time went on, Edward became more curious about the young woman whom he wanted to make the mother of his children. He started pursuing her with a relentless determination. Despite knowing how Micaela felt about having a relationship with her boss, he persuaded her to go out with him on a date.

"Hey, Micaela!" Edward motioned her to come into his office.

"Good morning, Mr. Sims," she greeted him politely.

"They are having a dance contest at the pub... I know you like dancing and I thought you might want to enter the contest and win us two hundred dollars...What do you think?" he asked looking at her with excitement and anticipation seeing how she would respond.

"Do you dance?" She asked him looking at him as if to say, 'where is this coming from.'

"Well, a little bit but we can start practicing until the day of the contest...what do you think?" He insisted.

"Well, I don't know, I have to ask my parents and look for a place to rehearse." She added a bit uneasy at the proposition.

"Well, you do not have to worry about that. My daughter is taking ballet classes and I converted one of the guest rooms into a dance rehearsal studio in our house," he added.

Micaela felt uneasy about the prospect of going to her boss's home to rehearse, but the idea of dancing and winning some money became more attractive than her fears and apprehension she had felt at first. She also became intrigued as how this dance studio was set up in Edward's house as she thought of going there to practice. She could not believe that someone with so much authority and older than her would be interested in bringing Micaela to his house to practice for an insignificant dance contest. *Stop being your mother and stop being suspicious*, she thought to herself.

"You have a dance room in your house?" she asked perplexed at the idea.

"Yes, is that so strange?" he asked with a smile on his face.

"No, but you must have a big house?" she added.

"It is rather large for the three of us, but we manage," he went on sounding sarcastic.

"Where is it anyway?" Micaela asked him curious about the location of this 'rather large house.'

"I live in Palos Verdes," he answered nonchalantly.

Palos Verdes, an affluent neighborhood set on the cliffs overlooking the Pacific Ocean where houses are in the millions of dollars and only very wealthy people live. This was the place where Micaela never dreamed she would live or even have friends in that neighborhood. However, she was starting to realize that this man wanted her and was trying his best to make her see him in a romantic light. She could not believe it. This only happened in fairy tales not in real life.

She became intrigued at the possibility of living among the well to do. Then all of a sudden she felt a chill run down her spine and thought to herself *How about if he only wants to get in my pants and then leaves me?* The ever prudent and wise part of her made her think these things and she smiled to herself about the way she analyzed everything and everyone in her life.

"Hello, is anybody there?" Edward asked waving his hand in front of her face.

"I am sorry, I just thought that you living in Palos Verdes it must be very hard for you to commute all the way down here to Los Angeles," she told him trying to hide her feelings of being unable to be romantically involved with this man who had everything and could not possibly want this young Hispanic woman who only dreamed to be a writer and a novelist in her own right.

"No, it's not...it is only about thirty minutes on the Freeway and since I come early in the morning, there is hardly any traffic," he went on telling her about his commute.

"How about the little ones?" she asked him about his children.

"What do you mean?" He asked back.

"Well, who takes care of them in the morning when you come to work so early?" she kept asking.

"My mother helps me with them...She takes them to school and I pick them up after work," he explained.

"Well, you are a very lucky man to have a mom that helps with such a chore," she went on.

"I guess you are right about having someone who helps me with them but I do not know if I am lucky," Edward added with a pensive voice.

"Of course you are lucky. You have your mom helping you with them instead of a nanny or someone unfamiliar to them," she added.

"That is why I do not ever want to have children," she went on to tell him how she felt about motherhood.

"You don't want to have children at all?" he asked her interested to know about her dislike for children.

"Nope!" she answered quickly.

"Well, you totally baffle me," he told her.

"Why?" she asked him while he thought about the question.

"Well, is it because I am Hispanic and we are all supposed to be barefoot and pregnant?" she asked him and this time she looked at him with an intent to see how he would answer the question.

"No, no it's not that at all...but you are so cute and young...and seeing how you acted with my two little ones, you are a natural... You will probably change your mind as you get older," he added hoping not to upset her with his comments because he knew how outspoken she could become in speaking her mind.

"Nope!" she reiterated.

"Why not?" he asked wanting to know.

"Well, because I think children require too much of your time as a parent and I do not want that kind of responsibility," she told him shrugging her shoulders.

Edward thought that maybe she was not the best person to take care of his kids as he had originally thought, but he had become smitten by her demeanor and zest for life. The way she talked and moved about was just too inviting and refreshing for him to stop now. She was everything a man would want in a woman. She knew where she stood in life and the things she wanted out of it. She was her own person and wanted so much to achieve her dreams, despite having the parents that could not let go and support the blossoming tender flower. But he also thought that she was young and with time he could mold her into changing her mind about kids and she would learn to love his, he told himself.

"I hope you change your mind someday, because you probably would make the best mom a kid would want," Edward told her.

"Are you trying to convince me?" she asked him.

"No, not really...just stating a fact that it will happen as you get older," he added.

"Let's talk about something else, please." She said it with determination.

"I didn't mean to upset you or anything like that," he added apologetically.

"I just think it is not your business nor anyone else's to tell me that I will change my mind about something I feel so strongly about...it is not right to try to make people change their minds about a personal feeling or conviction, you know?" she went on.

"I am sorry... I didn't mean to intrude either," he responded.

"So, how about the contest?" he asked.

"Let me think about it, ok?" she smirked at him and left his office.

They went their separate ways and didn't speak much during the rest of the week. Micaela started to wonder whether he changed his mind about the contest or maybe he never meant to be in it at all. The weekend came and went but on Monday afternoon when she came to work, Edward called her into his office and told her, Marisa, Micaela's friend, had entered them in the contest and they needed to rehearse. He invited her to come to his house and check out the dance room and then go out for dinner to his favorite restaurant near his neighborhood. He gave her directions to his place, and Micaela asked him if she could just follow him instead. Edward agreed and opted for the scenic route which Micaela loved since she relished the drive through the winding roads up Pacific Coast Highway looking at the ocean with its lustrous sunset promising nothing but beauty and solitude as the afternoon became night.

They entered the city limits and the lush winding roads gave way to the beautiful and spacious mansions lined up along the road showing how their breathtaking exteriors shone in the afternoon light.

They entered the big gate of his home and after a long drive into the front garden, the house painted a soft maize color with eggshell accents, stood amid a lush garden. The jasmine fragrance touched her nose as she got out of her car. Edward opened beautiful wooden double doors adorned with custom stained-glass windows that made her think of why he was so interested in a poor little Latin girl like herself. She entered the house and it was a beautiful place with high cathedral ceilings and long windows accentuating the long walls. The windows arched at the top with no curtains allowing the light from the ocean to mesh with the sky and come through the house and shine on the marble floors that were embellished with intricate Art Deco designs that reminded her of the old 1920's dance halls. Fitzgerald's "Great Gatsby" entered her mind and she thought she was in heaven. As she entered the dance room, she was in awe at the views that one could see from the windows. She saw her reflection in the wall of mirrors and saw this small framed young woman with dreams and aspirations having all that she was seeing come to fruition by her own hand. She knew of places like this and they could be yours if you worked very hard at what you love. She knew she would have a place like this because of her own labor of writing books.

The figure of Edward behind her made her think about his intentions and questioned why he was so interested in her. She could not fathom the reasons why this man who could have any woman, would want her for his girlfriend. She was young and at times, she probably sounded immature...*So what in the hell does he see in me?* She kept thinking to herself.

To make matters worse, things at home were becoming strained with her parents expecting her to follow in the Hispanic cultural traditions that were as impediments for her to become an American girl living in America. At twenty, she still needed chaperones, she was not allowed to go to the movies, she must remain a virgin and marry into a Hispanic home especially of Spaniard or South American descent. Micaela felt trapped in the traditions of both cultures and just wanted to be her own person. Why should her Hispanic background matter in the new country in which she now lived, she often thought to herself. She wanted to adhere to the cultural traditions of the new place that were less constricting. Micaela felt that in America her independent and outspoken nature could lead her into the writing world where she wanted to have a voice. However, she was always made to feel guilty for trying to be American. "Trying to be American" is what her Latin friends would tell her. She just wanted to have the freedom to think for herself and pursue her creative endeavors, while her mother, Paloma, kept asking her about Fabrizio.

"I do not know what happened to him, Mami Paloma," Micaela responded to her mother's question.

"What do you mean? He never calls or comes by anymore. What did you do to him?" she asked Micaela in her reproaching manner.

"I did not do anything to him. He just stopped talking to me. That is all," Micaela said it nonchalantly. She seemed not to be bothered by the fact that he just dropped off the face of the earth with no explanation whatsoever. Micaela had even forgotten about the last time they were together. Moreover, his absence upset Paloma, something that made Micaela rejoice contemptuously.

"That's strange!" Paloma exclaimed.

"He seemed to be more cultured with better manners to do the family this way," she added.

"Well, it does not matter to me, Mom," Micaela added.

"What is that mean, mom?" Paloma asked her looking intently at her daughter.

"What do you mean?" she asked back.

"Mom? What does that mean?" she repeated.

"Oh, that is *mamá* in English," Micaela responded.

"Well, I figured that but I do not want you to say that to me," Paloma told Micaela in a stern way.

"Why?" Micaela dared to ask her mother.

"Well, because that is not how you talk in this house," she retorted.

"Mom, is the English word for mama. Mom...what do you mean I cannot say it?" Micaela wanted an explanation from her mother to no avail.

"Just do as I say and do not question me, do you hear?" Paloma added sternly.

"Ok, I am sorry, Mami Paloma," Micaela resigned herself to her cultural "respectful" plight.

"Micaela!... Phone is for you," her younger sister exclaimed.

"Maybe it is Fabrizio wanting to ask me to marry him, who knows!" Micaela said it out loud as she walked away from her mother's sight.

"Don't be disrespectful, you hear?" her mother responded.

Micaela smirked as she reached the room where the phone was and in which they were allowed to take calls. She picked up the receiver hoping it would be Blake asking her to go to the prom and she would tell him "No, no...no can do," she smiled and motioned to her sister as to who was it. Her sister shrugged and walked away.

"Hello, this is Micaela," she answered politely.

"Hey, Micaela, sorry for calling your house, but you did not show up to work today and I just wanted to touch base with you about practice...Are you coming to the house again?...My children will be here this weekend and I thought maybe we could have a picnic down on the cliffs. What do you think about that?" Edward said all in the same breath. Perhaps trying to get everything in and not giving her any time to say no.

"Well, I do not think it is a good idea to get the children involved in our practice," Micaela told him.

"Why not?...You seemed to like them and I know they definitely liked you," he told her.

"Well, it's not that I don't like them...nothing like that...it is just that I feel uneasy," she explained.

"Why uneasy?" he asked.

"They are impressionable little kids and they might get used to our time together practicing and when the contest is over they won't understand that I would disappear...I do not know what it is, but I feel uneasy," she tried to explain herself and her feelings.

"Well, I thought you might like having a picnic...Maybe we can practice mid-week, when they are with my mom's," he said it sounding sullen.

"I guess it will not hurt to spend time with them once. Let's not make a habit of it, though, okay?" she pleaded, puzzled at the fact that he had made her feel guilty and out of this guilt she succumbed to spend the afternoon with his children.

Micaela could not understand why she felt obliged to accept the invitation. Was it because he was her boss and she did not want to lose her job or was it because how impressed she was with his large house? Knowing he liked her made her think that there was a possibility of leaving her parents' seemingly crazy house of pain to a larger and nicer place with the freedom she wanted to experience so desperately. The thought of being in that rich and immaculate neighborhood clouded her judgment about everything the future was to hold for Micaela, and in her most accommodating ways she started to become a permanent fixture in what would become her gilded cage.

She found herself liking the little girl, but could not make herself like the little boy. She felt badly at the prospect of becoming their stepmother lacking the emotions required to be a mother and already doing something that should never be done like picking favorites between children. That is something her mother did and she did not want to act that way, but the more she tried to like Edward Jr. the more she failed. They started spending weekends together with the children but she was telling her mother, Paloma, she was going to the library. It was becoming harder and harder to leave the nice beautiful house with its manicured gardens and panoramic views of the Pacific Ocean over the cliffs.

Micaela loved to have an early dinner as the sunset displayed its array of hues just in the right amounts creating a wonderful feeling only to be enshrouded by the warm orange shade that the sun far away in the horizon emitted and with, what seemed like nature's deliberate intentions, it slithered its way up to the cliffs leaving traces of yellow and orange to dance with the motion of the blue/green sea below. Darkness permeated bringing silence to the night. It was a sight that every time she saw it made her feel as though it was always the 'first time.' Micaela never took for granted the beauty, the joy, the suffering and all of the emotions life bestowed upon her. Besides all this beauty, she felt she would like to live there and have all the comforts that Edward would provide for her. She started to feel like she belonged in this area and was becoming a part of the community's in-crowd.

They won the contest and Edward took her to a nearby Italian eatery so she could enjoy one of her favorite dishes *Panini di mortadella* (Italian bologna sandwich) and *cappuccino* with lots of sugar. She felt comforted by his attention. No one ever in her life, other than her beloved *Mamita* María José, had paid this much attention to her likes and dislikes. This older gentleman started to make her feel wanted, yet she wasn't sure whether she was feeling love or more of an appreciation for all the things he was doing for her. However, she became enthralled with the way he started to cater to her. The new semester started and she needed to go back to school and it meant that she could no longer work the same hours and have Edward's attention. She felt like a spoiled child about to throw a tantrum, she smiled and told herself, "whatever will be, will be."

Edward on the other hand, took every moment possible to see her and spend time with her. He cunningly and very astutely started to put in motion the ways he would shape and manipulate the unknowing young girl who would be the caretaker of his children freeing him to do as he pleased. He did not mind trekking to Westwood in the middle of the day so they could have lunch together before she started her afternoon classes. Edward pretended so well to be smitten by Micaela's young refreshing attitude that he at times believed it himself. To him she embodied compassion, zest for life, and an optimistic outlook even in the most negative of circumstances. She was lively and always full of energy so much that at times just watching her go through a day was refreshingly exhausting. He knew exactly how to embellish the ways of entrapment to calm her down once they were married and she had a child of her own. He was pretty sure of this, when he went looking for a promise ring. He waited for her afternoon class to get out and decided to take her for French pastries and *latte* at the nearby café in town.

"Hey Micaela!" Edward called out seeing her coming down the stairway.

"Hey, what are you doing here?" she asked surprised.

"I was just thinking about you and thought I would just come by to say hello," he smiled at her taking her small hand and placing an old-fashioned ring with a half karat diamond on it. The most luminous and clear diamond Micaela ever saw.

"Oh my gosh! What's this for?" she asked him surprised and feeling very uneasy at the prospect of being engaged at the young age of twenty-one.

Micaela thought to herself, *my life is about to change but can I be a mother to those two little ones when I do not even want to have one of my own?*

"What are my parents going to say about this?" She heard herself say out loud.

Edward looked at her inspecting the ring very closely. He realized that she would know the quality and how much he had spent on this ring, since her father was in the diamond business. He asked her pretending to be embarrassed at being ostentatious with a ring of that quality, knowing too well, it would be the bait to catch the family and especially the father with the final word.

"Do you like it?" he asked hoping to read her expression of approval.

"I cannot accept this ring," she answered taking the ring off her finger.

"It is only a promise ring," he told her putting it back on her hand.

"What?!...all the more reason why I cannot take this ring," she went on.

"Why not?" he asked.

"Well, because it could easily be an engagement ring," she told him.

"Well, if you want to be engaged, it is okay with me" he grabbed her soft curly hair bringing her close to him, and giving her a kiss, that asked in a pleading way.

"Please accept my ring, and let's give each other a year to get to know one another and then we can get engaged. I love you Micaela I wanted you in my life from the day you could not pronounce Burger Keen," he smiled and gave her a long embrace.

Micaela was dumbfounded and overwhelmed at the prospect of getting serious with this man. Her parents did not even know he existed in her life. She knew that they would be so upset and they probably would send her back to South America so she would forget about the nonsense of getting married. All this time they thought she was studying at the library. Paloma, her mother, would call her a liar and deceiver of sorts, *But aren't I, a deceiver of sorts?* She thought to herself.

Despite her guilty feelings, Micaela could not wait to see her mother's expression at the sight of such a delicate and expensive ring and what it meant. The more she thought about it, the more appealing the prospect of being married to this man became, if only to spite her mother. She would not want her to do this and what about dentistry she would ask. Devilishly she thought how triumphant she would feel at springing this move on her, *Check mate, now you cannot touch me!* Undoubtedly, she later would regret the choice she was about to make.

"A promise ring, huh?" she said looking at the beautiful piece of jewelry. "My father is going to be impressed with this piece… the diamond is of good quality and the setting between the two delicate diamond baguettes creates an elegant vintage look…plus the size of the stone is too much for a promise ring, I know he will find it ostentatious," she added.

"I really do not care what your father thinks about the ring, I bought it for you without even thinking about the fact that your father is in the jewelry business" he lied.

Micaela looked at him and very proud of her father's trade, she told him, "You know he is a diamond setter...so I know you bought this for me without a thought of my dad, huh... I just do not know what to say, we've only known each other for what?...six months?" she told him.

"Do you like me?" Edward asked her.

Micaela thought that it was odd to be asked if she liked him as opposed to love him.

"What do you think?" She responded.

"I know you like me and with time I know you will also learn to love me...You come across as a very sensible girl, whom I trust with my life and the life of my children. I am hopeful that before the year is over you will be in love with me and accept my proposal of marriage." He told her as matter of fact.

"You seem so serious," she told him poking his ribs tickling him and giving him a hug as she would give one of her brothers.

"Of course I like you and I even dare to say I already love you and your children," she told him thinking about what her mother always told her. "The man who really loves you will respect you and never ask you to do things you do not want to do." Edward had never ask for more than hugs and kisses. He seemed to want to get physical with her many times but as a gentleman he always exercised caution and prudence. Micaela trusted him that he would never be out of line and she could be with him knowing that she would not have to guard her virginity.

The year went by so quickly and in the mean time she told her parents about Edward but leaving the news of the promise ring to herself. She never wore it around her parents, and for other gifts that Edward had bestowed on her, she had asked him for a jewelry box which she kept in his bedroom. He always asked her why she left them there instead of wearing them.

"You know? You are a strange bird" he once told her.

"Why do you say that?" Micaela asked him with an ingénue face.

Edward loved to see her that way because her beautiful exotic features became softer to a delicate form that only made her more sensual and an attractive creature making one want to hold her and love her passionately to bring out the woman he knew she had never been, but Micaela had told him about the promise she had made to her mother and many times he thought it was silly but he also did not want to make her feel uncomfortable enough for her to become aware of his true alternative motives. So he would wait thinking morosely about the virgin girl he was about to own. It made him resentful deep down inside knowing too well she did not love him. *Has she ever fell in love? I guess she is too young and sheltered for that?* He would think to himself.

"Most girls would love to show the presents a boyfriend has given her to all her friends and family...You, on the other hand, leave everything behind and only wear it around me," he told her waiting for her to explode at being questioned like that.

Edward had seen this side of her, and he thought she was definitely a fiery young woman with a passion that she would not ever be able to contain as she got older. He knew what the future held for this young girl who was unaware of how creative and ingenuous she was, and who he most desperately wanted to possess. To his surprise, Micaela in a composed and nonchalant manner and looking intently into his eyes told him, "I am not like most girls, and do not compare me to any that you might know."

Edward grabbed her by her waist and told her, "You drive me insane. Why don't you just marry me now and get it over with already. I want you to be with me always, and my children could definitely use a young and beautiful mother like you."

"So you want a sex slave and care taker for your children, is this what I am hearing right now?" she asked as she pulled away running from him as if playing a cat and mouse game.

"If I get you now, you will never escape me and you will be my slave forever," he told her as he ran to catch her and laughing to himself for those where exactly his intentions.

"Catch me if you can!" laughing and going to the back yard, Micaela ran out the door.

Edward saw her turning to the swimming pool area and aware that she did not know about the short cut, he met her around the corner and getting hold of her, he gave her a kiss that she did not resist. For the first time, Micaela felt an energy come alive in her body and the thought of her raging hormones starting to act up stopped her in her tracks and she pulled away from him. Edward did not fail her; he respectfully stopped, let her go and walked away.

"You need to leave. It is almost nine o'clock. Your parents are probably wondering why you are not home already," he said in a serious supervisory voice.

"Oh my gosh. It is almost nine o'clock!...I better hurry home. Mom will kill me," Micaela started to pick up her bag and sweater.

Edward came from behind her and gave her a hug making Micaela feel comforted and warm. She felt he really cared for her and although she did not feel or at least did not think of how one should feel at the thought of been married, the security he provided at many levels should be enough for the lack of the 'in love' feeling most people professed at the time of getting married. Micaela thought about what was of the most importance...the chance of getting away from an overbearing mother for whom she could not do anything right. Moving to a neighborhood where everything is so beautiful providing ample space to be inspired to do some real writing...That is what made Edward attractive to her.

Under Edward's tutelage, her life would be a better life with the freedom to do what she wanted; like going to school to study the subject of her choice without having to answer to anyone but herself, and of course, her husband. *Husband? that sounds strange!* As all of these thoughts came into her mind, she began to resent and feel the anger as result of her culture and the mediocrity her parents had chosen for themselves. Her father was a brilliant artisan that could make the most beautiful pieces of jewelry and could have set up shop for himself, but instead he chose to work for someone else using half of his potential. Her mother, had demurely stopped her own dreams, only to be subservient to the whims of her mediocre husband. So much potential and creative energy had been wasted away, overshadowed by keeping up with the cultural idiosyncrasies that did not belong here, but rather in the country where they came from.

"Are you okay?" Edward asked, seeing her in deep thought as she got in her car and looked around the beautiful gardens.

"Yeah, I am just thinking...why do you really want me?" she asked him hoping for a true answer.

"I think you are a beautiful young girl who can learn to love me and my children with time," he answered reaching to stroke her cheek.

"I love you and want you to be my wife," he added.

"Can you really love me in such a short time?" she asked him.

"Is there really a definite time in order to fall in love?" he asked back trying not to show that all he really wanted was a subservient mother for his children.

"Well, I do not know," she answered, unable to fathom what they both had said.

"So that means you do not love me, but you would like to love me one day?" Edward asked, forcing her to answer what he needed to hear.

"Of course, I do!" she said it so quickly, regretting saying it so fast without a thought of the consequences her feelings would have for this family as well as her own. She knew her family would not approve of her marriage to someone that did not belong to their culture. Her parents were not aware that she had been dating him. It would be a scandal as soon as her mother found out that she had been secretly dating this older American man.

She got home and her mother, Paloma the inquisitor, was at the gate looking at her daughter get out of her car. "Where have you been?" she asked Micaela.

"Nowhere," she responded coldly, knowing that with that statement she had started World War Three. It was such imprudent, disrespectful, and uncharacteristic of the obedient young woman her mother expected her to be.

Scolding her as usual, "I told you many times, you cannot be disrespectful to your parents who provide room and shelter for you to live comfortably until you become a dentist," Paloma said all in one strict tone of voice.

"Well, then your lucky day will soon to be here. I have a boy friend who wants to meet dad and the family to ask for my hand in marriage," she said in a flat nonchalant demeanor waiting for her mother's volatile response.

"What!" Paloma yelled at her daughter demanding a full explanation to her what.

"Well," taking a deep breath Micaela continued, "He is thirty one years old, has been married before and has two of the most precious little ones you could ever set eyes on. He lives in Palos Verdes in a home that overlooks the ocean and wants to marry me at the end of my sophomore year of college...Shall I go on?" Micaela asked.

"What are you talking about, you insolent stupid girl!" Paloma yelled again.

"What, what mom?" Micaela asked her mother expecting a slap across her face but was surprised that it did not happen.

"Your father will not hear of this!" her mother retorted walking away from Micaela.

"Yes, I shall tell him that finally a financial relief has come his way and he does not need to bother with the expenses his family incurs for one of his daughters." Micaela said it out loud feeling anger at the fact that her father always complained about having to spend money on the girls. She released a lot of pent up anger, feeling confident that her mother's lack of English would make her not be able to understand the degree of her contempt for her parents, culture and the frustration she had felt starting school in America.

"What did you just say?" Paloma turned and looking intently at her daughter, she repeated her questions at which point Micaela knew her mother would be in an attacking manner.

"What part, mother, what part do you want me to repeat?" Micaela insolently retorted back

"You better stop with that attitude...What has come over you?" Paloma was not able to compose herself seeing the defiant attitude in Micaela. An attitude she had never seen before.

"If you think that because you have found a fool to put up with you, you can come and treat me with disrespect you are quite wrong, you stupid girl!" Paloma retorted angrily and realized that she was angry with her daughter to the point of raising her hand, slapping her across her face.

"Mami, stop please!" Rebeca, her younger sister screamed out loud.

"Let her hit me! The physicality of her act will not hurt as much as all of these years of indifference and put downs. The lack of compassion and her critical demanding ways have hurt far more than calling me a stupid girl or slapping me." Micaela just let go of her pent up anger exploding in the most cathartic way for she knew that one day she would have her say so in life and the dreams she had harbored quietly all these years.

"You better stop!" Rebeca told her sister.

"You stay out of it, you do not tell me what to do, do you hear?" Micaela told her younger sister.

Paloma started to feel overwhelmed and one of her fainting spells was about to come over her. She grabbed a chair and started to cry and feeling sorry for herself, she told Micaela how ungrateful she was. After all she had done for her. "How can you leave me here with your younger siblings and my inability to speak the language?...Who is going to take me to do the errands on the weekends, huh?" Without even realizing how selfish Paloma sounded, she got up from the chair, and approached Micaela and pointing her finger at her continued blatantly, "Your father is not going to be happy with your choice of a husband, I can tell you that right now!"

"He might send you back to South America so you can forget about this crazy idea to marry an old American man," she added.

"I am twenty-one years old and you cannot tell me what to do any more" Micaela retorted back.

At that moment, her mother suffered her fainting spell and all the anger Micaela felt became a feeling of despair, anguish and mostly guilt. "How can I get away from all this when she needs me so?" Micaela whispered to herself as she picked her mother up and with the help of her younger siblings, they managed to lay her down on her bed. Micaela ran for the first aid kit and broke open a package of smelling salts to bring her mother to consciousness. Her younger siblings watched Micaela change into this soft and tender woman, the perfect Florence Nightingale to take care of her mother's hysteria. *It never fails,* Micaela thought to herself, *Anytime things get out of your control, hysteria ensues and a fainting spell appears and the damsel in distress enters to destroy everything I worked so hard to get for myself. Does it ever end?*

"What happened?" Paloma asked looking a bit disoriented.

"Nothing really, you just fainted, but you will be okay," Micaela answered with a caring voice. "I am sorry for getting you upset," she added.

"Get out of my sight!" Paloma exclaimed realizing that it was Micaela caring for her.

"I am not going to repeat myself!" she exclaimed again, pushing Micaela out of her way.

"Where is Rebeca?" Paloma asked trying to get up and looking around the room.

Rebeca, looking sadly at Micaela leaving the room, answered back, "I am here, Mami Paloma."

Micaela wanted to leave, to run away from all this. It would be so easy to get in her car and drive away, to drive so far away that no one could follow or find her. She could go to New York City and start anew where no one would know of her or where she came from. She could write a novel about her mother's hysteria, and the reason she had to run away. It could easily be a tear jerker. She smiled as she went into the kitchen to start the tea kettle, to make the chamomile tea for her mother's nerves. Micaela thought back to South America and added to her thoughts, "Pretty soon, Dr. Navarro would get here to make sure she is okay bringing the little green pills with him." Micaela's younger brother appeared by the kitchen door, and asked if the tea was ready.

"Nope, tell her to get up and make it herself," she told him jokingly but in a serious tone.

"Ooh, I am going to tell her you said that!" he added.

"Go ahead! She will faint again and this time I am not picking her up off the floor," Micaela told her younger brother with an attitude he had never seen in her before.

"Are you OK?" he asked her with genuine concern.

"Yeah. Why?" she looked at him with a smile and gave him a reassuring hug.

"Mom, will be okay too...You know that...She does that all the time, but she will get up and she will be okay," Micaela told him, rubbing his head.

"Here, take the tea with you. It is already lukewarm, ready for Mom to drink," she said.

It would be the last time Micaela came running to her mother's aid. She decided that she would marry Edward. She would leave this house and all the dysfunctional drama her mother insisted on creating. She felt relieved that she would no longer have to be under her every watch. She would be her own person, do her own thing. Confidently deceiving herself, she thought marrying Edward would be her way out. Micaela delved into the wedding preparations by herself knowing in her heart Paloma would not be there for her. The ominous feeling of long ago, the letters found in *mamita* María José's trunk, the stories told with figs and cheese stirred up great agitation around the deep corners of her soul and with much trepidation she embarked on her deliberate attempt to escape her suffocating life circumstances that would become the perilous road leading only to darkness and despair.

The Ugly Duckling's Pluckiness

Her wedding-or rather her way out-was a small family affair similar to her Sweet Sixteen, her *Quinceañera*...no fanfare, no pink invitations, not even a cake. It had been a bittersweet experience because compared to Isabel's big *Quinceañera* festivities in the old country, and also her wedding in the new country, Micaela's were both very much ordinary days. Her mother did not make the big fuss that this event required. Her wedding did not have a reception but simply a dinner. Besides having no bridesmaids to fill her day with enthusiasm, the traditional waltz with her father was excluded. Her gown was bought at a small boutique and it was rather simple and quaint. She had an antique cloche as her veil with baby's breath to the side. She look very much like a bride from the roaring '20s and she was happy about this look.

Micaela was certain that had there been a reception in a hall or restaurant, her father would have complained about the cost to him. Therefore, to hurt her father's sensitivities, the reception was held at Edward's opulent mansion in the affluent Palos Verdes neighborhood. Micaela's father was so upset that she had decided to do all this in such a short time without consulting her parents, that on the day of the wedding, he forgot to pick up his tuxedo and was late to the church ceremony. He never walked Micaela down the aisle and was not part of the wedding festivities. As such, marriage to Edward Sims began, Micaela's way out of her culture and her suffocating parental home.

The wedding night was another disaster. Unaware of her alcohol intolerance, Micaela drank too much champagne. On her wedding night, when according to her culture she would become a 'woman,' it did not happen and instead became just a blur. The women often talked about the importance of being a virgin and becoming a woman on that wedding night. Micaela often thought and asked herself, *What am I, a boy, until then!* She thought that was the most absurd notion the women of her clan back in the old country had, and now among the Latin women whom her mother had befriended in the States. Being intoxicated, she never knew when she and Edward had become intimate and if she had had any pleasure, pain or whatever you are supposed to feel on that night of transformation from child to woman. It was nothing but a blur and awkwardness.

The next morning, as she found herself next to the man who was both her boss and husband, she jumped out of the bed to make sure she had stained the sheets. The idea she had about the "wedding night" when one loses the precious virginity were that of her mother's soap operas, where the virgin would stain her sheets and the older women of the clan would be proud of the bride's dignity and honor. Instead, for Micaela, this was the 'night' later down the road that Edward would recriminate about not soiling the sheets as expected of a virgin, and thus he started questioning whether she had been with another man before marrying him.

The summer ended with her new title of Mrs. Micaela Sims. Soon it was time to go back to college and finish what she had started. She took a medium load of classes because she was fond of Edward's kids and wanted to provide a stable home for those two little ones that now made her life complete as their mother. She tried very much to love her husband. She liked him very much but deep down inside Micaela knew that it was not love she felt for this man. Needless to say, things were not turning out as she had anticipated. The responsibility of his children was becoming too intrusive in her college routine and increasingly, she was not able to balance the two. It seemed that Edward did not want her to finish her college education because her courses were becoming intensely harder; she needed more time to spend away from home doing the necessary research needed for some of her scientific projects, he would make-up an added chore with the kids preventing her from attending extra sessions to help her with her class material.

"This weekend my biology class is going to Palm Desert to do some research on the fauna up there, I need to leave on Friday and I will be back on Sunday... Maybe we can meet up there after the class and take the kids for a hike," Micaela told Edward.

"I don't think that is going to be feasible because Marie has a recital and I need to go back to work for some preliminary research on the new job that is coming up," he said

"What about your mom?" she asked.

"What about my mom?" Edward looked at her in a strange way.

"What is the matter with you?" Micaela asked annoyed at his attitude.

"Nothing is the matter with me, but I think you will not be able to go do your research...You have to take care of the kids this weekend." The tone of voice he used reminded Micaela of her mother.

"Well, I hate to disagree but I think my school work is just as important as your kids and you should be respectful of that," Micaela said with a stern voice.

"You are not going anywhere this weekend except to take Marie to her recital and take care of the children while I am away in LA." Edward told her, making Micaela think is this Jekyll or Hyde, hmm?

"Since when do you talk to me this way?" Micaela confronted him.

"I do not want to get into an argument with you but you should do as I say...Do you hear me?" he added.

"And if I don't?" Micaela retorted.

"Do not go there Micaela, you will regret it!" He approached her as if to slap her but seeing her reaction to this outburst, he backed off. Marie was nearby, in full view of the scene, unfortunately witnessing her parents fight.

"Daddy!" Marie yelled. "What is going on daddy?" Marie asked as tears started to fill her eyes.

"Nothing is the matter honey...go back outside... Micaela and Dad are just having a conversation, OK?" he said guiding Marie toward the patio.

Micaela did not know what to make of his behavior, but she felt like she had asked for this by marrying a man just to get away from her family. It was a victim's way to think and she recriminated herself for having this thought in the first place. She had only been married about two years and already she was feeling as though she would never be able to care and love this man as she had hoped she would the day she got married. Not for lack of trying, but his attitude towards her did not make her want to love him. Instead, his controlling ways were so disappointing and very unexpected. She thought she was crazy thinking that only Latin men were male chauvinists. She had fallen prey to a stereotype and now Karma or life would have it that it was going to show her a lesson about being prejudice and classifying people according to some man-made stereotype.

"I will have to arrange it with my professor and see how I can make this research paper up" Micaela told Edward conceding to staying home to care of his children.

With time, things got worse. Her obligations to both families, hers and Edward's children, interfered with her studies. She stopped attending her family's functions, and unbeknown to her, Paloma worried about her daughter's behavior and her new life in the splendid house with the many servants. Micaela purposely kept the fact they were being discharged one by one since their marriage creating more work and house hold responsibilities for her. Micaela seemed to be more detached from the family which caused Paloma to be concerned about her independent, carefree and full of life daughter. It was her younger sister, Rebeca's birthday and Paloma called Micaela to ask about bringing a dish, in hopes that she would feel obliged and make an appearance. Micaela agreed and showed up for the birthday party without Edward or the children.

"I am so glad you are here joining your family like old times," Paloma greeted her child.

"Hello, Mom," Micaela said giving her mother the dish of sautéed mushrooms.

"I hope you like them, I did not feel like cooking this morning, so I did them in a hurry!" she told her mother entering the old kitchen adorned with knickknacks everywhere. Strangely, she felt at home. She thought about how much she had hated her parents' decor, and now that she was visiting, it was endearing to her all of a sudden.

"You look pale, Micaela" Her mother told her as she placed her hair behind her ear. Micaela found it strange how her mother was so warm and tender with such a touching detail and a loneliness crept into her soul that brought a big lump in her throat. *What is going on?* She thought. Paloma the stoic, cold despot caressing her hair while noticing her paleness. *Who has taken my mother away and placed this impostor in her place*, she kept thinking as she smiled realizing how much she had missed her family and the little house they lived in.

"You think?" Micaela asked looking around.

"Yeah, you look pale," Rebeca added coming from behind Micaela giving her a big hug.

"Hey girly, happy birthday, I brought you something. It's in the car, go get it!" Micaela told Rebeca.

"Where are Edward and the kids?" Rebeca asked.

"They had planned something months ago and decided to go there instead. I am sorry," she said trying to hide her tears.

"Micaela, come sit here and tell me...What is going on with you?" her mother asked again.

"Is everything okay?" she asked truly concerned about her vivacious daughter being sullen and reserved.

"Well, it's just a lot of work with school and all. The kids have a lot of things to do and they trust me to take care of everything so I cannot disappoint Edward and them, you know?" Micaela started opening up to her mother, forgetting how she really was. All of a sudden, Paloma's demeanor changed and she told Micaela, "I told you, you will regret marrying that American man."

Trying to make Micaela feel guilty she added, "You could have finished school, become a dentist and have had your own life. You think life is easy! It's not but you looked for the easy way out with this rich man and his cold ways." Paloma went on saying what Micaela knew first hand to be true. But now, the truth was even more complicated. She was young, confused and to top it all off, she was pregnant with that, "Awful American man's child," as her mother would say.

"Micaela, you look so pale!" her father exclaimed.

"Gosh, everyone in unison, go ahead repeat after me 'Micaela you look soooo pale!'" Micaela said trying to hide her pain. She did not want to be pregnant. She never wanted to have children of her own. But now in her situation, the chances of finishing school, much less changing her major were becoming nil. Then without a moment for Micaela to compose herself, she heard her mother ask her the ultimate question, "You are not pregnant, are you?"

Micaela wanted to run and hide and never be found. She blushed and surprisingly her father gave her a hug. Paloma looked at her husband and daughter hugging and she started to cry.

"Why are you crying?" Micaela heard herself ask her mother.

"Are you crying because I am having a child with the awful American man or because a child makes the marriage to the awful American man supposedly stronger?" she went on.

"Hush, don't be disrespectful to your mother," her father scolded Micaela.

"Why do you say that, Papi?" she asked. "Why do you all have to look at me like some stranger, just because I married out of our culture and now I am pregnant...It is not like he is from outer space or I married from some other species...People are people no matter where they come from...no matter what language they speak. They hurt just like anybody else and they become happy just like anybody else. What is wrong with you people?" she kept asking and her questioning became uncontrollable sobs she had been storing for months.

Paloma stopped being the stoic matriarch and for the first time she was genuinely concerned about the well being of the pregnant woman in front of her, her own child.

"How long have you been this pale?" Paloma asked Micaela as a matter of fact.

"I do not know, maybe a month?" Micaela answered, regretfully wanting to be comforted.

"Have you gone to see a doctor. When was your last menstrual cycle?" Paloma continued with the physical questions.

"No, not yet...I guess it's been a while since I have had a period," Micaela said covering her face with her hands trying to hide the fact that she was embarrassed by the questions her mother kept asking her. They had never shared such intimate details in conversation. She was confused and astonished at her mother's real concern about her health.

"Well, tomorrow you need to make an appointment and make sure that you are taken care of," her father said.

"Yes, Papi," Micaela said rolling her eyes, thinking to herself, *a bit late for all these feelings of filial love.*

Micaela was not feeling well and felt like vomiting at the sight of the dishes that the guests were bringing to the party. She was surrounded by a lot of people but deep down she felt very alone and not cared for by the man she had chosen to marry. She thought, *things could be so much better if he would understand how much I loved to be touched and caressed by him...Why can he not understand that all I want is to be a good mom for those two little kids and teach them manners and culture? Why doesn't he let me be their mom? They don't even call me Mom...They call me by my first name.* These thoughts caused her nausea to intensify.

The more she thought about her marriage to Edward the more lonely she felt, because she had realized two years ago at that moment of "I do," she had not loved him and all she had was hope for success in a loveless marriage. She remembered how at the reception in Edward's home, one of the supervisors, a friend of Edward had told Micaela after several drinks, "It is never going to work between you two...you are far too smart and lovely for him." Micaela heard the words but did not want to accept the weight of them then. But now two years later, she felt she was losing sight of everything she had wanted to accomplish and she was also losing sense of herself as a young girl becoming a woman with the prospect of expecting a child that she did not want.

The next day just as she was about to arrange to see her gynecologist, she felt a crippling pain in her womb. She got scared and ran to the bathroom to see what was going on. She was bleeding vaginally and got very dizzy. She fell down and hoped Clara, her housekeeper, would come soon enough to help her.

"Mrs. Sims! Where are you?" Clara called out.

"I am here in the bathroom!" she yelled back.

"There is a courier in the hall way waiting for your signature on a delivery," Clara announced back to Micaela.

"Can you please help me? I am in the bathroom...Hurry!" she pleaded.

Clara and the courier ran to see what was going on.

"Thank God for you," Clara told the courier as he picked Micaela's small body out of the bathtub and whisked her into the bedroom. She was bleeding heavily and was becoming incoherent.

"Do you have her husband's number? You need to call him and tell him to get here at once," the courier told Clara.

"Ma'am, I am sorry but we need to call 911," he told Micaela.

"No, please call my husband at work...The phone number is on the fridge written in crayon for the kids to see," she indicated to him.

"I think it's best if we call an ambulance," the young man replied.

"Just call my husband first, please," Micaela pleaded.

"OK, let me get the number," he conceded.

As he was walking down to the kitchen, Clara appeared telling him she had contacted Edward and he instructed her that the kids needed to be picked up by three and needed for Micaela to follow through with this.

"Did you tell him, she is bleeding?" the courier asked her in disbelief of her husband's coldness.

"Yeah, but he said to get the kids first, then she can go to see the doctor," she told the courier, shrugging her shoulders.

"Well, then I guess I need to leave and continue on my route," he told her.

"Thank you for helping me get her up," she thanked him kindly.

When Clara went to see Micaela, she was trying to sit up in her bed, unable to do so since the pain in her womb had become stronger. She looked very fragile. Clara felt great sympathy for this young woman who laid on her opulent bed overlooking the Pacific Ocean, unable to move and without a husband to come to comfort her at this time of great distress.

The telephone rang, "The Sims residence," Clara answered.

"Hello, Mr. Sims. Yes, sir. She is on her bed but she is fainting and she cannot get up…What should I do?" Clara asked Edward who had called to see if Micaela had gone to pick up the children.

"I told you Mr. Sims, she is bleeding and I do not see it stopping any time soon. She is crying out in pain. Can you please come and help your wife, sir!" Clara pleaded to no avail and he became annoyed and told her that he would have to leave work in order to pick up the kids.

"I am sorry, Mr. Sims, but I do not think Mrs. Sims should move at all. She does not look good," Clara informed him.

"Let me go get the kids and I'll be right there, as soon as I can! Call the doctor and see if he can make a house call," Edward finally told Clara.

Minutes seemed like hours and hours seemed like years to poor Clara, who stood by Micaela in one of the worst moments of her life. Being pregnant, the feeling that something was wrong had come over her a few times early on, but she had chosen to shrug it off as just a figment of her imagination. At one moment she was lucid and asked Clara if she had called Edward to tell him about her condition.

"Yes, ma'am," she answered politely, feeling so sorry for the young woman crippled by her pain.

"He told me he was going to pick up the kids for you," she added.

"Oh, my gosh! I totally forgot about the kids," Micaela tried very hard to compose herself and attempt to get out of bed.

"Please, don't get up!" Clara tried to keep her down. "Maybe, you should put your feet up and not move," she added.

"Oh no! I can't, Edward will get mad at me for not picking the kids up and it will be hell to pay around here for the next month…I have to go pick up the kids," Micaela exclaimed.

She tried very hard to get up and put on some shoes with the help of Clara but when she started for the bedroom door, the pain became excruciating and she needed to get to the bathroom. Something was compelling her to go, a terrible cramping in her lower back spread like a wild fire down to her vagina and she hurt like she has never hurt before. Instinctively she felt her world going dark. "What is going on? She heard herself saying out loud.

"What did you say Mrs. Sims?" Clara asked.

"Nothing, let me go to the bathroom, I'll be okay," Micaela told her.

Clara waited but heard nothing, she felt a lot of anxiety at her inability to help the young woman who was in so much pain. All of a sudden she heard Micaela scream at the top of her lungs, "CLAARA! PLEASE HELP ME!"

Clara ran into the bathroom and saw Micaela had fallen to the floor. Blood was gushing out of her as if someone had opened a faucet. She looked as white as a ghost and everything about her indicated something was terribly wrong.

"Clara, something came out. I can't look. I am so sorry, but can you look for me? I did not flush the toilet," she said amidst her inconsolable whimpering.

Life as Micaela had known it was passing her by in slow motion, and she regretted all she had done so far. Not being able to have the power of being…the power of being the strong woman she knew she could be. Instead, trying to be the peacemaker...gentle, non-confrontational woman everyone wanted her to be. She had forgotten about herself and her dreams. She was letting her life pass her by, diverting her off the path she knew she needed to re-enter it before it was too late. She had married to free herself of family and when she needed family she knew she could not reach out to them. She needed the stoic embrace her mother would provide at this very moment when she knew that a piece of her being, literally and figuratively, had been expelled out of her womb.

Was this the punishment for all those times when I said I would never have a child? she thought to herself. She felt the warm blood coming from her vagina burning her soul, impeding her senses and she started to cry at the infinite loneliness she felt, only to be appeased and comforted by the Central American indigenous woman, Clara, who after picking the very small still life from the toilet and wrapping it gently in a towel went on to embrace Micaela in her arms caressing her forehead as fever ensued in her fragile and trembling body.

"I called Mr. Sims, but he was not available." Clara told Micaela.

"Was he in a meeting or picking the kids up?" Micaela managed to ask.

"Don't worry about that, I called your mom instead and she called your father. They are on their way." Clara told Micaela as she placed a cool damp cloth on her forehead.

"Thank you for being here with me, Clara... I am never going to forget you," she told her as she clung to her arms and buried herself in the housekeeper's bosom like a lost child waiting to see someone familiar come to her rescue as she fainted.

Micaela's father appeared in the bathroom doorway and rushed to pick Micaela up.

Right behind him was the ambulance, and its crew was very surprised at Micaela's strength since the hemorrhage was intense and she could have died had they gotten there any later. Edward, who was well aware of his wife's terrible plight of losing their baby was nowhere to be found. Her father had never liked Edward. His insensitivity with his daughter destroyed any chance of an emotional tie he could have made with his son-in-law. From the moment he saw Micaela left alone by the man who should take care of her, he decided never to come visit Micaela at this house. He always waited for Micaela to come to his home, which was to become more frequent as time went on.

Several months after her medical emergency, she went to see the same doctor who had performed the DNC to stop the hemorrhaging. She had told Micaela to come back in six months to make sure she would use some kind of contraception. In the mean time, Micaela decided to adopt the only approved 'rhythm method' by the Catholic church, something Micaela was not sure was a hundred percent guaranteed. She had a calendar and 'religiously' marked down all the dates that were safe and made sure, she stayed away from Edward on the unsafe days. On January 2nd, Micaela knew she was ovulating, Edward had approached her about being intimate and when Micaela told him that it was not safe, that she could get pregnant, he told her,

"Oh! be quiet. You do not even know how to count." Micaela being a good Catholic wife proceeded with the obligation of pleasing her husband, knowing damn well she would get pregnant. Nine months and five days later, a beautiful baby girl, Annabella was born.

She had been unsure and very frightened at the prospect of having a child grow within her, and much more at the immensity of the task of being a loving and understanding parent. Micaela was afraid that she would be like, Paloma, her mother, but swore she would try to love this child not like her mother had loved her with many conditions and guilt. Instead, she prayed she would have a compassionate heart to love this child unconditionally as her belly had grown stronger and bigger. "Motherhood is such a huge responsibility, I know I am not cut out for such a formidable task," she kept telling herself. At times she thought back to that awful day of the miscarriage, and did not want to lose this child as well. Thus, when she missed her first period, Micaela made the appointment to see the same doctor who had helped her on that horrible day. She wanted to go back to her since she was a woman, and Micaela would feel more comfortable sharing this new experience of motherhood with her, but fate would have it and Micaela would be wrong again.

"Hello, Mrs. Sims. Please come in." Dr. Sloan told her.

"So, what are my test results?" Micaela asked in a timid voice.

"Well, it is positive," the woman doctor told Micaela in a very aloof, detached sort of way. Micaela found it strange that there would not be any kind of polite excitement. What followed the blunt announcement of the results being positive caused a reaction in Micaela that she could not help. She was shocked by the bad bed side manner of her doctor. Dr. Sloan had such an accusatory tone about Micaela losing the first baby, as though she had intentionally tried to abort it and the 'home made' abortion went wrong.

"So, what do you intend to do with this pregnancy, Ms. Sims?" the doctor asked.

"What do you mean? What do I intend to do with this pregnancy?" Micaela heard herself ask as the pent up anger toward Edward surfaced. He had not been there for her when she lost the first baby, and never even said that he was sorry for his absence. Her emotions started to percolate with an added fury that made her lash out at the woman standing in front of her.

"I do not understand the question, Dr. Sloan. What amazes me the most, is the terrible bedside manner you have. I would think that as a woman...and a professional woman at that...the more polite and preferred comment would be CONGRATULATIONS, MRS. SIMS." Micaela found herself screaming at the doctor. "What kind of a woman or a doctor are you to insinuate that I had anything to do with losing my first child. That was the most painful and lonely experience I have ever had in my entire life and for you not to be empathetic and considerate of those feelings is like adding salt to an injury that is just starting to heal, you insensitive excuse of a doctor let alone a woman!" Micaela told her and continued by saying, "If you expect payment for this visit, you are quite mistaken. I will report you to the Medical Board before I pay for your callous and in-compassionate way of making something as beautiful as the miracle of life into something one discards as if it were nothing." Micaela grabbed her coat and purse and marched out of the room exhaling months of uneasy and tormented feelings that she had been harboring making her feel as if she was a time bomb about to explode. She never realized how much anguish losing a child could cause and how much guilt she felt about not caring enough for herself that caused her to lose her first child. She got home and Edward was there waiting to see what the doctor had said.

"I do not know how to count, huh?" Micaela told him reproaching, and still feeling angry at what the doctor had said to her.

"So are you positive?" he asked.

"I am positive that I am going to have a healthy baby, if that is what you are asking...Yes, I am positive. I am positive that this time I will take care of myself first so that this child does not suffer the same fate as the last one. Yes, I am positive. I am positive that I am going to reclaim the person that I once was and be stronger for the both of us...YES, I AM POSITIVE!" Micaela yelled out as she left the room.

"Micaela, are you sure you want to keep this baby?" Edward asked out loud.

"I am going to my parents' house to celebrate my news. I will be back later on tonight. Do not wait up for me," she told him. As she opened the garage door to leave, she felt very powerful. The child in her gave her a newly found force that made her invincible. The power of being was back in her. She would remember the 'jungle' of her childhood; she would plant a honeysuckle bush and would teach the child growing inside her how to extract and taste of the sweet juice, and they both would laugh at the feeling of pleasure this simple task brought to those who cherish life and all it offers. The unborn child was already transforming Micaela's life and she felt beautiful and wise.

September 7th came along and Annabella was born with the same fire of the hot afternoon. Seeing the tiny babe awaken as the nurse placed her in Micaela's arms, she had an overwhelming sensation of being in an unknown territory and she asked herself, "Am I strong enough to take care of both of us?...Am I going to be your light in moments of despair or am I going to extinguished the life I just gave to you?...I am sorry if I ever in this journey of our lives come to hurt you in any way my little one." Annabella seemed to coo, opened her eyes and the connection was made even stronger than the past nine months inside her belly. The child with the big brown eyes who danced with the witchery of love suckled from her mother's bosom demanded the life and zest she knew only Micaela could give. It restored her confidence; it demanded her strength with every suckle she took. Time passed and between birthdays, Christmases and all the day to day routines small children require, Micaela focused on the task at hand, her daughter. She knew how self-sacrificing motherhood was, but now it was a moment to rejoice and not resent, Annabella was her own baby. She had come at the most opportune time in her life and although giving birth had helped her remember her dreams and aspirations, these would just have to wait until Annabella would enter Kindergarten, Micaela thought to herself.

Meanwhile, she realized that the relationship between her and Edward had become more estranged even from the time she had lost their first child. Edward was spending more time at work and the responsibilities of all three children now was entirely left to Micaela. She knew she was going to have a hard time taking care of and being a mother to Edward's kids; this was all the more reason why she was starting to fret for Annabella. She was growing up in a home where the two older children had little if any respect for the mother figure. "Marie, you need to clean your room up...It is a complete mess and you are old enough to pick up your dirty clothes and put them in the dirty clothes basket." Micaela was not surprised at the answer she got.

"You are not my mother. You cannot tell me what to do!" Marie shouted back.

"I know I am not your mother, and I am not telling you to be clean from mother to a child, but rather from a clean person to one who seemingly wants to be a dirty one," Micaela retorted back.

Rolling her eyes and walking away with the middle finger up in the air in a rebellious form Marie said, "Whatever!"

Annabella was just a little girl and asked Micaela, "Why is Marie so mean to you, Mommy?"

"She is just been a teenager, sweetheart...she does not mean anything bad," she graciously explained.

"I am never going to be like that with you, when I get older," Annabella told Micaela.

Her child's promise reminded her of her own promise she had made to her mother a long time ago. Micaela could not help correct her child and without thinking pulled Annabella to her and told her very sweetly "Don't ever say never...always be true to your little self...respect Mommy and every adult you encounter in life, but never make promises that you might not want to keep, do you understand?" Annabella, laughed an uneasy laugh seeing her mother being so serious, said OK and out the door she went. Micaela could not help ponder what the future would hold for them with the way things were happening. She could not raise her child in a home where there was no respect and no loving relationship between mother and father. Edward was becoming more of a tyrant and more disrespectful to her. At times, he became so verbally abusive that Micaela was rather afraid of how much he had changed in the last seven years. She was afraid to tell him about his children and how impudent they were with her. Edward Jr. had gotten in some trouble at school, and Micaela was the one to go to talk to the principle in order to straightened things out. Edward seemed to be unaffected by the way his young son was getting in trouble. Micaela had suggested taking him to a counselor, but Edward just laughed making the ignorant statement that his child was not crazy. Micaela did not want to overstep any boundaries so she chose to say nothing. The arguments between Edward and Micaela about his children were becoming more frequent and abusive in their manner. Micaela had gone to her parents' home one day after a dispute only to hear her mother advise her to become more docile and put up with her husband's antics because that is just the way married life is.

"You knew what you were getting into when you got married. There will be no divorces in this family, do you hear Micaela?" Paloma said every time she had complained about how strained her marriage was becoming.

As life would have it, by the end of their eighth year of marriage, Micaela could no longer be the submissive wife or the disrespected stepmother. She started to drink her worries away, until the afternoon of New Year's Eve, when she had already had one too many screwdrivers. Edward came home finding that she was a bit inebriated he was furious knowing company was soon to arrive at their home.

"What the hell is going on with you!"

"What do you mean?" Micaela sounded disoriented not realizing the angry tone in his voice.

"Look at you! You are a mess! You are all disheveled and drunk!" he told her, grabbing her by the back of her neck and taking her to their bedroom.

"Hey! Don't grab me like that! You are hurting me!" Micaela exclaimed angrily and all of a sudden became aware that Annabella was crying.

"Where are Marie and Edward Jr.?" Edward asked.

"The hell if I know. They do not tell me where they are going or what they are doing!" she answered back.

"I am surprised you would even ask about them, when you do not care what the hell they do or say!" she continued moving toward Annabella who started to sob at the scene of her parents becoming violent with one another.

"Shh...Mommy is okay, baby girl. Don't cry," Micaela tried to console Annabella who could not control herself and continued to sob.

"Can you make her stop crying!" Edward said without thinking about Annabella's anxious feelings.

"People are going to start coming soon and look at both of you. What a mess!" He started to reach for Annabella and at this point the child clung harder to Micaela and grabbing with the force of a man, Edward took the child away from her and pushed Micaela so hard she landed like a rag doll near the table in the hall way.

"Daddy, stop!" Annabella screamed.

"Shut up!" he told her back. Walking toward Micaela, he grabbed her by the arm, twisting with such force that Micaela having not eaten all day and getting drunk in the afternoon, felt as if she was losing consciousness. Due to the extreme pain the whole scene caused her, she was about to have one of those fainting spells her mother succumbed to every time things didn't go her way. *Oh my God. Is this how she escaped all the painful moments in her life? I can't be her...I never want to be her. Please God, please help me, help me for Annabella if not for me!* She cried thinking to herself in her drunken stupor.

Never in a million years would she have seen herself in such a deprecating and deplorable way. She regained consciousness and walked into her bathroom and what she saw in the mirror was devastating. She saw herself very disheveled and wretchedly drunk. A drunk...Is this where she was going? The responsibility of entertaining people did not stop her from drinking too many cocktails. She saw herself and she did not like the person she was becoming. The loneliness and a loveless marriage were not good enough reasons to forget about who she was, and where she had come from. All the 'women' in her life stood beside her as she examined her face and torso in the mirror. She washed her face and started to cry. She felt as though she had fallen off of some small precipice with no one in sight to catch her. She entered the shower stall and let the hot water slide down her small frame as she wrapped her arms around herself to sustain all the pain inside her. She started rapidly saying the Lord's prayer three times pleading for the holy spirit to enter her soul and help her put her life back on track. She got dressed quickly and called her younger sister to come help her and then called Clara who told her she would be there as soon as the bus came to pick her up.

"Edward, can you please come here?' She called out.

"What!" he answered without coming to see what she wanted him for.

"Annabella, where are you sweetheart?" Micaela started to look into her child's room and saw her lying on her bed fast asleep. She closed the door and went downstairs to the living room where she saw Edward cleaning up the mess she had created that afternoon.

"I don't know who you think you are, but if you ever lay a finger on me again, it will be the last time you see me or your daughter in this house. Do you understand what I am saying, Edward?" she asked him calmly yet with an authority in her voice that she knew she was being embraced by her beloved *Mamita* María José's spirit and even the stoic embrace of her mother she felt in this moment.

"Whatever!" Edward responded walking away.

"I am serious," she said and started to the kitchen to get the party started.

People began to arrive and would comment on how nice she looked. As she politely said, "Thank you," she thought, if they only knew how good her cosmetics were. The people started to drink and be merry as the passing year was coming to its end. People admired her beautiful home and how everything was in perfect juxtaposition to make the pieces of furnishings be in harmony, creating a warm and serene place to be, the place where Micaela felt it was her sanctuary away from the strict hold of her parents. However, remembering the severity of the previous moments with her husband, she ironically thought how much she missed the small house surrounded by stucco walls that separated the neighbors' houses on both sides.

In all the commotion of the party as the anchor man on TV started counting down the last seconds of the year, she realized that Edward was nowhere in sight. She wondered if he might have stepped outside. Looking for him in the gardens, she could not find him. It seemed strange that when she went back inside and saw all the people embracing and wishing each other a Happy New Year, she realized her cousin, who had come from South America to spend time with the family during the holiday season was missing as well. She went upstairs, looking in every room. As she entered their bedroom, there they were, Edward and Raquel, in her bed kissing and fondling each other with no care of where they were or to whomever may have walked in on them.

"Raquel!" she exclaimed. "What the hell do you think you are doing?" she continued.

Raquel jumped up, picked up her clothes and ran to the bathroom. Edward stayed in bed looking at Micaela like there was nothing wrong with what she had just witnessed. He smirked and told her, "I will be down in a minute."

Micaela did not know what to think. She stood there shocked by the scene, transfixed in time and thoughts. She regained her composure and as she turned to leave, she saw Clara down the hall way. The old woman came to her aid again. Looking at her, she grabbed her hands and told her, "Come here, my child. Everything is going to be okay...If you could survive him five years ago, then what you saw tonight will prove you can survive this with grace and dignity. I am sure of it. You have a great heart, capable of forgiving anything. This too shall pass and you know it," Clara went on.

"Can you make some tea, chamomile tea please," she asked Clara.

"Anything for you, *mi niña*," she responded looking with great empathy into Micaela's sad eyes.

Micaela tried to put on a pleasant a face and went downstairs to the kitchen. She started to drink the tea when her friend came in asking what was going on with her, "No one drinks chamomile tea on New Year's Eve, girl!"

"Where is your champagne?" María continued as she reached for a glass to give to Micaela.

"Now this is New Years Eve, you know" María kidded.

"I am fine, María. I do not want any liquor tonight," Micaela told her friend.

"Something is definitely wrong with you girl!" she added.

"I could not agree with you more." Micaela hugged her friend and wished her a Happy New Year.

In their embrace the friend who knew Micaela quite well, pulled back and intently looking at her face asked, "What is going on?...You can tell me...You know that?" she added.

Edward came downstairs fixing his hair and right behind him was Raquel, smiling at the guests who immediately figured out what had happened and why Micaela opted for the chamomile tea instead of the champagne.

The year started on a such a bad note that Micaela knew her marriage was over. She just needed to place all her ducks in a row and decide how she was going to leave this situation without having her dear mother intervene for Edward. They never said a word about that night. Micaela couldn't bring herself to sleep in their bedroom again. She often stayed with Annabella or opted for the den. During one of these nights, Edward came down and woke her up.

"What the hell?" he asked as he shook her awake.

"What!" Micaela heard herself say.

"What are you doing?" She woke up to his fury. Trying to assess the situation, she quickly got up from the sofa.

"What is wrong with you? Micaela exclaimed at the top of her lungs.

"Why don't you come to bed?" Edward questioned her.

"Because I saw you with another woman in our bed, and I decided that night was the last time I was going to share my bed with you...so go back to it and leave me the hell alone!" she screamed at him. What she felt next was something she had never experienced since the long ago afternoon in the Middle School hallways. Edward slapped her across her face leaving a distinct burning sensation on her skin but mostly in her heart. She could not take the abuse. She knew she had made a huge mistake by marrying him and then having his child, but to be verbally abused and now slapped around, Micaela knew she could no longer stay in her gilded cage overlooking the Pacific Ocean.

Her power of being, the force that was always with her came over her body and she walked away from him to pack a bag for her and Annabella. Edward followed her through the hallway and blocked her from trying to get things out of her closet. Annabella started to cry, Micaela picked her up trying to comfort her. Annabella wrapped herself around Micaela very tightly knowing something was terribly wrong. Edward tried to pull the child away forcefully, and in desperation Micaela tried to hold on to Annabella with all her strength. Edward grabbed Micaela by the arm and flung her across their bed and chaos ensued. Annabella, crying inconsolably, seeing her mother being pushed away by her father cried out, "Don't hurt Mommy! Please you are hurting her, stop!" Micaela tried very hard to compose herself and calmly she got up and told Edward, "Give me Annabella, right now...She does not need to see all this. Look at her! She is hysterical."

"Well, then stop all your stupid nonsense," he retorted.

"Fine, but you do not need to be so cruel. There is no need for you to be so violent," she said very calmly and serenely. She walked down the hallway toward the living room. As she got to the phone, she tried calling 911, but Edward came from behind her and yanked the phone cord out of the wall. He started whipping her with it, screaming and yelling at Micaela without realizing that Annabella was watching with horror.

"Stop, Daddy. You are hurting Mommy!" Annabella cried out.

"Stop!" Micaela yelled.

But to no avail, Edward kept hitting her with the cord grabbing her by the hair, and said, "If you ever think about leaving me, you had better forget about Annabella because you will never have her. Do you hear me?" he yelled at her pushing her up against the wall.

Micaela started to cry feeling very frightened at the thought of having no way out of this situation. When Edward pulled the phone cord out of the wall, she thought the call never reached 911. However, Micaela thanked her lucky stars, because as she was trying to come up with Plan B, the police came knocking on the door.

"Good evening, officer, may I help you?" Edward sounded very normal answering the door.

"Good evening, sir. We had an emergency call come from this address...Is everything okay?" the officer asked looking past Edward into the living room.

"My wife and I are having an argument, but nothing to be concerned about," he went on.

"May I speak with your wife, sir?" the officer added.

"Sure. Micaela could you come here please?" Edward called.

Micaela picked up some clothes for her and Annabella and placed them in a duffle bag, then went down stairs. She took the opportunity to make things right for her once and for all. Among the beautiful things surrounding her with no love or affection from the man she called her husband, this was no way to live a life. She felt strong at this point, the same strength of the women she had heard and watched in South America as she grew up, seemed imbued in her own being. With this energy in her spirit she came down the stairs.

"Good evening, ma'am...is everything okay?" the officer asked.

"No, and thank you for coming so soon...I want to report a case of domestic violence and go to a safer place with my daughter." Micaela told the officer.

"Is this correct Mr. Sims?" the officer asked Edward turning to him.

What! You don't believe me? You fool! Micaela thought to herself as the officer asked Edward.

"No...just a little manhandling that is all. A husband and wife quarrel. She exaggerates," Edward responded.

"Well sir, how tall are you and how much do you weigh?" the officer asked

"What does that have to do with anything!" Edward started to get agitated.

"Answer the questions, please!" the officer retorted.

"Six four and two hundred pounds." Edward answered.

"How about you ma'am?" the officer asked Micaela.

"I am five feet and four inches tall and one hundred fifteen pounds." She answered.

"Well, I don't see how you can call this just manhandling sir. She is too small for you to be manhandling her. You could really hurt her based on these proportions, sir." The officer informed Edward as he went inside the house and saw the phone sprawled on the floor and the room in disarray. "Didn't anyone ever tell you not to ever hit a woman let alone your wife?" The officer asked.

"Ma'am, do you have a safe place to go or someone we can call?...We will be glad to take you there," the officer told her in a very kind sympathetic voice.

"Yes, I can call my parents," she told him.

"Come with me. Everything will be okay," he added reaching to help Micaela and Annabella with their bags.

It seemed rather unreal to leave this beautiful house with its manicured lawns as she opened the police car door and let Annabella enter the vehicle. "It's okay baby, Mommy is going to call mami Paloma. I will be right back." Micaela went to near liquor store and made a phone call to her parents' house. She became even more frightened at the possibility of her mother's ire. She called her brother first, hoping he would come get her, but he was not home. So she tried her only other choice. As the telephone rang she felt a cold sweat come through her spine dripping down her back knowing the energy and strength she needed to leave her house was no longer there when she heard her mother answer the phone.

"Hi, Mom. It's Micaela," she said softly in the phone.

"What is wrong?" she added quickly with a recriminating voice.

"I need to come to your house for the night. Edward and I have ended our marriage in the worst way. I will explain when I get to your house." She went on.

"What do you mean, ended the marriage?" she asked raising her voice.

"We had a real bad fight. He hit me and scared Annabella. Can I please come and spend the night at your house?" she added fearful of the answer.

"I do not understand. You can't leave your home in the middle of the night...Husbands and wives have problems all the time, but they do not call the police and leave their home." She vehemently disapproved of Micaela's actions, making her feel ashamed of what she was doing.

"Mom, I know you do not understand, but it is not safe for us to stay here. Do you understand that?" she asked becoming annoyed at the lack of empathy her mother had for the situation.

"I think you should calm down and talk things through before you rush out of your home like this in the middle of the night," Paloma responded.

"Fine, Mother. I will stay and talk things through," Micaela told her mother holding back her tears and her bruised heart as she hung up the phone. The anger she felt for this woman who gave her life was the same anger Paloma must have felt with her own mother's disdain that awful day she had asked for her blessings. *How can people who have this bond of mother and child be so mean and cruel to one another and why has it trickled down to me? Why can't she be loving and understanding? Why not stop the madness, instead of perpetuating this awful behavior? Is this the way she has always tried to rid herself of that anger?* Micaela thought to herself.

"I can't get a hold of anyone I trust at this moment, but I know there's a shelter for battered women down in Manhattan Beach. I know they would take us for the night...Can you please take us there?" She asked the officer timidly yet stoically holding back her tears.

"Sure ma'am. Come on little one. Get in the police car so you can see how we protect the city at night," the kind officer told

Annabella with such compassion making the child feel safe. "Let me help you with your seat belt, sweet girl."

The police car went very slowly through a dark and ominous looking back alley. Trash and a few homeless people lay to its sides. Micaela reached out for Annabella to comfort each other but she seemed fine next to her. The officer looked back in the rear view mirror and told her, "You are a brave woman, everything will be okay. I can see it in your eyes...Don't be afraid, there is a lot of light in them."

Micaela thought it odd that he used those words but somehow it made her feel a little bit better. He stopped the car in front of the shelter and opened the door for Micaela then letting Annabella out she ran to her mother. The officer opened the door of the shelter. A light went on and a woman in her early forties, a resident of the place, came to open the door. The officer registered his name and the incident on a form and smiled at Micaela empathetically and left. Everything seemed to be happening simultaneously and she was frightened, but she became strong with all the emotions she felt as she realized what the officer had said. She turned to see where he was and said, "What about my eyes?" but he was gone.

The woman led them down a hallway and opened a brown overly painted door to the small dark room with two twin size beds laying perpendicular to one another with hospital sheets folded on top of the beds. Micaela thought nothing for a moment. Physically limp and void of emotion she made the beds and tried to make it comfortable for Annabella as the light went off and the room became even darker and somber. *None of this was supposed to happen to me. What happened?* She thought to herself. *Was I that bad as a child? Was it bad to be a dreamer? I did not ask for any of this...What is the purpose? I must find a purpose in all this!* Micaela kept thinking to herself as she caressed Annabella's hair making her feel at ease and rocking her to sleep in her arms. The warmth of the child made her feel safe and out loud she said, "Thank God for you" placing a tender kiss on her child's forehead. A knock on the door dissipated her whirlwind set of emotions.

A social worker appeared and with great understanding asked Micaela to come out and talk to her for a while.

"Mrs. Sims, I have checked the information you have given us and we cannot keep you here more than just tonight," the social worker informed Micaela.

"You come from a very resourceful and financially secure background and this shelter is for women of low economic means," she added.

"I understand. I could go to a hotel but I am afraid that my husband will try to harass me there...He turned out to be more violent than I would have ever thought...Please let me stay here until I can make the necessary arrangements. I can give a small donation if that will help," she begged the social worker.

"In that case, I will talk to the clinical director and see how long we can let you stay here since this is not a repeat situation, but we cannot let you stay too long." The social worker added.

"I understand...First thing tomorrow I will make the arrangements to leave," Micaela told the woman.

She went back to her room and got in bed with her sweet innocent daughter, who was sleeping peacefully. She did not want to disturb her, so she lay down and stayed very still just trying to hold on to the innocence permeating from her little girl. Many thoughts went through her mind. The noise she thought came from the shelter was all in her head. So much heartache, so much pain and it wasn't coming from this lonesome place which had an eerie silence almost trying to hide all of its inhabitants from the atrocities no one dare to tell. She knew then as she had known when she was a child asking her mother questions about the street converging at its end and getting no satisfactory answer, knowing that her questions were unimportant, knowing that the answers will not come easily. Nothing thus far had come easily to her. She knew she had fallen into a treacherous dark hole of her own doing. Climbing out of it was going to be a challenge, but she would take on that challenge and triumph in the end. Micaela would call on all the 'women' in her past, present and future and they would help her go through the perilous trek she was about to embark on. Her power of being would lead to her pluckiness and from all of this pain the 'ugly duckling' would start shedding her young innocent plumes to make way for the beautiful swan to be born.

Uncharted and Poignant Territories

The life she had come to know after her marriage to Edward had ended, were the most lengthy four years of her life. She had gotten a divorce, had walked away from all the luxuries and to make matters worse, Edward had enough money to buy the lawyer and the judge who gave nothing to Micaela after her eight years of marriage...no alimony and no financial reward for the abuse and oppression to which her marriage had escalated. However, she shed the plumes, and although she unfortunately had become another statistic, she managed to get on with her own life...a single mother in a low paying job, juggling life as well as she could. It was a brisk spring morning that put Micaela in a pensive mood. She never thought of how this relationship would end or how another one would begin, however, this morning she was thinking about her date from last night as she got up and went into the bathroom.

"It is not going to go anywhere," she muttered as she took a long look at herself in the mirror. Making a face of cynical disgust she said to herself, "Cause you ain't putting out, little missy."

She looked hard at herself in the mirror and asked, "Why must you always be such a prude?" She winked at her mirror image, "men don't want that! They want action, they want fun!" she reproached herself out loud.

Wriggling her body and sensually caressing her sides, she continued, "Can't you be fun? Come on! Be a fun girl. Give a little; maybe you'll get a lot!" The cat meowed slinking around her legs and her daughter's "Good Morning, Mummy," interrupted the conversation with herself in the mirror.

Micaela picked up the cat, caressed her daughter's hair as they both came looking for food.

"Hey Mommy, I'm hungry" Annabella pretended to whine like a baby and in the same breath her ten year old daughter, surprisingly sounded like an adult asking about the night before.

"How was last night? Did you have fun?" She asked with a scrutinizing voice, and added "you look weird today. Are you OK?" sizing up her mother.

"Yeah, what makes me look weird, honey?" she asked back.

"Dunno, you just feel weird today," Annabella said shrugging her shoulders.

"OH! Now, I really feel weird, that doesn't make sense, can you explain?" Poking at her daughter's sides.

"Mom!" She shrieked playfully moving away towards the kitchen.

"Come on. You know. You were talking to yourself in the bathroom making faces and all. Isn't that weird?" she said as Micaela saw her put her little fingers in the strawberry jam container.

"Ah! So you were spying on me?" Micaela asked as she retrieved the child's fingers reprimanding her for her daughter's lack of manners.

"No, but I overheard what you said, and what is not putting out?" She looked attentive as she asked such an impertinent question.

Trying to be nonchalant and not patronizing to her poor child, Micaela told her, "Don't worry about that. That is grown up talk and you will soon enough be a grown up!"

They both ran out of the kitchen and jumped onto her bed. She looked up at the clock and realized she was running late for work. "Oops! We better hurry up!" she hurried off the bed and went to the closet doors nearby.

"Come on, come on let's get ready to go, sweet love of mine," as she gently threw her daughter's school uniform across the bed.

Micaela put on a frumpy pleated cotton twill skirt, and the oversized, hand-knitted green sweater she loved so much. It was made of a tweed merino wool in the prettiest kelly/mossy green that reminded one of Irish plains at the end of summer about to meet fall. It was rich in color and texture and she loved how people always complimented her for the way it was made and the whimsical way it made her look and feel, as if she lived in great comfort, imbedded in the sweater threads echoing the wind of faraway lands.

She arrived a little late to work, and the feeling that something dreadful was going to happen set in her heart. She always hated to feel that way because she could feel deep down that overwhelming sensation of the unknown. She thought maybe she would be reprimanded by her late arrival but that wasn't it.

She thought her ex-husband might call her and tell her he would not be picking their daughter up like so many times he had done in the past, but no that was not it either. Uneasy she made the sign of the cross and went about her day. Placing God in her heart by that simple motion made her feel a little bit better. It had always worked so as she sat down at her desk, she did another sign of the cross and said a Hail Mary in her thoughts.

Micaela's office was on the second floor and she shared this windowless space with her coworker, a young woman about her same age who was from Thailand. She was the logistic production manager of the company and her name was Rosie. Micaela always thought that it was a bit strange for a woman from the South Pacific to have such an ordinary American or English name. Why wouldn't it be Taipei or Mei Ling, or something exotic like the place she came from? Micaela asked her one day "Why did your parents give you the name Rosie?"

"That is my American name, "she said with a strong Asian accent.

"What is your Christian name, or your Tai name given at birth?" Micaela insisted

"It is too hard to pronounce, just call me Rosie," the coworker replied.

Rosie was abrupt and kept to herself most of the time. The other times she was too busy looking at herself in the mirror although she was not very attractive. Her features were really pronounced and her upper bite was extremely exaggerated. She was aware of this detail and she always talked with her hand over her mouth. She was very small and thin and had little bitty eyes that were not as almond shaped as most Asian eyes seem to be, but bulged out making her look like a little tiny frog of the prettiest cinnamon brown color.

They sat catty-cornered in this rectangular space. Micaela's desk was placed perpendicular to the wall that faced Rosie's desk, and it also ran along the entrance to the space they called an office. From her seat, Micaela could see clients come into their office. She would greet them and show them around the place. Her desk faced her supervisor's office which had a large window separating the two spaces. The next office was their boss's; he had a very large space with an alcove next to it that was arranged like a den. In the afternoon, Mr. Pollack would go take a nap and would ask not to be disturbed. This was Micaela's favorite time to think about the many ways she would disturb the man if she could. She needed the job so she could not play prankster with her boss, not at her age of thirty-two, she thought with a smirk on her face.

It was right before Mr. Pollack's usual nap time that he called from his house to say he was taking the afternoon off. So Micaela and Rosie were free to do whatever they needed to do, which for Rosie was to be on the phone with the many men she entertained from the companies providing the transportation services. Micaela frowned at her lack of professionalism that made her date and receive gifts from all these men. She used her position with the company for leverage with her personal liaisons. Micaela was in charge of keeping the database and greeting the customers. It made it easy for Micaela to do as she liked, so she would write sometimes. She would also sketch Rosie or one of the flower arrangements Mrs. Pollack would place throughout the rectangular space they called their office.

The morning continued unsettled as it had started. Lunch time seemed never to arrive. They had been talking about the new guy Rosie was going to 'use' for his services. His name was Richard and he was short like her and a little bit pudgy. He had come by a week ago, representing a company, and had taken her out for dinner. Rosie's telephone rang and Micaela turned around at her desk to resume the sketch she had been working on as she picked up the eraser, and when her heart finally seemed to settle down, she saw out of the corner of her eye the figure of a man looking into the glass door that was an emergency exit instead of a door. There was a sign on the outside that read "NO SOLICITING. FOR SHOW ROOM ACCESS, PLEASE GO THROUGH BOTTOM FRONT DOOR, EMERGENCY EXIT ONLY."

She turned and looked at this tall man in a khaki linen suit touching the window with his nose as his hands arched above his eyes, blocking the light, so he could see through the glass door. She looked at him and got up from her desk to tell him that it was not a door, as she motioned for him to go around. She knew she probably looked funny and tried harder to make the man understand what she was saying.

At that point, Micaela looked at Rosie and asked, "Where are the keys?" Rosie took the keys out of her desk and threw them to Micaela.

Rosie was talking to Richard and did not want to be disturbed. *When the cat is gone the mice will play*, Micaela thought to herself, rather upset seeing Rosie's apathy for the poor man outside looking in.

Micaela opened the door. As he entered he stood in front of her. He was tall, very handsome with a sparkle in his eyes that made Micaela weak at the knees. She could not understand what she was feeling. It was as though she had been taken away to a far distant land where time stood still, and all she could see was this Adonis of a man standing in front of her.

He started to apologize for lurking and startling Micaela as he looked through the glass door, "The sun is so bright. I could not even see the sign which says to go around. I beg your pardon, for knocking at this door," he said.

He had a southern drawl that made Micaela think of mint juleps and white porches all fenced in with the biggest and whitest hydrangeas on a hot summer night in the Deep South; where the mansions of an antebellum past would be the only witness to the torrid affair that was about to unfold. The sound of the telephone ringing gave her a jolt that stopped her day dreaming.

Rosie, who refused to play receptionist if Micaela was there, did not pick up the phone even though Micaela had a good hunch that this call was for her. Instead, Micaela heard herself saying, "Please come in. You do not have to apologize. There is no need for you to go all the way around when you are here all ready."

"Well, thank you ma'am," he responded in a voice reminiscent of the dreamy southern accents in "Gone with the Wind."

She directed him to step into the conference room nearby knowing Rosie, who liked to feel important, had anyone who arrived wait in the conference room for her grand entrance. Once in the conference room she extended her hand to shake his and told him, "I am Micaela Sims. How can we help you?"

As in a movie played in slow motion, his hand came into hers with a strong, sensual embrace. Again, she was transported to that far-away land where time stood still. The anxiety and uneasiness of the morning materialized viscerally, with a bitter sweet feeling of foreshadowing the future; she felt a griping warmth yet coldness with a sad feeling in her soul. She felt confused and astonished to feel so much turmoil and many overwhelming emotions at the mere touch of his hand. *What is this?* She thought, trying to let go but wanting to stay holding hands a bit longer. She knew at this moment she did not want to leave the place in which only the two existed, but that ominous feeling always nagging at her heart always, had just crept in.

This is weird, she thought. *I have never felt this way before meeting a man. Is this déjà vu? Do I know him from a previous life?* All these thoughts rushed in a whirlwind, creating abstract visions in her mind. With the savvies of a diplomat she retrieved her hand trying to hide all the feelings and emotions. She felt uneasy again as she introduced Rosie who had entered the conference room, curious to know why Micaela was taking so long to tell her who this person was and announce her entrance.

Micaela apologized by saying, "I thought you were still on the phone, I did not want to interrupt," Rosie excused herself away to the Ladies' Room and Micaela asked this beautiful stranger, "Would you like a glass of water or a soda?"

"A glass of water would be fine," he responded.

As she walked away to get the water, she became frightened at the question in her mind, *Is this love at first sight?* Is this what her friends have talked about so many times and to which she had laughed saying it was pure bullshit and it would never happen to her. "It does not exist," she kept telling herself. Yet the feeling was there and she could not explain all the emotions she was feeling; her stomach was being torn apart from the inside out not from the 'butterflies' but from a sadness she predetermined was in her near future.

She always used comedy at times of great distress and she thought to herself, *Coffee, tea, or me?* She smiled at him as she placed the glass of water in front of him.

"Much appreciated," he said, again in his twang dreamy accent of his southern roots weakening her knees once more.

In the adjacent room, Rosie was putting on lipstick and arranging her hair. Richard had asked her to lunch so she was on her way out, however, he had called her and was unable to make it. This was really no problem for her since she wanted to stay and see what this gentleman had to offer. She came into the conference room.

They exchanged pleasantries and Micaela went back to her desk. From her desk she could see every movement of his body. She felt like she was falling into a vortex falling in love with every feature of this man's being. She felt like a stupid school girl trying to get a glimpse of him to see if he was feeling the same overwhelming feeling that she was experiencing. Micaela found herself calling María, her best friend, and telling her about this man and most importantly, about the way she felt. Rosie and the beautiful stranger talked in the conference room for what seemed like thirty years but it was only thirty minutes!

Rosie came out of the conference room and like many times before when men from other companies came to do business with their company, it was Rosie who got to go out on these obligatory business luncheon or dinners. She informed Micaela that they were leaving and to let Mr. Pollack know where she went if he came in. At this moment, Micaela knew what the green-eyed monster called jealousy was like. She felt infuriated that it was not she who was going out to lunch with him. Politely she remarked, "I will let you know if he calls, of course."

"What do you want me to tell Richard, if he comes in?" she asked as though trying to mark territory for Richard's sake. She knew it was more for her own sake to prevent Rosie from wanting this beautiful stranger.

"Oh, do not worry about him. I already called him." Rosie replied.

The two left the office and Micaela wanted to follow them. The lunch hour became an eternity, but at least when they return, she would ask Rosie what he was like. Maybe Rosie would set them up on a date...she smiled at her desperation.

"I'm Gonna Put a Spell on You," she found herself doing Nina Simone's rendition of the song of the same name. The warmth of his hand was still in hers and she found herself caressing her tummy and letting out a big sigh, but anxiety was starting to set in again.

Rosie returned from the lunch date and she told Micaela about the beautiful stranger for she knew Micaela was expecting it.

"His name is Stavros Pappas, he is from Raleigh, North Carolina and is recently divorced from an ugly witchy woman," she said with a smile on her face.

"I saw how you looked at him," she added.

"He is kind of cute in a southern sort of way, isn't he?" Micaela said it trying to be nonchalant about her feelings. "Stavros Pappas?" she added in disbelief.

"Stavros Pappas, are you sure?" she asked again.

"Yeah, here is his card, you can have it" she responded, "I do not think I will be using him," she added.

"What do you mean, he is not coming back?" Micaela heard herself saying out loud in dismay.

"You need to make him come back," she added sounding a bit disappointed and urging Rosie to make him come back.

"I cannot believe that Stavros Pappas is his name, I have always been enamored with Greek names like Callas, Costas, Pappas, and Pappas has been my favorite like Irene Pappas remember, the Greek actress of the sixties?" she told Rosie.

"I always thought that Micaela Pappas had a good ring to it, don't you think?" she said with a child's innocence.

"Look, Rosie, I do know what is going on but I have to have this man. Please make him come back and take me to lunch so I can meet him in a non business situation." She was almost pleading to Rosie.

"I wrote a poem about the way I felt when I first saw him. Do you want to hear it?" unaware of how much this would cost her in the end.

"Sure." Rosie agreed.

Like a proud student reciting her work, Micaela let Rosie know exactly how she had felt at the moment of opening the door and touching his hand.

> In the tender touch of your handshake,
> I knew of faraway lands that are warmed by the purest sunlight beams,
> bringing rejoice to tired hearts.
> In the tender touch of your handshake,
> I saw my future full of delight,
> as one day in the twilight of morning anew
> I will love you so deeply, so gently your heart will throb as much as mine did
> when your eyes met mine.
> In the splendor of our nights
> my body will burn in your love with the intensity of the purest sunlight beam,
> bringing joy to my tired and lonely heart.

It was a mistake Micaela would regret for a long time, for Rosie seemed to show excitement at the prospect of setting another appointment with him. She let Micaela think she was going to set up a casual meeting where they could be re-introduced. Unfortunately, Rosie had seen how Micaela had reacted from the first moment, so she had arranged to see him again that night, something she decided to keep from Micaela. Stavros would later tell Micaela about this easily forgotten detail after Rosie came back from lunch.

That night, Micaela could not sleep thinking about how Rosie was going to set up this meeting. She wondered as she tossed and turned all night, how soon would it be, and how long is he staying in town? She could not wait to get dressed, go to work, and start plotting the ways she was going to 'put a spell on him.' She washed her long hair and let it air dry so the sensual curls that framed her oval small face would dance invitingly for the new man in her life.

She put on a white cotton Fishermen sweater and a blue silk polka-dotted pleated skirt. She loved this outfit because it made her feel like a movie star of the '30's. The billowy pleats embraced her small waist allowing the curve of her hips to sway and rustle the pleats as she walked. The bulky sweater was just the opposite to the softness of the skirt and it gave her that look that was only hers...kind of tailored yet with an 'artsy' flair. "Roman Holiday" always came to mind every time she wore this outfit and the streets of California's South Bay area became the cobble stoned narrow streets found in Rome as she walked imaginatively through the ruins of such a place and the breeze of the ocean nearby filled her heart with joy.

"Silly you!" She whispered, as she put a blue ribbon in her hair and a little make up on her eyes and Vicks Vaporub on her lips. "He really is going to want to kiss grandma, with the smell of menthol on her lips," she thought smiling and looking in the mirror as she walked out of the house.

When she got to the office, Rosie was there telling her that last night he had called her and that they had gone out. Micaela felt like a bucket of ice water had just been poured over her. Then she felt her face turn red in anger about the conniving ways she instinctively knew this woman was working to show her that she would win this competition, in which Micaela never wanted to be a participant. She had read the poem in which she professed so much love for this man. *What kind of person does this? Doesn't she realize that this hurts? What a vermin!* She thought.

Rosie told her, "Tonight, we are meeting after work again, and maybe you want to join us."

"No, thanks," she replied trying to hide her anger.

"I don't want to take away from what you have going on with this guy," Micaela added. "Plus, he is Greek and God forbid I go out with a Greek guy. They are perverted you know?" She heard herself saying this and to her own amazement she found herself convinced of the words she was saying. Actually, she always wanted to be connected with Greece in some way. What better way than to marry a Greek man with a Greek last name like Pappas? Her favorite last name in the world had been Pappas, yet it would never be hers. She could see Rosie making sure of this!

That conniving little bitch! She pretended to care and made me believe she would set me up with him. I can't believe it. She thought to herself as she walked toward her desk and sat down. She started to do some work but the heavy feeling in her heart sat along with her.

Rosie continued telling her about the night before. They had gone to dinner and she had taken him home to introduce him to her uncle. He was a pharmaceutical chemist with a prominent corporation. *Why is she telling me this?* She thought.

Rosie said that he was really nice and that he had already invited her to visit his home in Raleigh. Micaela said to her, "That was quick! What are you going to do with Richard? So this is your new catch? But, I saw him first, Rosie," she grimaced a pouting gesture pretending this was a joke.

In reality, all Micaela really wanted to do was to rip her frog-looking eye balls out of their sockets. *Now, now that is too brutal. Put them back,* She thought to herself smiling at Rosie and saying, "I guess that doesn't matter much does it? Well, I hope he does not turn out to be one of those Greek men that abuse women and make them walk three steps behind them." She chuckled and walked away knowing that he was not like that.

Around 2:00 p.m. in the afternoon, Rosie got a call from a relative who told her that a cousin had been in an accident and she was needed at home. Micaela remembered what Rosie had told her about meeting with him again after work and thought maybe fate was on her side, only to discover that what she thought was a fortunate opportunity would become the most poignant moment of her adult life. She was about to find out how much being in a state of grace would cost. How painful would it be to succumb once again to the 'pressures of love' when you think you love someone and the feeling is not reciprocated. She would know firsthand how lonely one could feel even when surrounded by people, how helpless one becomes even when kindness abounds and most important how ignorant we become in the presence of knowledge, but it is only for our innate power of being to make things right for all of us in the end.

Rosie had to leave in a hurry and told Micaela, "Stavros is going to call to tell me where we are meeting tonight," then added, "Please relay the message about my cousin and that I will meet him later at my house." She gave these directions to Micaela without thinking or maybe really thinking about the pain it caused her.

She went about her business and there in the middle of this tiny space they called an office she stood flaccid, feeling faint and sure that her body at any minute with the smallest gust of wind would make her plunge into a deep and dark precipice. She sat down and as she did, she felt like a lump of clay void of shape and form much like her heart...void of feelings and emotions, only to be restored by the picture of her daughter on her desk staring at her. It was a blessing to see those little pudgy cheeks, big brown eyes smiling at her, reassuring her everything will be okay by the mere presence of the two-dimensional space surrounded with a flowery frame of tulips and sweet peas.

She arranged her bow and told herself everything was going to be okay. She had a beautiful daughter to take care of and so she did not need a man in her life. So she had fallen in love at first sight, so he was Greek with her favorite Greek last name. "I bet there are other Pappas around town that I will find and marry," she said to herself licking her wounds.

She proceeded to mentally get up from the disappointment and do as she had always done...put any painful episodes aside and let the pain roll off her back continuing with the task at hand. She needed to make money so she could finally start doing the things she really wanted to do--buy a house and not live in an apartment, give her daughter the piano lessons she never had and the pretty dresses her daughter did not even want. But those things would make her happy she knew, so who cares if he is the one to own her heart yet his would never be hers. *I can still love him and make him mine with every breath I take. He will enter my soul and stay as the painful ache that no medicine can take away, and in this way, he will always be mine,* she thought to herself knowing this was going to be true for a long time.

She tried to stop thinking about the conniving ways of her coworker, but she could not. She kept thinking how she had poured out her heart to her with her poetry, and told her that this is the first time she had ever felt this way. Rosie had smiled and said, "Oh my gosh girl, you really have fallen for him."

The telephone rang and every time it did her heart trembled. The anxiety encapsulated her body making it go hot and cold at the same time. And when the voice on the other end wasn't his, she felt relieved. She did not want to hear his voice, because she knew if she heard it again it would make her envision the way he smiled his handsome brown eyes. She tried to keep busy, making lot of calls to clients that needed to come and visit the warehouses or the showroom. Anything she could do that afternoon, got done so the thought of him would not enter her mind. She had just managed to forget about him when the telephone rang and she answered it with her sweet professional way which made clients tell her that it was her soft spoken foreign accent that made it a delight to call the company.

She froze; it was him saying, "Hello, may I speak with Rosie, please?" She did not know what to say. After seconds of complete silence and being flustered she came back to her senses and apologized for not speaking right away. Micaela fixed everything with laughter and she made a joke to which he laughed making her heart skip a beat. She composed herself and ever so charmingly she answered. "I am sorry, you caught me at a moment when I could not answer right away."

"That is okay," he replied and persisted, "is Rosie there?"

"Oh, I am sorry again. No, she is not here," she heard herself saying, "she left a message for you..."and before she could finish the message the screeching sound of tires and a sudden stop played in her mind and she thought if Rosie wanted to play dirty after knowing how she felt about this guy, she could too.

"She said she would meet you at Mr. Frogs and that if you cannot meet her there she would call you later. Do you know how to get there?" She asked him.

"No, I don't believe I do," he answered sort of disappointed.

His disappointment became the dagger piercing her stomach tearing her apart. It was true they had spent the time together that Rosie said they had.

"Do you know how to get there?" he added.

"Sure, matter of fact I was going to go there this afternoon after work for happy hour," Micaela said nonchalantly.

"I can probably meet you there if you'd like and wait with you until Rosie gets there." How wicked she had become from the moment she met this beautiful man she thought with a devilish flirtatious smile on her face.

"Sure, if you don't mind," he answered.

Micaela almost dropped the phone, fell to the floor and died. However, she kept her composure and said charmingly, "Well, take the 405 South to Long Beach. About 30 minutes down the road you will come to Bellflower Street. Take a left, get in the far left lane right away and you will see a 'street named desire.' Just kidding," she said sheepishly. He laughed and that made her happy.

She continued with the directions making her voice more sensual and soft, "The name of the street is Studebaker in which you will make a left and you will see the big canopies overlooking the ocean. She told him about the killer Piña Coladas they make and he told her that he preferred Strawberry Daiquiris. "That is a girl's drink. What are you talking about?" She kidded with him.

"Well, I guess I like girly drinks," he said playfully.

She could not believe her ears at the tone of his voice playfully talking to her. Heaven!...she was touching heaven. "Silly girl," she told herself, "he wants you..NOT!"

Rejoicing from their conversation and meeting him later, Micaela forgot about the wicked way she had decided to relay the wrong message. This is a prospective service provider and here she was playing with fire. But the love bug had bitten her again after all these years and she was delirious!

Micaela made arrangement for a baby sitter, hardly believing her good fortune.

"So, I'll see you around 5:00 or 5:30 p.m." She hopefully waited for a response.

"That sounds good," he replied.

She looked at the time and it was about 4:00 p.m., so it was only about an hour and a half that this torture would last until she came into his presence and succumbed to whatever the future was preparing for her. Work came to its end and full of anticipation she left the building. It was a warm and lazy afternoon, promising nightly delights with the sun setting far away in the distance. She got a glimpse of herself being highlighted by a phosphorescent gleam of light reflecting from her car window. Her light olive skin became a glimmering bronze making her curls and their shadows dance around her face. "Oh how beautiful the shapes and colors of nature are," she whispered to herself.

The scene made her think how beautiful this picture of a woman running to see her lover would play out on the big screen.

She often fantasized about the many facets one finds in nature that can easily become slogans with pictures that tell a thousand stories. "Well, art imitates life. That is where we get all the inspiration," she told herself.

She smiled and entered her car, rolled down the windows allowing the breeze to come through and rearrange her hair. It made her look more like the sensual creature she was feeling at the moment in anticipation of meeting with Stavros. She remembered the change in her being since touching his skin in their handshake. Words started to appear in her mind filling many pages of her journals. Feelings were becoming more sensual than the previous ones. She found herself looking at her breasts and thinking of him caressing them ever so gently. At night, she would lay aching with desire while thinking of how it would be to lay next to him and smell his natural scent mixed with her sweat and French perfume after loving him like a wild creature meshed in this great love he inadvertently invited her to feel.

Is this what loves feels like or is it just lust? She thought to herself. "You never felt this way. Even at seventeen, your hormones never raged like this. Why now and not then. Why him and not any other? A tear rolled down her cheek thinking of times in the past when she had desperately wanted to feel this way, but the thought of her mother admonishing her was ever-present. *You have to be a good girl!* That was what she always thought to herself until now, until Stavros came along. Now the passion flowed through her veins and she felt alive.

She felt like she could conquer the world. She became strong and just wanted to be with him, embrace him to let him know how he made her feel in such a very short time...her heart inflamed with desire and her senses numbed with expectations. Micaela drove down Pacific Coast Highway with the breeze caressing her hair and the music on the radio promising romance. She arrived at the place in Long Beach. She entered a bit uneasy at what the future held with this stranger who had come into her life disrupting the goodness and sense of Victorian propriety she had always held dear.

She sat down at the bar next to a gentleman who sized her up and down with an approving wicked smile as he got closer and offered to buy her a drink. "Hi, I love your outfit. Are you from here?" he asked.

"Yep, from Redondo," she said looking over his shoulder, hoping to find Stavros among the crowd.

"Oh, a local girl. But you have an accent? He continued.

"Where is it from, France? It sounds French or I dare to say Mediterranean?" he went on.

"Nope, it is Latin American. I am from South America." Still looking over his shoulder paying no attention to the way he looked at her.

"Let me buy a pretty South American girl a drink," he said with a fake conviction.

"No, thanks, I am waiting for someone," she added getting up from the stool moving away from the bar and him.

"Well, if he doesn't show up I am going to be here waiting to buy you that drink!" he exclaimed a bit loud. Micaela smiled back knowing that men wanted her and hoping Stavros would feel the same about her.

The sunset of an hour ago was disappearing rapidly and she always loved to see all the different hues encompassed by the redness of the sun's more vibrant light. The ocean started to get dark and the red/brown sunlight flickered in its movement.

"Hey! How are you? I have been looking for you and was about to leave 'cause I didn't see you," the voice with the lazy twang southern accent came from behind her. She wanted to scream out loud, "Let's get out of here so I can love you forever."

She turned around feeling something gripping her tongue so that the words wouldn't come out, until he said, "Are you okay?"

"Oh, yeah, I am sorry, I was thinking about the sunset and the awesome colors it makes on the water," she added in disbelief that she was telling him things that were very dear to her without even thinking. "My thoughts are already his," she said it to herself in disbelief once again.

He looked at the horizon and said, "Yeah, that is very pretty, but it is getting darker."

"Do you want to have a drink?" he asked, dismissing her observation of the beautiful hues and tonalities of the night appearing before their eyes.

She felt a sort of sadness, and trying to dispel it, she answered, "Sure, I bet you I know what you want," she added very sweetly, alluding to the way she had remembered what he liked to drink by the conversation they had had earlier.

"Oh, so you remember?" he added patronizingly surprised.

"Of course! When a strong man like you likes a sissy drink like that, of course one remembers," she said smiling a big flirtatious smile.

"Thanks a lot! So is that what California girls do? Call people names from the first time they meet them?" he said it in a reprimanding comedic tone.

"No, I am sorry. I just wanted you to know I remembered our conversation earlier," she added painfully showing regret.

"I noticed," he added again dismissing her regret.

"What do you want to drink?" He continued to ask.

"I'll have what you are having," Micaela answered immersing herself into every form and plane of his olive skin and dark brown eyes sparkling with a brightness that made her feel dizzy, falling in the same precipice as the morning.

She pretended it was just the two of them dancing throughout the room. She saw his natural smile that accentuated a dimple in his cheek viewing his face, she saw his chiseled nose...a nose sculpted better than Michelangelo's "David," she thought. He was her Adonis incarnate and she would be the goddess that would succumb to his every desire she thought as she walked behind him wanting to grab him and be with him in the twilight brought by the disappearing sun.

The sound of Caribbean music, "Reggae," to be exact started to fill the room. She thought to herself how appropriate the music was with its simple syncopated rhythm making the sensual melody be reminiscent of the short sexual strokes one takes leading to the crescendo of a climax in the arms of the one you love. She already loved him so sweetly that along with the music, she craved to be dancing this dance of love and to have these moments engraved permanently in her heart and soul.

Abruptly, he gave her the drink, "Try it, see if you like my sissy drink," he added winking at her.

"Do you like the music?" she asked him as she reached for her drink.

"It's all right. I really have not heard this music before," he added looking around.

"You are kidding me, right?" she exclaimed in disbelief.

"Not really," he answered as he looked and sized up a girl walking by.

"I am sorry, but Rosie is not able to meet us here tonight," she delivered the bad news as to get even with him for checking out the other girl.

"Oh, she isn't coming?" he asked in response.

"No," she said and continued to explain what had happened with the cousin.

"Oh, is her cousin going to be all right?" he asked.

"I really do not know. She is going to try to make it later, she told me," Micaela lied.

"Maybe, I should call her," he added.

Micaela saw herself in the window reflecting her image and heard herself say, "What are you doing. You do not belong here. Why don't you leave now before it is too late and you get in trouble at work?"

"Did you say something?" he asked.

"No, just thinking out loud," Micaela responded.

"Why don't we go outside, so I can hear what you are saying!" he said loudly and seemingly interested as he invited her to go outside.

"Sure!" she answered moving about the crowd and having guys look at her as she passed by.

"So what happened with Rosie's cousin?" he wanted to know.

"I really don't know," she answered upset at his insistence.

"All I know is that she got a call and then had to leave early, then I talked to you," she added.

"Then right before I left work, she called again and she said she cannot meet with you but will try if she can later." She lied again and felt bad that she had to resort to this type of underhanded action on her part to meet up with this man who came to disrupt her safe and untouched world.

"Oh, well!" he sounded resigned.

"So tell me how long have you been with the company?" he asked wanting to know about her, Micaela sensed.

"I have been there only about a year, but Rosie has been there for about six years or so, I think she told me once," she responded to the real question.

"Oh, do you get along with her?" he asked her, detecting the annoyance in Micaela's voice.

"Oh, yeah!" she answered quickly.

"I have not found a person yet that I do not like," she said with a smile.

"Is that right?" he sounded patronizing.

"Yep! I tried to find the goodness in every scoundrel that comes my way," she added.

"Oh, scoundrel huh?" he questioned and winked again.

"I feel it is better to find the goodness in people, until they prove you wrong," she added.

"Rosie, is a nice girl. A bit flirtatious...she has too many men calling her," she said in a factual way letting him know he would be wasting his time with her.

"Oh!" he responded in a way that Micaela couldn't read.

"For example, right now she is seeing one of the salesmen of a local transport company," she continued snitching on her coworker.

"Who is this guy?" he asked.

"I don't know just some local salesman, but enough of Rosie. Tell me about you," she asked excited to know about his life.

He went on telling her that he had been born in South Carolina but attended college in North Carolina, at Chapel Hill, and had majored in political science. Once he earned his degree, he married his college sweetheart, Penny, only to see her die a year later. He looked pensive but not sad.

Micaela thought that was an awesome way to remember someone you have loved. He was not sad but in his pensive mood, she saw him longing for her. It made her love him more because of such a delicate way he remembered this woman he once loved. Enumerating the catastrophes he had gone through after that moment in time, it came down to the evil woman he just divorced with whom he had two beautiful children but had made his life hell.

Micaela thought to herself, "Foiled against the sweet woman his deceased spouse had been, the second one had no chance." They had settled in North Carolina after graduation and he had made a life for himself in sales.

"How come you are not working or running for office?" she asked jokingly.

"I do not know," he answered looking around and annoyed at the noise.

"Do you want to have another drink or do you want to go someplace else?

"Well, how many strawberry daiquiris is this I am about to finish?" she asked feeling a bit hot due to the alcohol starting to mix in her blood.

"I am not counting, are you?" he responded as he grabbed her hand and pointed toward the exit.

"I guess we are leaving," she said following him and wrapping her arms around his waist.

"Where to?" he asked.

"There is a bar down the street that plays southern rock for those out-of-towners like yourself," she said winking at him.

"You are cute, you know," he said looking intently at her.

Micaela felt as if she was floating on air. Not being able to feel the concrete floor of the parking lot, she realized they were walking toward his car.

"Do you want to drive two cars, or do you want me to drive you around," he asked.

"I do not know. What do you think?" she responded.

"Well, I think we better go together 'cause you know where we are going and can direct this 'out-of-towner' around," he said it playfully getting very close and opening the car door for her.

"Get in, little girl. Let's blow this joint," he said laughing.

Micaela started to feel a little tipsy from the alcohol. She opened the window to get some fresh air. She knew she could not handle alcohol very well and as the sad drunk she had a habit of being, she wanted to sober up a little bit.

They got to the place nearby called *Night Secrets* and he laughed at the name, asking her "How often do you come here?"

"Every night, of course," she answered playfully.

"I bet," he responded as he opened her door.

"You are such a gentleman. Are all southern men like this?" she asked.

"I dunno," he shut the door behind her.

They went into the place and not a soul was in the house. Stavros playfully said, "Are they waiting for you to start partying or is it like this every night?"

"They are waiting for me, of course!" she added winking at him.

They went to the bar. He ordered a Scotch and soda and asked Micaela what she wanted to drink. As he sat there waiting for Micaela to answer, she could not help stare at him wanting to be in his arms whispering sweet nothings like she had never done before. She thought for a while about her new manner. She was not the "typical" Latin girl who is often referred to as hot; Micaela was much more methodical, calculating and less compulsive than this. But this night, she was out of control, feeling urges that were totally out of character with her refrained persona, if mom could see me now she would not like this one bit! Was this stranger, whom she hoped would become the one and only in her life, the reason she was being so audaciously refreshing? She believed then, that this man was the one she would love the way most people talk about the love of their life, something she had never experienced. The total giving of oneself without thinking about the consequences of such actions, and without even thinking about the three strawberry daiquiris in her system, she responded. "I'll have my usual...gin and tonic, please," she sounded like a spoiled child about to get her way and how delicious that feeling was.

She moved to the dance floor and signaled him to come over with her little finger. Stavros got up from his seat and as he approached her he teased her.

"Someone has had a bit too much to drink, I think, 'cause that is the wrong finger to use," he told her grabbing her by her waist and pulling Micaela toward him getting very close and they started dancing the slow song coming out from the jukebox.

Micaela could not believe this moment was happening. A long time ago, she had conquered a young man and persuaded him to be her high school sweetheart. The feeling tonight, although it had a taste of conquest, felt a lot different. It was not a capricious feeling trying to take from Rosie the man she already had lassoed in the night before, but rather it was an overwhelming feeling that she had arrived at the core of her own being. Micaela felt a passion never felt before. It flowed through her veins burning with a heat that reverberated in her heart, clouding her senses as she wanted to love this man like she never had loved before. *Have I loved him like this already? Has he been in my life once before? Why do I feel so close to him?* She found herself asking as he let go of her, going toward the bar where the drinks awaited them.

"You dance very provocatively," he said in a weary sort of admonishing way.

"There is a sensual wickedness about you that I better stay away from," he added with a smile, which was much more than what Micaela tried into read in what he was saying.

"Do you approve or disapprove of my new sensuality?" she retorted.

"What do you mean, new sensuality?" he asked perplexed.

She moved gently close to him and found herself telling him, "I have never danced with such strong feelings of sensuality; a sexual urge came over me as you got closer."

"Before tonight, I have danced to the beat of the music. Now, however, it was not the music I danced to...it was to your beat. I wanted to feel your body next to mine to take away its heat making us one using the music as a disguise," she told him with a sincere emotion, feeling the trembling in her lips.

The anxiety she had experienced before became the force of an avalanche inside her heart and she continued trying very hard to be cautious, but failing terribly. Fearing the worst or the best she got close to his face and she touched his mouth. Playing with it, she exposed its delicate, moist, rosy flesh and stole a kiss from him. She had longed for this moment from the first time they shook hands and now it was hers. The fear and the anxiety turned into fierce desire. She moved back and looking into his eyes, she whispered in Spanish *"vas a romper mi corazón, pero no importa. Esta noche quiero ser de ti."*

He grabbed her waist and pulling her from the stool they left the bar, as if he understood what she had just said, "I know you'll break my heart tonight but nevertheless, tonight all I want is to be yours." She felt like she was running to paradise where sweet manna and the embrace of her beloved promised an eternity of bliss. Reality hit when they came into the parking lot structure, found his car and opened the door for her to get in. As he got in, he motioned to get close to him. Micaela knew she would play this moment time after time again and again for the rest of her life. She knew that she would regret what was about to happen, but she did not care. At this moment, she knew she wanted him like she never had wanted any other man. The raging hormones of a deprived youth, the admonishment of her mother always insisting she needed to be a good girl, the name calling of her ex-husband of being a goody-two shoes bitch...all of these times in her young life were present at this moment becoming the agitators enticing her to be in the rapture of the moment which Micaela so desperately wanted to be a part of with the company of the beautiful stranger sitting next to her.

He stopped at a liquor store, before going to his hotel room and bought some champagne. "I have never been with a Spanish girl and never, never have I been wooed in a foreign tongue," he said with an excitement matching her desire that only added fire to an already flaming one.

"You are a beautiful woman. Why would you want to be with the likes of me?" he asked not in disbelief but rather in acknowledgment of his good fortune.

They arrived at the hotel and entered the room. He started to open the bottle and offered her to change into one of his shirts. "Get comfortable, girl!" he instructed her with excitement.

Micaela liked being called "girl" the way he did in his southern twang. For the first time in her life she felt like a woman. A young woman, reckless and in love, full of unknown passion reverberating in her mind, asking her to stop at times and then wanting to go on. Although, in the midst of her inebriated state Micaela knew she was where she wanted to be. She wanted him like she had never wanted anyone before and she did not care to intellectualize the fact that all this could be only for this night and never more.

"The chance exists that he will never feel the same way you are feeling now, you know?" she told herself out loud and he asked her "What are you talking about?"

"Nothing, never mind," she responded quickly and added,

"How do I look, *c'est si bon*"

"What is that...Spanish again?" He asked.

"No, this is French," she said reaching for the glass of champagne he was offering now.

"How many languages do you speak?" he asked curious and interested in knowing.

"All the Romance languages, I suppose," she answered not interested in divulging her knowledge.

"Come here, girl," he grabbed her and gently threw her in the middle of the King sized bed and started to kiss her. Opening her shirt he stared at her small frame and surprisingly with a tone of approval he said, "you are white."

"What do you mean, 'You are white?'" She repeated feeling annoyed.

"I am not white, but I am a fair skinned Hispanic maiden. There are many of those around, you know?" she told him sounding bothered by his insinuation of approving her skin tone, yet trying to dispel her annoyance to continue loving him. Because no matter what, that night she was going to love him like she had never loved anyone else.

"You smell so good, and I like the way you feel. Your skin is so soft," he said very gently, cunningly going down her stomach and kissing it so sweetly yet demonically going down into her 'wetness' kissing it ever so gently and entering her with the witchery of fierce desire. Despite the intensity of the moment, Micaela felt uneasy since they had danced and frolicked and she wanted to bathe before they made love. She tried to move away, "I need to freshen up" she added.

"I do not want to smell soap or anything that will take away from the smell of you, so let me love you the way I see in your eyes you want to be loved, girl!" he told her pulling her opened legs closer to him.

She relinquished her body and soul and the ecstasy of his caress came rushing like a tumultuous wave of fire burning her senses, making her cry because it was the first time she had actually climaxed from the touch of a man. She knew he existed and that all her pent up emotions of being a good girl for mom would be dispelled in the primal scream she would share with this man. Stavros lay next to her bringing to fruition every fantasy she had contained in the deep corner of her soul with the passion she had only known and craved in a previous life.

Micaela wanted to love him back the way he had just loved her, sitting up and reaching for his enlarged penis she placed it in her lips. The feeling of ecstasy she felt a moment earlier left her hearing his voice say, "I am sorry, honey, you are just too hot...I could not stop myself."

Micaela stopped him and said, "Please do not apologize, you have done what no one has ever done for me."

"I just wanted to love you back," she added and went on to kiss his groin, as she got close to his extended penis some of its sperm was still spilling onto her lips. She never thought she would do something like this. She caressed him and the rest of the liquid from her fingers she place on her lips watching him and loving him she said, "The sweet manna has been given to this mere mortal, my beautiful Adonis."

"You are something else and your melodrama just makes you more enticing, you know?" he exclaimed as he chuckled and sat up at the top of the bed motioning her to come closer.

His tone of voice and choice of words told her that this was not supposed to have happened. She knew this was the one night stand she would talk about in her lonely moments. She knew it was not what she had hoped for...it was done. *Tomorrow will come and it will be another day,* she thought to herself as she saw herself finding refuge in the arms that will not hold her like this ever again. In a sweet embrace they fell asleep.

She woke up early in the morning and asked him to take her back to her car, to which he just sounded a bit annoyed, "Now?"

"I need to get home. Maybe we can see each other later," she added hoping for a positive response. Unfortunately nothing was said, so they went out into the morning light without speaking a word. When they got to the parking lot, her car was the only one there amidst the lines demarcating the parking spaces, unable to be seen at a distance for the fog coming from the ocean made them disappear in the distance. She felt sad unlike the night before in those brief moments of complete happiness and euphoria. She identified with her car, left all alone and unattended in the desolate parking lot amidst the enshrouding fog and cold ocean breeze.

"I will call you later," she found herself saying.

"Okay," he responded nonchalantly.

All the other times when she had a break up, there was always a song on the radio that coincidentally paralleled with the circumstances of how the relationship ended, however, this time there was no music, only the news telling the bad things happening around the world, foreshadowing the anguish and disillusion she would come to feel. She arrived at her apartment complex to see her neighbor watering her plants.

"Good morning, Micaela!" the old woman yelled out.

"Good morning, Ms. Stein," she responded with a smile, trying to ignore the look of her neighbor at her disheveled appearance. She opened the door and went into the living room. The sound of the T.V. was loud in the other room. As she peeked into the den she saw her daughter dressed and her hair done in ponytails.

"Hi, Mummy," her daughter was up and greeted her with a hug.

"You look terrible. Why is your hair so messy?" grabbing her tangled tresses as she planted a big kiss on Micaela's cheek.

"Did you stay with Maria again? I know how those Italian girls are," the child said with a disapproving tone that made Micaela feel ashamed for showing up like this for her daughter to see.

"No, I went out with other friends and we had a ball. I danced the night away, just the way mommy likes, you nosey little thing," she responded tickling her, feeling a bit sad having lied to her poor innocent child.

Squirming away from her, Annabella exclaimed, "Don't tickle me, Mom!"

She felt lonely and tried to comfort herself by loving her young child, but still the loneliness started to creep in.

The baby sitter announced that she would no longer be able to baby sit because of school, but told Micaela that she had a friend that could.

"Well, that is too bad, Rachel. I am going to miss you and so will Annabella," Micaela heard herself saying but without any feeling as if she had been emptied of all emotion. Feeling as if she was in a box containing parts of a human being that resembled her. It was a strange feeling that would never go away.

"I am going to miss you, Rachel," Annabella whined.

"We both are going to miss you. You have been a great help to me," Micaela added as she got closer to Rachel and gave her a hug.

She held Rachel as if it was Stavros she was saying good bye to. Rachel looked at Annabella with an expression of what is going on?

Annabella shrugged her shoulders and went into the kitchen. "Do you want some coffee, Mom?" she asked.

"No Sweetie, I am fine I picked up some Chai tea on my way home," she added.

Annabella left the room and as Micaela opened the door for Rachel to leave, standing in the threshold, Rachel asked Micaela, "Are you okay, Ms. Sims?"

"Yeah, why?" she answered.

"You seem to be miles away."

"I am hoping this day will go by fast. There are many things I need to do, so I am just going over them in my head...I am sorry for making you worry about me. You are a very sweet young girl. Don't lose that empathy for people, you hear?" Micaela responded feeling a melancholic mood coming over her.

"Thank you, I will remember that. See you around," Rachel said as she walked away.

"We do not have school today, Mommy," Annabella told her mother as she came back into the living room.

"Why is that?" Micaela asked her child.

"I told you already and gave you the paper the school sent home. Did you forget already? You silly goose!" the child added.

"That is right, holy cow! I still have to go to work and now I am going to have to take you to grandma's," she started to get breakfast ready and in a rush had forgotten that Annabella was not going to school.

"Come on Annabella, I can't be late for work because of your dawdling," she admonished her daughter as she took her sweet time getting ready to go to her grandmother's.

"What is wrong Mom?" Annabella sounding annoyed.

"I told you I do not have school today…Are you here today with us on earth?" she added.

"Don't get smart with me young lady!" Micaela tried to dispel her sadness for she knew she was regretting the night before and was becoming scatter brained with the awful thoughts in her head.

"Hurry up. I still have to go to work and I need to take you to grandma's," she told her child still distracted thinking what she would tell Rosie once she became aware of what had happened.

"Can I take my backpack with my toys?" Annabella asked.

"Of course. You know the drill when you go to grandma's," she retorted.

"Here Mommy. Can you zip it up?" showing the open back pack full of stuffed animals.

"Looks like you're taking your whole bedroom here!" Micaela exclaimed annoyed at her own misdirected anger she displayed toward her daughter.

"You said I could take my toys," Annabella retorted.

"Yes, but not your whole collection!" she added at her child's insistence.

They went back and forth until the phone rang. It was her mother, asking precisely what time was she bringing Annabella.

"I am coming right now, because I need to get to work," she told her mother.

"Okay," Paloma said coldly and went on to give Micaela directions on what to do before she came to drop her child off.

She asked her to stop by the bakery on the way and get some bread for the night supper so they could have a family dinner.

"Well, Mom I don't know if I'll be able to stay," she spoke into the receiver.

"Okay?" she added.

Paloma, was telling her all about the dinner she had planned but she needed to leave in order to make it early to work.

"Mom, I need to hang up now, I will see you in a bit and with your bread for tonight, okay?...Bless me," she told her mother sounding a bit annoyed.

It had been a tradition from antiquity to ask for your parents' blessing every time you say hello or good bye to each other. Her other siblings sometimes forgot to ask for the blessing and it was Micaela who kept the tradition alive. Micaela felt comforted by the gesture when her mother would make the sign of the cross on her forehead.

She went into the bathroom to get ready and in a rush, grabbed the first thing that came out of her closet. It was a pretty dress made of the lightest yellow hue in silk charmeusse cut on the bias and gathered at the waist. She added a big bulky black belt and the black low heel patent leather shoes made the whole ensemble. She put a little bit of make-up on and let her curly hair naturally air dry. She went to the bakery wondering why was her mother so intransigent to request things at such odd times. She only requested them from Micaela, as to test her daughter's patience and devotion to her and sometimes the requests were outrageous.

Micaela got to her mother's house, exhausted thinking about Stavros and the moments they had spent together; wondering whether he would want to see her again or not. Trying so hard not to think of his kiss and his touch, she found herself answering questions and more questions from her inquisitive mother and requests by everyone. She felt exhausted.

"Hello, Mami Paloma," Annabella said as soon as they opened the door to her grandmother's house.

"*Hola, bella,*" Micaela's father greeted Annabella.

For Antonio Galarza, Annabella was his *bella*.

Micaela felt so good to hear her father refer to her daughter as beautiful, as though living vicariously through her child's camaraderie with her father, which she missed as she was growing up in South America without him.

"Good morning Annabella," Paloma greeted her granddaughter coming out of her bedroom.

"Hi, Mami Paloma," the child answered.

"So where is your mother going and why you are not going to school?" she asked as if there was a conspiracy and she needed to know about.

"Mom, I told you over the phone…I forgot that today they do not have school and I did not make prior arrangements. I am sorry for putting this on you at what seems to be at the spur of the moment." Micaela saw herself as the chastised child apologizing needlessly to her mother and letting in her feelings of despair reverberate, coming with a force of a tidal wave bringing her off into the torment of guilt and anxiety that her mother always managed to do so well.

"Well, you know what your younger sister says to you every time you manage to have one of your emergencies," Paloma admonished Micaela.

"Yes, Mom!…I know, 'My irresponsibility does not constitute her emergencies.'" she told her mother. Her younger sister was helpful but it was always conditionally done. Everyone in her life had made her feel how they loved her beyond reason as long as she 'behaved and did' the right thing, 'loved' the right people, 'went' to the right places and whatever they all felt she should be thinking and feeling.

"Well, you better be going now, Mica or you will be late," her father told her pointing to the door and winking at her daughter with a cue to escape.

"Thanks, Dad!" She smiled tenderly at his understanding for her to be out of there and get to the office on time.

"Behave for grandma," she told Annabella.

"Bye, Mommy," the child answered.

She got in her car and checked herself in the rear view mirror as if waiting to exhale as soon she approved of her looks. She smiled and told herself "Be kind, you deserve as much love as one can possibly have."

She wanted to get to work to see if he had called and left a message or to see Rosie's face and see if she knew about it already, since it had become obvious that they were communicating much more so than with Micaela.

"Good morning, Rosie," she cautiously greeted her coworker.

"Hi!" with a solemn aloofness.

"How is your cousin?" Micaela asked Rosie.

"Fine, thank you for asking," she replied.

"So how was last night with Stavros?" Rosie asked.

"He called me early this morning and told me you both had met...and he was sorry about me not showing up," she told this to Micaela well aware of how much hurt she was inflicting. Without any regard she continued by saying, "We are meeting tonight for dinner...Would you like to come?"

"No, I don't think so...I do not have anyone to watch Annabella...Thank you for asking anyhow," she said it trying to cover her jealousy toward Rosie.

"Well, if you change your mind, we are going to be at the café where you met yesterday... Stavros liked the atmosphere and wants me to check it out. Isn't he nice?" she added.

"Very nice, I think he likes you a lot," Micaela answered back in a nonchalant way that even she was surprised at how well she acted on cue, guarding her feelings.

"Why do you say that?" Rosie asked intrigued at Micaela's comment and demeanor.

"Well, for starters he kept asking about what had happened with your cousin even though I told him time after time that I was not sure." Micaela told her about the times he asked but she embellished it and exaggerated at the times.

"I am sorry, for the way things turned out after all," Rosie told Micaela.

"Lies, lies, lies." Micaela told herself, "Do not worry about it. You can have him...I think he 's a bit too on the brown side, ethnic and he is not my type after all, you know," she told Rosie.

"That's right!..He is not your type," Rosie conceded.

"You like blond and blue eyes," she continued.

"Yep!" Micaela turning toward her desk said it with a coquettish smile.

"You really don't care?' Rosie asked.

"Care about what?" Micaela responded with a question.

"About that he wanted me and not you." Adding more salt to the wound with no regard for Micaela's feelings.

"Rosie, listen...everything is fair in love and war," she said looking straight into Rosie's eyes.

"The fact that you asked him out the night we all first met, because you had his card and not I, gave you the upper hand. You have his attention. Well, then...enjoy the ride." Micaela's strength came over her. She thought of her mom and how she would react to what was going on. *Indifference, indifference is what is required at this time,* she thought to herself. "Indifference kills always remember that!" She could hear her mother's voice.

"Well you are taking the situation far better than we expected," Rosie added in disbelief.

"Well, there you have it! What is done is done...and if you want to hear you won. You've won! Happy?" she added.

"Well, I do find him attractive and he likes me too, so I guess that makes me the winner." She said deliberately knowing Micaela was hurt.

The day became an eternity and after their morning talk all Micaela wanted to do was to leave and never come back to see this insensitive woman who just had so much hatred in her heart and wanted Micaela to feel the same way! Micaela knew this, however, she was still in so much pain knowing that her Adonis, the one she had stolen a kiss from and had entered her heart would never be hers.

The telephone rang and Micaela felt as if her whole chest cavity fell down to her knees making them be flaccid and weak. The pain of having this gaping hole in her chest cavity became intense. Had she ever been aware that she could feel so much pain? Where had she been all these years, how much protection could she have had? Micaela managed to pick herself up to answer the call, knowing ahead of time it was him, Stavros, on the other line, asking for Rosie and not for her.

"Thank you for calling, Pollack Enterprises, this is Micaela how may I help you?" she managed to say all that without a much desired whimper.

"Hi, Micaela" the voice was Stavros but the demeanor was unknown, he sounded a bit embarrassed.

"Hey, Stavros how are you doing today?" she answered trying to be chipper and happy and under the same breath she said, beating him to the punch of asking for Rosie, "She stepped out for a moment, but I will let her know that you called, okay?"

"Oh, oh okay," he said incredulous to hear Micaela not be the typical scorned woman.

"Have a nice day, good bye!" she said trying at any cost to sound unhurt by his rejection.

"Micaela, wait... I want to apologize for the other night." He said it sounding truthful.

"Oh, do not worry, we are consenting adults right? So I consented to be hurt by my irresponsibility and throwing caution to the wind. I hope you do not think too badly of me." Micaela said it in a matter of fact that only she knew it meant she was trying to convince herself.

"Are you okay?" he asked sounding rather honestly concerned.

"Yeah," she answered back.

"Listen, I never meant to hurt you. You have to believe that!" he said sounding a bit anxious and nervous.

"I understand, please do not worry about me...I will be fine," she said trying to hold her tears back.

"Well, then tell her I will call her back at home tonight," he said it with no respect whatsoever for Micaela's feelings.

"Thank you for calling Pollack Enterprises. Good day," she said it as she hang up the phone.

Micaela could not help but feel intense betrayal by the people who seem to be concerned about her feelings. She knew she had made a big mistake trusting her coworker, trusting in her own feelings of desire for this stranger who had come and disturbed her world like no other. She did not know who he was or what he was all about, and the thought of giving to him the way she did that night made her feel bad but surprisingly enough she was not ashamed. It was all so overwhelming and confusing, she wanted to cry but couldn't, she wanted to scream yet not a whisper came out of her. She felt stripped of a layer that had prevented her from feeling different emotions. She felt shaken to her core where dusty memories had been awaken to let her feel all that life had to offer whether good, painful or pleasurable.

Micaela became aware of how she had pushed all these feelings away and hid them in the corners of her being so as not to ever feel this most awful vulnerability she was now feeling. She felt stupid, empty and most of all lonely like many times before when life had tried to show her its many lessons. There she stood feeling always alone. But with the same frenzy of the night she loved Stavros, the images of papers and the many poems she had written and the acclamation of her high school literature teacher, the notebooks Dr. Rodriguez had given her all appeared in her mind as if calling her to come back to herself. And with all those images, Micaela wanted to start writing again. She forgot where she was and looking for paper she sat down and started to write with a quivering motion, trying to stop herself from crying. So much pain she thought, *Why now? Why with this man?*

"Poem for letting go," she wrote at the top of the piece of paper.

For you, the thrill is gone,
but your sweet scent remains
making me long for you
making me want you all the more...
For you, the thrill is gone,
so is my heart,
gone, lost
succumbing only to the beat of yours...
For you, the thrill is gone,
so it seems,

*but truth be told,
deep down running through my veins
you are my thrill
bringing desire, bringing that tumultuous passionate fire
that keeps me longing, waiting
'till the day you'll come
to quench that thirst
that can't ever, ever be gone.*

She finished writing and reread what she had in front of her eyes and it was a poem that flowed with an ease she knew was there and it had been a long time since she became aware of how happy writing made her feel. "Poetry at this time? You are such a peculiar bird!" She told herself pushing her curls back and rereading the poem. "Not bad for an amateur," she whispered. She got up and went to the ladies room, making sure she looked okay. She went back to her desk and continued her work. A layer of feelings, old feelings, bad feelings had been stripped off and she felt the cold air conditioned room raise her skin and as if she had been asleep from a long slumber, she awaken from a complacency ready to tackle the obstacles that would be in her way of becoming a writer.

The morning was a very long morning and it did not matter how hard Micaela tried to keep busy and focus on the task at hand, the night she had spent with him kept coming into her thoughts. How she wished she would have never met him or had at least tried to handle the night in a different way. The telephone rang. It was now becoming painful to answer knowing it could be him at the other end.

"Good morning, Pollack Enterprises. Micaela speaking," she answered politely.

"Hi, Micaela!" her best friend was at the other end. "Listen, tonight we are invited to the Comedy Club in Hermosa and I went ahead and accepted for both of us...aren't I a good friend?" Maria said it with her thick accentuated Italian accent.

"I can't tonight...Don't have a baby sitter," she answered.

"I have everything under control. Tonight is Girl's Night Out and you are a girl and it is your night to be out!...not moping over a one night stand, excuse me! Half of a one night stand, because according to your account there was no intercourse, no consummation of any sort...so it does not constitute a full fledged one night stand." Maria went on to tell Micaela with a scolding playful attitude about that night. Maria had called Rachel and had her friend agree to babysit Annabella for the night.

"Well, then, if that is the case, I still need to go home and feed the cat and make sure Annabella is going to be okay with me going out tonight," Micaela answered her friend and as she looked up she realized that Rosie had been there listening to the conversation with Maria. "Hey, Maria listen...I have to go now, I will call you later."

"You are going out with Maria, tonight?" Rosie asked sounding a bit resentful like many other times before realizing that although divorced and with a child, Micaela had a tremendous ability to connect with people, to go out and enjoy her singleness without sacrificing her time with her child, Annabella. As opposed to Rosie who having all the men lacked a female connection to share the good times with.

"It looks that way...I do not know how you girls do it?" she said nonchalantly as she shuffled some paper work around her desk.

"You both crack me up. You and María have the ability to have your way with men and to have them lavish you with gifts. How does one do that?" She looked up and looking in Rosie's eyes directly she asked her outright, "What are you going to get from Stavros?"

It was a question she will regret having asked because she could see the ire in Rosie's eyes, which with a deliberate contempt in her voice told her that for tonight she would have Stavros wine and dine her and afterwards he would take care of the entertainment. Little did Micaela know how conniving Rosie could be. It was about five o'clock. As they started to straighten up the office, the telephone rang, Micaela walked away from the reception area into the small break room, Let her answer the phone, *it's probably HIM!* She thought to herself.

She heard Rosie answer the phone and started the conversation in the most flirtatious way, then went on to finish by saying, "Most definitely, that would be fun sounds like a plan to me. I will be ready. See you later Stavros."

She looked up to make sure Micaela was aware of whom she was talking to. The indifference Micaela was taught by her mother proved to be her ally at this second, because with great indifference she said, "Bye Rosie, don't keep the Greek waiting too long. He might get mad and break some of your dishes as the night goes into the entertainment part. And tell him, I said hello, would you?"

She laughed with an infectious laugh, the one she used in times of great stress to make sure no one knew how she really felt. People would always comment to her, "Are you ever in a bad mood? Cause you are always so happy and energetic." *If they only knew*, Micaela would always think to herself.

She left work and went home to get Annabella's things ready for school the next day and make sure the babysitter would know the drill of what to do in case of an emergency.

"Hello, Micaela," Maria appeared behind her in a pretty black dress.

"Hey, what are you doing here so early?" she answered with a question.

"Nothing, I figured you probably would chicken out, so I came to give you a little push to come out and play," Maria told her as she reached out to give her a hug.

"You always smell so good. What are you wearing?" Maria asked.

"The usual, "Magie Noir" by Lancôme," she answered.

"Well, that is what you need tonight a little bit of black magic," Maria told her laughing going into Micaela's apartment.

"What are you going to wear?" Maria asked excited at the prospect of going out for the night.

"What you're looking at," Micaela answered feeling a bit languid and disenchanted with herself.

"What is the matter, Micaela?...Please do not tell me you do not feel like going out?" Maria desperately grabbing Micaela by the arms.

"NO, it's not that but what is the purpose of going out. Men do not look at me...they look at you. They buy drinks for you. I always feel so inadequate and now a bit lonely and disgusted with myself. But I told you we would go out and out we are going okay?"

"That is the spirit!" Maria cheered on.

"Hey, Mom!" Annabella appeared.

"Hey Sweetie, how was school?" Micaela asked.

"It was long and boring. I got into a bit of trouble, Sister Angelina will be calling you about my music fiasco," the child tried to explain.

"What happened?" she looked concerned.

"Nothing, I just did not want to draw the same thing that everyone else was drawing so I did a poster of Sister Angelina, which was more than a caricature and she got upset. I was listening to my headphones because we had permission to bring them, but she said I should put mine up after she saw what I was doing. I protested and then I got sent to the director's office." Annabella told her story with such conviction of being wronged by the nun at her school that Micaela felt she was going to have to really keep an eye on this child of hers. She was not going to be demure, respecting all the rules and convention of society. This child of hers will be totally different from what she had been as a child growing up as sheltered as she was.

"Well, I guess I better be prepared for the nun's side of the story, huh?" she told Annabella grabbing her and giving her a big kiss and tickling her as Annabella squirmed out of her embrace going to her bedroom, yelling nonchalantly, "What time are you coming back? Do not stay out all night you hear, little missy?" the child yelled out to Micaela.

"Are you going to let your kid talk to you like that?" Maria asked.

"Oh, please do not be my mom!...I hear that all the time from her...as if she does not have a mind of her own to express how she feels," Micaela told Maria as she rolled her eyes at her.

"We better hurry up. The boys are going to be waiting for these damsels in distress...but not for too long," Maria said it jokingly as she started to redo her makeup.

"I really don't feel like going, Maria...There is something lurking in this night and I feel so unsure about going out tonight," she told her.

"Oh, come on. There is nothing that lurks except in that head of yours...since you have been with that man, you are not the same." Maria went on criticizing Micaela's attitude from the last two nights.

"It is almost as if you were keeping yourself for him to come one day to this apartment and whisk you off to a foreign land where you would be his protagonist and the play would only be about the two of you... I know how you are when you start thinking about writing your play, your novel or whatever it is that you want to write about." Maria continued.

"Ok, that is enough, Maria...If it makes you happy we will go out like we said." Micaela got up went to the bathroom took a quick shower and came out with her curly hair still wet. She put on a pair of black rayon palazzo pants and a white bohemian tunic made of worn out linen that moved along with her small figure. Her soft body and the determined stance she took as she walked flowed in harmony with the rustle of her clothing as she moved about her apartment getting ready for this night. She looked like a gypsy girl ready to go out there and sell her goods with the most fervent passion in order to survive in a world where deceit is a norm and apathy reigns. Rachel's friend got there right on time. Micaela explained everything to her and Annabella seemed content to be left with the new baby sitter, so off they went.

Maria and Micaela, the two M&Ms as they were called by their closest friends, got in the car and started off to Anza Boulevard making a turn on 190th Street heading to the beach. They turned on Pacific Coast Highway and came to the hustle and bustle of Hermosa Pier where the Comedy Club awaited the two fair maidens unaware that deceit lurked in the midst. They entered and got a table near the stage. A young girl came and asked them if they wanted anything to drink.

"We'll have two gin and tonics," Micaela said looking around the place.

"I told you it was going to be a full house," Maria told her.

"I know. It is kind of crowded isn't it?" Micaela responded.

"Look over there, Micaela. Do you see that couple? They are kind of odd! Aren't they?" Maria told Micaela as she pointed out the couple entering the place and scoping it to see where they could sit down.

To Micaela's disbelief, the couple were none other than Stavros and Rosie. She felt like a smoldering fire entered her being and replaced the blood flowing in her veins. Out of all the places they could have gone in the vast city of the Angelinos, they were here! Among the crowd she tried to hide and then a feeling of power came over her, the kind that comes in at the most desperate times. She felt like staying there to make a point. She chose to do the unexpected and with a big grin she yelled out, "Stavros, Rose! Hey you!...Come sit with us!"

Stavros' olive face turned red, obviously embarrassed by the whole situation and looking at Micaela as to say, I am sorry I did not know you were going to be here, he said, "Hello, ladies!"

Micaela made the introductions, "Maria, this is Rosie, my coworker and Stavros, her friend."

"Nice to meet you," Maria politely answered, but could not believe that Micaela with such a graciousness could introduce everyone and keep civility among the characters of this little piece of Shakespearean tragedy where betrayal ensues as the characters play on and prepare to see the show about to begin.

"I did not know you liked comedy?" Rosie asked Micaela.

"She not only likes comedy but she is quite the comedienne herself," Maria added, smiling at her friend.

"She is shy, and does not speak up as she should," Maria added.

"Oh is that right?" Stavros asked back.

"Stop it Maria!" Micaela motioned to her friend.

"Why?...because it is true?"

"I think the show is about to start. Maybe we should be quiet," Rosie interjected.

"Maybe we should do a lot of things, but we don't," Maria continued to say, looking intently at Rosie.

"I think it is best that we sit somewhere else, I really came here to see the show and don't care for the commentary of the people around me," Rosie added.

"Of course you don't like it!" Maria added.

"I am sorry, but is there a story line here that connects us... or am I missing something?" Stavros asked a bit annoyed at the display of cattiness.

Micaela deep down loved Maria for being the outspoken Italian girlfriend who she knew would defend her with her own life. If she could only have a man to love and protect her like Maria did, Micaela would never need anyone else in her life. "Too bad I am not a lesbian," Micaela would joke and Maria would retort, "too bad you are not my type." They would end up laughing like teenagers at the silly remarks they often had for each other.

The show started but the intensity of Stavros and Micaela's angst and feeling uncomfortable could not be overlooked by the other two characters of this play. They tried to laugh at the jokes being told but nothing could deter from the fact that the more Micaela looked at Stavros, she felt her heart being torn out of her chest and every bit of her blood run out of her body, leaving her with only the last breath to which she would use to let him know how much she cared for him, or how much she longed for his caress of the other night. How much pain it caused her to see him with Rosie knowing that after the show, they would go home to screw and that struck her at the core of her being leaving her totally drained. She needed to flee the place and never return to see them ever again.

"I am sorry, but I just realized that my little girl has a project due tomorrow and I neglected to tell the baby sitter about it. Maria, do you want to stay or leave with me?" To make matters worse, Micaela realized that Stavros was holding Rosie's hands, and at that moment when her heart was about to leave her body the inexplicable strength came over her as she was lit up by a spotlight.

"To the lady about to leave, can you please tell us a joke before you make your exit?" the MC asked Micaela.

Much to her amazement, she was able to approach the stage and she felt armed with the invincibility given to her by the women of her past as she experienced the lights warming her face. It made her feel better somehow and she saw herself as the many times before as a child with her cousins on the play stage singing the songs of her favorite Spanish singer. Life was giving her a chance to act upon that strength that could make her shine as she had always wanted to shine but never could in her sheltered upbringing. She felt naked and exposed yet comforted by the warm light and perusing through her thoughts with the ease of being the social butterfly, which would make her mother very proud, Micaela had the crowd laughing and applauding. She stopped in her tracks as she saw Stavros and Rosie leave the club and the sweet taste of revenge touched her lips. It gave her back her heart, the pulse of the blood running back in her veins let her know that she was alive and had always had the power of being. The power of being a victor; despite the awful circumstances that often caused her to be the melancholic and detached woman unable to love herself at times. "Thank you for making my debut as much fun as I thought it would be, Thank you, thank you," Micaela proceeded to tell the crowd and to her surprise they asked her for an encore and this time she sketched out something personal, something from her daily routine and with perfect timing, she delivered it to cause the crowd to applaud more vehemently.

"Who knew we had a natural in the crowd?" the MC told the audience.

That night, Micaela realized she had a gift far richer than the beauty of some women or the ability to manipulate men in buying them drinks and things that they could easily get for themselves. She might not have had that ability to have men succumb to her beauty or play mind games that makes them treat women like trophies only to be discarded at their whim when the taste of the conquest is no longer fresh in their mind. She knew all along that the power of words would rescue her from some of her anxieties and mediocrity of life. She knew that with pen and paper she would be armed to tackle being a single mother and to hell with what her parents and society at large thought of her. She would pursue her most beloved creative endeavor, writing and getting a literary education, and then wait to see what the future had in store for her. Maria hugged her for a long time and told her, "I am so proud of you. You are so funny and beautiful. Don't let this jerk take away the goodness that you contain in that lovely heart of yours."

"Thank you," hugging her back.

"I know. I know you are sorry you are not a lesbian and yes still you are not my type." Maria tried to dispel the intensity of the moment with their one liners.

"I know, but if I were a lesbian you would be mine you know." Micaela told Maria.

"I know that too, but truth be told what you really need is a geeky brainiac of a man with a strong vocabulary to hold you in the middle of the night asking you to paraphrase the latest novel you read or wrote and for that matter, not a very simple crazy woman like me," Maria told her giving her a kiss on the cheek. "You deserve the best, Micaela and you know it," she added

"I love you for being such a good friend to me, Maria."

"It is you who brings the best out of most people, and your true concern for your fellow men is what makes you awesome. Go inside and write. I know that is what you are itching to do right now."

She went home and could not wait to write a little comedic sketch that had come to her in the middle of delivering her first joke. Micaela entered the room and saw the new babysitter reading a book. Looking up at Micaela, she motioned that Annabella had just fallen asleep. She had George Benson playing on the radio and Micaela asked the young woman, "You like him?"

"Shit yeah!...He is totally cool, I like the selection of records you have," the young girl told Micaela.

"Well, coming from someone your age, I think that is as cool as shit!...right?" she smirked.

"María told me you were cool. Never would I have thought you were that cool!" she exclaimed back. "I love your top," she added.

"Thank you," Micaela answered making a curtsy.

"You are funny!...Can I stay here for a little while longer?" the baby sitter asked.

"Sure! But it is rather late and I want to do some writing." Micaela found herself saying.

The words were music to her ears. Writing, to be able to sit down and put your thoughts on paper, devising ways to make a simple sentence have the vibrancy of life that upon one reading it, it can make someone cry, laugh or think back to a time unknown to any other, that was the gift of writing to have the power of words to create pictures for everyone to share. She could wait no longer.

Patty, the baby sitter, gathered all of her belongings and decided to leave. Micaela closed the door behind her and walking toward the stereo she wanted to play the last song on the album. She looked about her small apartment and appropriately enough the music that began to play was George Benson's "Everything Must Change." She dimmed her living room lights and with his crooning she walked about her apartment making sure everything especially the most precious gift of all was OK; as she approached Annabella's sweet face, she heard Benson say, "Young becomes the old, mysteries do unfold..." and right then and there the mystery of how this young child came into her life was unfolding before her own eyes. She reached softly and placed a kiss with the sign of the cross on her little forehead and left her to rest in the innocent slumber of childhood.

Micaela went back to the living room and heard Benson as if he was singing to her... "Everything must change, nothing stays the same, everyone must change nothing stays the same... young becomes the old, mysteries do unfold, there is always a time that nothing or no one goes unchanged..." She started to dance to the music and for the first time in her life she was in her place, where she knew she had to change, because nothing or no one stays the same; we do not go unchanged. She sat down and started to write the prologue for her book. She started to sketch out the characters and some of the painful moments of her own life that would add vivacity and credibility to her characters. Filled with an uncontrollable emotion to fill a page she started out. As she reached to turn the desk lamp on, she realized that it had been lit up all along. She was surprised because she could not remember turning it on. *Hmm, that is strange*, she thought.

She reached for her pen and paper and the light flickered with an intensity that she was not used to for that lamp to be so invitingly bright, yet it was. It had a welcoming feel as if to prompt her into the writing fest she was about to enter. She wrote a farewell poem for Stavros and placed it in her lingerie drawer and with a devilish smile continued to change in to the turn of the nineteenth century antique night gown she had bought long ago, specifically for the lonely nights she would write her books and poems, and with the spirits of 'old' she sat down and pretended to be one of the Bronte girls. Every night for the next year she did nothing but write her novel, tweaking and creating this wonderful world of fiction in which she transported herself to live the moments she wanted to have lived herself. In one of these lonely yet fulfilling days, she found herself applying to UCLA. She was accepted and finished her Bachelor's Degree in the Humanities, much to the dismay of her mother for not going into the dentistry field, "I do not understand the obsession to be a bohemian writer instead of choosing a profession that is more like you," Paloma, her mother would tell her every chance she got.

"I don't think you know who I am to know the profession that best suits me." Micaela finally found the courage to confront her mother, which ended up costing her so much in the end. Paloma chose not to talk to her daughter as she started to write short stories for the college newspaper. One day out of the blue an agent for a standup comic sought her out to write some of the sketches for his client. Micaela's world was changing and with every change, every day she grew stronger; the force that saw her as a child walk in the "jungle" was getting fierce. Stavros, although not yet a distant memory, became her muse. The pain of his disdain and unrequited love gave her back the voice and inspiration to fill her pages with prose, poetry and even short comedic playwrights. She was in heaven realizing that with patience and persistence the world is attainable. Her world of literature was coming to her threshold dressed in the most luminous bright light that at times she was blinded by and forgot about the world around her only to see and have a genuine concern for the little girl with the big brown eyes who danced with the witchery of love, her daughter, Annabella her reason for being.

Part Four

Transformation from 'ugly duckling' to triumphant swan.

Enlightenment

In the middle of a humid, sultry afternoon, the cab made a screeching sound and stopped in front of a beautiful turn-of-the-twentieth century Neoclassical apartment building still being renovated by its present owner. It was not New York City but Athens, Georgia and this would be her living quarters especially since the University of Georgia had accepted Micaela's short story and wanted her to do her Masters in Literature on campus. It meant she would receive a substantial stipend for her studies and she would actually get to write and achieved her most precious dream. Micaela grabbed Annabella's hand as they both stood in awe of the building before them.

Without realizing how the excitement of being away from all she knew and with the chance of starting over affected her, Micaela squeezed her small child's hand. The child exclaimed, "Mummy, you are hurting me!" trying to pull away from her mother's grasp.

Still in a trance she spoke to Annabella, but in reality telling herself

"NO, darling! No one is ever going to hurt us again." Snapping out of her thoughts she knelt down and said, "This time I will take care of us...and all the goodness in life is just awaiting for us to have and enjoy."

Looking intently at her small child and directly into Annabella's big brown eyes, she told her "Promise me that whenever you are unhappy, you will come and confide in me...We both will make our booboos go away. Promise me that. I don't ever want you to feel lonely...okay?"

Annabella's questioning look went undetected by Micaela, as she responded to the question "Yes Mummy. Whatever you say."

In unison, they both grabbed their respective luggage and started to go into the beautiful white painted building. It had two grand columns which time had chipped some of the paint away yet still provided the support for the portico leading into the main hallway. Next to the columns there were some fancy carved banisters awaiting to look new again by the magic of a few coats of paint. They opened the door and a musky smell of old hit their nostrils but they both looked at each other with approving smiles as they saw, in awe, the beautiful newly renovated banisters leading up the stairs where they would find their apartment. The new place would take away everything painful and they both sensed the powers that be awaited their arrival. There, Micaela knew she would become stronger, invincible..."fighting the animals in the jungle" of her youth, where the touch of her child would be sufficient to let the love for herself blossom and flourish as time will go on letting her write her novels, her poetry and where her imagination would finally release all that had been contained within her.

Feeling like the world was at her feet, Micaela heard herself again in unison with Annabella say, "Look at our door. It is our favorite number, number two like you and I together, we are two." They laughed and both felt the connection that would keep them together through it all.

The apartment was smaller than what Micaela had anticipated but it was quaint with three big windows overlooking the busy avenue. Her first thought was how much smaller is going to be once her furnishings arrive. Nevertheless in great anticipation, she began to think and brainstorm. Many thoughts and ideas started to come, as well as episodes of her life began to appear as vignettes of a play.

She smiled but the knock on the door brought her back to the real world. It never fails, when I am most inspired looking for a muse, the door bell, telephone or something else rings! It was the landlord welcoming Micaela and her daughter into the apartment building and the community in general. Jerry Hall was his name and he was an associate professor at the University. He was tall and very handsome with a clean cut manner about himself. Sporting a worn T-shirt of his old alma matter and jeans made him look younger than his fifty years.

"We finally meet!" he told Micaela extending his hand to shake hers.

"Indeed! It is so nice to meet you, Dr. Hall," she responded.

"Wow, I would not have expected such a strong shake from a petite woman like yourself," he added, surprised at just how strong her handshake was. He thought, This woman has hutzpah.

"Well, thank you for the strong and petite compliments. You are very kind," she told him letting go of his grasp.

"Listen, first forget the Dr. Hall part. Please call me Jerry. Second, there is going to be a get together next door and I would love for you to accompany me as my guest," he asked her very excitedly.

"Well, I would love to but I just got into town. I have my little girl with me and I don't want to leave her with a stranger from the get go...I hope you understand," she looked at him intently, hoping that he would be dissuaded by her comment.

"Oh no! You can bring her with you. This is a family affair, so everyone is invited," he added.

Micaela saw Annabella peeking from behind the curtains with a smile on her face as though pleading to accept the invitation for her. Thus, Micaela accepted mainly for her child's sake.

"Well, in that case, Jerry you have made my daughter very happy. She loves a party just like her grandmother...Please come here Annabella."

"Jerry this is my daughter, Annabella. Annabella this is Dr. Hall."

"Nice to meet you Annabella, that is a beautiful name."

"Thank you, likewise Dr. Hall."

"I hope you find this place is to your liking," Jerry added looking intently at Micaela.

Micaela felt uncomfortable having her child in front of this stranger who looked at her in a most inauspicious amorous way. Prompting Annabella to make a move, she smiled at her in their secret way, and out of the 'mouths of babes,' Annabella proceeded to say, "Mom you better get cleaned up or no single man is going to ask you out," winking at Jerry.

"She is a precocious one, isn't she," Jerry added.

"Well, she is something!" Micaela concurred.

"Now, now. Don't you start talking about me like I was not in the room, I find it very rude and cumbersome...can I use cumbersome in the context of this situation Mom?"

"Yes, you may," Micaela looking at Jerry smiled shyly.

Jerry finally decided to go and left the two girls who started to laugh, falling down on the nice wool rug that lay in the front room.

"Did I do well, Mom?"

"Yes, honey. You took care of Mom and the big bad wolf," caressing Annabella's cheeks.

"He is kind of cute, in a nerdy way, you know," Annabella said it with a nonchalant way that made Micaela see herself in this child.

"Come here you big girl. You make me so proud the way you think for being such a whippersnapper. You, you, you, love of my life…Don't ever change you hear?"

They both starting unpacking, looking for what to wear. They finally got dressed for the party that could be heard already as people had started to arrive. Micaela wore a white linen shirt-dress with a white silk embroidered collar that made it softer, more feminine with a straw boater hat decorated with ribbons and lace making it feminine to match her girly stride. Annabella upon her mother's insistence wore a seersucker summer dress that made her look like a character of many children's books much to her own dislike, because she would have preferred a T-shirt and shorts to what Micaela had chosen for her.

They met all the neighbors and they all seemed friendly and welcoming. The buzz all around them was that no one had seen Liam. Liam was another post graduate student that lived in the neighborhood, however, he had not made it to Athens yet, but everyone seemed eager to see him.

"Who is this Liam Griggs?" Micaela asked one of the young women who happened to be yet another student.

"Oh, he is one of Jerry's other tenants," she answered.

"Oh, does he live in Jerry's building?" Micaela asked intrigued and trying to find out why he was liked by everyone.

"Yeah, he is helping Jerry with the renovation…He is quite the handy man…plus Jerry and he go a long way back to Liam's undergraduate days," she added.

"They are good friends?" Micaela kept asking questions about this stranger, who everyone was looking forward to his arrival.

"He must be a really nice guy, huh?" she asked totally intrigued by the mysterious man.

"He is one of the most likable fellows you could ever meet," Jerry told her annoyed by her insistence to find out who he was.

Annabella saw Jerry's annoyance and grabbed Micaela's hand squeezing it the way Micaela often times did in order to get her to behave. She looked at her child understanding yet another signal between them. Micaela stopped asking so many questions and returned to enjoy the music some people had started to play. Once in a while, as she mingled with the people, she felt caressed by a breath of fresh air. This energy, she felt, had a name; the name of the mysterious Liam Griggs. Unexplainable, she thought how this stranger could enter her mind and make her wonder about him without even knowing him. However, there he was faceless, imageless but entering her thoughts, entering in her brand new world.

"Hi Micaela, I am Biloxi Blue, nice to meet you...I live in apartment four...welcome to the building and the area."

"Biloxi Blue!?...what an interesting name...nice to meet you too."

'They tell me you were all the way from Ecuador. How does it feel to be in the States?" she asked looking at Annabella's dumbfounded look.

"Originally, I am from Ecuador but I have lived in the United States for more than a quarter of a century so I guess that kind of makes me an American, no?" Micaela said it accentuating her Spanish accent.

"Oh! I am so sorry, I did not mean to be imprudent. I didn't know that you have lived here for that long. Professor Hall told me that you came from Ecuador so I assumed you were one of the foreign students in the program... So where was home before coming here?" Biloxi asked politely and sort of apologetically.

"We came from California, Palos Verdes to be precise." Annabella answered with a disdainful attitude that everyone could tell she did not want to be there.

"Yes, we lived in Southern California...I lived there for twenty five years, got married, had Annabella...The marriage did not work out so here I am...Only time will tell what gifts I will find in this place with its fine, hot, humid weather and its antebellum past," she said looking around at the huge pecan tree that spread out its limbs to give shade and shelter to those gathered around it.

The afternoon was a delight and she felt comfortable with the people around her. Annabella made friends with an African American girl who lived two houses down. Her name was Trixie and Annabella thought that was the coolest name.

Unfortunately, it started to rain and everyone darted for shelter. Micaela and Annabella ran home and when they got there, the telephone was ringing. It was Annabella's father, Edward, wanting to know when it would be a good time to come pick Annabella up for the summer to stay with him as he was granted in the divorce decree.

"Hi, Daddy!" Annabella excitedly greeted him.

"Hey girl. How are you...How is your new home?"

"It's okay," shrugging her shoulders. "But, I like my old house better...I made a new friend so that's nice and her name is Trixie... Can I change my name to something cool like that?"

"Well, you will have to ask your mother."

"Do you want to talk to her?" she asked with trepidation in her voice.

"No! Just wanted to know when I can pick you up and bring you home."

"Hold on k?...Mummy when can dad pick me up?" screaming out loud Annabella asked Micaela

"You do not have to shout...Give me the phone!"

"Hey, how are you doing?" Micaela said coldly.

"Fine. Just tell me when," Edward said it in a despondent tone.

It had been four years since their divorce but he was still angry with Micaela for walking away from their marriage and having full custody of Annabella. Micaela had warned him every time he threatened to take Annabella away from her that it would never happen. She had told him that if he ever dared to try and take Annabella away from her, all his family's dirty laundry would be brought out in court and perhaps she would be able to take custody of the other two children who needed a stable home which is not what they had with a grandmother addicted to pain pills, who despite having a maid never kept a clean house and the list of dysfunctional habits extended a mile long. Micaela made it clear not to touch Annabella in any negative way. If she ever detected Edward using her as a pawn in the divorce negotiations she would go for the jugular only for the child's best interest.

"Well, you have a copy of the court papers. It states right in them the days she is yours, so whenever it is convenient for you... You can come any time...just let me know when and she will be ready...Let me let you say good bye to her. Take care of yourself," she added with genuine caring for the father of her child.

"Hey Daddy! I love...what? He hung up on me," Annabella reported.

"Well, maybe he was in a hurry to get here to pick you up...who knows!" Micaela told her winking at her.

"Mom, why are you so nice after all the things he has done to you and me...You still pretend he is a good guy?" Annabella said to her mother, scolding her.

"Annabella! Please, be kind! He is still your father and I know it is hard to understand but you must love him for that...Just the simple fact that he is your father is the reason you should always respect him and love him despite his idiosyncrasies, *n'est pas?*"

"Oh no! Not French again!" Annabella went into her room. She liked how her mother would try to teach her another language but pretended to be bothered by it.

Edward came a few weeks later and took Annabella back to the West coast for the summer. Micaela had mixed emotions letting go of her child, but also she felt free to complete the task at hand which was to unpack a lifetime of possessions and memories in this little place and get ready for an arduous study schedule about to begin. She felt a bit apprehensive and scared about the uncertainty of the future, but also felt strong and happy about being far away from all she knew to make her own song, her own life.

She started to unpack. As she opened some files, she realized that she only had an hour to get ready for a meeting at the English Department and had not even had a chance to get to know the campus or where she needed to be. She brushed her teeth put on a hat and went as is; old and worn out linen palazzo pants and a knitted cotton tunic that made her look like she just arrived from Madagascar. She loved this particular outfit because it had the look and feel of an old safari ensemble. Her fishing hat just completed the *je ne sais quoi* way she loved to dress. She rushed to get there on time. Not having a car nor the money for a cab, she walked about three miles down the road to where she was supposed to be. The temperature at ninety seven degrees with ninety nine percent humidity made her soft olive skin glisten becoming lustrous and defining the bone structure of her small face. She was quite beautiful. She glowed as she walked down the stairs of the main library going to Stanford Road and turning right toward Lumpkin Street where the Joseph Brown building stood.

"Excuse me. I am a graduate student who needs to go to orientation at 11:00 in room 234."

"Yeah go up the stairs and someone will direct you once you are there," a heavy set woman eating pork rinds directed Micaela.

"Thank you," she said, in her mind judging the woman's eating habits.

As Micaela started to go upstairs the same heavy set woman eating the pork rinds informed her that she could take the elevator instead and pointed to her its direction.

"No, thank you, I will take the stairs. It is only one flight up," she said politely, smiling at the pork rind-eating receptionist.

"Hello. You must be Micaela Sims." An older gentleman greeted her as he showed her the way to Room 234.

"Yes, and you are?" she asked politely as they got to the entrance and realize that she was a bit late. Seeing Jerry out of the corner of her eye coming her way, she rudely stop the introduction and turned to Jerry.

"I am so sorry about my tardiness, Professor Hall," she apologized to Jerry who was conducting the small gathering of graduate students.

"Hey, Micaela...Don't worry you are fine...I saw you walking and thought of asking you if you wanted a ride but your stride told me you needed to be left alone," he said winking at her.

"Well, thank you for not asking me...I did want to become familiar with the neighborhood and decided to walk...It is a lovely place with all the trees and azaleas blooming everywhere," she told him.

"So, you are the beautiful Micaela who Jerry can't stop talking about!" the older gentleman told her.

"You are much too kind, professor?... I did not catch the name," Micaela told him reaching for his hand to shake and realizing how rude she had been.

"Professor Hughes...Langston Hughes." He said almost apologizing about the greatness of his name, being that he was not 'the' Langston Hughes.

"Goodness, what a name!" Micaela's grand smile made the old man approve of her and told her she was going to fit in fine.

Micaela was puzzled by the remark but dispelled it as she sat down to get on with orientation. Everyone seemed rather young.

Here she was a woman in her mid thirties trying to become a female literary writer of sorts. She was as happy as happy gets. The university hallways, the homework, and assignments were as if a child had been sent to a candy store with a lot of money in her pockets to get anything she wanted. Micaela was in heaven and for the first time in a very long time, she became aware of her being and how good it felt to be in her own skin feeling whole again with the invincibility of the child who roamed the 'jungle' in her youth. Some sort of roster was read out loud by Jerry who was conducting the session and from the back of the room a question was shouted, "So where is our beloved, Liam Griggs?"

Micaela's head turned so fast that it made everyone looked at her, like what was that about? She felt embarrassed at her lack of decorum and obvious interest in this Liam Griggs.

"I am so sorry about my curiosity, but who is this Liam Griggs?" She asked trying to dispel her intrigue about the stranger.

"He is our major star. Every time he writes a grant proposal we get the money so his art of persuasion keeps us working here at the department...thus, he is our god!" the male voice came again out from the back.

"So you might be one of his groupies...So much devotion!" Micaela said this in a sweet, but funny voice that made everyone laugh.

"He would like to be his groupie, all right!" another voice from a girl this time added to the conversation.

"Paul is right," Jerry added seriously and everyone turned around to see what Jerry had to say.

"Liam is one of our protectors. His art of persuasion and his eloquence are just phenomenal, and what makes it more interesting is that the man has no clue of his wit and clever ways. He is very down to earth." Jerry said it so ceremoniously and grandly that everyone became solemn and made Micaela even more curious about this Liam Griggs.

In all the meetings of the summer, the mysterious Mr. Griggs never appeared. Summer ended and Annabella was coming back home to begin the new academic year in a completely new school. The semester started. Weeks went by Micaela was very busy trying to be mother, student, daughter from a distance and friend to everyone who came to her for advice. She was teaching a multicultural literature class as part of her graduate work. She liked to teaching this class, so she could introduce some of the Spanish authors not well known in the South. The work load was becoming tedious and overwhelming. She could not wait for the holidays to come so she could perhaps relax and get back to writing her novel.

She had started to write this novel about a woman awakened by the "light" surrounding her and she had put it off but now that she was in the literature program she had made a vow to get it finished and perhaps she could even use it as part of her academic work.

She had a class in comparative literature where Walter Benjamin and his thoughts on ideology and observations on *camera obscura* proved to be a bit much for her brain. She was in awe of this class wishing she had more time to do the necessary research to become proficient and eloquent in the material. Instead her daily routine made it really hard for her to get a strong grasp on the subject matter. To top it all off the teaching assistant for this class still had not made it back from his out of the country obligations. The ever elusive Liam Griggs was the teaching assistant for this class and he was still MIA.

Months had passed and fall was starting to peek through, bringing with it the dropping of leaves and morning chills that neither Micaela nor Annabella were used to. One Monday morning, rushing to get Annabella to school, gathering up all the papers he had graded but first making sure they all had been put in the grade book before passing them back to her students, Micaela got dressed in a hurry and without even thinking twice she went out the door trying to put her coat on before hitting the chilly morning air. Her sweater was inside out and backwards showing the tag in the front. She wrapped around her neck an alpaca hand knitted scarf that Annabella had given her. She was so proud to wear this thoughtful gift from her daughter that in her haste the pretty grey soft scarf hid the tag and her hat had been placed to the side making her have a disheveled "high fashion" look that was a sight to see. Annabella looked at her and instead of telling her the truth about how she looked, she only saw her with the same unconditional love she knew Micaela had for her and added, "Mom...I love you...you are the best!"

"Well, where did that come from?" Micaela looked at her puzzled.

"Hurry up! We are going to be late!" she added.

As they hurried from their apartment, slamming the door behind them they noticed an attractive man entering apartment Number Three across the hall. He muttered a hello under his breath and Micaela thought to herself, *Could that be the elusive, too good to be true, grant writing guru, T.A. par excellence?* He finally made it home.

Barely seeing him, she thought, *I guess he is kind of cute.* She gave no more thought to the man who just crossed their path, trying to hurry so she could get Annabella situated in school and then off to school herself.

"Shit! The paper is due today!" she muttered.

"Hello, Micaela!" Jerry waved as she made it into the faculty conference room.

"Hey Jerry!" she answered.

"So are you ready for your sustained exposition on your characters for the novel you are writing or is the paper for my class more important at this time?"

"What paper, are you referring to? Your *camera obscura* nonsense paper? Is that the paper you are talking about?" she went on making faces and showing him the pages of the paper she wrote in a hurry trying to meet the deadline.

"Why are you having such a hard time with the subject at hand? You are the quirky, ever questioning, overanalyzing kind of woman. What is your problem?" he grabbed her by her shoulders pulling her close so he could give her a warm embrace as he always tried to let Micaela be a part of his life.

"Oh, Jerry if you only knew how good it feels to be held the way you are holding me, but I would be a brute of a lover, an insatiable student forever and a bad cook, so you do not want me!..Just take the paper, be kind and give me a passing grade...no questions asked." She winked at him and he gave her a brotherly hug which made Micaela feel secure in the fact that Jerry was finally getting the point that she did not see him with romantic eyes.

"Well, do not give it to me. Liam finally is here and he will have the task of reviewing all that for me," he informed her.

"Is he the guy in Apartment Three who arrived this morning?" Micaela asked full of anticipation and she did not like that feeling.

"Yep! The rascal went out last night and did not make it back in until this morning," he sighed.

"What does that mean...Is he a ladies' man?" She asked.

"Well, he is beautiful as you probably could see," Paul sneaking into the conversation giving his ever unwanted opinion.

"Is he a ladies' man or not?" Micaela just wanted a straight answer.

"Well, well...I see he has already gotten under your skin and he has not even talked to you. Wait until that happens," Paul added with a mischievous wink in his eye.

"He is not that great from what I saw this morning, if that is in fact who I saw," Micaela went on to drop her paper in Mr. Griggs's box.

She went to class. As she started passing out her students' papers, she realized that she did not turn in her class paper instead Micaela had mistakenly interchanged her paper with the prologue of her novel she had been reviewing,

Holy shit! I turned in the wrong thing. Maybe he did not pick them up yet, she thought.

She told her class she would be right back. She ran across campus like a mad woman, waving to students and friends that looked as if they were saying, "There she goes...always in a hurry, whirling like the currents of the wind, becoming a whirlwind herself," she smiled back, puzzled sometimes at the way they looked at her. She made it to the English department and hurried to the mail room to retrieve her prologue and hand in the correct paper for class. She realized that in her haste she had become rather hot and started to unwind her scarf as she went up the stairs. The pork rind-eating receptionist looked at her in a weird way and Micaela responded, "What!"

"Nothing, nothing" she looked away with a smile.

"You people are so weird! Haven't you ever seen a woman on a mission?" she said it out loud pulling the paper out of her satchel and low and behold! There he was the same good looking man from this morning. She became self conscious and did not know what to say. The ever eloquent Micaela went numb and paralyzed as if she had been given a shot of that serum given to Michelle Pfeiffer in the movie "What Lies Beneath" where she could see what was going on, but could neither move nor talk being unable to escape her predicament. In Micaela's case, Liam was reading her prologue with a concentrated look and did not become aware of Micaela's arrival in the room. All of a sudden they both became aware of each other's presence and Micaela abruptly asked, "Are you Dr. Hall's TA?"

"Yes, I am Liam Griggs...Nice to meet you, and you are?" he extended his hand to shake hers.

"Oh, excuse me..I am Micaela Sims nice to meet you too!" she added full of energy becoming a whirlwind again.

She felt like she was being whisked away to some 'far away memory,' but remembering back how sad the feeling had left her, she tried to dispel it not ever wanting to go there again. She had fallen for a pretty face with aquamarine eyes that made her miss her prom, an exotic Adonis of some sort with classical features beautiful olive skin making one long for feta cheese and long winding roads on a private Greek isle once before, and it never went well; she was conformed to write her stories but would never be the protagonist who is loved by a man the way she wanted to be loved in real life, *Too much crap to deal with to think about this man in a romantic way*, she quickly thought.

"Is this yours?" he asked as he pointed to the paper he was enthralled with.

"What does it say?" She asked shyly.

"It is quite good," he added not wanting to relinquish it to her.

"What do you mean, quite good...It is quite good not just good?" she asked wanting to know this real opinion of her work.

"Oh I see, it's you!" he said giving her the paper back and looking at the tag of her sweater showing right behind the unwound scarf.

"What?" she asked, perplexed at his look.

"You are the girl who left this morning in such a hurry that you put on your sweater backwards, Did you teach the class like that?...and no one pointed out to you that it was inside out?...You have made an impression, I dare say," he grabbed the rest of his papers and left.

Micaela ran to the nearest restroom and looked at herself in the mirror and there it was, her sweater inside out with the tag showing, she turned beet red and started to laugh nervously and felt like a child as she scolded herself like her mother would have, You cannot even dress yourself anymore! What is wrong with you? can a simple task be so hard for you to handle properly? And tears started to flow but she did not know why.

"Are you okay?" one of her students that happened to in the bathroom asked her showing concern.

"Yes, thank you...A little bit overwhelmed by life, that is all," puzzled at the emotions she felt right then.

"So, professors have lives too!" she winked at Micaela, touching her shoulder and giving her a Kleenex.

"Yes, unfortunately or fortunately, we do have lives as well... and when we cut ourselves we also bleed," she smiled at the young girl who continued to laugh as well.

"That's good, you are also the witty Professor Sims."

"Well, thank you...Remember the paper, needs an outline so the assignment can be complete," she told the young girl with empathy.

"Nothing gets past you, does it?" she added.

"Nope!"

"Can I come by tomorrow so you can help me with it. Is that okay?"

"But of course. Just come after class and we can go over your whole argument and why the outline will help present your ideas more clearly OK?" Micaela started to assist her student which helped dissipate the anxiety attack she was about to have.

That afternoon and consequently that evening, Micaela could not concentrate at all on the most simple tasks. Annabella came into the room with her new collection of books she had just received in the mail and did not get the response she would have gotten from her mother some other time.

"Mom, you seem to be miles away," she told Micaela.

"What?" she responded as though trying to assimilate what she had heard her daughter said.

"You see what I mean?" she added.

"You are not okay?" Annabella insisted

"I'm sorry. I am fine. It is just school, work and having a beautiful young girl who is about to be a pre-teen weighs very heavy on my heart...but don't you worry, okay? Mom is going to be fine," she reassured her daughter by holding her and caressing her the way she would have liked to have been caressed by her own mother.

Micaela kept thinking about the things she had not had a chance to tell her mother before she left home. Why was her mother in her thoughts at this time and place in her life? "Why is she on my mind so much lately?" Micaela said out loud.

"I think it is crazy, Mom, talking to yourself," Annabella added looking at her mother with a smile on her face.

"I am sorry, but thoughts keep coming in my head that I have to stop myself from saying out loud. Do you know what I mean?" she told her child as if she knew what she was thinking.

"Yeah, whatever you say Mom," Annabella shrugged her shoulders and went into her bedroom.

Micaela wanted to be a little lady bug and zoom across the hall to see for herself what he was doing right now. Everything was so quiet and Paul hadn't called her to tell her about the suave Mr. Griggs. *Why are you thinking about him so much? He probably does not even remember you from this morning or afternoon whenever it was when you talked to each other*, she thought.

She went into the small kitchen to make some sort of dinner as she realized they had not eaten yet. She put on George Benson's best hits and "Give Me the Night" came on filling the room with the rhythmic tune to which Annabella knew Micaela would be dancing away as she made dinner. She came out of her room and went to see what her mother was doing, and as expected Micaela was moving to the rhythm of the song cutting the tomatoes and placing a slice of it in her mouth as the juice ran down the side of her hand to which she started to lick it off and out of the corner of her eye the figure of a man standing there making her turn in such haste that half the slice in her mouth went flying across the cutting board. She froze staring at this tall handsome blond haired man with the bluest of eyes that gave her goose bumps.

She caught her breath and asked him, "How long have you been standing there…spying on me…in my own home?"

"Not as long as I stood in front of your door knocking like a mad man with no answer, because Benson is giving these two young ladies the 'Night,' so I jiggled the door knob and it was open. I peeked in and this beautiful child looked at me. Thank God she did not scream or call the police. Instead she introduced herself to me, allowed me to do the same and told me you were in the kitchen making dinner and dancing away. So I had to see for myself," he said it all at once.

"What the hell, Liam. What planet do you think you're from?" she asked cleaning her hands with a cotton towel she just pulled from a drawer.

"From Earth but as I walked into this room, I seem to have gone to heaven and I am in the presence of two angels," he said it in a most complimentary way. Micaela started to laugh.

"Are you the Harlequin novelist people talked to me about?" she smirked.

"At least I do not go to work with clothes inside out and disheveled hats, running around campus like a mad woman. Oh but we were on a 'mission,'" he added.

"Well, I see we are not only a Harlequin novelist but also a fashion critic and gossiper," she retorted.

Micaela and Liam seemed to be going tit for tat at their own witty speed as Annabella watched her mom being transformed from a harried stressed out woman to a softer gentler feminine creature she knew she always was, yet her strength could not be veiled because she protected herself with the same zealousness as she protected her daughter.

"Mom, can I go play with Trixie before dinner is ready?" she asked.

"Oh! I'm so sorry babe. Dinner is ready," she responded.

"How about me leaving you two girls alone and I can come back with dessert?" Liam said winking at Annabella.

"How about you having dinner with us girls and taking us for ice cream afterwards?" Annabella said it using Liam's tone and mannerism as she spoke.

"Annabella!"

"I think it is a splendid idea!...Out of mouths of babes. She really is a smart one, isn't she?" Liam told Micaela pulling up a chair to sit down.

"And it is best you don't refer to me in the third person when I am in the room, because I find it not only patronizing but rude, Professor Griggs," Annabella informed him as she started to set the table.

"I am sorry about that, I see nothing escapes you...I will make sure not to be rude in your presence, madam," he said it ceremoniously.

"Apology accepted!" Annabella concur.

Micaela rolled her eyes not knowing what to say at their camaraderie from the get go, she was glad but weary at the same time.

She did not want her child or her to get attached to anyone at this time. It had been too painful to go through the one way relationship she had recently experienced, and even more painful was the loveless marriage she had escaped from, knowing she had never been in a symbiotic loving relationship. She became sad at the thought that this had always evaded her life and trying to stop herself from tearing up she thought of her book, poetry and her work. She made herself think she did not have enough time to play those kind of romantic games people play. Annabella went out of the room leaving them alone, they just stared at each other in wonder of one another with a silence that spoke volumes. There was a tenderness coming from Liam that made Micaela feel very exposed yet she liked being in that moment with him, unaware that she was falling for his blue eyes not in the same way as before but a conscious knowledge of who she was and what she was willing to give up. Caught in the assessment of themselves, finally Liam broke the ice that was between them for a second or two.

"I love the way you eat tomatoes," he said flirting with her.

"Oh is that so?" she blushed.

"I am sorry for being so forward with you, but this morning when I first saw you, I thought, "WOW she is everything people had told me about her'?" looking at her very intently.

"Who are the people that have been talking about me?" she asked curious about the response.

"Just people in the department," he added.

"Well, don't believe everything you hear," she said placing Chicken Alfredo on the plates.

"No, I don't make a habit of gossiping or believing everything people tell me, believe you me!" he said helping with the dishes being brought to the table.

"Oh my gosh! That is my expression. Please tell me they did not tell you that I say that all the time and that is why you are using it," she scolded him. "Please try to be original in my presence!" copying Annabella's insolent behavior of minutes before.

"I would not even dare to copy your language little missy! I could not even begin knowing how to go about emulating that accent of yours!" he said flirting again.

"So now we are going to be insulting?" she added sounding mad.

"I would never! You are too fair a maiden to have anyone insult you with those dark brown eyes of yours," he said it approaching, arriving in her personal space.

"Wait a minute, mister!" she said putting a hand to his chest and feeling weak in her knees.

Micaela felt a tremendous sense of guilt and apprehension and wanted him to leave yet she also wanted him to continue with his advances. They had met just that afternoon after glancing at each other in the morning, yet the energy she felt and knew he was feeling for her as well could not be denied.

"I am sorry, but you do not understand...All summer long before coming to work, I had this faceless image of you entering my thoughts, appearing in my dreams and it became taunting at times...in a good way of course!" he said holding her small hand that still spread itself on his chest.

"What?" trying to pull her hand away from him.

"Please do not take it wrong. Jerry has talked about you a lot, and the pictures he created in my mind while I was away are nothing compared to the real person that you are," he told her ever so gently.

Micaela had never been complimented like this before, *Was she dreaming or was it real what this beautiful man with the bluest of eyes in front of her was professing his admiration,* she thought.

She felt anger and confusion at the thought of not knowing how to act. She wanted to flee yet she wanted to embrace him, *Don't let the teenage angst and the adult bad choices you've made thus far take away from this joy. Please don't!* She thought. She could not help becoming teary eyed and looking at him intently she heard herself say, "I do not know what to say or what to do with this information, Mr. Griggs, but I tell you right now, walk away 'cause I am not the one you want...please," pulling her hand away she opened a drawer to get the silverware out.

"Mom, are you OK?" Annabella interrupted concerned about her mother's disposition. She had seen the anxiety in those loving eyes and she could not understand why that look was in her mother's semblance again.

"Oh! I am sorry baby. Professor Griggs is just sharing the plot of this novel he is writing, and it is heart wrenching. Maybe if you heard some of the lines, he would have you crying too." Micaela tried to dissipate the concern that appeared in her daughter's eyes.

"I am not buying it, Mom," Annabella responded.

"You are the most precocious little child I have ever met!" he added.

"Thank you, but can you please leave my mom and I alone for a while?" Annabella asked politely as she reached for his hand showing him the way out.

"She is going to be all right, I assure you," Liam said worried about what Annabella would say to her mother to dissuade her from seeing him.

"I know, Professor Griggs, but just let me talk to her...In the mean time she likes Rocky Road ice cream go figure and I like Chocolate Mint with lots of hot fudge and nuts!" Annabella told him pushing him out the door but letting him know to come back with the promise made of dessert.

"You are going to be my angel, aren't you?" he caressed her cheek.

"We will see,"

Annabella returned to the kitchen and as expected, she knew Micaela would be crying and soon would be looking in the old photo album to look at pictures in which she was as a young girl, where painful moments of her loveless marriage were captured in the images. She looked at them often only to be reminded that she had been and always would be unlucky in love. She felt the need to look back at these memories to subconsciously sabotage the new people and experiences in life. Annabella had seen her do this on several occasions and as she was growing up she started questioning her mother much like Micaela had questioned her mother at the same age.

"Mom, why do you do this to yourself?"

"What do you mean?" She asked reaching for a Kleenex.

"You know what I mean!... You have to let go of the past to find some peace and harmony in your heart! You tell this to your friends and yet you do not follow your own advice."

Micaela hugged her daughter and holding on as if it was the last time they were to see each other she started to sob.

"When did you become so mature and understanding...You are nothing but a baby," she told her.

"Now, I am not going to take that personally because you are too upset to know what you are saying, however, I have you as my mom...and at this young age I know so many things because of you. Aren't you the one who told me I was an old soul?"

"Yes, you are!"

"Then, wouldn't it make sense to be this way?"

"Yes,"

"Is YES all you know how to say? She asked, smiling at her mother.

"You silly girl of course not I know how to say no as well!" Micaela said wiping her nose and picking up the untouched dinner off the table.

"Say no to the sadness that consumes you at times and yes to the ice cream Professor Griggs is about to bring us and just be his friend. He seems lonely to me," Annabella very sweetly told her mother and giving her a hug and kiss she got up and went to answer the door.

It was Liam with a brown bag and a smile that Annabella knew in her heart this man was the one she would approve of. What more can a girl ask of a mother's boyfriend than to bring ice cream?

"That was fast. You owe me big time, Professor Griggs," she said reaching for the bag and taking it to the kitchen.

"May I come in and start all over?" Liam asked sheepishly.

"Of course, I am sorry for my emotional outburst. Please come and join us in this overcooked Alfredo," Micaela tried to apologize

"Don't worry about it...I just do not want to appear pushy or forward...but it is true, I have imagined you all summer and now that I have you in the flesh, I want to know more. I think I'll pass on the Alfredo and have some dessert instead," he told her sitting down next to her as Annabella passed out the bowls full of ice cream, fudge and nuts.

"Now if you really want to make my mom happy, the food she loves when she is getting acquainted with someone is figs and Mozzarella cheese and a good Pinot Grigio," Annabella informed Liam.

"Well, thank you. I will keep that in mind."

"Annabella, one cannot disclose everything all at once, little bits of information are better."

"That is not true!" Liam and Annabella said it at the same time and everyone laughed.

On this fall evening, with ice cream and laughter, Micaela and Liam's lives would change forever. They knew it but they kept quiet trying not to disturb their new found destiny and the love that would forge Micaela to blossom into the eloquent and savvy writer she knew she would become when she had walked the city streets of her native country, and then, in the immense boulevards of Los Angeles, California. She felt at ease yet a nagging feeling appeared in her heart...*this is too soon,* she thought. They played a game of Pictionary and when Annabella started to yawn. Everyone decided to call it a night.

"This was really delightful. I am glad I got to see you eating tomatoes," he grinned making his blue eyes sparkle with the luminosity that attracted Micaela like a magnet.

"What? Do I have ice cream on my face?" he asked puzzled at the way she kept looking at him.

"Oh, I am sorry for staring, but I have never seen such a beautiful shade of blue in anyone's eyes." Micaela said it a bit shyly and tried to dispel the great joy she felt being so close to him.

"Well, thank you. They are my mother's eyes," Liam told her.

"She must be stunning."

"Well, thank you again for the stunning part," he grinned again getting really close to her.

"Well, I meant your mom, not you!" She poked him without realizing she did it.

"Ouch, that hurt!" grimacing pain.

"Oh, my gosh! I am so sorry!" she exclaimed, embarrassed at the idea that she had done something so personal.

Grabbing her hand, he laughed and gave her a big hug, and proceeded to give her a brotherly kiss on the cheek, to which Micaela felt uneasy not knowing why.

"You are going to be easy!" he told her.

"What?" she exclaimed.

"I don't mean that kind of easy, but easy to pick on, you silly woman!" he told her as he walked to the door. "Well, this has been the best return home, I can honestly say I am happy to be back," winking at her.

"I am glad you are here, too," she said it very softly, realizing that she meant it.

Micaela was glad to have this man just a few steps away from her. She felt such an ease to be in his presence. She had been guarding herself from the time with Stavros, not letting anyone come close to her. Yet this stranger had managed to do just that in the few hours they had shared. Micaela could not help feel so close. She was curious what this man would mean to her future. She also felt a goodness that he exuded not to mention how comfortable he made Annabella feel. *Maybe that is a sign. After all only with her blessing would I approach this relationship...if there is to be a relationship,* she thought as she closed the door and started picking up the pieces of paper scattered on the floor from the game.

A very peaceful feeling overcame her as she picked up the glass of wine he had been drinking and bringing it to her lips, she started to think of a time where she had not been yet. Micaela saw herself in a landscape where the different shades of green of the trees and bushes went in harmony with the light emerald green color of the fresh cut lawn after a rainy night. She saw them walking hand in hand on a walkway, making plans she didn't know at the moment but nonetheless the couple in her mind walked making plans. "Micaela don't dream so much, you do not want to be disappointed again," she said it out loud as she placed the wine glass in the sink letting the water run on the glass and her hands. *Something about water and its cleansing effect. Maybe he is the water to cleanse me of all my awful past experiences, who knows!* She thought.

Morning came and the hustle and bustle of another day came rushing through her door. "Mom, get up we're late!" Annabella was trying to wake her up.

"Holy Cow! Babe what happened? We both overslept," she sounded disoriented.

"What time did you go to bed, huh?" Annabella smiled.

"Listen!"

"Just kidding Mom. For the first time I truly like this one from the get go."

"Well, thank you but I do not think you need to think about him so much."

"Why is that? Don't you like him?" Annabella looked at Micaela intently. "It figures, the first guy I like and you don't!" She added.

"Hurry up we are late, already!"

They came out of their apartment and closing the door behind them, Micaela wished that he would be there waiting for her.

"Please. Let's stop being a teenager!"

"What?" Annabella thought she was talking to her.

"Never mind."

After dropping Annabella off at school, she hurried to her class but could not concentrate. Micaela went to the department offices and read some papers in the faculty lounge hoping to get a glimpse of him, but to no avail Mr. Griggs was nowhere to be found. She saw Paul and as much as she wanted to ask about Liam she kept quiet, hoping that Paul would give some information about his whereabouts. Nothing!

"Micaela, this is not good at all!" she told herself.

The day came to an end and she hurried home to see if she could see him, but he was not there either. "Man! Where the heck is he?" she asked out loud.

"Mom, are you okay?" Annabella asked.

"Yes! Just have a lot on my mind," she said it nonchalant.

"Well, did you see what is on the counter in the kitchen?" Annabella asked and added, "You are a space cadet, lately you know?"

"I am sorry, honey just too much crap!"

"No, Mom you have too many thoughts about #3, and his whereabouts, but if you would listen to your daughter, you would go into the kitchen and see what someone left for you on the counter near the fridge." Annabella pushed her in the direction of the kitchen.

Micaela was so surprised and an immense feeling of happiness enshrouded her she felt as if all the women in her past were there looking at the pretty still life in front of her. Liam had brought her a ceramic bowl full of figs, a bottle of Pinot Grigio and a card that read

"Thank you for last night. I thought I would appease the foretelling goddesses with their favorite food. Fresh mozzarella is in the fridge. Call me when you get a chance, Liam."

She started to cry and felt wanted and revered by the simple gift of remembering her favorite food. "Should I make this tonight?" she asked Annabella.

"If you want?" she responded.

"No, I will make him wait. I will do it this weekend. What do you think?" she asked again.

"If you want," she responded.

"What is the matter, baby?" she asked.

"Nothing, maybe I could go to Trixie's this weekend and spend the night so you and Liam can have some private time," Annabella informed her, more than a suggestion.

"NO, I don't want you to spend the weekend out," she added.

"Why not? Mom!"

"Because I said so and I would miss you terribly when you are gone!"

The week took longer than most weeks to end. Micaela rejoiced in the fact that she felt all those feelings of falling in love again. She laughed unexpectedly at the silliest things, and cried when a fly got trapped in a spider's web. *To feel alive again is what love brings, only to kill you at the height of its splendor*, she thought and smiled at the passersby as she sat among the young crowd sitting on the steps of the Main Library. She read her prologue often, thought of the many things she should add and the things she should take out. All of a sudden the shadow of a man appeared on her pages and it made her look up only to be blinded by the sun in her eyes. She could not discern who was this man; standing in front of her, but she could only hope it would be him.

"I would not change a thing," Liam said.

"Hey, thank you for the figs and wine," she told him.

"You forgot the cheese," he added sitting down next to her, whispering in her ear.

"One cannot forget the cheese, that completes the dish, right?" he said with a smile adding that sparkle in his blue eyes, making Micaela want to dive into them and let all decorum and propriety fly out the window and have her way with him right there on the steps. The thought of making out on the steps made her laugh.

"What? Did I say something funny?" He asked.

"No, just thinking about many things...how are you?" very politely she asked putting some distance between them.

"So, we are going to be civilized and behave properly, because we are part of the faculty, because we are a boy and a girl, or simply because you feel uncomfortable knowing I know how you eat tomatoes." Getting up and dusting off his pants, he extended his hand to get her to stand up.

"What? Are you leaving?" she asked him.

"We both are, I want to show you this place where I think you should place the protagonist of your book when she falls in love with the male lead," he said.

"How do you know she falls in love? Maybe she is already in love with a lover who comes in the middle of the night to make hot, passionate love to her, huh?" she added.

"You are very beautiful when you flirt, and you should not do it because I can flunk you right now and the seminar is very important for your thesis," he chided.

"So...I see how it is going to be...professional jealousy and pressure...Come on let's go to this mysterious place where she falls in looooove," Walking right behind him, making the faces she made as she walked through the 'jungle' of her childhood years.

They drove down Highway 441 South to a small town named Madison. The only town General Sherman did not burn in the Civil War, the reasons why no one really knows, so the speculations are wide and farfetched. One being Sherman's mistress lived in Madison. They drove into town noticing a row of run down houses leading to the large well-kept mansions of the antebellum past. Micaela sadly thought of the people living here, some having it all and the others with not so much living in unison on Main Street or were they? She knew this was the South and the separation of classes was nothing new to her, still it gave her a lump in her throat to think of the atrocities human beings perpetrate still on one another.

It started to rain when they reached the first light in the town while looking for a place to park near this awesome old brick building, Micaela loved the place. She squinted her eyes and turned to Liam, "Hey, if you squint your eyes and don't look at the modern cars, it becomes a twilight moment and you are back in time. I hope I don't get lynched or anything like that! What do you think?"

"Stop! It's not like that anymore. We've come a long way baby. Plus you are not Black but Hispanic," Liam informed her a bit annoyed at her rhetoric.

"I don't mean anything bad by my comments, but you never want to put the unacceptable actions of others to the side and become complacent, allowing history to repeat itself, you know?" she told him with conviction.

"Are you always this honest?" he asked.

"No, I am not. Sometimes I have to bite my tongue," she added looking around at every building, at every detail in this small town.

It continued to rain, heavily now, like cats and dogs, as they say. Micaela was surprised at how much the rain and the small town made her think back to South America. The torrential rains they had there would eventually stop and soon after the sun would come out, glad to see the rain had dissipated. They entered the restaurant which was very quaint and old. It seemed to be buffet-cafeteria style, around the corner it continued into a large room with a vault to the right of the entrance. "What was here before?" Micaela asked.

"Didn't you notice the bank sign outside?" Liam asked her.

"Oh, yes. So this is the inside of the white marble building, huh?...Very interesting," Micaela added as a young girl showed them to a table Liam pulled out her chair.

"Thank you," she told him smiling, telling him with her eyes she was glad he had brought her there.

"I hope it stops raining because I want to walk around town for a bit if you don't mind," Liam told her.

"Sure! But I need to get back to Athens, Annabella is soon to be out of school and she would wonder where I am," she informed him.

"Okay, let's have lunch and we will go back," he added.

"They have the best pork chops ever, and you must try the sweet potato soufflé," Liam told her excited about the southern cuisine. They enjoyed the delicious southern food, as they were finishing their meal the rain stopped and the sun started to appear.

The young waitress came to the table bringing them their check and Liam handed her a twenty dollar bill adding, "Keep the change."

He got up to pull Micaela's chair out for her. She took a long look around the place it was really cozy and full of history, Liam had been right this was the perfect place to have the protagonist come and have dinner. She laughed to herself. They walked toward the car and as though nature was telling Micaela everything is going to be okay, she looked up at the sky noticing it as was as blue as his eyes and further down the street a line of old brick buildings with newer faces stood there waiting for the rainbow to catch her glance, conspiring with the old memories of South America that fled through her heart. She felt a kind of homecoming. She sighed realizing she was glad she had made the move to the East coast. New York would have to wait because she was ready to make her life in this small Georgia town where the sun peeking out showing her an awesome rainbow ended in the directions of Athens, "Is that where my pot of gold is?" She asked Liam out loud.

"If you believe in those things, I guess that is where it will be." He said it almost waiting for a response that would help him make his next move. He really liked this woman the way he had never felt about any other. He loved the spunk of her eleven year-old daughter with a fifty year old mentality. He liked the way Micaela delivered her lectures and especially how she ate tomatoes.

"I don't. That is bunch of malarkey. You are the controller of your own destiny, so no I don't believe in fairy tales of any kind," Micaela said it trying to convince herself, but deep down she knew that this small town with its beautiful antebellum homes, somber torrential rain, that gives way to skies opening up to a brilliant sunny afternoon presenting the wonders of nature in such a magnificent rainbow was a giant welcoming sign for her. She knew that after she finished at UGA she would stay in this area. Little by little, the ugly duckling was giving way to the swan. Annabella would be raised among the Georgia pines, sultry summers, spectacularly colorful falls and frigid winters. She would know all four seasons and with the passing of each of them she would also write new chapters in her small life and would surely blossom in love like Micaela would have wished to have had for herself.

They arrived back home and there they were, Biloxi and Annabella, pretending to be upset at their lateness and unknown whereabouts, "Where did you go mom?"

"I went to Madison a small town, very quaint very *je ne sais quoi.*"

"Why didn't you call? I was worried, you know?" Annabella pouting now.

"I thank you for being such a sweet worrywart, but Mr. Griggs was a fine gentleman taking good care of me and was kind enough to bring me back home safe and sound." She turned around to thank him, finding out he was not there. "Where did he go?" she called out.

"He is a gentleman and he ran as fast as he could!" Annabella said with a big grin.

"Liam, what are you doing? Where are you?" Micaela asked.

"I am sorry Biloxi for the delayed, thank you for keeping an eye on this little chick."

"No need to thank me, delighted to stay and talk to this cute child of yours, I got to go now. Bye." Biloxi went into her apartment.

Coming out of his apartment, Liam said, "I remembered that in order to appease the gods, the small goddess that is, mint chocolate chip ice cream would be an excellent idea. What do you think Ms. Annabella?" extending a paper bag with the goodies inside.

"Indeed, you are a gentleman!" Annabella exclaimed going to the kitchen to dish up the sweet treat.

"That is going to be your bait to lure her into your good graces, I guess, huh?"

"Does it bother you?"

"No, I just don't want her to get too close to you and then you go off to another precious little girl," she said taking a contemplative stance.

"Is that what you think of me?" he asked annoyed at her concern.

"No, but it happens." Micaela reflected on what she was about to say. "I don't want my daughter to get hurt in any way, I know she is smart and precocious. All the more reason I don't want her to suffer any more. She has been hurt enough already."

"I don't intend to hurt either one of you. Just relax and enjoy the ice cream," he said looking beyond Micaela, ready to accept a glass dish full of ice cream and fudge.

"Nicely done, my sweet ice cream angel," Liam said gratefully to Annabella.

Micaela did not want to interrupt the friendship between this man who thought tenderly about her only precious gift, Annabella. They sat down on the front porch watching the passersby as they ate their ice cream on this sunny late spring afternoon, promising Micaela sweet manna from heaven to appease the foretelling gods.

The end of the school year came and Annabella headed out to the West Coast to spend time with her father for the entire summer. It made Micaela sad to have her child travel to and fro to the two homes across country. It was the result of her actions and the poor child had to pay for it. She always felt melancholic and guilty at seeing her daughter leave. *Thank God for work!* She often thought because in the mean time, Micaela would immerse herself in her class schedule while trying to finish her novel.

There was going to be a competition in the department with a chance for the winner's work to be published as well as a fellowship to the prestigious University of Oxford in England. She jumped at the chance and tried to finish her novel to submit it with the hopes of an objective hard critique, if nothing else. Her classes were demanding but she was able to delve into the research. Reading the required material meant trying very hard to stay away from Mr. Liam Griggs. The obstinate pride that kept her away from Blake long ago, the same one that helped her walk away from Stavros, was making itself at home in her heart. She did not want to be hurt again even though Liam seemed to really care about her and Annabella.

"Hey pretty lady, whatever happened to those figs I brought you, the Mozzarella and the Pinot Grigio and the promise of a kiss? Omit the last one," Liam exclaimed as he got closer to her in the teacher's lounge.

"Annabella ate the figs. We both had *Pommodoro Alla Caprese* and the Pinot Grigio is aging as we speak in my fridge. Would you like it back?" she sarcastically asked him.

Liam looked at her as to say, "Where did that come from?"

Not giving up he added, "I would love to have a glass with you when you get a chance. I never get to see you anymore. Many evenings I have waited up for you but you come home so late...moonlighting somewhere?"

"Yes, on the corner of Pulaski and Clayton, Why?" she answered smirking back.

"Oh, no wonder I don't see you anymore...very hard working woman," Liam said getting closer to her only to feel her deliberate cold shoulder.

"Are you okay?" he asked.

"Yep. Why?"

"You seem upset, I really don't care if you ate the figs and cheese without me, I just want to have a glass of wine with you tonight," Liam retorted.

"I can't tonight. I have papers to grade and I'm turning in a paper myself in the morning. Sorry," she lied.

"I would rather you tell me the truth, I am a big boy and don't shy away from getting hurt," he added cynically.

"Good for you! I have to go now. Excuse me," Micaela darted out of the room as if a tornado was about to sweep her up and take her to that place that she had never wanted to return.

"Micaela!" Liam called her.

"I have to go, bye," she yelled as she kept moving.

When she got home she started to cry at the absurdity of her actions, all he wanted was a glass of Pinot Grigio for heaven's sake, why was she so afraid. Why was she so full of excitement and anticipation one moment but then full of anxiety wanting to run away from it all at other times? The more she tried to understand her own feelings the more she became angry at her mother, who had refused to speak to her because she had moved away from the family circle. She found out she had been sick, so the times she had called home that was the reason she had not taken her calls. Her father always made excuses for her but Micaela knew better. It was Paloma's disdain and indifference that was eating at Micaela's heart stopping her in her tracks from accepting the gifts this new place and her new life were bringing her way.

She realized she was pushing Liam away due to her misdirected anger. How can someone so interesting and educated, with a heart of gold, want to be with her? *My mother wouldn't even talk to me. What would he want with me,* she thought.

A tear ran down her cheek, she quickly wiped it away. The telephone rang. There was one of her students calling, "Hey, Professor Sims, a bunch of us are going to this new night club tonight. People were talking about how much you like to dance and we thought we would ask you to come with us."

"Thank you Jenny, I would love to go but I can't tonight. There is a big paper I am presenting this weekend," Micaela said.

"Well, I told Dr. Hall that you were probably busy and would not be able to come, but he insisted I ask any way," Jenny told her.

"Who else is going with you guys?" She asked wanting to know if Liam was going.

"No one else from the department," Jenny said trying to cover her lie.

"Are you sure? Did Liam put you up to this?" she asked directly.

"I swear, it wasn't Professor Griggs, but Dr. Hall was adamant I ask you." Jenny said

"Thanks, Jenny. Let me call Dr. Hall and see what he has to say."

"Please don't make me look like a fool."

"Don't worry. You go have fun, okay?"

"Good night," Jenny said sounding disappointed.

Micaela called Jerry and there was no answer at his apartment. She called the school and there was no answer as well. A few minutes later as she was making some coffee, there was a knock at her door sounding loud and with urgency.

"Hey, Micaela!" Biloxi was at the door.

"Hey, What is it with the urgent knocking?"

"I got gossip to tell ya. Do you want to hear it?" She said going inside the apartment and helping herself to a cup of the fresh brew that permeated the room.

"Well, I went to drop some papers at Paul's office and I overheard a conversation between Jerry and Paul, talking about the novel that Liam had just finished, the one he is going to enter in the competition, Jerry was telling Paul that one of the chapters was really heart wrenching and that it had been changed in the last three months. That it was brilliant how Liam had changed this chapter without interrupting the flow of the whole book, which was already finished but the chapter he changed has a new character that seems to be based on none other than YOU!" Biloxi said pointing to Micaela .

"You are kidding right?" Micaela asked in astonishment.

"Nope!"

"Have you read the work?"

"Nope!"

"Stop it!" Micaela told her annoyed at her lack of knowledge about the book but also intrigued by the facts just presented to her.

"Do you know about the students going out tonight?" Micaela asked Biloxi.

"Yeah, the whole department is going and I also heard Paul telling Jerry, Liam couldn't go because of some paper he is presenting this weekend at a symposium in North Carolina."

"Are you sure?" Micaela looked at her intently.

"Nope!"

"You drive me crazy with your nopes! What do you think? Should I go and try to find out about this changed chapter?" Micaela's wheels were spinning as she saw herself in front of her closet picking a dress to wear to go out for the night.

"Are you going?" Biloxi asked in anticipation.

"Well, the whole department is going except the elusive Liam, so why can't I be there too?"

"Awesome, we can go together!"

Too many things were happening all at once. Her mother not answering her calls, her father was not telling her if Paloma was actually sick or in another one of her hysterical phases. Annabella had not called in days and now she finally realized Liam's good intentions were genuine and she had managed to push them away,

"Why didn't he tell me about the book?" Micaela asked herself looking in the mirror. "You've done it again, you managed to completely push him away!" she scolded herself.

In the whirlwind of getting dressed, she also realized it had been a year since she had moved to Georgia and school had proved to be everything she had expected but now little obstacles seemed to be presenting themselves in a time when she needed to focus and put her work in the competition. Now that Liam was entering it there was no chance she would even be given an objective critique.

She got in a vintage 1930's stripped black and white rayon dress and placed a thick red belt accentuating her small waist and perky breasts despite having breast fed Annabella for more than twelve months. Her hair was mid length to her shoulders and the curls glimmered in the heat of the summer night, she wore a little bit of makeup with red lipstick to match her sandals and belt. Micaela took a last look of herself in the mirror and she felt sexy, secure in her own female sensuality that made her exclaimed, "Boy, you still got it!" She walked downtown where she saw Jerry and Paul. Jenny was talking and carrying on like a child without a care in the world. Micaela felt a bit out of place.

She tried looking for Liam discreetly but Jerry approached her saying, "Wow, you look marvelous. If I had any chance with you, I'd marry you right now!"

"Stop! Jerry tell me this little secret you have had and never bothered to tell me," Micaela looked at him trying to detect any emotion that might disclose important information.

"What are you talking about?"

"Liam's novel…what is it about?"

"Oh! That paper…I know about it as much as you do. The little prick is telling me I have to wait to buy my own copy to find out what it is about! I was the one who taught him the craft, yet his masterpiece I have to wait to buy. Can you believe it?" Jerry said looking around the crowd.

"Is he coming tonight?" Micaela asked trying to be coy.

"Do you want him to come tonight?" Jerry asked winking at her.

"Stop, I tell you!"

"No, he is not coming, unless someone already went to tell him you are here then I suppose he would come. Matter of fact, he would definitely make his way here, the little prick! He's going to get the girl, too." Jerry becoming a little tipsy was starting to tell Micaela everything she wanted to hear.

There were people coming and going, laughing and enjoying themselves. Micaela's thoughts, however, went back to the first time she had gone to this kind of place, a bar, pub, discotheque … whatever they were called. She had been twenty-seven at the time, married, and had a child. As these thoughts raced through her mind, a feeling of loneliness became very palpable with the tension of expectancy much like the time when Blake broke her heart. She felt sad in anticipation that the same turn of events would be with Liam this time, *I can't go there anymore*, she thought.

Suddenly, someone yelled out her name, interrupting her reverie and she was back in Athens, in this place called the Caledonian. It was a tiny space for a night club, very obscure but it had a 'young' feel to it with movie memorabilia all over the walls,

"Hey Biloxi! Come here girl!"

"Hey Micaela, I am about to blow this taco stand. Do you want to come or stay?"

"Let me finish this drink and we can go home."

It was very late and people were starting to leave. The music had mellowed out and the feeling of loneliness became more prominent. George Benson's Masquerade was playing on the juke box and Biloxi asked Micaela to dance, "You're crazy! People will think we are lesbians. How will we ever meet the man of our dreams, Biloxi?"

"Oh someone is tipsy. Maybe I can make you mine tonight?" Biloxi said flashing a devilish grin.

"You are silly!" Micaela said as she got off the bar stool, getting closer to Biloxi's open arms.

Out of the corner of her eye, she saw Jerry coming over announcing he would buy another round to celebrate his apt pupil's accomplishment. Liam had gotten another grant prepared, sent and accepted by a major foundation that would help the Department's next academic year in a big way.

"Where is your brilliant master mind?" Micaela asked looking around.

"He was at home with an old girl friend of his. They seemed to be reminiscing or some shit."

Micaela let go of Biloxi's hand so abruptly that it made Jerry laugh.

"I got you! I wanted to see your green-eyed monster come alive and I see, it is not a pretty sight," continuing to laugh.

"You jerk!"

"But I am right, ain't I?" He said hugging her in his brotherly way.

"No, you are not!" She said pushing him away.

"Micaela, you do not need to have your guard up with me. I can see it in your eyes how intrigued you were at the first mention of his name. I also saw how intrigued he was about you at the first mention of your name. You both were meant to be together, but you both are fighting it, you more so than him. Whatever your issues are, let them go. Be happy. All work and no play is not good for the soul, Micaela. Life is too damn short," Jerry said sounding very sullen.

"Thank you for the advice, Jer." Micaela told him.

Looking for her purse, she was getting ready to leave. The sound of the DJ announced the last call and a voice asked for Marvin Gaye's Distance Lover. Biloxi announced that it was her favorite and asked Jerry to dance. They went off to the dance floor leaving Micaela watching them. The place became even more empty. Paul came over to ask if he could buy her another drink. "Are you guys plotting to get me drunk or something?" Micaela asked looking for her purse.

"Are you looking for this?" She had not been aware that Liam had been standing there all along watching her, holding her purse.

"Well, well, look what the cat dragged in?" She pretended to sound annoyed.

"It was on the floor so I picked it up for you," he said giving it to her.

"It doesn't have a lot of money in it."

"I know, you couldn't even buy me a drink."

"What makes you think I want to buy you a drink?"

"Well, that's right. I'm sorry for my presumptuousness, but I believe you owe me a glass of wine," he said smiling at her.

Micaela loved to see him smile. It made his blue eyes sparkle with the intensity of the bluest ocean gleaming from the sun. His blond hair in disarray made him tender, fragile yet strong. *Really girl? You see all this in him?* She thought continuing to answer out loud. "Yup!"

"I think you had a little bit too much to drink, why don't I walk you home?" Liam asked, trying to hold her hand.

Micaela pulled away, looked directly at him, and said in a hurtful way, "Please stay away from me. I am not ready for any kind of relationship, not even a fuck...oops!...a one night stand, I mean." She sounded inebriated but spoke with a sting that was felt by Liam. He reached out his arm to hold this fragile yet strong woman up who was becoming an enigma he needed to sort out, needing to know how this piece of the puzzle would fit in the intricacies of his life. He wanted her.

"Please stop and don't say anything you might regret tomorrow Micaela," he said letting go of her hand.

The DJ announced that the last song was dedicated to the girl who captured someone's heart but it will be a challenge to make her his. "For all the hardcore Eagles fans, this one is for you!"

The music started to play *One of These Nights* becoming Liam's anthem to Micaela, for he was about to find out 'what turned her lights on at night.' He already knew it was the writing but he knew there had to be more. He would have the pleasure of challenging her intellect but most importantly he would have the patience to see her go through her emotional upheavals having him there to come and repose. She is beautiful and cute and extremely provocative, "Why are you single?" he heard himself ask Micaela as he got her by her waistline and swept her onto the dance floor whispering the words of the song into her ear.

"Shit! I am falling for you. I know I am and I don't want to stop," she told him.

"I'm glad. I am going to be there to catch you always, just wait and see," Liam told her as he embraced her in a very stoic stance, desperately trying to become one with her.

"Stop! This can never be. I am going home." Abruptly she broke away and started for the door. Biloxi ran after her, "Stop Micaela! We will walk home together."

The two girls walked all the way up to Pulaski St and turning on Prince Avenue, Micaela saw Liam and Jerry holding Paul by the shoulders, walking behind them. With an anger brought on by her alcohol, she turned to Biloxi and asked, "Why are those bozos following us?"

"Because we all live in the same apartment building, you silly woman!" She told Micaela holding her by the waist to stop each other from tripping.

"I think I drank a little too much. I haven't gotten this way since I left Annabella's father. Isn't it crazy?

"Shh, just rest your head. We are almost there."

They managed to get to her place. By this time Micaela was coming to her senses and felt totally embarrassed by her behavior, wanted to run to her apartment and hide.

"Thank you guys for a great night. The drinks and now for this sleepless night I am about to have with this drunken idiot," Jerry exclaimed opening the door to his place.

"Good night girls and boy!" Paul yelled as Jerry stopped him and pulled him inside his apartment.

"Good night, Liam." Biloxi and Micaela said in unison.

"One of these nights, Micaela." Liam waved to them as they opened the door and disappeared behind it.

"Oh my goodness! You are a very popular lady, look at all these messages on your machine."

Micaela went to the phone to check the numbers of these messages. They were all her parents' phone number. Just as she was about to pick up the receiver to make a call, the telephone rang simultaneously with her motion. "Another disruption, why can't I get a break, HELLO!" she exclaimed as she answered the line.

"Micaela is Rebeca, we have been trying to call you to no avail. Are you okay?" Her younger sister asked sounding genuinely concerned.

"Hey Beca, I'm fine thank you and you?"

"Is everything okay with all of you? Have you seen Annabella, and how are mom and dad. Why are you at their house? I thought you found an apartment and moved out. Did Mom make you feel guilty about it? Tell me she didn't!" Micaela sounding agitated and rattled asked all the questions in the same breath.

"Micaela, are you drunk?" Rebeca asked in an accusatory tone.

"A little bit. We were celebrating this new grant we just got... sorry," she apologized.

"You need to come home. Mom is not doing too well," she added.

"What do you mean? Did she faint and you are out of smelling salts?" she asked sarcastically.

"Micaela, this is serious. She has been sick and has gotten worse, she is in the hospital and doctors don't think she will make it till the end of the week. When do you think you can get here?" she asked sounding very upset.

"Don't worry, my little Beca, everything will be okay," she answered trying to disguise her own concern.

She looked around her small apartment among the craziness of each day, her books, her papers, her child's personal belongings that added a whimsical tone to the ambience, she found peace, harmony and understanding, all wrapped up in her precious quiet solitude, yet a phone call from mom's house and my place gets topsy turvy and my world turns upside down, she thought as she heard herself saying, "I will catch the next plane out of here. I will call you when I can with an itinerary okay? Don't cry...she will pull through this one too, she is as strong as an ox!"

"We need you Micaela, you should have never left us."

Farewell

Micaela found herself once again at a crossroads. Her life had been full of them and now she had that familiar ominous feeling gripping her heart, which was trying to pull her into another abyss. Perhaps it was true that her mother was dying. Paloma always spoke about her death, and how relieved she would be to leave all behind and rest. Micaela also thought maybe at this time she would no longer have her critical eyes on her. But as she realized Paloma was giving up on her own life, she knew somehow her mother would not only manage to make Micaela feel responsible for her dying but also guilty for savoring the new accomplishments she had started to enjoy. Amidst all these feelings of resentment and remorse for an uncommitted crime, she felt also great angst about the upcoming writing competition. It was so important to her at this time in her short scholastic career.

She hated leaving her unfinished manuscript to take care of her mother. "But she is your mother, and no matter how hard this relationship has been, you must be the ever protective, strong and obedient daughter. You must. You know there is no way out!" She told herself, looking at her freshly washed face as she prepared to go to California later that afternoon. She moved about her apartment with a headache not so much from last night's drinking, but more so with the turmoil of not having finished the last pages of her book to enter the competition.

"Just half a chapter is missing. Why didn't I work on it last night instead of going out? She reproached herself out loud.

"Because you were a bad little girl," she answered in the voice pretending to be the old man in the trunk of her grandmother.

That is weird, I haven't done that voice in such a long time. Wow... eerie, uncanny...are we gathered here for a reason? Are we going to find out more secrets, as she lies in her dying bed? The Galarza Díaz epic continues with secrets from the past! Micaela thought as she put on an over sized cotton mustard colored sweater, matching linen pants and striped white and black espadrilles.

She had lost some weight and her oversize sweater looked a bit large for her small frame. She put her hair in a pony tail, picked up her small suitcase, and a silk scarf and out the door she went.

"Hey Micaela, where are you going so early in the afternoon? I figured you would be sleeping your drunken stupor off from last night!" Jerry said to her smiling.

"I got a phone call from home and I am summoned to appear immediately."

"Oh! Is everything okay?"

"No, not really. I guess my mother is a bit under the weather, and she needs to see how the black sheep of the family is doing in the South."

"Well, tell her that Jerry Hall is quiet impressed with her production and this version of her lovely daughter, however, what about your manuscript for the competition?" Jerry asked looking a bit concerned and disappointed for her.

"Well, maybe next year there will be another opportunity," she added.

"Micaela! Opportunities in this field are scarce. So why are you doing this? Can't you go check on her, see how she is and come back next week? How long are you going for? What about the rest of your classes this summer?"

"Jerry stop! I have made sure everything is taken care of. I have managed to get all the assignments done, and for the one class I am teaching, the papers can be sent to me and I can grade them as they arrive. I also took the liberty of bringing you my manuscript so you can tell me honestly why it would not have made it in the competition, especially when one of my main rivals is pretty boy across the hallway with his spectacular novel that you already have given your blessing. All I want to know is what do you think is missing for it to be a best seller. Please take the time to read it while I am gone. I know I am asking a lot of you, but I consider you more than a mentor, a teacher, a friend. Please Jerry I will only ask this from you one time," she said holding the large envelope in her hand.

She got close and gave him a kiss on his cheek, whispering, "I will be in your debt."

Micaela walked down the portico steps, got in her car and scanned the facade of the building in which she had found sanctuary. She did not want to leave. She was encroached by that ominous feeling again and was afraid to go home to see her mother. It had been almost two years since they had seen each other. She was glad that Annabella was in California. She would have someone who would be happy to see her.

She arrived tired. Taking the 'red eye' after a previous night of celebration did not help. She felt old and ragged, and her cotton sweater and linen pants were all wrinkled and in disarray. Her scarf was falling off her neck making her look like she had been in a scuffle and lost. She hurried out of the airport to get to her parents' house to see if everything was okay there. She would assess the situation before going to see her mother at the hospital. Stepping out of the cab, the house seemed dark and lonely, if one can describe a building as being lonely, but it was lonely... unkempt with the rose bushes in the front yard dying from lack of water. The lawn was overgrown and weeds were in the flower beds. Micaela wanted to cry.

"Why did I leave? Am I so selfish, not to have realized that this would have happened?" She scolded herself.

She knocked on the front door but no one answered. The next door neighbor, Mr. Powel came out and yelled to her, "They all went to the hospital, your mother is very sick!"

"Thank you!" she yelled back.

"Could I use your phone to call a cab to take me there?" she asked.

"Of course! Come in...come in?"

"You wouldn't happen to know which hospital she was in would you, UCLA or St. Mary's?"

"I believe she is in UCLA Medical Center."

"Thank you, I'll call my Dad there."

She felt the bitter juices from her stomach creep up into her throat. Something was terribly wrong. She felt it and the fear that her mother might require her help indefinitely weighed heavily on her. After all, she was the one without a husband to take care of, or a home respectable enough for her not to leave. She lived alone with her daughter far away from everyone, so God only knows the vagaries people thought she was committing. Micaela could hear her mother's strong criticism of her. "*Hola*, Papi?" she greeted her father.

"Micaela, where are you?" her father asked.

"I am here at Mr. Powel's house. No one is at your house."

"Can someone pick me up? If not, I can call a cab?"

"No one is here *mi hija* so you better call a cab"

"I am on my way. Is everything okay?"

"For right now," her father answered in a very despondent way.

She called a taxi and headed out to Westwood to the hospital. As they got on the 405 Freeway, Micaela started to cry. It seemed that her world, her small new world three thousand miles away in Georgia was going to be destroyed by a mere request from this woman...the woman who instead of loving and supporting her daughter as a mother should, had done nothing but be her biggest obstacle, painfully reminding her of how ugly and awkward she was as well as needling her, saying her boisterous inquisitive ways were not lady like at all! "Why does she have so much power over you, why do you allow her to treat you this way?" She said it out loud, and she noticed in the rear view mirror the cab driver looking at her puzzled but with a benevolent smile. He said, "It's okay, that's nothing compared to what I get sometimes."

"I am sorry, there is a family member that needs my help and I have so many other commitments. How do you say, 'No,' I can't help this time?" she asked him.

"Well, just like that, like you said, 'I am sorry but I have so many other commitments right now, I can't be of help.'" He sounded supportive of her plight.

"Oh my gosh! It has been an eternity since I have seen Westwood. I loved to come down here and eat at the little Middle Eastern eatery, oh! The memories!" She cried looking around as the monumental grounds of the UCLA Medical Center appeared at the top of the hill.

"Thank you so much. You were a big help."

"No worries. You are a pretty woman and always should keep in mind that you are number one and if you do not take care of number one, no one else will!" The cab driver spoke with such a conviction, Micaela wanted to kiss him.

With trepidation and trying to make sure she did not forget herself in the process, she went inside. All the memories of when her baby brother was born in this same hospital came rushing back; how she was kept from going to school to help Paloma with his care and the resentment followed by guilt rushed again through her soul. She thought how she had stayed away from these corridors when she was studying Pre-Med and her feelings of resentment of being forced to study something she did not want began grabbing at her heart the same way they did back then as she found herself in the elevator getting closer to the room where her mother was, the one with all the power, waiting for her. She saw people outside the room, some family, friends and Froilán who approached her as she was walking toward her.

"Hey girlie, you finally made it!" Froilán told her giving her a warm hug.

"How is she?"

"She is lucid today. Issy arrived from South America yesterday. She and Dad are with her right now. No more than two people can be with her at once."

"Why?" she asked looking around and smiling at their friends who were waiting patiently for their turn to go in and see her.

"Well, they don't want her to get excited because it is not good for her heart," Froilán said it sounding very concerned.

"I am sorry, I know you do not like to see her like this, but she is going to get better, you'll see." Micaela sounding empathetic to her brother's feelings returned his hug.

"The doctors don't think so." he answered very sullen.

The door opened, and her father came out looking relieved that she had arrived but did not say a word about her condition except for "Hi, *mi hija*. When did you get here?"

Micaela walked to him and she embrace him, she told him, "Just a few minutes ago, Papi. I did not realize it was this serious when Rebeca called me to tell me the news. Can I go in to see her?"

"Yes, go in," he said opening the door.

Micaela wanted to see her mother but the feelings of guilt and fear were encroaching. She saw her mother frail and very skinny. Her olive skin was dark in a sickly way. Areas of purple from bruising appeared on her arms and Micaela for a moment lost all the resentment and anger she had for this woman. The mother, who now she realized she would be staying to take care of. The mother who was letting Micaela know in her own way that she needed to sacrifice all she had built in her new life in Athens, Georgia and get back home. Issy came over to give Micaela a hug. After exchanging pleasantries with her estranged sister, Micaela turned to her mother to say hello and gave her a kiss on the cheek.

The words that came from her mouth were like bricks hitting her all over as if she was being stoned for committing a crime, "Look at you, look at your hair. It is all disheveled and messy. Did you just get out of a boyfriend's truck after spending the night? Didn't I teach you better than that? You always had to have your own way and not follow any rules of civility!"

"It has been a little less than two years since we have seen each other and you have chosen not to speak to me when I call the house and this is how you greet me, your daughter! I may not be Snow White or the exotic beauty that your other daughters are to you, but I am also one of your daughters. I have traveled across the country and dropped everything that means anything to me to be here with you to see if I can help out. I do not know what else to say or do for you to be civil to me, Mami!" She responded all in the same breath without leaving Paloma the chance for rebuttal. It was a mistake Micaela soon realized.

"Get out! You are not going to come here and treat me this way. Who do you think you are?"

"Please don't get upset Mami," Issy started to appease her mother just as the nurse entered and asked everyone to leave.

"Do you see how you are?" Issy added.

"How am I, Iss?" Standing tall, she looked directly in her sister's eyes.

"I am not the one who left the family and never came back to share in the good or bad times. Am I like that?" Micaela stood there without moving a muscle in the corridor of the hospital, where everyone was looking at them.

"I am sorry, for the scene, but it isn't very pleasant to arrive after five hours of traveling to be treated like I just got out of jail or something!" Micaela told her family's friends and relatives who waited outside in the hospital corridor. Gloria, a good friend of Paloma, came over and greeted her with such an understanding tenderness that made Micaela give her a hug with such strength that it surprised both of them. "Thank you, Gloria, it is nice to see you too. How are you?"

"Everything is fine, just saddened by the news of your poor Mami," she responded.

"I am pretty sure she is going to make it. She always does and then she will have a party to complain about all the nurses not being kind to her and make jokes about the poor doctors who helped her with her malady." Micaela heard herself say all these things with a hint of anger and resentment as if telling on her would make up for the painful greeting Paloma had given her.

"We know, your mother is a fighter," Gloria added.

"That she is!" Micaela agreed.

After saying hello to the crowd, Micaela wanted to go back in to see her mother, and apologize before it was too late. For the first time, she was scared about her mother's health. She did not look well to her. Even when she was telling her off, she felt a genuine frailty in her mother's spirit. Micaela felt that for her mother the end was coming and there were so many things she wanted to tell her, explain to her and make her see that she should be glad that her middle daughter was a force to be reckoned with. Paloma should be glad that the same spirit of the Díaz family, proud and stoic, reigned in her being. She should be proud of the accomplishments Micaela had forged, and all on her own. Sadly she also knew Paloma would never acknowledge her accolades but would always be ready to criticize and show contempt for her middle child, the 'ugly duckling,' who was becoming the beautiful white swan. She was becoming a woman with an indomitable spirit and a formidable power of being. She decided to walk away and come back the next day.

"Mica! Wait up!" a voice from the past was calling her by a nickname only known by her inner circle.

"Oh my gosh! Could that be DOCTOR Bezhad Mohammed?" she exclaimed.

"Well, for a beautiful woman like you it is just Bezhad," he said with a big grin and a hug that Micaela reciprocated with the same verve.

"How long has it been?" she asked him.

"Too long. We were just babies the last time we saw each other," he said looking at her with a questioning look and a smile.

"I know, at your apartment on Slauson Street right?" she told him answering the unasked question.

"You always could read my mind, and you have not lost your touch, witchy woman!" he added seeing the more self-assured woman in front of him.

"You still think of me as a witch? I thought that rumor was dispelled when I could not make you disappear, remember?" she laughed.

"Ouch!"

"I am just kidding. You know I loved you more than words could have said, but it was not written in the cards for our lives to be together, so we went our separate ways to be better people, always being true to ourselves even in our youth. Won't you agree?" she told him holding his hand pressed against his chest.

"You...you still have those bewitching ways!"

"Stop!" letting go of his hands. "So tell me, how are you? When did this happen?" flicking his tag Dr. B. Mohammed, Clinical Pediatrics.

"You know, my family would never forgive me if I did not became a doctor!" he said laughing, as he mocked Micaela's plight of long ago.

"That is mean!"

"I know, I am sorry. Well, I stuck with it and then I started liking it and when I did my internship in the children's wing, I fell in love with the children and the rest is history, as they say." He said becoming a bit sullen.

"Anything else, you want to tell me after all these years?"

"I really fell in love with the children, after my wife became ill and we found out we could never have children of our own. She is the head of pediatrics, here," Bezhad told her with a dignified resignation in his voice.

"I knew you were my Persian prince then and now. She is a very lucky woman. Please let's all get together before I leave."

"When are you leaving?"

"As soon as I can. I have too many irons in the fire in Georgia, where I live now, to stay here and care for the hysterics of an old woman."

"I am so sorry. She is still hard on you, isn't she?" Bezhad said to her as he approached to hug her and plant a kiss on her forehead.

"You are so beautiful, even more than before. You and your mom are going to be fine. Just stand your ground like it seems you already have."

"Thank you. Let me know when is a good time for me to meet Mrs. Mohammed."

"There is no such person, I am married to Dr. Beth Carlton," he said winking at her.

"Right on! I like her already."

"Give me a call before you leave, *ciao bella*!"

She kept walking the corridor and thinking back to what the cab driver and now Bezhad had just told her after all these years.

"Stand your ground. She can't hurt you anymore. You are about to earn a Masters in Literature and maybe publish a novel by the end of next year. She cannot hurt you. Please don't let her," she said it all under her breath looking around to make sure no one had heard her talking to herself.

She got a cab and went back to her parents' house where her younger sister was there waiting. She had a strange look on her face which Micaela could not decipher, "Are you mad at me for some unknown reason?" she said getting closer to her sister, extending her arms hoping for a hug or even just a response.

"I am so sorry about the way Mom treated you this morning, so I heard!" she exclaimed starting to cry uncontrollably.

"It is okay. Don't worry about it. Mom is Mom and I know how she operates," Micaela responded caressing her sister's long hair.

"Why is she so mean to you? I was hoping now that she is dying she would be kind and loving to all of us," Rebeca continued.

"I don't know why and I don't really care to know," Micaela said walking about the house, touching the old trinkets, removing the dust from some of the furniture and looking at pictures trying to see if she would find one of her and Annabella. Much to her surprise, a portrait of the two of them that Micaela had given to her parents one Christmas stood in a very nice frame with the image of St. Anthony next to it. She smiled and turning to her sister she said,

"Look! Mom is praying to poor St. Anthony to bring her lost daughter back, I wonder which way I am lost to her?"

"You know which way Micaela. Don't pretend you don't know!" Rebeca said in a rigid way.

"No, I don't know, you tell me. She has my address, my phone number. Annabella comes here every summer and tries to spend time with her. So how am I lost?"

"I am not a drug addict nor a whore…not anything immoral she might not approve of, so physically nor emotionally am I lost." She went on walking back and forth through the small living room with the light coming from a lamp that had been in the very same spot since they moved into this house from South America.

"I can't believe she has kept that lamp this long!" Micaela said looking at the vintage amber glass hanging lamp in the corner of the living room. She went over and turned it on, with the yellow-brown reddish hues reflecting on her face, Micaela became contemplative and without much thought she turned to Rebeca, "What have I done to her to be so insensitive toward me?"

"I don't know, Mica, but if this is any consolation, you have always been a good daughter. I know she is proud of you. She's told people about the stories you write and moving away to get a higher degree with such pride that I don't understand why she would not tell you these things. She does love you, I know she does. She just wants you back with us," Rebeca held her sister's hand.

"I know that!" Letting go of Rebeca.

"You see what you do? You pull away every time someone tries to get close to you. You act just like her! You both are two peas in a pod. No wonder you are so critical of each other," Rebeca told her as she left the house. "I'm going back to the hospital. Do you want to come with me?"

"Okay, I guess I won't hurt her too much with my presence."

"Stop feeling sorry for yourself."

Soon after arriving at the hospital, Rebeca realized she needed to leave to tend to some business with her boyfriend. She approached her father who looked uncomfortable and very tired.

"Hi, *mi hija*. Have you talked to Annabella? She has been trying to get a hold of you."

"Don't worry Papi, I will talk to her later. Are you okay?" Micaela asked giving him a hug.

"Yes, I am okay but your Mami is not."

"What did the doctor say?"

"Well, she is not getting any better. They are going to try a new medicine and if she does not respond to it then that is all they can do for her, so she will stay here until she..." he broke down and started to sob.

Micaela was shocked at her father's break down. She had never seen this man fall apart. He had stood by Paloma all his life and quietly had managed to control every move his wife made after coming to America. She knew they both controlled or rather "loved" each other so much that they always did for each other and their alliance was quiet but very strong between the two. However, Paloma made him look very detached and she was the one who controlled the reins. It was so confusing growing up with their marital idiosyncrasies, that now at the end of her mother's life Micaela's father did not know how to act or what to do. She sensed an unresolved sensitivity that made Micaela just want to take care of her father to make things right with her mother.

"Don't worry. She will respond okay to the medicine and you both will be going home before you know it, and then you will be saying, "Your Mami is impossible. She is always wanting things I cannot give her. Am I right Papi?"

"I hope so, *mi hija*," looking around to see if Froilán had arrived from seeing his in-laws. "Froilán said, he would spend the night with your Mami tonight, but I do not see him yet."

"Don't worry. If you need to go home and rest, go ahead. I will stay here and watch over her. There are plenty of us to look after her don't worry, Papi," she told him, trying to ease his anxiety.

"You are very thoughtful, *mi hija*. Please don't let your Mami's anger toward her own mother be the torment in your adult life. She loves you...she has told me so," he said in a sweet voice as if he had heard her cry the many times she had asked herself the question, "Does she love me?"

Micaela's felt her head exploding. Why did he tell her this now? Why not all those many years ago? Suddenly the commotion of the nurse's changing shift brought her out into the hallway as she saw her father walking away. Froilán was nowhere to be seen and the nurse approached her asking who would be staying with the patient, "I am. I'm Micaela Sims, her daughter."

"Are those her linens to be change?"

"Yes, I am going to change her linens and make sure she has enough liquid for the night. She is also in a lot of pain so I'll be administering some more pain medication."

"Is she going to be okay? What do you think?" She asked, knowing she probably would not be given a straight answer, but was hopeful anyway.

"You need to ask her doctor," the nurse answered very coldly.

They went into her room and Micaela saw Paloma all alone, stiff and fragile, so fragile that her heart ached. The skinny old woman laying with all the needles and tubes and machinery taking account of every breath she took, was not the woman who raised her. Paloma, the one who could not show her the love she so much needed, was full of life, full of resolve, laughter and beauty.

"Why are you here lying in this bed dying, when there is so much life to be lived yet, Mami Paloma?" Micaela said it under her breath.

She saw the nurse very insensitive and matter of fact rushing to lower the bed to change the linens.

When a grimace of pain came from the small mouth of her mother, Micaela kindly asked the nurse, "Can I help you change the linens for my mother? I know she probably would like me to do that for her."

Softly Micaela approached her mother's bed and saw her olive skin glistening from the fever the doctors were trying to bring down. There was an infection that could not be contained. She was in pain in many ways. Only Micaela knew because there was that unspoken connection the two had had all these years. A love-hate relationship, mother and daughter, envious friends...Micaela could never pin point all the feelings the two had for each other. She caressed her face and touched her fragile hands and the overwhelming sensation to hold her in her arms made her cry and slowly, trying not to wake her up she planted a kiss with such vehemence that the nurse told her, "You are a sweet woman, her infection is very contagious you should not get so close to her or you can put on a mask."

"I am okay. She is my mother and I have been away for so long, that I want to make up for the time lost."

"I know how that is. Well, here are the linens. Go ahead and change them. I will be back with her medicine."

The nurse left. An eerie silence filled the room and there they were...the two of them both looking fragile physically and emotionally. They had hurt each other for what seemed like an eternity of sorts. The rhythmic sound of the machines making sure her vital signs were okay disrupted the silence and Micaela very slowly started removing the sheets from underneath the small yet heavy weight of her sick mother lying there, gone in the euphoria of pain killers. Micaela felt all kinds of emotion...guilt for having left, resentment because she knew it was the end, anger because she would never know why she had been so critical of her, pity for the pain she felt her mother was in as she grimaced in the stupor of her medicated mind. She managed to pull the dirty sheet out from under her and started to place the clean one on. As she moved her mother's head and shoulder, Micaela heard her say, "Hi Issy, you've come back?"

"No, Mami Paloma, it's me Micaela." She said full of fear.

Silence, the eerie silence again. *Did she hear me or is she back into her medication?* Micaela thought.

She continued moving Paloma's body to make room to extend the new sheet underneath and trying very hard not to wake her or cause her any discomfort as she saw the painful grimace on her face. She managed to change the linens, placing the one on top of her to cover her body and she heard her say again, "Issy, when did you get here?" reaching for Micaela.

"No, Mami Paloma it is me, Micaela. I am here to change your linens and keep you company for a little while." She bent down to touch her mother's arm but to her painful acknowledgment Paloma withdrew her arm and in that demanding voice she knew so well she asked, "Where are your sisters?"

"I think they are at home but they should be here first thing in the morning. We are taking turns to spend time with you and look after you. Is that okay?" She said sheepishly in the teenage, young, frightened voice of long ago.

She had forgotten how afraid of her mother she had been all these years. No response increased the fearful angst her mother always had caused her to feel and Micaela's eyes filled with tears as she reached for her head to put back the pillow and make her feel comfortable. She felt the intent look of her mother's eyes on her and she became the eight year old wanting to know things from her mother but afraid to ask, followed by being told how impertinent she had always been. But with the resolve of the woman now, she asked, "Are you okay? Doesn't that feel better?"

Paloma looked at Micaela with a lucidity that could not be denied and said, "Oh, it's you. I should have known...Why must you always hurt me?" and with the same swiftness that she had come to, she left to her unconsciousness becoming flaccid and immobile as her heart and pulse became so agitated that the nurse came in to check to make sure she was okay.

"Are you okay, Ms. Sims. You look like you have seen a ghost. Your mom is fine. It's the medication we just gave her. Don't worry. She will sleep fine for the rest of the night. Are you okay?" the nurse asked again as she saw Micaela come undone, literally, at her seams.

Micaela's head could not process what her mother had just said and the nurse questioning her brought her back to reality. The painful reality that the last words her mother would ever say to her was *Why must you always hurt me?* "Really mom, I always HURT YOU! How? Tell me how?" she screamed and turning around so fast to gather her scarf and purse, the scarf got caught in a chair ripping it in half, but she fled anyway.

She had to run from all the hurt and meanness, telling herself, "The hell with you, the hell with your family traditions, the hell with your culture and your fucking pride, the hell with all of you!"

She ran through the corridor looking for the elevator realizing in her anger and hurt she had gotten lost in the labyrinth of the hospital corridors. She felt lost. She felt she had no one to ran to and felt so hurt, "Why did she say that. Why, why?" She kept saying as she looked for an elevator or a sign where she could exit. She wanted to exit her life as she found herself standing in front of the chapel with a cross in front of her to remind her that she needed to assess the situation and rethink her words. She genuflected, made the sign of the cross and whispered, "I know you love me, so please get me out of here. Please give me the strength to forgive her for the pain she's caused me and if I had ever hurt her in anyway, dear Lord, give me a sign to tell me that I am forgiven. That's all I ask...get me out of here." Micaela kept walking and somehow she found a big sign showing her the way to the elevator that would take her to Conde Street where she could walk to Westwood Boulevard to catch a cab.

Micaela got home and everyone-her father, brother and two sisters-were sullen and looking at Micaela, they approached her very concerned, "Is Mom, okay?" they all asked in unison.

"Are you okay, *mi hija*?" her father asked looking as though he knew something was up.

"I am fine--just a bit tired from the trip. All the emotions from seeing Mom so fragile and sick, just makes me hurt for her. The nurse told me to leave and get some rest that the medication she was on would make her sleep so there was no need for anyone to be there." She said in a monotone and flat voice. No emotion just the words came out and it was as though it was not she who was talking.

"Micaela, you could have stayed just in case," Issy added with a reproaching tone.

"Well, you and you and all of us could have done this, should have done that, but no one is going to take responsibility for what could have or should have been done and frankly I am too tired to tell you exactly how I feel, so I am going to continue being the black sheep of the family and make my exit now." She collected her things, called a cab and left to go see Annabella at her old house, the 'gilded cage.'

Upon arriving, Edward answered the door saying, "Hi, Micaela. What are you doing here?" surprised to see her there.

"I am here to see Annabella, and see if you would let her come with me and spend the night."

"Are you going back to Lennox?"

"No, I am staying with Maria here in Torrance," she lied.

"Well, Annabella is asleep and I really do not want to wake her up. She is not a happy camper when she is awakened."

"I understand totally. You are right about that! I will be back first thing in the morning to pick her up to spend the day with her, if that is alright with you. Did you have plans for tomorrow? If not, can you tell her I'll be here around nine in the morning and we'll do breakfast?"

"Sure," he said with a questioning look.

"Thanks." Micaela left Edward's 'gilded cage' and walked through the gardens as she had done many times before. The smell of jasmine was still there. The beautiful night laying over the landscape of Palos Verdes with the millions of little lights demarcating the shore still made her smile. She told the cab driver to drive to Manhattan Beach and let her out at the pier. She would catch another cab from there back home. She explained this to the cab driver as if he cared of her whereabouts. She chuckled a nervous chuckle to which the cab driver gave her a look of pity.

It was about eleven thirty at night and still there were many passersby as she walked to the end of the pier. She thought back to the times she and Blake had walked the old wooden planks, these old planks full of texture, full of stories of the many jilted lovers that explained their way out of the painful circumstances of their break up. She stood there staring at the deep darkness of the horizon feeling the cold breeze on her cheeks. She caressed her face and thought, *Has the air always been this cold in the summer months? I don't think so. I think it's Paloma's way of saying good bye to you; the woman is so powerful she can make the air that you breathe feel as icy cold as her feelings for you, but don't despair help is there. You see? You rhyme! You speak in poetry...your prose continues and your spirit, depleted as it feels now, will rise again tomorrow...you know it, I know it, everyone knows it! You need to seek therapy, Mica. You are thinking crazy things to yourself.* She walked around the pier smiling and thinking back to when she was young how Blake had hurt her feelings and when she had gotten home, her mother added salt to the wound.

She felt lonely like that night long ago. She stopped for one moment, feeling warmth coming from the lamp up above her. She smiled again to know that light was so important in her life. Light being natural light from the sun, light from lamps, light from the books that she had read, all these 'lights' helped her find her way. *That is why 'light' is the one thing needed in my life; for it enlightens my soul, helps me find my way and in the cold nights of good byes always brings me warmth.* She thought, as she grabbed her arms and kept walking toward Hennessy's Pub to get to their phone and call her dear friend Maria, who in a matter of minutes was there to get her and give Micaela a place to stay.

"Girl! I am so sorry about your mom. Is she okay?" Maria asked holding Micaela in an extended embrace.

"She is okay for now, but I don't think she is going to make it."

"Oh I am so sorry,"

"You're sweet. Thank you for coming and picking me up and letting me stay with you tonight."

"No need to thank me. Would you like something to eat or drink?"

"Something to drink, if you don't mind,"

"Here or at my house; I have your favorite and some limes.

Do you want a gimlet?"

"No, just on the rocks will be fine at your place."

Once in the house, they headed for the kitchen where Maria poured a glass of Micaela's favorite gin handing it to her she sat down and looking intently asked, "Okay! Now tell me what is in that head of yours. I know you have been crying and you look like shit!"

"Thanks!"

"I am so envious of the way you are. You are single, so pretty, not now of course, but there you are walking into Hennessy's looking like that, and you don't even care. Do you know how many opportunities you missed?"

"You are crazy! Men are the last thing on my mind, they all suck anyway and not in that good way either!" she laughed making Maria laugh.

"You are amazing! Despite your pain here you are laughing and making me laugh. Do you ever have a bad moment?" Maria asked sarcastically.

"Nope!"

They went to bed and Micaela lay there unable to make sense of her mother's words. It still weighed heavily on her heart and she was unable to sleep that night. All through her life she had craved her mother's love and attention. She had always tried to gain it, doing exactly what she thought her mother wanted her to do.

Micaela was in her mid-thirties and all her dreams and aspirations had been put on hold or discarded totally for the sake of her mother's well-being. Why, at the most crucial time to make one's life have purpose, had Paloma chosen to repudiate Micaela even more? In her inability to sleep, while tossing and turning Micaela had an epiphany. She realized that she had a false sense of security when it came to her mother's love, but conversely, she also had the protection of her mother's over critical eye which pushed her to always do her best. Now when she may soon be leaving this world without saying good bye to Micaela, Paloma inadvertently lifted the veil and Micaela saw herself as the 'ugly duckling' shedding her last ugly dark plumes giving way to the 'light' of the beautiful white swan she felt she was becoming. She will have no one to answer to but herself. She will have no one for whom her dreams would be put on hold nor would there be the question: "What fun would that be?...to travel the world and write about it." There would no longer be the person who would say, "That's crazy Micaela. You are not good enough...You would starve to death as writer!"

"So I would starve to death but I would know how exciting it would be to travel the world and write about it." She said it realizing she had not slept a wink all night. She got up, got in the shower and cleansing herself emotionally, she let the water flow through her body. She cried like the nights when Pablo, Blake and Stavros left and she thought this pain would pass as well as the pain of being left behind with no one to answer to. It does not matter who abandons you or the reasons why they do so, the pain is still there. Your hurt vanity remains, making you question every move you have made in the past and those you are about to make. She became angry in her resolve and she no longer questioned why. Micaela knew that now the sky is the limit. She would be all alone with big responsibilities. She would be her authentic self, loving herself by reclaiming her gift of writing. She can love as she wants and do everything she can for that precious gift she has been given, Annabella.

Micaela got out of the shower and went to make coffee. Maria came out from her bedroom and giving her a hug told her very gently, "You are going to be a power house. I can't believe all these years you felt so alone, experiencing so much sadness. I wish I was a better friend and had felt your loneliness and been there for you."

"What are you talking about? You're the best ever and to prove a point, look around. I have taken over your apartment, made myself feel at home, used your shower, and by the way you need more shampoo and I am about to make breakfast with your best stash of coffee. So you see, you have always been there for me. You are a good friend whom I can always call in times of need and I know you will be there. I love you and thank you." Micaela embraced her friend.

Maria held her tightly and then pushing her slightly away to see Micaela's face, she said, "You are going to be fine, 'cause you are an awesome woman, mother, friend and most of all a dutiful daughter!"

"Stop! The coffee is ready. Do you want a cup?"

"Micaela, please don't deny yourself anymore. Accept the gifts life gave you and put your pride aside. Life is too short," Maria said, picking up a note from her telephone stand.

"Annabella called last night but you were asleep, so I decided to keep it until this morning."

"Oh my gosh, I forgot about the poor thing! I told her father I would have breakfast with her." Micaela reached for the phone and called her daughter.

"Hey, Honey, how are you?"

"Hi Mom, finally I get to speak to you. I've called you several times. You are one hard lady to get hold of."

"Sorry, honey, but Mami Paloma is very sick and I have been taking turns staying with her," Micaela said sounding in a hurry.

"I know, I talked to *tía* Beca and she told me about it. Do you think she is really sick or do you think she is just having one of those fainting spells?" Annabella was well aware that this had been her grandmother's history.

"Don't talk about your grandmother like that Annabella," she scolded her.

"I am sorry, but I know how you suffer because of her," Annabella sounded ten years her senior and disclosed feelings Micaela did not know about.

"Oh baby, please don't say that,"

"What Mommy?"

"Never, mind. I am coming to pick you up and spend the day with you. How's that?"

"Mom, I have something else to tell you. Jerry called and he left an important message for you."

"Jerry Hall in Athens?"

"Yes! Something about you need to get back ASAP because you are about to become very important."

"What? I am important already, wouldn't you say?" Micaela said laughing.

"I know, you know but soon the world will know, Mom. Call him right away, and then come and pick me up. I think we need to celebrate with ice cream and a soda. I love you!"

"I love you too, sweet girl. See you soon." Puzzled by her comments.

Micaela dialed her work number the second she hung up with Annabella, the receptionist answered in that soft slow twang of the old south, "English Department. May I help you?"

"Hi, Bertha, it's Micaela, is Jerry in?" sounding full of anticipation.

"Hold on, Miss Sims, he is with someone in his office, but told me specifically if you were to call, to stop everything and get him on the phone. Something is goin' on,"

"Like what Bertha? What do you think is going on? Am I in trouble?"

"Oh, no, ma'am! Nothing like that! He has been singing your glories along with Mr. Griggs. They spent much of their time looking

at some paper of yours and going, 'Micaela is something else, isn't she?'"

"Who said that Bertha?"

"Well, both of them ma'am. Here he is. Hold on please."

"Micaela! How are you? How is your mom? When are you coming home?" Jerry sounded excited and in a hurry for Micaela to come home.

"WOW, if I did not have you as my mentor, sort of colleague and teacher, I would say you love me and miss me," she said sounding sarcastic.

"You need to bring your ass home as soon as you can. Many things have transpired recently and you need to be here at once. A lot is at stake if you do not make it here by next Monday morning."

"What is it? What could be so important that I need to leave my dying mother, for what Jerry?"

"There is too much to tell you over the phone. Liam has done a disfavor to the department and no one can tell him to stop what he has put in motion."

"What did Liam do?" Micaela wanted to know because the agitation in Jerry voice was genuine.

"He better explain that one to you himself. I am not at liberty to tell you, but maybe he will listen to you and stop this madness."

"You are being very dramatic and unfair since I am so far away and cannot talk to him now."

"I am sorry, but he is being irrational, just because he feels he loves you!" Jerry said with an indignation in his voice Micaela did not know how to take.

"Are you in love with Liam?" She asked not wanting to hear the answer.

"For heaven's sake, that is the stupidest thing I have ever heard!"

"No, I am not in love with him! He is a hell of a catch, however, he is not my type, plus since you have been in the picture, all he wants to know is about you! But you are so wrapped up in yourself you cannot even tell how much time he has invested in you. Am I in love with him? How silly girl. Once he met you, no one had a chance."

Micaela could not believe her ears. Had Liam put Jerry up to this? How insensitive of them to pull this kind of crap at a time like this with my mother dying and all. "I will try to get things in order here and call you tomorrow with the time and date of my arrival home, okay? Whatever Liam did, I am pretty sure it can be undone, do not despair," she told Jerry as if she was talking to Annabella. The compassion in her voice trying to appease him from miles away was heartfelt and Jerry realized how wonderful and sincere this woman was even though she knew nothing about what was taking place.

"Sure, just get here please."

"I will see what I can do. Relax...have a cup of tea and get some lunch...bye Jer."

Micaela finished getting dressed as did Maria who was kind enough to drive her around town and take care of all the necessary arrangements so Micaela could leave without making the family too upset. Micaela picked up Annabella who was waiting for her by the gate. Her almost twelve year old daughter was becoming so pretty and grown up that Micaela wanted to keep her close without stifling her like her parents had done. But how does one manage to do this? She wondered as she extended her arms and hugged Annabella tightly, "Hi, my love. How is my pretty girl?"

"Oh no! Are you okay? Every time you treat me like a toddler, I know something is wrong," Annabella protested.

"Oh, she is becoming a teenager!" Maria yelled out from inside the car making Annabella roll her eyes.

"Stop it, babe. I just haven't see you all summer and have missed you terribly, plus I leave tomorrow night for Athens. I want to ask you...would you rather wait for summer to end and return then as scheduled or do you want to come with me now?"

"Well, Dad and I have plans for the rest of the week. Is it okay if I stay a little longer?"

"Sure, babe." Micaela hugged her again caressing her very gently as if she was stroking her own 'inner child.'

They got in the car to go see Paloma and see how the family was going to handle Micaela leaving early, not waiting for her mother's total recuperation. As they drove down Pacific Coast Highway, Micaela perused her thoughts, seeing herself driving these streets and boulevards not too long ago yet feeling like it had been an eternity. She thought of the many times she felt like she did not belong. She often felt abandoned and alone amidst all the people she met. Was it her culture, her upbringing that separated the locals from the *loca*?

Indeed Micaela's family thought of her as crazy for wanting all that life had to offer whether she belonged or not in this new place she was making her life. They drove by her beloved Manhattan Beach Pier. In the early morning haze and from the distance, she saw the round desolate building that held so many memories for her. That picture of the structure standing alone yet strong with a feeling of loneliness but also with hope that the sun would come out and the pier would be filled with passersby as the day becomes night with lovers promising love or saying good bye like she had done once before...all these memories and feelings gave her a sense of closure because she knew at this moment that the pier, the strand and the breeze of the ocean with its salty smell would become a long distant memory in this chapter of her life. Maria got on the 405 Freeway north headed to another world where a different set of memories awaited Micaela.

The dark ominous cloud of coming to terms with her mother's imminent death weighed heavily on Micaela's heart. They pulled into the parking lot laughing and teasing each another. As Micaela and Annabella got out of the car, they waved Maria good bye to and heard her say to them, "See you later girlies, CALL ME IF YOU NEED ME OK?"

They went into the frigid cold air-conditioned lobby of the hospital. It was a prelude of what was going to greet them when they would enter Paloma's hospital room. Micaela looked at Annabella with a look of watch out! Here we come again! Annabella, as young as she was, felt her mother's angst and caressed her hand while pressing it ever so gently. Both had tears in their eyes and their nonverbal communication was sensed like so many times before. Micaela feeling secure in her child's love, knew that it was a bit late to expect her mother's love and affection. They knew Paloma was near life's end.

"Hey, Micaela, where have you been?" Rebeca asked with resentment in her voice.

"I called the nurse's station this morning and they told me she was stable and I could take my time getting here. I also had to pick up Annabella. I am a mother too, and have responsibilities of my own, so stop with that tone of voice."

"Well, you seem to disappear and not be accountable at times of need." Rebeca added.

"She's always done that! Wandered off and then Mom had to send Froilán to fetch her," Issy added with contempt.

"Well, at least I was there for Mom when she needed family the most, when Andrés was born. I did not choose to leave the country and take care of myself first. Please do not get me get started on who has been more unfair to Mom or who was treated better than the others. I do not want to be petty at this time of great stress for Papi. His two dutiful daughters must take into consideration that their father who is about to become a widower will be left alone and now who is going to carry that torch?" Micaela said it with such conviction that she knew the strength of the women of her family was coming to her. It never failed her, imagining the women of her clan embracing each other telling each other and now telling her that everything was going to be okay.

"Hi, Papi how are you?" extending her arms to her father.

"Fine, thank you *mi hija*. Oh before I forget, someone from Athens called you last night and he said it was important for you get back to the University." He said holding her arms in such a way as to say, "But you must do for family first."

"Don't worry. I talked to them and everything is fine for now. I do need to get back. This is why I came here to make sure Mom doesn't leave me at the most important time in my life. So I need to see her and talk to her."

"Are you insane? She is not talking at all. She is so sedated that she's not lucid for any length of time!" Rebeca added.

Ignoring both of her sisters, Micaela turned to her father,

"Can I see her please?"

"Sure, go in but she is not answering to any of us."

"She talked to me a little while ago." Issy said it boasting.

"You lie!" Rebeca added.

"Splendid! Are you trying to keep her from me now too? We are no longer children and you no longer have any power over me. So go back to being the most unsympathetic and selfish brats that you both are. I could never see myself calling you my sisters...you both disgust me and it's better I tell you this now to your face!"

"Micaela, stop it!" Her father exclaimed.

"This is ridiculous!" Micaela went in the direction of the nurse's station and asked to see the doctor in charge of her mother.

"Dr. Robinson is not here yet but you can talk to his intern. He can also tell you about her condition."

Micaela went looking for him and had a long conversation with the young Physician's Assistant, who told her that Paloma was stable but he believed she would not make it past September. However, if she needed to take care of her business in Georgia and come back for the final good byes, he felt sure that there was enough time before Paloma passed away. Micaela felt better that she could leave, take care of her professional affairs, and come back to stay by her side until she left them all.

"Papi, do you want to come inside with me?" Micaela asked her father.

"No, you go ahead. You need to be with your Mami alone."

"Thank you," she said, reaching for his cheek and kissing him ever so gently as she had done with every goodbye they had shared in their lifetime together.

Holding hands, Micaela and Annabella went inside the pristine hospital room noticing right away the noise of the machines helping Paloma stay alive. She was not the Paloma everyone knew. Her decimated, pasty brown/olive skin no longer showed the vibrancy it had as Micaela had seen growing up. Micaela remembered seeing her frolic and move with the elegance and agility of a gazelle. Annabella gasped in terror and ask to let her go outside,

"I'm sorry mom, I can't look at her like that!"

"It's okay, baby go on. I will be outside in a little while."

"Hi, Mami Paloma, I know you are there, listening to everyone who comes through that door. I know you check out what they are wearing and let's just hope they are dressed to your standards. I always thought that was funny on your part but now that I have Annabella, I understand and give thanks for the sense of beauty and perfection you have given all of us."

The noise of the machines seemed to sound louder but the stillness of Paloma made Micaela ache as no other ache in her life before, "Are you okay? I know you are in pain but if you can understand what I am saying please let me know. Open your eyes, make a gesture...please I beg of you. I know you can hear me, I know you can!"

The nurse came in and asked her to move aside as she increased her pain medication. "Why are you doing that now? Is the medication given randomly or did she tell you she is hurting?" Micaela questioned.

"When she becomes agitated, that indicates pain or discomfort. We check the last time she was given the pain medication, although right now it seems we just gave her something to stay calm, but her vitals show agitation." The nurse said, leaving abruptly after administering it.

"So, is the agitation because of me Mami? I know you are mad at me, and you think I hurt you every time I deviate from what you have decided my life should be, but now please let me know you accept me and love me for my crazy ways. Please don't leave me without letting me know that I am right in following my bliss. Please I beg of you, open your eyes, squeeze my hand, don't let me go without saying good bye to me. Please don't Mami! I have loved you and respected you my entire life. Your pains were my pains, and your joys were mine ten times fold. I saw you...the abandoned child, be triumphant in taking care of us. That is all I wanted...to be as strong as you are! Can you please tell me you felt the same for me as I did for you? I know you know we are both one in the same, aren't we Mami Paloma!"

There was only silence from her still body, no movement and the noise of the machines accompanying her pleas, so it seemed. A set of nurses and an intern came in to check every port and looking at her eyelids, turned to Micaela, asking her to leave. *Are they siding with her or do they know something she didn't?* She thought, as she exclaimed, "I can't leave now she has not given me her blessing, you see it is important for a parent to bless the child at this time in her life. SHE CAN'T LEAVE ME WITHOUT HER BLESSING!" She yelled causing a commotion with the nurses that looked at her in the most strange way.

"I'm sorry, Ms. Sims, she really is becoming agitated, and she was just given a strong doze of sedatives. It is kind of abnormal for the vitals to be so out of whack!"

Micaela knew it was she that was causing the agitation. Perhaps her mother wanted to say something or perhaps Paloma wanted her to leave. She would never know nor would she ever have a chance to have her mother's blessings. It seemed to Micaela that at the end Paloma was avenging what had been done to her by not giving her the last blessing, leaving Micaela in despair. Paloma's poignant choice of departure left Micaela knowing firsthand what her mother felt at the young age of eight when her own mother had refused to give her the blessing. She hated to leave without saying all the things she had wanted to tell her all their life. Paloma was bestowing on her poor broken heart so much pain, so much turmoil. She knew she must leave to appease her mother's 'vitals' even if it meant the painful knowledge that even close to death, Paloma would not accept her daughter's love and devotion. Micaela knew that this was the last time she would see her mother in the same pain as she had always made her feel; the result of Paloma's contempt for Micaela.

Now, as Micaela looked at her life, she would strive to make a happy, stable life for her and Annabella. She would always let Annabella know how much she loved her and that love was unconditional! She would repudiate the obstinate pride, the absurd contempt Paloma had for the new culture in which the family now lived. She would become 'Americanized.' She would even change her citizenship and become an American citizen delving into the culture her mother prohibited her from becoming a part of and that way she would sever all ties with the woman who had offered nothing but disdain giving her the reason to have many moments of self doubt. *My little apartment full of books and stories would become my sanctuary where slowly all the left over insecurities would be plucked away to let the beautiful swan come alive, I owe it to Annabella. Thanks to you Mom...A new chapter in the life saga of the Díaz's girls would start with your death, I owe it to myself,* Micaela thought as she left the room. She saw Annabella standing and waiting for her. Both reaching in silence for each other's hands, they walked the hospital corridor without saying goodbye to any of her family members who stood in awe seeing them leave without saying a word.

Peace Restored

Micaela left the hospital ready to embark on a new chapter in her life. Annabella was her most precious possession, besides her books and literature, and the only person who mattered in her life. As she saw her life now, she was an independent woman, a 'free agent' with no one to call the shots for her. The only person to ever have had a hold on her was about to leave this earth. She did not want to rejoice in this fact, but she did feel a large weight lifting off her shoulders, a weight that had held her back with little explanation as to why. She would make sure she remained a free agent because now her life was all her own. She went to a nearby cafe and called Maria to come and pick them up. As they drove to Edward's house to drop Annabella off, the feelings of fear and doubt dissipated. There was no more worrying nor questioning that part of her life. She had made amends with Annabella's father so she felt free of any guilt at the break up of a marriage that should have never taken place. Looking at the sweet, loving face of Annabella was the only positive thing of that ordeal and she was so thankful for that child.

"Annabella, do you want to stay with your dad or do you want to come back to Georgia with me. I am leaving first thing in the morning."

"I thought I told you that Dad had plans and I want to stay with him, if that is okay with you. Do you need me?"

"Oh, it's okay sweetie and I don't want you to sound so solemn with me, okay? I am fine. It is the order of things, and we are born to die so do not fear for me. I am fine and I want to make sure you are fine through all this, okay?" Micaela caressed her daughter as the gates of the beautiful house opened. She watched her daughter walk in and disappear in the luscious gardens. Getting back into the car, Maria started with the questions, "So what is the verdict, my dear?" Maria looking intently at Micaela.

"She is stable but probably only has about two months or so."

"I am sorry."

"Thank you. You are such a good friend. Everything is going to be okay. I need to get back home and take care of some things before I can come back here to wait for her to pass on, I guess."

"Oh my God! Did you hear what you just said?" Maria was incredulous.

"What?"

"You just said, 'I need to get back home.' Since when is Georgia home?"

"Since every move I make is not questioned there."

"So you really feel like that is home?"

"Yes, it is kind of strange that in a place where the races are still separated, I, a woman of color does not succumb to that idiosyncrasy. I can make a life surrounded by all kinds of different people, with different likes and dislikes and most of all enjoy the sultry hot summers of the antebellum south. I can stay in a state of anonymity because of my color. What more could I ask for?"

"Wow! I never thought of you as a Southern Belle!"

"But of course I am, or at least I think I have the strength of Scarlet O'Hara, and the resolve of Rhett Butler because *finally my dear, I don't give a damn!*"

They hugged one another laughing as they had done many times before and Maria straightening her hair told her, "I know you are going to be extraordinary, don't forget the little people along the way to the top, like me okay?"

"Stop, you are not little at all. You are a giant among men with a heart of gold, and not to mention that mean spaghetti you make!"

When Micaela got to Maria's place she started packing for her trip home, the next day. They went out for a quick drink and came right back. Maria opened the door to a ringing telephone. When she answered the voice on the other end was that of Jerry asking for Micaela. Reaching for the phone, "Hey Jerry, how are you?" Micaela said, rolling her eyes.

"When are you coming back? You need to call Liam and tell him not to do what he is about to do!" He exclaimed.

"What is it, Jerry?"

"I can't go into details but you need to stop him. He will listen to you. Can you just give him a call? Today!"

Micaela sensed the urgency in Jerry's voice but could not pinpoint what would be so important to call Liam this late at night. She wondered about all the things that could possibly go wrong and there were none to have such a sense of urgency, the way Jerry was making it sound. "Jerry, I bet whatever it is, it can wait till the morning and furthermore, I am leaving in a few hours and will be there in the afternoon." She said trying to appease him.

"No, Micaela! You need to call him now." Jerry pleaded.

"Fine, I will call him and if he gets mad at me for calling him at three in the morning it will be your fault! *Capisce?*"

"Thank you, I knew you would do it. You are such a doll! Just tell him that you talked to me and that you think it is a terrible idea. Please don't do it Liam, I will never forgive you if you do!"

"What?"

"Tell him exactly like that."

"What is it that I will never forgive? If you want me to call him you better tell me now or I'm not calling, Jerry this is ridiculous!"

"I can't Micaela, but I know you are a dedicated student and will do as I have asked you to do. I've got to go now. Have a safe trip and I shall see you later today."

"Je...rr?" Looking at the phone after realizing he hung up on her.

Micaela dialed Liam's number to no avail; he did not answer then nor the couple of times she tried reaching him later. She finally decided to leave a message repeating *per verbatim* what Jerry had instructed her to say. She could not sleep that night. Tossing and turning, she tried to think what it could be that she needed to stop Liam from doing, but nothing came to mind. After a long perusal of work ideas, she returned to the matter at hand that weighed heavily on her mind...it had a bittersweet feeling to it, though...her mother's health and her refusal to talk to her when she had had the chance. Micaela so desperately wanted to be inside her mother's head and see what she was thinking right now, as she lay there dying. Trying to dispel all her morbid thoughts, she got up, took a long shower and left a note for Maria.

The drive from Torrance to Los Angeles International Airport seemed like an eternity. The light of dawn was appearing in the East and her heart quivered at the thought that she had spent a life time on the West Coast filled with mostly sad memories and was leaving it all behind to capture those beautiful hues of soft purple mixed in the deep orange dissipating into a white light of the splendorous mornings of the South. It has always been the light, be it natural light or from any other source that had attracted Micaela to think of it as a metaphor...the light that guides and lets us see our way, the light that can be warm in times of cold, the light that enlightens us as we become aware of new thoughts and experiences. The light and its association with God and all that is omnipotent had always been in her soul as the source of her strength. At times just lighting a candle in the middle of the many nights when she questioned herself gave her so much solace by the flickering movement of the flame. She knew as long as she could turn on a light, or see natural light and feel the 'light' opening her heart, opening her soul and embracing everything that came her way, she would be all right.

She was leaving the West Coast for a better life in the South. She would become an American citizen and would always give thanks for her parents giving her the choice to love the place where she had been educated, for it is not the land in which we are born but rather the landscape in which we grow and blossom. It doesn't have to be the family that one is born into that helps achieve our dreams but the ones who support us in achieving those dreams. Her family and her mother had failed her in this task. She only hoped with the light becoming brighter that her future on the East Coast would not parallel the one on the West Coast but they would become permanently perpendicular to each other and the crossing of those two lives she was experiencing at this moment as Sepulveda Boulevard was taking her to her new beginnings one more time.

She arrived at Hartsfield International Airport in Atlanta, Georgia. She felt happy it had rained and now the sun was showing its graces. As she got on I-285 toward I-20 East she exhaled. She wanted to hurry but did not want to get a ticket. She was soon entering rural Morgan County, with the splendid splashes of green and wild flowers in the mid section of the freeway. The trees along the highway covered in Kudzu were telling her she would soon be at home.

She stopped at a liquor store and got some red wine and olives. *Really red wine and olives?* She thought to herself smiling as if she knew now she could do that; there was no one to stop her or question why she made any of her choices.

It was five o'clock when she got to her apartment in Athens. Micaela had a bad habit of always or at least almost always leaving her apartment door ajar. This time was no different. She took her shoes off and her bra went flying across the room landing on her bed as she headed for her small desk near the kitchen. She saw the many messages on her answering machine and tended to them taking notes. She stopped, being very still staring at the phone with her hands holding her small oval face. There were many emotions running through her mind. She was tense and had a worried look with desperation at the same time. Sadness pervading the overall softness of her face made her vulnerably tender. Blowing her imaginary bangs off her forehead she dialed Liam's number. She could hear the phone ringing across the hall, but still no answer.

"Hey Liam I am back and I have a bottle of your favorite red wine, a jar of olives and I do not know what to do with all that? Do you want to come over and give me a hand with it?"

"Why didn't you come knock on my door?" Liam said standing in the threshold letting himself in.

"Hey, why didn't you answer?" Being flustered and nervous at the sight of this tall beautiful blond man with those piercing blue eyes, she turned abruptly and getting up from her chair too quickly, she got tangled in the phone cord making her loose her balance. Micaela had never really looked into those eyes the way she did at this moment and she did not like how they made her feel. She did not want to feel anything, not now.

Liam smiled and came to her rescue before she fell. He reached for her arm but she pulled away harshly, "Don't be a pertinacious damsel in distress, all I am trying to do is prevent you from falling," he added letting go of her.

"Are you calling me annoyingly stubborn?" She asked, freeing herself from her convoluted phone cord.

"You look cute, all wrapped up in the cord. Are you trying to make a connection?" He laughed, walking toward the kitchen.

Trying to cover up her precipitous desire to know all about this man, and getting so close to him that the air surrounding them would not be enough to withhold their being and in that trance she would touch him, caress him and seeing herself in the 'crystalline waters' of his blue eyes she would know how the shape of her body would conform to his, "Don't you dare come into my place and make fun of me, do you hear?"

"You're still cute wrapped around the cord. Maybe that is the answer to the riddle...somebody better lasso you in and keep you hostage. Putting tape on your mouth wouldn't be a bad idea either, but then those lips, those inviting lips would not be seen and that is a crime in itself," Liam exclaimed from the kitchen.

"You shame all the romantic writers, and you the poet, tragic story writer that you are would make Shakespeare turn in his grave!" She exclaimed back trying to fix her hair and making sure she did not look too bad, *Why are you doing this? It is only Liam!* she thought to herself.

"Let's start again, okay?" Liam said extending a glass of red wine and a plate of olives adorned with little umbrella picks stuck on each one of them.

"Okay, you go first!" looking at the plate of olives and trying not to laugh.

Looking intently at her he said, "Hi, Micaela. I am glad you're back home. How was the trip and most important, how is your mom?"

"Hey Mr. Griggs, I am fine thank you. I'm also glad to be back, the trip was overwhelming and mom is dying."

"Oh, I am sorry." He said, getting closer to her but very cautiously.

"Thank you, but no need to get any closer and get all mushy on me okay?'

"Deal!" He moved away from her but wanted to hold her to help ease the angst this soft petite seemingly fragile woman exuded at this time.

Rolling her eyes, she told him, "I was trying to get a hold of you, because Jerry called me in great desperation to ask me to ask you not to do whatever it is you were about to do!"

"What? Jerry called you when?"

"For the last two days, so whatever he does not want you to do please don't do it and tell him I pleaded with you, okay?" She said it with a frivolity in her eyes making her look sexy, fragile yet child like.

Making a funny face, "Of course, I will tell him that you begged me like you are begging me now and I could not help but to accept your begging and I agreed!" Liam said, almost laughing.

"Agreed to what?' What is it that Jerry does not want you to do?"

"It is nothing. He shouldn't have involved you in it."

"What is it?"

"Nothing. How is your mom, really?"

"She is dying any minute now; I will get a phone call saying come to the funeral."

"How can you say that so matter of fact?"

"We are born to die and so what's the big deal?"

"Micaela! I do not believe that cold attitude is coming from you. Are there unresolved issues there?...Was she that horrible to you?"

"You have your secrets and I have mine, so let's not worry about them right now, okay? And let's enjoy this wonderful wine." She sat down next to him realizing the anger and fear of the past few days became too much to hold in. She knew she wanted to get lost in the euphoria of the wine.

"Cheers to your strength is all I am going to say." Liam raised his glass.

"Thank you, my kind sir!" Touching his glass to hers.

"I am glad to know that I am your 'kind sir,'" Liam took a sip of his wine.

"Well, don't take it too seriously. I am on a mission for Jerry and want to make sure you agree to whatever he does not want you to do." She said it looking at him intently and taking a long sip of her wine.

"Easy on that, Micaela, or I just might take advantage of you!" He tried to take the glass from her.

"Wait! Don't do that." She got up and continued to finish her whole glass.

"Do you want me to leave?" He asked a bit annoyed at her.

"I want to be alone. There has been so much commotion this past week I just want to sleep it off for a couple of days," she poured more wine into her glass and took another long draft.

Liam got up and headed toward the door, "You don't have to come to the departmental meeting…I think we can manage without you there."

"Wait! What do you mean, 'we can manage without you?'" She looked puzzled.

"I don't mean anything. All I want you to do is get some rest so you can deal with everything that is going on in your life right now, okay?" He said taking the glass away from her and pushing her gently to the sofa and handing her a pillow and a throw.

"Thank you. You are my kind sir." She smiled and started to doze off.

"Am I...your kind sir?" Liam said, getting closer and gently kissing her forehead. "Go to sleep, I will call you tomorrow."

Liam watched her fall asleep, her face not only showing turmoil but a sadness permeating through her motionless body. He wanted so much to keep caressing her and tell her he had loved her from the moment he had read her manuscript. Her prose was like no other...the vocabulary elegant-complex yet managing to reach a diverse audience-her wit, clear declarations in perfect sentence structure. He had not seen that in all the papers he had come across, and there have been many. She was a writer and her passion for the craft showed in her manuscript. She had to know how good she was, *Why hadn't she submitted it before leaving for L.A.?* Liam wondered. He extended the throw to cover her whole body and as the blanket touched her face she moved her arms across her face in such an innocent and childlike way that he quickly left trying to avoid falling for her even more.

Moving and nuzzling the pillow, Micaela muttered, "I love you...umm..."

Liam stopped quickly and turned to see if she would mention a name, hoping absurdly it would be his, but Micaela slept peacefully. He knew that once she knew he had taken the liberty to submit her manuscript instead of his, he might lose her all together but for the woman he knew he wanted in his life even if the chances were nil, he would do much more.

Micaela woke up to the ring of her telephone and answering machine. She heard Jerry's voice on the line, "Hello Micaela, Liam tells me you two had a lovely time last night, but your power of persuasion failed to stop his absurdity and all I can say now is, I hope you are happy?" She sat up looked at her wrinkled clothes and watch seeing it was past eleven o'clock and without a second thought she registered Jerry's message with a pronounced frown on her face.

"Crap! I missed the departmental meeting!" She exclaimed trying to get up but she slowed herself down thinking about the night before. Examining the glasses in front of her and the empty bottle of wine. "Oops! Maybe I drank it all! Was that after or before Liam left?" She questioned herself. She got up slowly to take a shower. She cried in the shower another cleansing cry like the one a long time ago. Too bad no one was here to compare her to a diamond like her father had done, but she knew she was a diamond, the ugly duckling plucking away the dark and somber plumes leaving her to expose all the beauty within. She came out, taking a long look at her small apartment, trying to put things in perspective. She started to tidy up the place knowing she would have to leave for California at a moment's notice. In the kitchen, she started to wash the glasses which made her remember back to her youthful days when she had to do the family's dishes and miss school. Her mother made her be truant many times. Micaela smiled a sad smile thinking, "You're crazy! The poor woman is dying and here you are blaming her for your lack of responsibility!"

Biloxi Blue was knocking at the door and being herself,

"Room service! Thai with Japanese beer for me that is!"

Micaela hurried to open the door, "Hey Blue! Should I beware of 'Greeks bringing gifts, or bearing gifts, however that goes!" She smiled at her friend while grabbing the bag of food.

"So, tell me. How is your mom, how is Annabella and how is Liam?" Biloxi asked placing plates on the small table.

"How should I know about Liam?" She asked with a big frown on her face.

"He was so happy this morning, proclaiming that you were a 'funny' drunk last night."

"What!"

"Just kidding! Girl don't get your panties in a wad!" Biloxi laughed.

Micaela sounded annoyed and trying to get to the bottom of what Biloxi Blue knew, "Can you make more sense? I am lost here!"

Biloxi Blue looking intently at Micaela asked her point blank, "You do know what Liam is up to, don't you?" She placed a big piece of egg roll in her mouth and continued to say, "The guy is nuts about you. Everyone can see it ever since we went out that night before you were summoned to Cali."

"What?" Micaela asked in sort of disbelief. She had sensed the sexual tension from the day she found him reading her manuscript, but with everything that was happening right now, a new place to live, new job, new friends, her mother dying, she had tried to push it all to the back of her mind. But now Biloxi, who was into everyone's affairs, was confirming what she had felt all along. "Don't speak with your mouth full, and tell me what you are talking about?"

"Liam is crazy about you and everyone in the department knows about it, but it seems that you, you of all people, have missed it!" She said laughing out loud in celebration of watching these two people who had so much in common yet worlds apart, to have been placed at the right place at the right time.

"You are crazy. Liam loves only himself and no other. He is the most narcissistic male I have ever met!" Micaela said trying to convince herself.

"I beg to differ!" Biloxi said with a conviction that had piles of information untold.

"Why do you beg to differ?" Micaela looked at her with a seriousness that was asking for the truth and nothing but the truth.

"And don't you dare leave anything out! You hear me?"

"Well, here it goes: this morning at the meeting Liam was a little bit late but made up for his tardiness by bringing us blueberry scones from Jitter Joes'...YUM!"

"Biloxi stop and give me the important information, now!"

"My goodness! Micaela, can I be descriptive in my disclosure?" She smiled knowing that Micaela wanted to know what was going on, and by her demeanor, Biloxi knew she had no clue what she had been put up to. "He was so chipper telling us he had seen you last night and he had shared a bit of red wine with you. He said you were so excited at his proposal to reaffirm the submission of your unfinished manuscript with the condition that you finish the last chapter before school ends at the end of the year, calendar year that is...not academic year. My dear you have about three months to finish the chapter so they can look at your work and deem you publishable or not, which Liam attests to and he swears that your work is so superb that it will bring more to the department, much more than his would...and that is the truth!" Biloxi bowed and made a curtsy unaware of the reaction her revelation was to have on Micaela.

"Son-of-a-bitch! I can't believe he did that!" She went to the kitchen and threw the dishes in the sink, breaking some of them, "I just didn't think Liam would do such a stupid thing. My manuscript is not only unfinished but the work everyone was expecting to be turned in was his. The big grant coming to the department next year is all about having his novel earn the University that much wanted and needed Peabody award. Why did he do this and most importantly why without telling me about it so I could object! No wonder, Jerry is pissed at me. I could tell he was by the message on my machine this morning." Micaela said all this, then threw herself on the sofa reaching for the throw, she placed it over her face and started to cry inconsolably.

Micaela's crying astonished Biloxi Blue. She could see how much pain the news caused her, but why? She should be happy for someone to care about her that much to sacrifice his own work to give exposure to hers. What Biloxi Blue was unaware of was that

Micaela, at this moment, was crying a lifetime of sorrows and disappointments. She felt overwhelmed by the emotions coming to her all at once...the brightest star to shine upon her was being cast at the time of great distress in her life. Paloma's death being so near weighed heavily on her. She did not have the closure she needed which should have been given by the person who was her biggest obstacle in life, her mother. She would always wonder, "Why did she not bless me when she had the chance to say good bye? She chose to shut me out and not give me her blessing, WHY?" Micaela screamed and like holding on for dear life, she clutched the throw.

Biloxi Blue thinking the worst was about to come asked, "Are you okay, Micaela? I didn't mean to upset you this way. Please forgive me."

As if coming out of a trance, Micaela looked at Biloxi, becoming aware that she had been there all along, "Oh! I am so sorry for my hysteria, but he had no right not to consult with me first. Don't you think?"

"Who did not bless you. Who is she who has hurt you so much in your life. Was it your mother?"

"What?" Micaela sounded disoriented.

"Are you okay? Do you want some water?"

"No, I am fine." Getting up and walking her to the door, she turned to Biloxi, "I thank you for lunch and your friendship, but I need to be alone and sort many things out." She opened the door and saw Liam come up the stairs and hiding behind her door, Micaela gave Biloxi a hug.

Micaela closed the door and started to sob again. She was alone in her apartment, so tiny that her big world of pain, had no room there. However, this was the first time that Micaela did not have the urge to flee like so many times before. She wanted to stay in this little place she called home. Her books, her recycled furniture and things she had acquired throughout the years... they were all hers. Her daughter, the beautiful child for whom she had fought for from her conception until now was hers. Annabella loved her mommy unconditionally. She knew Annabella was her world and her world was Annabella's. She would make life better for her from this small home. Micaela decided then, she would forgive her mother for shutting her out of her life the same way Paloma's own mother had done to her. But even Rocío had blessed her daughter. Why Paloma chose not to bless Micaela had to have some purpose in her life, something she would figure out later.

Trying to stop her whimpering, she thought of when her mother had called everyone to her hospital room telling them how special they had been to her and how much each of her four children had brought joy to her life. Micaela's siblings had mentioned to her that Paloma had said these nice things to them, but when it was Micaela's turn to see their mother, Paloma choose to shut down and all she could mutter to Micaela was, "Why do you always hurt me?"

Sobbing ensued like a wild beast that had been shot and in those last moments of holding onto life, she destroyed every trinket and gift her mother had ever given her. She went to her jewelry box and threw everything out, making sure the life of Paloma and Micaela would be asunder forever more. Micaela laughed a nervous laugh and putting on these big silver hoops that Paloma had given her because "they looked something only a gypsy would wear!" had been Paloma's comment. Micaela looked in the mirror and muttered to herself, "I would be the unblessed, carefree, black sheep, ugly duckling female of the Díaz family…the gypsy, as she often called me…but no longer would the words and attitude would be there to keep hurting they way they have hurt all these years!"

Micaela felt forcefully placed on a roller coaster with so much back and forth but she knew then, she would be the beautiful swan staying intact and becoming only a catalyst in the life of those who came her way. She would be happy with anything and everything, even the stupid way her novel was going to have recognition or not. She hated Liam for being perfect in so many ways, for making her feel weak in the knees and most of all, for proving her work would not be good enough to bring the accolades to the school as his would. This will be the final test of her talents and thank God, Paloma would not be here to tell her "I told you so!" Micaela exhaled and her sobbing demanded to come out to cleanse her soul, and cleanse her spirit of so much pain she still had to endure at realizing that with everything happening right now in her life, she would have very little time to revise and make her work as good as it could be. Paloma in her dying bed was not going to have the last word. Jerry's voice message on the telephone brought her back to reality.

"Hey Micaela, it's Jerry. I need you to come to my office as soon as you can. I know this is a terrible time but things need to be taken care of here as well." He sounded aloof, distant and annoyed.

"Oops! Your golden child has failed you big time, Jerry. That is why it is so important to trust no one," she said out loud. She picked up the receiver before he could hang up.

"Hey, Jer, sorry for the disappearing act," she said nonchalantly. "I was planning to go first thing tomorrow morning and see if I still had a job."

"Don't be so melodramatic. You and Liam make me nauseous at times," he exclaimed.

"Why is that, Jer?"

"You know. You two are so stubborn and think that what you want to do is what the rest of the world wants as well. Let me tell you, you are both wrong!"

"First, do not call me and start yelling at me without knowing all the facts," she exclaimed in a strong voice making Jerry think twice about his tone of voice. He had never heard so much resolve in this petite woman, "Second, you are head of the department which gives you every right to have stopped that decision, not with sentimentalities or nepotism, but with the facts. I am not ready to present my work, and I do not have the time nor the energy, mental energy that is, to bring the work to its final stages before presenting in January. You knew better and you had every right to say no. Why you chose to put me in such a delicate position and jeopardize the money coming to your damn faculty is not for me to ask much less to speculate!" Rubbing her head and trying hard not to unleash her wrath on the wrong person, she heard herself saying, "If you want me to resign and use me as your 'scapegoat' just let me know and I'll do it. I really don't care about anything right now. And most importantly, I don't want to work with two assholes that don't care that my personal life might have a crack or two. My mother is dying for heaven's sake, Jerry! I don't need any more aggravation. I will see you tomorrow…bye!"

Micaela hung up and really didn't care about what would happen at work. She needed to know how her mother was doing. She was sure Annabella wouldn't have any idea, but she needed to call her and let her know she had made it back home safely. It had only been one day but it seemed that she had been in her apartment getting drunk, crying and feeling sorry for herself for a life time. Enough of this crap! She thought as she dialed Annabella's number.

"Hey Mom, how are you doing? You sound like you've been crying. Are you okay? I miss you and wish I was there with you." Annabella said it so fast, it made Micaela smile.

"I am fine, love. I just wanted to let you know that I got home and wanted to check on you. How are things with you?" She asked trying not to sound somber.

"Fine. Dad and I are going to the Mojave Dessert and then maybe to Vegas. I will let you know of our travel plans, okay?"

"That sounds great. Has *Tía* Beca called you?" She asked, afraid to disrupt Annabella's world with the reminder that her grandmother was dying.

"Yeah. She told me everything was okay and that Mami Paloma might be going home." Sounding in a hurry she added, "That is good isn't it? I've got to go now, Mom. I love you, talk to you later bye."

"Bye, babe…I love you…too" She could not finish as she heard the dial tone.

Micaela hung up the phone and did not want to call her parents' house. She was afraid to know how her mom really was doing. She was worried that they would tell her that her mother was aware that she was not there paying vigil at her side. She knew Paloma would not take kindly to that. Micaela was afraid that she would summon her to finally give her the last blessing and find out she was on the other side of the country tending to her career. Most importantly, that she was entertaining a man that had managed to break the seal that Micaela put on her heart the last time she gave of it. All this would break her mother's heart. She had sworn never to fall prey to anyone's eyes, mouth or personality that would make her succumb to the 'pressures of love.' However, Liam had broken the seal and removed it. She would welcome giving in to his advances. She smiled and thought back to the task at hand to call home and see how her mami was doing.

"Hello," Rebeca answered.

"Hi, Beca it's me, Micaela. I just wanted to let you and Papi know that I am back home and trying to tidy up some loose ends so I can come to Cali and help you take care of Mom." She said hoping for something but not knowing what.

Sounding cold and detached, she responded, "Hey, Mica. I am glad you made it home okay. We are here just taking turns with Mami and looking after Papi. He seems to be fine with everything. You know how he is."

"Good, I am glad to hear everything is almost back to normal. What is the doctor saying about Mom?" She asked, waiting for the other shoe to drop.

"She seems to be stable but still on the machines. Papi is saying that Mami had told him that she did not want to be hooked up to them, so he is thinking of having them removed. Froilán is not going for that though and neither is Andrés." She informed her.

"Wow! But that has to be written by mami in order to do that, right?" she inquired.

"I don't know, but the doctors are saying to keep her hooked up for another week and see how she is doing then. She is still on pain killers and we don't like that." She added.

"She has always been on pain killers! What are you talking about? Remember the little green pills. Those were pain killers. You should know that by now." Afraid of the reaction Micaela told her sister not to be so naive.

"Well, I've got to go now. Bye, Mica." Rebeca's denial was obvious.

"Bye, Beca." She said sadly.

Micaela could not understand why all of Paloma's children made excuses for her and why they did not accept their mom's idiosyncrasies for what they were. She had everyone wrapped around her little finger. Her mother always had played the victim, had played the poor abandoned little girl...so what? That was her life. She should have embraced it and went on. Instead, she made you feel sorry for her and responsible for the damage done to her when she was growing up, "I don't think even after death she would stop." She said out loud.

It was about dinner time and she started to feel a bit hungry, going to the refrigerator she realized she needed to get some groceries. She hated this ritual of going to the supermarket to buy what was necessary for a meal or two. The many times she had gone with her mother had ruined shopping for her. The only sweet memory was of the handsome figure of Blake and his tantalizing smile that kept her going Saturday after Saturday to the grocery store, but now she hated it and what she hated more was the fact that she needed those groceries and there will no Blake to look at. She picked up a cotton sweater and headed for the door. She saw Liam coming out of his apartment. She quickly closed the door behind her trying to evade Liam. He pretended not to see her and off he went. Slowly she peeked out to see if he was there. Picking up her purse and car keys, she started to go down the stairs. Rushing out like a whirlwind, she saw Liam entering the vestibule. She had no place to hide.

"Hey Micaela! How are you feeling today?" He asked genuinely concerned.

"I am fine thank you." She tried to pass him on the stairs. "I am in a hurry, but we need to talk."

"Where are you going?" He asked.

"Are you my life patrol now?" Trying to be polite. She quickly reminded herself that this was not the time to speak. She needed to calm down a bit more and tend to her purpose. "I am going to pick up some groceries I'll be back in a few minutes," she answered coldly.

"Do you need one?" he asked with that smile that made her weak in the knees.

"What?" she asked annoyed.

"A 'life patrol'?" he answered.

"I'll be back." She left in a hurry.

The sultry afternoon was about to become night. The sky had a pristine spacious blue turning into a soft orange hue and in a matter of seconds it turned with a promise of rain. *How quickly things change. I think it is going to rain, so there goes my chance of grilling on my little bitty patio,* she thought. She got in her car and heading toward downtown, she pass by the Varsity where the idea of a chili dog made her salivate.

She parked the car and much to her annoyance there were people from her department waiting for her to say hello.

"Hey, Micaela! Congratulations! We heard your manuscript is the one to be evaluated for publication. That sounds so nerve wracking, exciting and promising, doesn't it?" Micaela heard someone say, "Yeah! I am sorry but I just got back from seeing my mom, and I am not totally informed of this matter, so I'd rather keep to myself for now. And, I am so hungry, please excuse me." She got in line where she could place her order. It was the aloofness of the Díaz girls that made everyone think she was a snob and out of touch at times. Micaela was aware of this but did not know how to change it. She was just a matter-of-fact kind of person going on with her tasks without much fanfare and excitement. It had been one of her mother's gifts, she often thought. She paid for her order and was about to leave and darn it! There he was. Liam in his worn out Henley shirt and jeans, slender, tall and with those blue eyes questioning why she had a chili dog in her hand.

"Hey Micaela, long time no see. I didn't know you liked American flair," he said flirting with her and shyly trying not to say what was on his mind.

"Micaela, likes American flair, does not need a body guard, nor a personal coach, nor a life patrol. You are wasting your time." She said it quickly and determined to be heard as she made her exit leaving her drink on top of her car forgetting she had put it there.

A few minutes later, Liam appeared at her door which she had left open on purpose, "May I come in?" he asked politely with an empty cup in his hand and a bag in the other.

Micaela felt like an idiot at the realization she had left the cup on top of her car knowing now the reason for the weird thump and brown 'rain' that splashed on her windshield was her spilled coke. She wanted to smile but she was too upset at this cuteness, bringing her the empty cup. "What are you trying to do, Liam?" She asked with a grave serious tone.

"What do you mean?" he asked back.

"Are you trying so desperately to point out the mistakes of my miserable life?" she asked with that same grave tone but this time an unspoken remark was in her body language as if she was saying, I have had that already. My mother points out all the bad choices and mistakes I have made in my life. She hastily grabbed the empty cup.

"I still do not know what you are talking about," he said pointing to the cup. "I just wanted you to be aware you spilled coke on your car and it may do some damage to the paint job. It's a guy thing, you know?"

"Really?"

"Really!"

"What are you doing here, really?" She asked him looking intently in those blue eyes hoping to catch herself in them.

"You said you wanted to talk to me," he answered pointing to the table and asking if he could sit there.

"Did you follow me to the Varsity?" she asked again looking at him intently.

"No, I felt like eating a hamburger and that was the closest place. I wanted to be ready when you came back from getting the groceries you said you were going to get," he told her as he took a bite of his hamburger. "Hey, do you have a coke or anything to drink?"

"Sure help yourself," Micaela said pointing to the fridge. Micaela liked even the way he ate and chewed his food, *Don't be silly! He is just making himself likable so you will forgive him for his arrogance. You've seen this type of stupid man before and stop looking at him like he is the first man you have ever seen!* She thought finding herself staring at him.

Quickly trying to dispel the trance, she said, "Well, then! I am dumbfounded hearing what you have done without consulting with me first!" Getting closer to him, she added, "How dare you to do such a stupid thing?" She immediately moved away, for the smell of his body was like an aphrodisiac. The masculinity he exuded was something that made her nervous and she effused about everything and anything. Micaela wanted to get closer to him to slowly feed him the French fries. She wanted to savor his food as she slowly and tenderly would take from his lips the kiss she knew he wanted to give. She looked at him devouring his food unaware of how much emotions he provoked in her convoluted being by all the things happening to her at work, at home and now in her heart, "The department was counting on your work for the grant, no way in hell am I going to make the same thing happen, you knew it and you decided to throw me to the wolves, how mean and insensitive on so many levels, Liam!" she told him.

Very calmly, Liam finished his meal taking a big sip of his drink and told her, "Do you hear yourself? It is not about you; it is all about the department, the contribution we might lose. So what if we lose? You will be in the limelight and you will see that your work is just as good as mine. I even dare to say, it is better than mine."

"Don't patronize me, by saying things that you think I want to hear, you hear me?" she pointed at him with her finger.

Liam came closer and grabbed her finger and looking at her lips while holding her other hand in place alongside her leg, he said, "I know this is the worst time, but I am going to take my chances with you because I feel I need to do this now. Please don't fight me Micaela. From the moment I saw your disheveled hair and sweater inside out and backwards, I knew I wanted you. When I read your work, I fell in love with the way you construct your sentences with such a naiveté yet raw honesty that the reader can smell, feel and touch your characters. To do that, you need passion! You need to have this," pointing to his head and letting go of her hand.

"You need to have that little brain of yours filled with experiences, emotions and to let your whole being be exposed, out there naked to be used and abused knowing that you do it for the love of the craft, and only then the creation is satisfying. All that I could read in your words, and I fell in love with the heart that wrote the awesome story. It wasn't the girl who runs in a whirlwind that I fell in love with first. That came later as I saw you live your life, full of passion and love for those who are lucky to be near you. I fell in love with you when you appeared in my dreams and told me to hold on, that it wasn't time for me to disclose my being yet." Letting her go completely and walking away from her.

He turned and told her, "You turned up in my dreams and told me things I cannot disclose now but you were the girl of my dreams who loves me so passionately, it hurts to wake up."

Clearly frustrated, he rubbed his hand over his face and exhaling he added, "Call me crazy but this is the truth: I love you and want to be there for you. You more than anyone deserve to be loved the way I know you love back. I have read many papers, written many papers and thus I feel I have a little bit of a license to know when something is good, and you my sweet Micaela, deserve to be introduced to the world at large. You have the potential of being extraordinary."

Micaela listened and she thought she was about to explode. Her heart felt a thousand fears and her soul rejoiced and then collapsed into those thousand fears, *What is he talking about?* She thought and heard herself say, "What dreams are you talking about?"

Without realizing it, she became demeaning like her mother and told him, "Are you a voodoo man? What that hell do you think I am?...a stupid South American woman who does not know when she is being taken as a fool by the handsome white man only to tear her into a million pieces so no one would ever know of her!" She went to the door and opened it with such anger and determination, "GET OUT! How dare you come to my house and talk about your dreams? You do not know about dreams and how they become nothing but ashes because you did not prepare yourself for a life that can destroy them, GET OUT!"

Liam saw a different side of Micaela's disposition and knew that the pain in one of her characters was her own. He felt badly for bringing all these feelings to the surface, but he guessed then that he did not listen to the girl in his dream who told him, Wait until the storm passes and when the mourning subsides. Then she would be ready to accept your love and admiration. He nodded his head as though thinking that Micaela should have known about this, but apparently not, "I am sorry, this is not what I was expecting."

Holding the door and waiting for him to leave, she said, "What were you expecting...that after you make fun of me I tell you I love you madly? You have some kind of nerve to submit my work without asking me, leaving me no time to absorb the responsibility now placed on me, plus having to deal with all that I am dealing with in my personal life. You tell me you like me!"

Liam grabbed the door and slammed it shut, "No I did not say I like you, I said I love you and yes I picked the worse time but the way things are transpiring I took my chance to let you know how I feel. Forgive me for my insolence but all I know is that I want you. I want you and your quirkiness and all the pain I feel coming from you. I want to help you bear it. Why can't you accept that?" He yelled and as he tried to open the door to leave, he had trouble with it because he had slammed it so hard. He looked back at Micaela, with her eyes full of tears. The childlike persona of yesterday's slumber stood there begging him to hold her and make the pain go away. He went to her cautiously extending his arms. The offering was too much, too precious for Micaela to dismiss and she fell to the 'pressures of love' in the sweetest, most innocent way she had ever experienced before. She held onto him and cried like she had never cried before in the presence of anyone.

Liam caressed her hair and quietly they stood there holding each other, swaying to a music as sweet as their souls and one that only they could hear. They swayed back and forth in silence uttering not a single word but telling each other a thousand stories and how they came to live every one of them. All of a sudden, Micaela slowly slipped away from him. He watched as she became distant and aloof as though they had not shared this moment at all.

"Please leave, and do not mention this to anyone. This never took place. I will present my resignation tomorrow and you and Jerry will clean up the mess you both have on your hands." Calmly she went to the door and opened it with a slight tug asking again, "Please leave and forget me. It is best this way and you will come to understand. I do not need a Svengali in my life."

"Really? Is that what you think of me, a Svengali. You're crazy!" Liam said, leaving abruptly.

Micaela closed the door and looking around at everything that she held so dear made her feel trapped. She was on another roller coaster presented by her life. She hated the unwanted invitations to be in a circus that life puts us in at times when we have to do the best we can. She would have to move, look for a job in whatever paid the most, like many years back and forget about her dreams and writing aspirations. She had Annabella to think about and provide for. She could not be selfish and just struggle as an upcoming writer leading to nowhere. Her biggest fear now that Paloma, her mother and tormentor, was near her end. She looked outside her window and saw the sky opening its announcement of rain with lightning that lit up the entire neighborhood followed by the thunder that opened the skies to a torrent of water, "Even the sky is crying. No one is happy ever." She said as she went looking for candles for the way it started to rain, Micaela knew the lights will be going out.

She went to the kitchen and poured herself a glass of white wine, lit a candle and sat down waiting for the lights to go out.

"I am ready, so go out and that will give me an excuse to do nothing…to stay still, quiet and see what such solitude brings… oohooohoohoohh," she tried to make a macabre sound but laughed at her inability to do so.

Sitting quietly looking at nothing, she started to stare at the way the candle light was reflected on the wine in her glass. With a loud clap of thunder the light started to flicker. She smiled as she kept on staring and tears started to flow quietly with the same stillness permeating through her. Micaela did not know why the tears came now, but she cried softly, quietly staring at the soft yellow liquid splashing against the sides of the glass making lines and forms with the light reflected on all the facets the movement of her hand softly swirling the glass created. She became aware of the liquid, and took a big sip, "White wine gets warm and then it is no good," she said out loud as she finished the whole glass in one big gulp.

She wiped her tears with a swift and rapid motion as to dispel the sadness creeping into her being. She set the glass down and got up looking for her manuscript. She sat down in front of her computer and started to write. She felt empty and blank...a creative block ensued. She closed her computer screen and there was a picture of her and Annabella at the time of her divorce. It seemed like a lifetime ago when she had had the nerve to walk away from it all and make her life her own.

"What is wrong with you now? Things are much simpler these days. All you have to do is pack, move your sweet little ass where no one knows you and start all over again. So you better prepare for an awesome departure."

She pulled out her favorite stationery and got her quill set out. She loved to write letters in an old fashioned way where ink, quill and parchment paper were a must. She got up and went to get a paper towel from the kitchen and realized that her candle had blown out. She looked puzzled at the candle light going out, "Hmm." She got the candle, setting it next to her, lit it again and started to write her letter.

"Dear Mom, Mother, Mami (don't know which one will make you more happy)," Micaela tore this one up and put it up to the candle light almost burning her fingers. She let go of the paper and saw how it burned slowly yet rapidly in the small flame becoming little black specks of thin charcoal shining in the hot wax. She pulled another sheet and started again,

Dear Paloma,

> *I always loved your name and I saw you as the beautiful winged animal that your name represents. You were the dove who flew so high, I could never reach or hold onto to feel your beautiful pristine white feathers so that I can let you know how much I loved and admired the way you could fly. You never allowed me to get close enough and for that I resented you all these years, until I last saw you not being the beautiful dove ready to take off. What I saw*

> upset me so because I could feel your pain. I have a myriad of regrets and there is nothing I can do about it to let you know how much love and strength you have given me all these years despite your inability to love and accept me.

Micaela started to cry and this time it was not a soft quiet cry...it was the sobbing and heaving cry that at times comes unexpectedly as though trying to cleanse oneself. "I ALSO HATED YOU AND I DON'T WANT YOUR FORGIVENESS FOR THAT! She yelled out, and as soon as she finished that statement the lights went out,

"Shit! She closed the lid on her ink bottle and cleaned her quill the best she could in the dark. She got up to refill her glass of wine.

"Now, I cannot do anything. So all I can do is sit here and cry my way out of the darkness into the light. That is all I have to do to forge ahead and no one is going to stop me. I will have to struggle a bit but the triumph will be all mine, without Liam, family or anybody that deems me good enough to give me a hand. So I put my dreams away for a little while. I can always go back to them because they are after all, my dreams!" She took another big gulp and sat there in complete darkness the candle having gone out again. Upset at the inability to keep it lit, she got up looking for the matches. *They were just on the table,* she thought, "Where are they now, damn it!"

Micaela annoyed at not being able to find the matches got up and went to the kitchen to get a new set. Coming back she started to light the match when the lightning and thunder seem to be laughing at her inability to do so. Finally, the match was lit and there in front of the window was the shape of a woman extending her arms out to Micaela. *Paloma?* She thought and without realizing the flame from the match had reached her finger, she felt the physical burning sensation of her fingers and simultaneously the emotional burning sensation of her heart beating so fast upon seeing in a flash the figure of her mother in the window. She looked around and everything was even darker, "How could this be? Stop the wine Micaela; you're starting to see things." She said out loud. She turned around examining the window pane and looking outside the torrential rain was flooding everything.

"It is nothing more than the leaves playing with the wind you silly girl!" She continued with her conversation out loud. She tried another match and this time it lit letting her ignite her candle on top of the small desk in front of the window.

The amber colors of the flame enshrouded her small space embracing the stroke of lightning that was simultaneously one after the other with its thunder breaking the atmosphere so hard and so close Micaela closed her eyes and sat down. Upon opening her eyes, there she was standing behind the window extending her arms like she had never done before. Paloma's figure was the age of 30 something and she was outside the window asking Micaela to come to her.

"Mami, is that you?" She said afraid of the answer.

"Mi Micaela, *ven a mi niña mia.*" Micaela could not fathom what the figure had said in such a tender voice. This could not be her mother looking young and beautiful calling her, "My Micaela, come to me little girl of mine." Micaela, in disbelief, looked around and for a flash of a second went back to her childhood when Isabel and Rebeca would play mean tricks on her, locking her in the closet when it stormed the way it was storming right now. She looked around and with the fear of her childhood years said out loud, "Stop!" She turned back around hoping that the 'vision' was just a fear of hers and it would be gone but as she turned it was still there looking at her with such tenderness that it made Micaela cry.

With trembling lips in disbelief she asked, "Who are you? You look like my mami back in South America when she was young and full of life."

"It's me Micaela, your mother the one who just realized that I loved you in the most capricious and absurd ways; I am here to ask you for forgiveness and hope you would let me explain why I behaved the way I did, so you can stop the circle of obstinate pride that does not lead anywhere positive." The figure of a younger Paloma said it calmly extending her arms out to her again.

"What! Who are you? Why don't you come inside you are getting all wet out there," Micaela said realizing that the figure outside her window was not wet despite the torrential rain she was in. Nothing made sense at this moment and she became very calm, looking at the figure in her window extending her arms insistently for Micaela to come to her. It was a very strange feeling for Micaela to see her mother in that stance of filial love. Maybe she was dreaming or the wine and the rain were playing tricks in her head, *That's it! I am hallucinating and should never drink too much white wine again,* she thought. She saw the figure start to cry and she became curiously perplexed, and asked to be excused as she got up and headed for her bedroom.

"Stop! Please come back I know this seems strange and illogical but for you Micaela it should not be so surprising because you have the gift of great intuition and clairvoyance. I know now María José has come to you in dreams and prepared you for things to come or appeased the fears engulfing your soul. I know you have been in others people's dreams doing the same. This is all clear now to me and I wish you could see the things that I am starting to see now," Paloma told her in a very calm and Zen-like attitude that was not Paloma's nature in the physical world. Micaela stopped in her tracks, turned around and came back and got closer to vision in the window.

"So tell me, why are you here besides asking me for my forgiveness, huh?" she asked with an insolent tone.

"You are so constant. The child in you still lives strong and with a power like no other." Paloma said it with a smile and acceptance.

"What?"

"Micaela, this is how old I was when I had you and the night that you came into this world was like tonight. I thought back then that the sky and life itself was announcing this child's way into the world. I knew then that you would be different, special in some way especially at the time of your birth. As you were coming out of my being, I saw a bright light encompass us both and as the doctor pulled you out and cut the umbilical cord, the light stayed with you. I did not understand what that meant then but I was told later that what I saw was the same bright warm light that my mother had seen at the time of my birth. Her heart was full of anger and hatred she did not care to know what it meant, instead all she could think to do was to squelch that light with blinding cruelty as she did." The figure with extended arms still very calm kept talking to Micaela who sat there stupefied looking at the young figure of her mother.

"Although in life, I was able to be successful because of *mamita* María José's love, under the precocious bravado of a wounded little bird, afraid that someone with the same power of a mother's love or hatred would strike me again and take away my success made me always be on guard. I was afraid of people not loving me for who I was. I was the product of rape, a perfidy and with the dark skin tone of the indigenous people of our country my life has not been easy. Too much prejudice, too much unwarranted hatred has filled my life and when you were born I got scared by the 'bright light' surrounding your small innocent spirit. I became even more afraid that you would grow up to be this beautiful woman with such fair and lovely skin that you too would despise me and not want anything to do with me."

The figure started to cry, and softly with a shameful look she went on, "I became so afraid of you at the beginning of your life as you were growing and with that spirit full of life, full of joy and your head full of questions that I did not know the answer for most of them, on the contrary to you, you with full of answers from early age that when you came into a room it was like a whirlwind because of your wit and thoughtful ways, I too stupidly and absurdly became my mother, wanting to suppress all the goodness in you. I became jealous of you, only to realize that the daughter whose spirit I tried so hard to quench, was the one who would love me so as to never ask for anything of me but my love and at the time of my death you only looked out for my comfort and well being. So much tenderness I felt coming from you as you stayed in the hospital looking after me. So much respect and kindness in your words and the way you held my hand. The peace of your heart, the warmth of your soul came to me with the same bright light that I felt at the time of your birth. I felt the same warmth in your protection making sure I would be guided with your light to see a much brighter one. This is why before I go completely from this world, I want your forgiveness and I want you to stop being obstinate like the women of our clan, be yourself and let love come your way. Don't be arrogant and don't be proud when people give of themselves to you. Say thank you and love them, love them, Micaela. Love them unconditionally, the way I should have always loved you but chose not to. I chose to be this despot that I didn't need to be, so please break the circle of obstinate pride and love yourself and let those around you love you and do for you because you more than anyone deserve that and much more. God be with you always and all my blessings are for you, my sweet girl Micaela and her power of being."

A crashing unexpected sound landed at her window almost breaking its glass in unison with lightning and thunder bringing Micaela to reality from what seemed to be a long but yet short trance. She looked at the figure of a wounded white dove flapping its wings in pain trying to compose itself after whatever had just struck it. "Oh my God!" Micaela exclaimed trying desperately to open the window only to realize that it was painted shut.

"Crap!" she exclaimed running out of her apartment without realizing that Liam was coming in.

"Micaela! Are you okay?" He exclaimed looking at her frightened look.

Micaela ignored him and out she went to a communal shed where she hoped she would find a ladder to reach the wounded animal that had slammed into her window right in front of her own eyes.

She opened the heavy wooden door of the shed and struggling in the rain she got the ladder out which was too heavy for her. Liam and Jerry came up behind her and tried to help,

"Micaela, what are you doing outside in this rain, girl?" Jerry scolded her.

"Nothing, leave me alone!" She yelled trying to be heard as the loud thunder followed its lightning companion. "Crap!" Again she exclaimed as the ladder was just too heavy for her to drag across the patio to her window. The voice of Paloma's young figure entered her mind and she heard it say softly again, "Let go of your obstinate pride...let Liam help you."

"Micaela don't be so stubborn! What are you doing with the ladder...What are you trying to do?" Liam asked annoyed at her chivalrous, stupid attitude.

Calm and resigning herself to obey or rather agree with her mother's advice she said, "A white dove that seems to have been disoriented by the wind or struck by lightning slammed into my window and now it is dying on my window ledge, and I can't get the window open." Looking at Jerry with a disapproving expression she added, "They are painted shut, very unsafe from an emergency point of view,"

"I have been meaning to have that taken care of, since the last time you asked me about it. I am sorry Micaela. I will get to it tomorrow morning first thing," Jerry told her as he and Liam carried the ladder across the small patio. Positioning it under her window, Liam went up the ladder and saw the small bird almost waiting for someone to pick it up to exhale its last breath. "I am sorry, Micaela but it's not going to make it!" Liam yelled as another lightning and thunder team announced the death of the small wounded dove.

"NOOOOOO!" Micaela screamed trying to get the bird out of Liam's hands as he stepped down.

Jerry and Liam were astonished by her screaming and could not understand why so much pain over the death of this bird. Micaela put the small bird in her hands and brought it closer to her chest. She sobbed inconsolably and her tears meshed with the rain pouring down and crying the death of her mother she succumb to let out a primal scream, "NO YOU CAN'T LEAVE ME NOW, PLEASE DON'T."

Liam came closer to her and holding her by her shoulders, put Micaela's limp body next to him. Caressing her wet hair he told her, "I'm sorry Micaela. She is in a better place now, and you know that."

Jerry couldn't help telling them both, "Are you nuts? All this over a bird that probably is infested with germs that you are both catching now. Let go of that thing."

In automaton motion both Liam and Micaela got up and went inside ignoring Jerry altogether.

Inside the apartment they both looked for a shoe box. Liam got a hand towel and they placed it inside the box with the bird. They put it under the lamp, both hoping the lights would come back on and the bird would come back to life. They stared at each other in the glimmer of the candle light and as soon as Liam approached Micaela in what could have been a romantic moment, the lights came back on. The art deco lamp came on and as though a miracle happened without them being aware of it, the bird started to flap its wings. Incredulous of what they were witnessing, they approached the shoe box. The white dove was coming to life with its wet feathers, hurt, broken but very much alive. "I knew you would do this to me. I knew it under that stoic aloof exterior my mother was there ready to love me," Micaela whispered. Liam looked at her, trying to get close to her but afraid of her rejection. He was surprised at her soft almost subservient demeanor and he asked, "Are you okay?"

"I am sorry, but in a crazy way this little bird represents my mom. It is a dove and Paloma, my mom's name in English means dove or pigeon. I know this is crazy and I would not blame you if you leave and never come back, but I know she has left this world. She is in a better place." Reaching for Liam's arms as though searching for a place to nestle and find peace, she held him feeling exactly that, a sense of peace, a sense of having returned home.

Liam could not verbalize all the emotions Micaela had made him feel from the first time they met. He had sworn never to be wooed by any female after his last heart ache. It would not matter how sexy, voluptuous, smart or everything else a man needed in a woman, yet in front of him, looking at the dove, this simple yet exotic girl with sensual lips and wet clothes was making him feel like a giant. The way she spoke, the way she looked at him, had never made him feel so much emotion. Looking at this petite woman with so much bravado, with so much tenderness, all he wanted was to keep an eye on her, be close to her and mesh as one in a moment of carnal rage. He wanted her to know of his body for he knew it would be a complete communion of the senses. He wanted to know of her soul for he knew it would be like touching heaven and he would not stop until she succumbed to all the love he felt for this South American *mestizo* girl with a spirit as immense as the sky itself. "I am going to be here for you no matter what, Micaela, this I promise." Holding her ever so gently he let her call all the shots.

"I am so tired, I know I have to prepare to leave tomorrow. I wish I could have had more time to take care of the fiasco you and Jerry created for me," she said, letting go of his hold and walking to the door.

"I know you must be very tired, so poor Jerry must be informed that you will not be coming back until you are ready."

"Thank you my kind sir," she said smiling.

"I am glad I am your kind sir and I hope I am the only one."

"Not now, maybe when I come back and you have pulled me out of the embarrassment I am about to face with my unfinished manuscript.

"Shhhh, not another word. Go to bed. I will check on you first thing in the morning. I am taking the bird to the Vet Hospital on campus ok, they will take care of it." Liam kissed her on the forehead.

"Thank you, good night." Smiling again an almost docile smile.

The rain had finally stopped. Lights came on and peace was restored for the moment. The grueling upcoming events were yet to come and Micaela feared going to her mother's funeral realizing that it was all over. No one ever again would have a say so in her life, and with the heaviness being lifted, she now felt the melancholic sadness having had closure with her mother through a dream, *Because all this was a dream, Micaela remember, just a dream,* she thought.

The morning came with a knock on the door which awakened her from a deep slumber. "I'm coming." Micaela went to the door and at the same time the telephone rang. She opened the door and there was Liam with breakfast on a tray.

"Room service, ma'am," he smiled. "How are you this morning?"

"Fine thank you. Just leave it over there," Running to the phone, she was a bit late. So the answering machine had come on. It was Annabella, "Mom, call me as soon as you get this message, please." There was turmoil in her voice. The first thing that came into Micaela's mind was, why would Annabella know anything about Paloma, she was supposed to be in the mountains with her father.

Liam came over and handed her a cup of freshly made coffee, and a plate of toast covered with butter and jam. She took a big gulp of the coffee and gesturing with her index finger to wait a minute, she started talking to Annabella, who was crying at the other end of the line.

"Hi, Mommy, when are you coming to get me?"

"Hi, love. Stop...take a deep breath and tell me how is my baby girl?"

"I am fine but I had an awful dream and I asked dad to take me home, but he said I need to wait another week. Is this so?"

"Well, I thought you were in the mountains? What happened?" Micaela asked concerned about her daughter's whereabouts.

"We did not stay the whole time. It was boring and dad's girlfriend got sick."

"Are you okay?"

"Yes, but I need to come home. Something bad is happening mom and I don't know what it is or how to fix it!" Annabella exclaimed.

"Settle down, I am coming as soon as I can get a plane."

"You are?"

Micaela laughed a nervous laugh, "Of course, you silly goose!"

"Mom, I think Mami Paloma is dead. I dreamed of her. She was very healthy and she was really nice to me and she told me to look after you. It was weird the things she told me, like be kind to your mother and don't let anyone stand in her way. She is my 'ugly duckling' that has turned into a beautiful swan. Do not let anyone hurt her and then she disappeared…so weird. I woke up scared, Mom. What does it all mean?"

There was complete silence and Micaela excused herself and told Annabella she would call her later on, "I need to call you later, love."

"MOM, what does it mean?" Annabella insisted.

"Mami Paloma was a very strong woman, and when you are strong like that you can kind of make people dream what you want them to dream. I believe she was saying good bye to you in your dream. She was a very special woman, your grandmother, you need to remember this, okay?" Sounding very sad Micaela added, "I have to get ready to come see you, babe. Let me go now."

"Mom, wait! What about the 'ugly duckling' part?" Annabella asked curiously.

"I will explain that later. It is something between your grandmother and me, something really silly."

"Did she really call you an 'ugly duckling'? That is not very nice!"

Silence...Micaela's world crumbled in that instant again. Why did her mother have to get Annabella involved in the most cruel passage of their life? Why did she have to bring such a mean memory back? Micaela felt the sadness she felt as a young girl when she first heard it and the rage she felt at her mother for making her feel so inadequate in those growing up years so much so that she felt she was not good enough for anyone when she felt her appearance was not commensurate with her intellectual capabilities.

"Mom, I am sorry, I think I made you remember something really sad at this awful time. I didn't mean to but you always say, 'Something good always comes out of something bad.' She did tell me in the dream that you are her beautiful swan and that is what happens to the ugly duckling...Mom! It turns into a beautiful swan. I think Mami Paloma was paying you a compliment. She wanted me to know that you are a beautiful, intelligent awesome woman and you shouldn't let anyone take any of that away. Mommy you have always been beautiful to me. I know I am an unruly kid sometimes but I love you always." And so, Annabella a bit perplexed and with apprehension tried to further explain her dream to Micaela.

"Annabella, you are not unruly. You are the best daughter anyone could want...I am so lucky and thankful because you are all mine!" She told her with genuine thanks in her voice and added,

"Thank you, my love. You are such a sweet girl. I think you are right she was paying me a compliment and telling you to be good for your mom. I think that's what all that meant." She said trying so hard not to start crying so Annabella would not be alarmed.

Micaela hung up the phone and started to cry. Her daughter had said the words she was afraid to hear making the reality so palpably true, yet she had also appeased her hurting heart. Liam came over and caressed Micaela. "You know she is right. You are a beautiful woman to everyone else, but to me you are the cutest girl. I prefer cute over beautiful because cute has character. Beautiful you can buy now a days." He said, holding her by the waist trying very hard to be her friend when in reality he wanted to also be her lover and taste such a fragile, sweet fruit.

"Thank you for being such a good...mentor, friend, brother," she said it thinking back to the conversation of Annabella's dream.

Liam realized she was not thinking of what she had just said, Brother? Where did that come from? He thought, trying not to be bothered by her comment. "Are you going to be okay? Is Annabella okay?" He asked truly concerned.

"Yeah, everything is going to be fine. I just need to call home and see how my mom is doing."

Liam looked at her, almost questioning, why? For Micaela already knew her mother had passed. He respected her wishes and excused himself.

Micaela in her automaton attitude went around her apartment picking up things she needed to take with her on the last trip she would make to her parents' home. She knew she would never go back there permanently. Not only to her parents house but to that whole side of the country that had given her many bad memories. Every time she went there it would bring back the memories of her young life's struggles, her sleepless nights being a gracious daughter only wanting to leave their home, so many heartaches by the boys who did not love her for who she was.

"Naugh, this is too much shit. I just need to leave it all behind." She said out loud as she picked up the phone and made the arrangements to fly out on that same day.

Across the hall, Liam waited until she came out of her apartment and came to say good bye. "Listen, if there is anything you need or anything I can do while you're away please let me know. I want you to know I am going to be there for you. Can I get a number?"

"Jerry has all my info. Tell him I will do right for the department when I get back, I promise." She said matter of fact.

"Don't worry about the department. Just take care of you and Annabella."

"Thanks." She left as the phone in her apartment was ringing off of the wall.

Micaela knew it was her family trying to tell her the bad news. She did not have time for that at the moment. She would surprise them with her arrival. Little do they know she came to tell me goodbye in her own way that was amazing, she thought as she started to drive on Atlanta Highway. She exhaled and prepared to see her father. That was going to be really hard. All the kids loved Papi but he was not there physically most of their lives and emotionally only on occasion. Did he somehow let them all know of his paternal love for each of them? *It would be like consoling a friend that you saw once in a while but deep down you had strong ties with, Strange, very strange this is going to be*. She thought.

Micaela arrived at LAX and took a cab to her parents' house after picking up Annabella at her Dad's house. It was comforting to have her daughter with her at this emotional time in her life. Micaela hoped somebody would be at the house when they got there. María, her good friend, was there already and Paloma's best friend Cecilia came all the way from South America to Micaela's great surprise. They were helping Rebeca and Isabel with the household chores. Micaela entered through the living room door, the same living room of her adolescent years with some changes but the same vintage amber lamp in the corner of the room. Some things never change, she thought and smiled to herself. They all looked at her in disbelief that she was standing there in the flesh looking around like a spectator of familiar surroundings where you notice only the things that are out of place or those that don't belong. "Where is Dad?" she asked in an aloof tone of voice.

"Oh my Lord. How did you know? We have been trying to get hold of you!" Rebeca exclaimed.

"I somehow knew and needed to be here for her anyway," she lied. Annabella and Micaela gave each other a quick glance both of them knowing "how" they knew.

"Fine time you decided to show up," Isabel said with sarcasm in her voice.

"Out of respect for Dad and the circumstances, I am going to keep my mouth shut. So stay away from me. Don't speak to me, do not address me in any way, shape or form. Do you hear me, Isabel? She said looking at her sister with the same look Paloma had worn many times before and Micaela could feel her mother's strength come over her. "I don't have a poor excuse for a husband to keep me in a gilded cage, I work for a living and do for myself, so don't you dare preach to me. Thirty some years ago you left this family, your mother, you chose to leave then, so now stay away from me!" She walked away and went to see her father who was sitting on the edge of the bed in silence, looking sullen.

"Hi, Papi. I am so sorry about Mami but you know she is out of pain now, right?" She extended her arms wrapping herself around him; she gave him a kiss on the forehead. There was a balmy moist feel to his skin, "Are you okay? She looked at him so tenderly that upon their eyes locking on one another tears flowed from both of them and in silence father and daughter loved and understood each other's pain. Micaela in a flash thought how wonderful it was to have been connected with her parents in a realm all of their own. It was such a special gift to be so intuitively connected with these two people that brought her into this world, gave her the means to survive and live a life with no regrets, almost no regrets like going to NYU but somehow they gave her the strength to follow her bliss the way she was doing now.

Froilán had asked her to do the eulogy. The congregation consisted of her family, friends and members of the church. Until the mass had ended and the procession starting with her mother's coffin, Micaela was surprised to see the church full of people, many of whom she had not even known were her mother's friends. She delivered it, full of respect and tenderness as if she was talking to the figure she had just seen in her window a few days earlier. She expanded on how much she really loved her mother and the strong character Paloma had forged in her middle child. Her speech was short but full of emotion, respect and admiration for the matriarch of this family.

Micaela had been so nervous and stressed out with all the funeral arrangements, making sure her father was okay, and not coming apart while delivering her eulogy she hadn't really paid any particular attention to all the attendees except for noticing Annabella who sat with the family like such a brave and mature young lady. As she came down the altar stairs holding her younger brother's arm and seeing the image of the *Resurrection* on the entrance wall of the chapel Micaela could not believe the familiar face sitting at the end of the last pew reserved for friends of the family. She was surprised beyond belief, trying to contain her tears as she was coming closer to the standing figure of Liam. The procession stopped for a minute to open the entrance door, and one of the altar boys dropped the incense ball making a crashing sound at which everyone turned to make sure he was okay. In the commotion she lost sight of Liam as the procession started to move forward again.

She wanted to run out of the church and disappear, but she did not know why. She wanted to spontaneously combust to get rid of all these feelings and with Liam's presence they became augmented, *What was he doing here? When did he get here and how did he know where to find her?* She thought. Stupefied and with a mechanical motion, she continued in the procession leading to the final resting place of her mother. The marble covered hallways of the cemetery had light coming through the stained-glass windows in various hues on both sides. It was a surreal feeling thinking that she would not longer see her mom. She felt that Liam was behind her but as she turned around he was no longer there. Was she hallucinating? These figures coming and going in her life were too much to take. Final words from each of Paloma's children were said as they closed the small marble slab with her name and its epitaph written by Froilán. It all seemed to be going too quickly for her. It all seemed surreal or unreal and now a very important part of her life was gone.

It was all up to her now to make the pieces fall into place to make her life full and rich as she had always hoped, "Stop the obstinate pride and let people love you," Paloma had just told her that but could Micaela believe it and do it for herself? Everyone came to her parents' house after the funeral and she could not remember any of it, she was now in the airplane sitting next to Annabella going back to Georgia.

"Are you okay, Mom?" Annabella asked.

"Yes, baby, why?"

"You seem to be in a place all your own. Papi Antonio was very concerned about you and he said, 'She does not seem okay. Watch out for your Mami, okay?' I am just repeating and now agreeing with him," Annabella said.

"It is not one thing yet...it is everything. I miss Mami Paloma. I have a lot of work, I worry about Papi and mostly you. I worry about you...You soon will be a teenager!" She tried to dispel her daughter's apparent fear and concern.

They slept the rest of the way home. Micaela realized many things had come to an end, and she also knew that the last sultry nights of summer were awaiting her in her beloved South. Soon the leaves would start falling. The earthy colors of fall would paint the landscape. The death of winter would hit, and the resurrection of everything dead would have its time again. The whirlwind of her life resembled these seasons and it seemed that her personal life was ahead of time and she was to rejoice of a personal spring especially now when she was going back to what had become her home. Everything was left behind and now it was time to move forward. She caressed her daughter's small head, stroking her baby fine hair and exhaling a calm cleansing breath.

As soon as they arrived home, Micaela was curious to see if Liam was at his place and dropping everything in front of her apartment door, she went knocking on his door. There was no answer and she was annoyed. Annabella looked at her upset demeanor and mumbled something under her breath. Micaela looked at her with the same look as Paloma would have given her and Annabella could not help but say, "You look like Mami Paloma right now, Mom. You are scaring me."

Micaela listened to the words as she was entering her apartment and taking a long hard breath, exhaling she added, "I am sorry baby, but I thought I saw Liam at Mami Paloma's funeral and I just wanted make sure I wasn't seeing things."

"He was there, I said hello to him and asked him what was he doing there?" Annabella told her nonchalantly but trying to see her mother's reaction.

"What did he say?"

"That he loves you immensely and that you are the only one for him and that if you do not go out with him, he'll die! And then you'll have another funeral to go to," Annabella said it with the same dramatics that Micaela used as a child.

Watching her daughter perform she smiled and said, "That's terrible, the poor guy deserves a better life, don't ya think?"

"I dunno!"

"Really?"

"I know he likes you a lot and everyone could see that at the funeral he never took his eyes off you and they all asked me who he was so I told them that he was your boss and classmate." Annabella said, making it sound like a pronouncement.

"He is not my boss!" Micaela said indignantly.

"What is he then, Mom?" Annabella asked intently looking at her.

"He is a colleague and we both love literature."

"That's all?" Annabella insisted.

"You are too young to ask me these questions." She looked annoyed at her daughter's inquisition. "You need to start preparing for the new school year. Stop worrying about me!"

"I don't worry about you. I just want you to be happy doing the things you need to do for yourself." Annabella sounded so grown up.

"Come here you little pipsqueak!" Micaela gave her daughter a hug that had more behind it than just holding her. It was a recognition of sorts at how much her daughter had grown up and a testament to her love for her dear daughter. *Out of the mouths of babes,* she thought.

"I love when you hold me like this. You are so warm, Mom." Annabella said with genuine appreciation.

The knock at the door dissolved the tender moment between mother and daughter and Annabella ran to answer the door,

"Coming!"

There standing in the threshold was Jerry with a bouquet of flowers and a bottle of champagne. Annabella and Micaela looked at each other in disgust then looked back at Jerry and his insensitive behavior. Micaela could not believe her eyes. "Are you out of your mind?" she scolded him.

"Forgive me, I know this looks really bad, but it is not what you think," he said looking a bit embarrassed by what he was about to say.

"What is it?" They both asked in unison.

Jerry looked at Annabella, annoyed at her meddling, yet surprised how close this pair of mother and child were. "Boy! I better be careful Micaela. You definitely have a supporter and body guard in this pistol of a kid!" he added. "This came as a shock to me as well as everyone in the department." Putting down the flowers and handing the bottle to Micaela, Jerry went on to explain, "You have been chosen for the Peabody Award with your novel and they want you to have it to the printer by January. That does not leave you enough time to finish and edit the chapters that need editing. I was hoping it all would be a ruse and Liam would be happy that he had tried for you but his manuscript would far outweigh yours and he would be chosen. But I just found out he never entered his to ensure your acceptance."

Micaela stood stupefied but Annabella made her come back to reality preventing her from releasing her wrath. "WOW! This is great, Mom. This is your chance to shine and really put your work out there like you have wished for a long time." She said it with such enthusiasm making Micaela smile at her daughter. "I bet you it is Mami Paloma that is conjuring all this up from heaven. I betcha!" Annabella came closer to her mother giving her a hug.

"What is she talking about?" Jerry asked.

"Nothing. Don't pay any attention to her. We are both very tired and sad. I don't know if you heard but my mother passed away and we just got back from the funeral and all the details that situation entails."

"Oh, I am so sorry. I have not seen Liam since the day of the storm. I really did not know that she had passed away already. I knew she was sick but did not know the extent of her health or lack of," Jerry added.

"It's okay. We will be okay. Sorry for the look of shock but I did not expect it to be so soon. I knew he had entered my manuscript but had no idea it would be considered." She said in a contemplative voice.

"Where is Liam, anyway?" Jerry asked.

"I don't know. Annabella tells me he was at the funeral but he never spoke with me. He is kind of strange, isn't he?"

"Strange is putting it mildly, but a super nice guy, though!" He added.

"Well! That is good to know," Micaela said, making a funny face.

"You know Micaela?" Jerry said getting close to her. "I have never seen Liam as excited and committed to a student's work before."

"I guess he has never seen a writer of my caliber!" Again Micaela making yet another funny face, mocking her writing abilities.

"He can tell what is good and what is mediocre in writing. That is why he is sought out by many universities. He has a keen eye for what makes a manuscript better than any other, so forth and so on," Jerry said looking intently at Micaela.

"Well, that is why you like him so much and that is good, but what has that got to do with me?" She asked him to see if she could tell something about Liam in the answer.

"I know, you probably think he is doing this because he likes you, but that is not how Liam works."

"How does he work?" She asked.

"I told you...when he sees something of value he puts that first and as you can see the faculty has agreed and voted for your work. He was able to tell that from the pages he read before he knew you." Jerry said it with such conviction that made Micaela think about what he just said.

"Really?"

"Really!"

"And how do you know this?"

"He told me when the year started that he had gotten a paper in his mail box and when he started to read it, he the master of reading great manuscripts, told me himself that he had become entranced with the story and the way it was written. It was done in such a baroque way that he was in awe and wanted to know what this paper was doing in his mail box. Then of course you know, the rest is history!"

Micaela thought back to that moment when in the haste of the day, she had made that mistake. Now about a year later all she could think of was the figure of that good looking man who looked at her questioningly and then surprised at realizing that it was her paper. She thought how those eyes, those deep ocean blue eyes had escaped her and now all she wanted was to see herself in them again. Unfortunately, all that would have to wait for she needed to take care of Annabella and herself before she could be open to love again. *It never worked in the past. What makes you think it can work this time. All he sees is your ability to write and do good for the department,* she thought.

"Well, Jerry, I do not know what to tell you but I am withdrawing from the program and looking for a job somewhere else. You need to advise Mr. Griggs to send in his manuscript and make that work for him," she said with that obstinate pride of the Galarza-Díaz girls. "I don't need his recommendation to get my manuscript chosen. All in due time, my words would be out there with or without his help."

"Are you crazy?" Jerry asked getting a bit upset, "This is the chance of a lifetime and you are going to be that stupid about it?"

"Excuse me?" Micaela exclaimed.

"Yes! You heard me. You or anybody else for that matter would be very stupid to let an opportunity like this escape." Jerry walked to the door and told her emphatically, "I don't care about your personal problems nor Liam's either, but you have a responsibility not only as a writer but a student and teacher to do the right thing for the educational system that is paying for the roof over your head!"

Jerry left and slammed the door behind him. Annabella ran out of her room and looking puzzled, wanted to know what had happened. "Are you okay, Mom?" she asked.

"Yeah, I am going to be fine. It is just people making choices for me that I can't stand." She answered.

She did not know what to think. All the events with Paloma's health and subsequent death had come and gone so fast with its inexplicable pain yet a calm that she had not had a chance to absorb it all. Now she found herself again in a whirlwind of a different kind, "Toto, are we home yet?" she said out loud laughing as she threw herself on the couch and covering her face with a pillow, she let out a scream. Everything now was happening so quickly that she knew if she did not act accordingly and steadfastly she could lose it all. She kept wondering if she could have won against him. Why didn't he allow the competition to be fair and see if her paper would have had the same weight as his? She did not want to ask nor have an answer to this question, yet she felt compelled to ask. "Why, didn't he trust me or my work to be just as good as his and stand on its own?...Damn it, Liam!" She said out loud. Annabella looked at her and seeing her talk to herself, she knew Micaela would be fine and went back to her bedroom, nodding her head with a smile.

Micaela waited for the whole evening to hear Liam come back home but he never did. The morning came and she was wide awake laying in her bed, trying very hard to hear any footsteps whether coming or going, but there was only silence. She tried to get up and start the day but she couldn't move. She wanted to stay sleeping, forgetting everything that made her question herself. She wanted to sleep and perhaps never wake up, but then she thought about Annabella and she could not nor would she ever do that to her, leave her all alone in this sometimes tough life. She tried to dispel the depression that seemed to be creeping in from her mother's death. She got up and went to Annabella's room and saw her laying there sleeping sweetly and peacefully. She got into her daughter's bed to snuggle with her. Stroking her hair, telling herself more than to her child, "Everything is going to be okay, I promise you that!" Still in her sleep Annabella caressed her mother's arm that was around her and softly said, "I love you." They fell asleep. A thunder storm was on its way and soon after it arrived, the thunder and lightning woke them up in the middle of the afternoon.

"Oh my gosh! It's almost time to eat supper!" Annabella said jumping from her bed.

"I am not hungry, babe."

"Oh Mom, come on! You need to eat, otherwise you will waste away and never get married again!" she laughed.

"Funny!"

"You seem distracted. I should call Social Services and tell them that you don't feed me at all," laughing again.

That is not very funny, you know." Micaela said angrily at having to get up and tend to herself more than Annabella.

"Remember how we used to eat ice cream for dinner back when I was a little girl? Why don't we save some time and have that for dinner tonight, huh, Mom?"

"Wouldn't Social Services object to that?" She ask smiling.

"Touché!"

Micaela went into the kitchen. She heard a commotion out in the hall way and she ran to see if it was Liam. Quietly and slowly she opened her door to see who was making all the noise. To her disappointment, it was Biloxi bringing in a desk. She was having a hard time with it and Micaela decided to help her friend and neighbor.

"Hey BB!"

"Hey Micaela, I didn't know you were back!" She said struggling with her desk.

"Hold on, let me come help you!"

"Thanks. Is Annabella with you?"

"Yeah, why?"

"Nothing, just wondering if you wanted to go for a drink after we get this stupid thing in my apartment." She said looking at Micaela.

"In this rain?" Coming down the stairs, she asked, "Are you crazy?"

"Yeah. What else is new?" placing the desk on top of the stairs and breathing out, "Congratulations on your winning manuscript...girl!"

"Thank you."

"I told you Liam had chosen yours over his. That to me is one of the sweetest things a man can do for the one he loves," Biloxi said as she huffed and puffed trying to lift the desk inside her place.

"What?" Micaela could not believe what she had just heard.

"What, what?" she answered back.

"What did you just say?"

"Nothing, except that it was a nice thing he did for someone he loves," she repeated.

"Who loves who?" Micaela pretended she did not understand as she also struggled with the desk.

"You know Micaela, for a smart woman, you are really dumb or is that what Latin women do to get their way?" She said it sarcastically as a matter of fact.

"Why would you say that?"

"For starters, the guy has been gaga over you from the beginning and I don't know whether you are playing coy or you really don't know how much this man has the hots for you!"

"He does?"

"Oh come on!" Finally, getting the desk where she wanted it,

"Now I know how sneaky you really are!" She smiled at Micaela.

"Who is sneaky?" Annabella said, appearing on the threshold.

"Your mom!"

"Oh! You just learned this?" Annabella said it smiling at Micaela.

"Hush, both of you! You don't know what you are talking about." Micaela said, pretending to be indignant.

They all laughed looking around making sure the desk was in the right spot. Micaela was in shock to hear what Biloxi Blue had just told her.

"I did not realize that everyone knew about our tension." Micaela said.

"I knew from the beginning and I told her and she did not believe me. He got us ice cream one time and he was so sweet about it. I knew then he liked my mom," Annabella told Biloxi.

"OH, I see…Ice cream gifts to the child, red wine for mother, and champagne with flowers for the writer, Hmm, and I just didn't know that he liked me." Biloxi said it imitating Micaela's ingénue response.

They laughed again and Biloxi crossed the room hugging Micaela, "If anyone deserves to be happy and have the nicest guy in the whole wide world, it's you, so don't let him slip away."

Micaela heard her friend saying those words and the image of her mother the last time she saw her came into mind, "Do not let obstinate pride get the best of you," she had told her. She started to cry. Both friend and child hugged her trying to console her.

"Are these happy tears or sad tears, because I know your mom is sick," Biloxi said.

"Her mom is dead." Annabella told her.

"Oh my gosh! I am so sorry!"

"It's okay. Thank you. I am going to be okay. She is at peace now. She was in a lot of pain, so she is better off." Micaela said it in a contemplative voice.

* * * * * * * * * * * * * * *

Months had passed since her mother's death and she hardly ever saw Liam. Micaela had learned that he had been at her mother's funeral because he had gone to California on business. How convenient Micaela thought but she could never get a hold of him to ask him all the questions she wanted answers for. It was almost as if he was avoiding her. She wanted to call him but still, she held on to that pride and she could not make herself available to him. He was always so busy or in the middle of sessions and she did not want to disturb him until one morning when she was stuck on her manuscript and really wanted to go across the hall and ask for his help. Instead she came up with all kinds of excuses not to reach out to him, "Crap, I do not know how to go about this part and I need to turn this in, whatever this is, tomorrow morning," she said out loud.

Annabella was reading and going over some notes for her homework. She looked up and saw her mother and asked her, "If Mohammed does not go to the mountain, the mountain must go to Mohammed. Isn't that the way the proverb goes, Mom?"

"What?" Micaela answered distracted.

Annabella reiterated sounding like she was trying to make a point to her mother.

"You are a funny girl, however, right now I do not need your advice."

"Maybe not mine but you need his. If I were you, I would use that to get close, hmm."

"How clever, you seem to be, my dear. Don't you think I thought of that already?"

"Nope!" Annabella got up and went into her room. "Because if you had thought of it and you still didn't do anything about it then I have to concur with your friend Biloxi, you're dumb. He likes you and he would do anything for you. Why can't you accept his gift?"

Annabella left and Micaela thought about their conversation and how much she really wanted to have contact with him yet she felt he did not want to help her with this paper. "He could have come over to say hello and see how I was," she said out loud.

She walked over to the vase of flowers Jerry had brought months ago. They were dead and crisp. Micaela looked down at the vase and there was a card. She looked puzzled as she opened the small white envelope with a card that read, "I am so sorry about your mother. Time is always of the essence. I hope to see you soon to help in any way I can with your awesome but incomplete manuscript. I knew you had it in you! Liam."

Micaela's eyes filled with tears and she did not know what to do, laugh or scream at her stupid behavior. She did not know if she was crying because he felt a genuine appreciation for her craft or because he had reached out to her in the most romantic way and she had missed it. Liam had been supporting her all along and she had managed to push him away, unknowingly though this time. "How stupid, I've been!" she yelled out.

She went into the bathroom, took a quick shower, got dressed and looking cute but fragile despite the sturdy look of her thick masculine gray sweater and a pair of old corduroy pants, she rushed out of her bedroom throwing a hat on her head. It was Sunday morning and Micaela went into Annabella's room and told her, "I'll be right back. Don't leave the apartment, sweet kid of mine. I am going to find Liam and tell him how stupid I have been, okay?"

"About time, Mom! Bring me something good for lunch, okay?" Annabella told her smiling.

"Deal!"

"You look super cute in that outfit. He is going to love you forever, I am telling you...listen to me. I would not steer you wrong, my lovely mother!" Annabella laughed in gratitude to see her mother be happy for once.

"You are very funny!" She yelled out as she shut the door with her satchel in her hand.

"Hey Micaela! Where are you going so early this morning?" Jerry asked.

"To make things right, and thanks for telling me the flowers were from Liam, you knuckle head!" She yelled out as she went down the stairs.

"He is at the library you know!"

"I know where he is, thanks!"

Micaela at that moment realized how much her mother's words meant now. Paloma wasted a lifetime with her absurd ways, ousted a daughter and died unhappy realizing her mistakes. Micaela knew she was not going to be like her mother. Life was too short to know your mistakes and not do something about them. Yes, we all have a past and some are not so good but the present is for one to change things and make a better future. This Micaela knew to be true all her life but she had allowed people, circumstances and herself to detract from her purpose in life.

She felt she deserved the accolades of her profession...her chosen profession, that of a writer. She deserved the love of a 'super nice guy' who would love her the way she wanted to love someone back. No more apprehension, no more self doubts...go for it and seize the day! Her mother in the most conditional way had shown her how to be brave and how to shed the plumes at the right time. From the entrance of her apartment building, she could see her surroundings with a fresh new outlook and it all seemed to be beautiful pictures that were no longer scattered about but rather put in order for her life to make sense.

She got in her car on this chilly Sunday morning headed for the Main library where she knew Liam would be preparing for next week's class he was teaching. It never failed she knew that on every Sunday, unless he was out of town, he would be at the same table next to the same stalls. Her heart raced as she reached the stairs going into the building. Laughter and conversation echoed in the walls of the vestibule and she saw him coming out talking and laughing with this beautiful blonde. Micaela's heart sank and she wanted to flee in the opposite direction only she was a bit too late...he had seen her and acknowledged her.

"Micaela, this is a nice surprise!" He was genuinely please to see her.

"Hey, Liam, I didn't know you would be here," she lied.

"Well! This is my church," he said, winking and smiling.

"Oh, that is good to know, I didn't think you were a religious man," she added nervously wanting to know who the 'blonde' was.

"Micaela, my niece Samantha. Samantha, a good colleague of mine." He said, introducing them.

"Nice to meet you, ma'am."

Micaela gladly extended her hand and added, "Nice to meet you too, Samantha but please, call me Micaela."

Telling on him, Samantha said, "My uncle speaks very highly of you and now I can see why. I love your outfit."

"I just speak the truth." Liam said smiling at her.

"Thank you. Both of you are very kind," she said trying to cover her desperate desire to hug him, hold him and tell him that she too has loved him from the day she saw him enthralled in her story, but she knew she had to play it cool. He was no match for her in the matters of pride. She loved knowing that he valued and respected himself enough to keep away from her, while thinking that she had choose to ignore him. And most of all how rude she had been by not acknowledging the flowers and card he had sent. Her silence and the thoughts raging in her mind made for an awkward moment between them and Samantha dispelled it by making it very uncomfortable for both.

"My uncle tells me you will be leaving for England come next year. Maybe you could stay in his cottage if you are fortunate enough for him to let you even get close to his sanctuary," she said, looking intently at Liam.

"Oh, I did not know any of this, but hopefully other arrangements will be made by the faculty. I don't think your uncle needs to worry about me disturbing his personal space," she added looking at Liam.

"You ladies are funny talking about me as if I wasn't here," he added.

"Well, you are just staring at poor Micaela, as if you hadn't seen her in years and aren't saying anything," Samantha added.

"I better be going. I need to pick up some books and lunch for Annabella, who is studying for an exam she has tomorrow, I hope."

"I would love to meet your daughter, Liam says she is quite a young lady, much like her mother, isn't that right?" she said, turning to Liam.

"Yes, she is quite something," he agreed and continued by saying, "What books are you looking for?" He asked knowing that Micaela would be caught in a lie.

"Oh, I forgot the title, I have it here." Looking into her satchel and showing the papers she needed Liam to help her with. "They are for Annabella, she'd kill me if I go back without her books." She said trying to sound truthful.

"Is that your manuscript I see in your bag?" He asked with uncontained excitement that made her happy.

"Yeah it is. I was going to read some of it here in complete silence, without the daughter asking too many questions...you know what I mean?" she said sounding relieved for not having to keep lying.

"Well, it was nice meeting you. Maybe I can meet your daughter some other time. I am heading back home early this evening," Samantha said hoping Micaela would invite them for lunch so she could keep watching these two people's obvious sexual tension.

"That would be nice, I will keep that in mind." She said.

"If you need any help with the manuscript just let me know. I know you are keeping to yourself for obvious reasons, but I would like to think that you thought of me as your mentor once and will continue to do so," Liam said touching her shoulder.

"Thanks, I will let you know." Sounding aloof and distant, she kept walking and then looked over her shoulder to see if he would turn and look at her, but instead she saw him putting his arm around his niece's shoulders and a bit of jealousy entered her heart.

Micaela put down her satchel and sat down in the same chair she knew Liam always sat in. *What? How old am I? Maybe I should carve our initials in this wooden desk to mark our love forever?* She smiled and started to read her paper. She could not concentrate and decided that it was stupid for her to stay there when she needed to go home and just make the changes herself. She went to the nearest store and picked up some lunch meat and ice cream to make banana splits. It had been months since she had made that for dinner. It would be a treat and Annabella was old enough now to know that this is not an everyday thing. She smiled again to herself thinking back to how far she had come since those days in the small apartment in Redondo Beach. "Now you have a small apartment in Athens, Georgia." She told herself as she paid for her groceries.

She got home and went near Liam's door to listen for noises but instead laughter came from her own apartment. She started to get annoyed at the thought that Annabella was not studying and had invited friends that further would disturb her preparation time. She was about to open the door but it opened as if it was waiting for her to enter. Liam came out of the kitchen with big bowls of ice cream. Samantha and Annabella were enthralled in a movie on TV.

"What is going on?" She asked the girls but they did not answer.

"Is anybody home?" She continued, looking at Liam as he gave each girl their respective bowl of ice cream. He grimaced to be quiet.

"They started to watch this movie. It is really good," he said going to the kitchen and getting a bowl of ice cream for himself. "Do you want some?"

"No thanks!" Micaela put down her groceries and pulled the ice cream she had just bought out and showed it to him making a face, "I have my own!"

"Well, then you can dish it yourself!" Liam said smiling, pretending not to care.

"I will!" she added.

"So did you get the books for Annabella's homework?" he asked waiting for Micaela's response.

"No, I forgot and left the list here," she lied.

"Yeah, a huh!" he smiled.

"What?" She asked as she put some ice cream in her mouth, leaving a drip on the side of her lip.

Liam got closer and said, "Wait, you have something here." Gently wiping her lip with his finger made Micaela feel weak in the knees.

"Stop, I can take care of my own mess!" she exclaimed.

"I know you can. God forbid someone might want to help you or even worse, accepting somebody's help," he said as he picked up a spoon and sat next to the movie watching 'zombies.'

Micaela saw him as being so comfortable in his own skin, so beautiful with his new hair cut making him look debonair. He turned to look at her and the blue eyes just made Micaela and the ice cream melt but she could not let him see how much of an affect he had on her, so she said, "I wish I would have known this was happening. I would have stayed at the library doing some more work."

"Annabella is ready for school and Sam is leaving as soon as the movie is over, so why won't you take a little break and join us in the movie," he said inviting her with those blue eyes she did not want to see herself in...not now any way.

"Shhhh," the TV watching 'zombies' said in unison.

"Shh," Liam said and signaled a place for Micaela to sit next to him.

Micaela obeyed, pretending to resist the invitation. As she watched the movie she started to doze off and heard Annabella telling Liam and Sam that she always does that. Liam got up found a throw to cover her up. A connection had been made. Micaela slept peacefully knowing that the deep ocean blue eyes were there watching, guarding her sleep. For the first time she felt safe having a male in her apartment with her daughter enjoying these simple circumstances. She started to dream of a cottage somewhere in Europe and she knew that for her the cottage would be surrounded by deep ocean blue waters to always remind her of Liam's eyes. Greece would actually be the place where she would find the cottage of her dreams.

The next day she was ready to turn her completed manuscript in after spending the rest of the night making the final changes to her 'baby' of three years. She could not believe that this paper which she had started so many years ago, as it seemed now, would give her the recognition she sought after all these years. Perhaps it was Paloma conjuring the spirits that had granted this gift, but she shook her head in acceptance that the gift was her work coming to fruition and nothing more. She did not want to accept Liam's recommendation making people think that's why she got in, but mostly because she was afraid of depending on a male counterpart to make her dreams palpable. She had it in her to follow her dreams, and to do them as she pleased. She felt free and unconquerable and it was the fear of losing all that that made her push Liam away. But Micaela knew now that she could give herself a pat on the back and delve into what she had wanted to do all her life, be a writer...the playwright she knew still needed to come out of her without Liam's help. She was afraid that needing his love would stop the power of her being and everything she wanted to be in life.

As Micaela was leaving her apartment, she saw Liam in front of his door as if he had been waiting for her to come out, "Micaela, I know this is not the time but I've really been thinking about and wondering if you would go out to dinner with me, just the two of us without anyone from the department."

"And why now, Liam?"

"Just to have dinner and get to know what goes on in that brain of yours, I want to find out what turns you on at night, remember?"

"I can't right now. There is too much I am trying to figure out for myself and I have about a lifetime of questions of my own. Please don't make me question this too." She said putting her satchel strap over her shoulder as she walked to the exit.

"Do you want me to leave you alone?" He asked firmly but also afraid of her answer.

"I want to be alone. I did my job for Jerry and the department so everything should be fine and dandy."

"So, that's it. We are done now?"

"Liam, stop! Do not make this any more difficult."

"Why is it difficult?" Following her and getting real close to her, he pinned her against the threshold of the outside door.

Micaela did not know what to do at this moment. She wanted to run away but she also wanted to hold onto him in a long embrace but too many emotions were hovering over her tired soul. She stood there thinking of all the things she wanted to do but was not acting on them. A tear fell down her cheek and although she felt an eruption coming through her body that was about to explode, but she knew it could not be in front of him. *Do something!* She thought and before she could decide what to do she felt Liam's arms around her waist going up her back and coming back down her arms to her hands. Holding both hands in her back, he pinned her against the wall again and gently placed a long awaited kiss…a kiss like no other. Micaela could feel him trembling and she had never felt any of the men in her life tremble the way Liam did at that moment. Softly and ever so carefully he let go of her hand to caress her face and letting his hand go through her hair. As he looked at her tears had started to fall, he told her, "I know I will find out what turns you on at night, even if it takes a life time. I don't give up too easily."

"You are going to need lot of patience with me, Liam," she said holding his face and adding, "I don't think it is fair to love someone as complicated as I am, because believe you me, I am," she said placing her forehead on his chest.

"Let me be the judge of that, won't you?" He said wanting to take her up to his apartment to consummate their long-awaited moment of love.

"I am going to drop the manuscript off and then I am heading down to Madison. Do you want to come with me and have lunch?" She asked quietly.

"Anything, anything you want, I want it too," he said excited at the prospect of getting close to this fragile yet strong woman who had come into his life like a whirlwind entering all his senses.

"I have to be back by three to pick up Annabella."

"I have a better idea. Let's have Biloxi pick her up so we can make dinner plans. I want to be with you today and every day," he told her nudging her softly on her shoulders.

"Okay, I have to go now. See you later, Mr. Griggs.

"See you in a bit *Micaelita*." He rushed up the stairs.

She yelled in surprise, "Wait! What did you call me?"

"Isn't that the name your father calls you at times?" He winked.

Micaela had never felt so wanted and Liam's pursuing her and nonchalantly beseeching her had managed to bring down her guard. She had never wanted to love like this again but his caring ways had made it easy to give in to his wanting and desires. Not admitting defeat, nor being resigned but with an open heart and clear sense of who she was, she decided to welcome his love. As she walked out to her car, Micaela felt the chilly morning breeze on her cheeks and the memory of her late mother entered her thoughts and she cried. They were tears of happiness, of utter happiness knowing that although the chilly Andean air had frozen her mother tears and her mother's heart, it had contained love in all its coldness...Paloma had given Micaela the greatest gift. She found herself walking in this chilly morning air crying with a happy heart knowing that we all have the power of being; victims like Paloma had chosen for herself to be or victors like Micaela was choosing for herself to be long before Liam's love came to warm her heart.

It had been a treacherous journey. There were many obstacles she had discovered and which she needed to overcome. As she dropped her manuscript, she thought in contemplation, *let love in without any expectations.* She returned to her apartment to fix herself in anticipation of spending the afternoon with Liam.

"Hey, Micaela, can I come in?" Liam was lurking behind the door.

"I am coming!" she yelled from her bedroom.

"Oh my gosh!" he gasped as she let down her hair. Her curls cascaded down to her shoulders, an invitation to touch and die in the craziness of being in love, "You look too cute for Madison."

"What do you mean?"

"You look like you should be on the pages of a magazine and you are going to be the talk of the town."

"Oh...Stop!"

"I mean it! Your soft olive skin and your dark hair asking to be stroked, those lips and the little eyes telling stories from old... there is no such a creature like that in Madison you know?" Liam said, approaching her and getting closer to her making her nervous.

"Come on, let's go!" She grabbed a hat and put it on her head.

"Oh, no, don't cover your hair!" he complained.

"Stop it or I am not going anywhere with you." She pulled away.

"You are not getting away from me ever!" He tickled her and pulling her close to him he made love to her only with his kiss, "I love you and I am never going to let you go. You're mine, only mine."

"Really! Let's see how fast you can run," Micaela let go of him, trying to run away from him.

Liam followed her around the small living room and managing to get a hold of her losing her balance, they fell on the floor near the small ottoman. Laughing and tenderly fixing her hair, he kissed her with the same trembling anxiety of teenage angst. Looking at her with loving eyes and slowly touching her somewhat exposed breasts, he told her, "I love the sexiness of your breasts. I want to make love to you like I've never done before."

Micaela felt her fast breathing become one with his, softly she embraced him and they kissed as if they had waited for this moment for an eternity. They stopped to catch their breath and they kissed again. She could feel their nervousness dissolve in the sweetness of their lips as she flavored his tongue entering her mouth. They knew this moment would come and with the pleasure of feeling safe and loved, he slowly unbuttoned her white silky blouse as she was undoing his jeans. Shoes went flying and a communion of body and soul happened as their naked bodies touched and all their senses meshed in the rapture of the moment they knew was theirs for a lifetime. She felt like a teenager and with the raging of her hormones she thrust against his body and he entered her ever so gently and slowly. She felt like she was in paradise. They moved slowly and then faster, they danced so flawlessly enjoying each other giving pleasure to one another. It went on for hours and the more he gave the more she wanted of his lips, of his thrusting against her. She came too many times to count and when he was about to ejaculate he stopped, "Wait, let's stop for a second. I don't want to come yet. You feel so soft and good inside, I don't ever want to leave. I love you, Micaela...Oh boy! Do I love you."

Madison never saw them that afternoon. Instead they loved each other as making up for lost time and they kissed and talked and drank from the same glass exchanging sweet nothings, regretting having to get up and be ready for Annabella to come home.

"Oh shoot! I better get up and you better leave, you naughty man!" She lovingly caressed his cheek.

Caressing her exposed legs, he sighed and looking at her he added, "These are the gate keepers of desire that drives your naughtiness to my wanting and the more I have you, the more I know I want you...all of you."

Micaela saw herself in those blue eyes. The sun rays from the lazy late afternoon coming through the window did not compare to the golden messy hair of his. She kissed him and a tear escaped from the darkness of her brown eyes breathing a calming sigh feeling how peaceful it was to be in his arms hopefully for a lifetime.

* * * * * * * * * * * * * * *

It had been five years since her mother had passed away and she had started to compile her memories. She had gone back and talked to her siblings about what they remembered most about the country from which they came and the mother who gave them life. It was interesting for Micaela to know that her four siblings had different memories of their matriarch. She started to put it all down on paper with added sentimentality to create a palpable story of love and strength amidst a life full of contradictions. She called it "Paloma: A Daughter's Story." She knew it would be a good story to tell but much to her surprise it became a bestseller and had the acclamation of people in the literary arts. She was a fully fledged published author which got her some notoriety but she felt shy about it. The signing and public relations were becoming too frequent but it was a necessity. She felt so thankful for the noise and the harried stance of her life at this moment. She wanted to resent this time, but how could she? All her hard work had materialized and people loved what she had to say. Although all of this took time away from Annabella, who was growing at the speed of light; Liam, her biggest fan and supporter, made it so easy for her to blossom the way she had wanted for her all these years. He made a home and became a friend to Annabella so she would feel secure. He never complained and he was always ready to catch both of them if they should ever fall. Their love did not need a little paper and neither one of them had ever asked if there would be a wedding.

As far as they both knew they were committed to each other, to loving Annabella, to continue writing and reading to each other, especially on Sunday mornings. Their love for the arts kept them busy with the many fundraisers they promoted. Annabella had chosen to become a fashion designer, had applied and had gone to a prestigious Fashion Institute. Micaela was so happy and proud of Annabella going to school in NYC, something Micaela had always dreamed of from a very young age only to have her parents take that dream away from her. The little ugly duckling of long ago had become the beautiful swan with the power of being a victor in all its glory. Her realm was full of memories, and the tangible gifts of standing firm to all the bad, sad and good times that made her who she had become.

In the excitement of promoting her latest book she felt nervous, happy and harried. She had found a cottage on a little island off the coast of Greece and she was to embark on a new chapter in her life moving to this island and living in harmony with the stars, the moon, the ocean and the sun that became eclipsed in comparison to the rays of sun found in Liam's blonde hair and the deep ocean blue color of his eyes.

"Come on Micaela! We are going to be late." He reminded her.

"I'm coming, I'm coming!" She came out of their bedroom looking youthful and more self assured than ever. She wore a vintage white pleaded polka dotted skirt with a silk navy blue dolman sleeve blouse and pearls of different sizes cascading down her chest. She had worn the skirt before but it had been a long time since she had pulled it out of her closet. She smiled to herself thinking back at the first time she had worn this lovely piece, *It all seems to be so long ago, yet the cloth is still in good shape just like me, thank God!* She thought with a devilish smile fixing the strands of pearls as she approached their living room and felt the weight of Liam's approving stare. She looked and smiled at Liam who looked at her full of love, full of pride to have this lovely woman as his.

"You look gorgeous. You drive me crazy after all these years," he told her getting closer, wanting her.

"Thank you, but we are going to be late! You said it yourself." She smiled coquettishly.

"You do drive me crazy," kissing her and playfully spanking her butt.

They arrived at the book store where many people awaited her arrival. They saw a long line of fans wanting their book to be signed. They looked at each other and a deep sense of satisfaction was exchanged in the squeezing of each other's hands. Micaela was introduced to the crowd and the applause fogged her senses as she became preoccupied with the signing of her best seller.

"Your name is?" she would asked and write something sweet, sometimes something long to which Liam would whisper in her ear, 'Keep it short, sweetheart.'

The line seemed to get longer, never shorter, as more people came to have their book signed but Micaela remembered that they needed to leave soon to catch a plane out of the country. She took a short break and walked to the table where some water and left-over appetizers still remained. Liam came from behind her and playing with her, he said, "Hey gorgeous one, if you are alone, I would love to take you to Greece and make love to you in the middle of the ocean blue. Would you like to come with me?"

"In a heartbeat! You are very cute! But I am with someone who has these tantalizing blue eyes that have offered me the same trip and I have accepted." She gave him a kiss that spoke volumes of passion waiting to be dispelled at his mere touch.

"Come on. We are going to be late and there are still some people in line that command your attention besides me!" he said smiling at her.

"Okay, okay!" Micaela went back to the small table and started asking again, "How would you like me to sign this?"

Micaela was immersed in this one note for a young woman who went on to say how much she liked her work. She explained at length how much she felt for the characters. As a result, Micaela was not even aware of the male figure who had been watching her all this time.

"Thank you, so much for your devotion," she told the young woman laughing with her for her presumptuousness.

Out of the corner of her eye, as she asked the next person on how to sign their book, she thought she saw a familiar figure that sparked a memory that had been long forgotten. It made her look around to make sure she wasn't seeing things. No one appeared and she looked down at the book and signed, *With lovely thoughts*, Micaela.

She looked up to give the book to the person she had just finished signing for and there he was. She could not believe her eyes. He stood there looking at her with a look that Micaela tried to discern but could not. Stavros was standing there waiting, last in line for her to sign his copy. The man who had painfully given her voice back stood there in awe of this young woman who he had let slip through his fingers. The man who now realized the grave mistake he had made, but as Karma would have it, it was too late for him now. Micaela was sitting there wearing the same skirt she had worn at their first meeting. The top was different but the way the skirt flowed and moved with her spirit he had been able to see as she took her break, was the same. They both looked at each other in silence. Telling each other all the things that perhaps needed to be said or not.

The beautiful swan with the power of being smiling at the Adonis of long ago asking, "How would you like me to sign?"

"You look radiantly beautiful, different yet the same in so many ways," Stavros told her ignoring the question and trying at this moment in time to have closure with the woman he had let go without a thought.

"Thank you. It's been quite a while hasn't it?" She said matter of factly. "How are you? How are your kids?" She asked wanting to know but a bit incredulous of how life made things happen for her. *So many blessings!* She quickly thought.

"They are fine. Thank you for asking," he answered still staring at her.

"Ms. Micaela time is of the essence. Can you please hurry," Liam told her.

"I am sorry. How would you like me to sign?" she asked again with a bitter sweet taste of triumph at the turn of events.

"However you want. I know it would be heartfelt because all along you were the 'good one' I had a major oversight, wouldn't you say?"

"Life is as it is and we must follow our paths with all the deviations and obstacles that appear at times…but we must remain true to ourselves. No regrets on my part."

"Micaela, sweet Micaela," Stavros said it endearingly and sadly.

"To Stavros," she started to write,

> *The man who came one day and awoke the senses,*
> *bringing pain to compare to future joys,*
> *bringing angst to look for peace,*

bringing confusion to learn to see clear,
bringing short-lived love;
a prelude to the constancy of true love.
Thank you for letting me feel again,
so I can put in writing all the love and passion
once contained.
Always,
Micaela

Micaela closed the book and gave it gently back to Stavros. She got up and leaning across the table and with a tender caress of his cheek she told him, "Thank you."

Liam holding the door open for her with her coat and bag in his other hand looked at her with the love and devotion Micaela had sought all these years and it all made sense now. She felt the presence of the women of her clan back in the old country. Most of all she felt the pride and love of her mother's spirit had become one with hers. She was not content...she was truly happy with a rich sense of peace at how her life had turned out. They reached the airport and boarded the plane. She fastened her seat belt and Liam caressed her messy hair, "You look beautiful but very tired" he said moving closer and placing a kiss softly on her lips.

The motion of his hand putting her hair back in place rekindled the memory of her aunt when she told her "You'll be something extraordinary one day."

She knew then that extraordinary for her meant to be true to oneself, always be humble at life's riches and to give of oneself selflessly to become immortal because only then the Meaning of Success by one of her favorite authors took on a personal note. She smiled as the airplane took off knowing Greece awaited her...

Meaning of Success

*To laugh often and much,
to win the respect of intelligent people and the affection of children,
to earn the appreciation of honest critics and endure
the betrayal of false friends,
to appreciate beauty, to find the best in others,
to leave the world a little better, whether by a
healthy child, a garden patch or a
redeemed social condition,
to know even one life has breathed easier because you have lived.
this is the meaning of
success.*

Ralph Waldo Emerson

Made in the USA
Charleston, SC
29 July 2012